To renew this book, phone 0845 1202811 or visit
our website at www.libcat.oxfordshire.gov.uk
(for both options you will need your library PIN
number available from your library),
or contact any Oxfordshire library

MY HEART AND I

by

Brian Elks

MY HEART AND I

First published in 2001 by Brian A F Elks
12 Cheshire Road
Thame, Oxon
OX9 3LQ
United Kingdom
tel: 01844 214361

ISBN 0 9540236 0 9

Cover design by Peter Aylward
18 Cheshire Road, Thame, Oxon

Set in 12-13½pt Times New Roman by Ian Goodman
7 Deacon Close, Winterbourne
Bristol   BS36 1DT
United Kingdom
tel: 01454 778248

Printed and bound by Antony Rowe Ltd.
Bumper's Farm, Chippenham
Wiltshire   SN14 6LH
United Kingdom
tel: 01249 659705

WERE THEY SINGING AS THEY WENT BY?

*'I WILL SURELY LOVE YOU 'TIL I DIE
MY HEART AND I, WAITING JUST FOR YOU
LONGING FOR THE LIGHT, ALONE NO MORE
MY HEART AND I – MY HEART AND I'.*

AUTHOR'S ACKNOWLEDGEMENTS

I am most grateful to EMI Music Publishing Limited for allowing me to quote the words of the song 'So Deep Is The Night'. [The additional words, from which the book title is derived, are my own.]

The poem which I have called 'At the gate of the year' was written by Miss M. Haskins in 1908.

FOR INSPIRATION

The Royal Green Jackets Museum, Peninsula Barracks, Romsey Road, Winchester, Hants for their excellent display of Great War memorabilia, in particular, that relating to the Oxfordshire and Buckinghamshire Light Infantry.

The 'Book of Remembrance' in the Oxfordshire and Buckinghamshire Light Infantry Memorial Chapel in Christ Church Cathedral, Oxford.

The supporters and staff of the Oxfordshire and Buckinghamshire Light Infantry Museum, Slade Barracks, Cowley, Oxford, who are working to keep alive the memory of the Regiment.

The Thame War Memorial.

The Thame Gazette, 1914-18.

Brian A F Elks, Feb 2001

OTHER BOOKS BY THE AUTHOR
Light A Candle

CONTENTS

INTRODUCTION

The story is set in Thame, Oxfordshire and other places appropriate to the war situation in the period from 1914 to 1918 and culminates on New Year's Eve, 2000.

A disparate group of Thame men and lads are gradually drawn into the war and the events around it. The war does not end by the first Christmas as generally expected but rolls on, slowly an understanding of the terrible reality of this war takes hold. From the very beginning men enlist and the townspeople throw themselves into supporting their soldiers and their country. Endlessly raising money and providing comforts, giving freely of their time, energy and support.

Slowly public understanding of the terrible tragedy taking place grows and events and circumstances draw together the men and lads to their date with destiny. As the war reaches 1918 the German Army launches one last desperate major offensive. Fate dictates that the men and lads are there to meet it, while at home the women must wait and hope.

Nor was this time from 1914 to 1918, simply about fighting an enemy. The whole population was drawn into the conflict, millions enlisted and even greater numbers laboured at home. The result was social change. Even where not obvious the seeds of change were sown deep and would eventually flourish. Such was the desperate need that women undertook roles and responsibilities beyond any previous understanding and acceptance. After the war there could be no going back; enfranchisement would have to be extended to all adults. Technology surged, medical knowledge grew apace, women's dress shortened. The forelock tugging classes quietly took their respect elsewhere and subservience started to die.

Almost every change we see in modern society had its roots in 1914-18. Naturally the change was often slow in the early days, nonetheless it was persistent, year on year until two decades later when social change was fashioned even further on the anvil of the Second World War.

Prologue: FOR THOSE OF COURAGE

In August 1914 the small quiet Oxfordshire town of Thame was thrown headfirst into the major conflict that came to be known as 'the Great War'. Within days of the declaration of war the first man was mobilised and very quickly forty-one reserve soldiers took the train from Thame for the unknown. Did they sing as the train pulled out? Very likely so. Songs kept the spirit from flagging on a long march. Songs were the common currency of comradeship. Songs were balm for the soul – 'Keep the home fires burning'.

No one thought to ask the townspeople of Thame if they agreed with that precipitate declaration of war made on their behalf but being loyal citizens, deeply respectful of their King and dedicated to their country, they gave their support. In any case the universal acceptance and understanding was that this war would last only a few months. Such was the belief in the power of their modern powerful weapons and armies! Those who didn't volunteer quickly would miss all the fun. Such excitement, a rare and strange commodity in a little market town. Very soon the Recruiting Sergeants would exceed their quotas. Meanwhile the townspeople raised money to equip the old Grammar School in Church Road as a hospital and staffed it with local volunteers. When the first casualties arrived in November 1914 the ladies of Thame were ready for them.

Throughout the entire war period there was a most wonderful upsurge of community spirit and the whole town set out to raise money, food and any manner of items that would aid and comfort our troops. A sense of community prevailed that was so strong that it began to transcend barriers of class, gender and religion. When the inevitable tragedies unfolded and were reported, the families bore their grief and heartache with bravery and fortitude; no aid from modern counselling and medicines. How did they cope?

From a total population of just under three thousand men, women and children, nearly six hundred men went to war. Nearly one in five. Sadly over ninety did not return. Thame was, in its own

1

way, a microcosm of events from across the whole country and paralleled the circumstances and consequences that prevailed in every town and village throughout the land.

The first British soldiers met the enemy on 23 August 1914. The Thame Gazette reported the first Thame casualty, Private William Robert Loosley, on 13 October. From my own research the last Thame casualty was Corporal William Bowler, who died in a tragic accident only six days before the Armistice in 1918. Hundreds were injured. One man, Bugler Arthur Robert Howland was born in Wollongong, Australia. There is no mention as to why he enlisted in Thame and joined the 6th Battalion of the Oxfordshire and Buckinghamshire Light Infantry. He died in action in France in September 1917.

So many lives lost or ruined at immeasurable cost to the future; a loss that can only be guessed at. A debt that can never be repaid. A debt that defies assessment or meaningful calculation.

Since time immemorial men and women have stepped forward in defence of their country when it is threatened. We cannot see into their minds to know the truth of their fears and motivations. One issue seems clear to me and that is the courage of those men and women. Surely it takes courage to step forward. Not great buckets of courage necessarily, but real courage nonetheless. And what of those who saw them off to war? Waiting at home, working, raising the children – waiting and hoping that all will be well, the future somehow secured. Surely that is courage also.

This story is set against a background of historical fact but is a fiction. I could not bring myself to write about the real people, even after over eighty years, I fear that feelings are still too raw for the full exposure of truth. It is a sad thought that when sufficient time has passed to allow the real stories to be written it will be too late. The memories will have gone. But that should not diminish our gratitude to the people who fought and died. That we are here today, is a monument to the fortitude, endurance and spirit of those people of the past, a monument built upon a foundation of courage.

They should not be forgotten. When it comes to the eleventh hour
of the eleventh day of the eleventh month, please remember them.

FOR THOSE OF COURAGE

The dearest thing on earth that man possesses is his life
should he stake or gamble it in war and strife?
But can men hold back while others take the risk alone
coldly weigh the risk of death and then their pride disown.
Not for those of courage.

And should the gamble fail what of those they leave at home
what happiness for them, a future bleak, the seed unsown?
But can women cling while others take the risk alone
blindly hold their men at home and then their pride disown.
Not for those of courage.

When life is done and tomorrow faced with daunting fear
pride dissolved and swept aside, whose memory stands clear?
Only those of courage.

THE THAME WAR MEMORIAL LIST : 1914-18 WAR

Allen C A	Hake F G B	Outing G C
Allen S	Hewer R T	Parker S
Bateman C B	Hemmings A	Price F
Bates T	Hicks W E	Price H
Baverstock W T	Higgans A V	Pullen R A
Birrel-Anthony H A	Higgans H R	Richardson H
Boiling C	Hinder J	Roberts S J
Boiling E	Honour W	Roberts W E
Boiling W	Hopkins F	Rush C A
Bowler W	House E E	Shaw J B
Bowdery G	Howes A J	Shaw D P
Brown J	Howlett J	Shrimpton H J
Burbridge D	Howlett S	Smith W
Cartland F	Howlett C H	Soames F L
Castle J L	Howland A R	Squires B
Chowns F	Howland A R (Bob)	Squires G
Chowns G	James E W	Squires J
Clarke W H	Keene F	Stevens H
Cozier H J	Keene J	Stockwell B
Crook G H	Ladbrook G E	Summerhayes J A
Cross A F	Lane A	Sutton A H
Cross F W	Lidington D V	Tappin S
Cross R I	Line Ralph	Trinder A A
Cumming A	Line R	Wallington W A
Dicker S	Loader G C	Wells M
Dover S D V	Loosley W	Wentworth W H
Drake W	Lovejoy J	Wilson H T
Eaton R	Miller G	Witney C A
Eele H	North F J	Wood C
Farnborough R G	Olieff J	Young A V
Fielding F W	Oliver H W	
Green A H	Ostrehan D H	

Chapter 1   1914: 'ON MOONLIGHT BAY'

Tomorrow was August Bank Holiday Monday so Samuel Peddelle knew that he and his family were safe for one more day. Even the bailiffs did not evict on a bank holiday. Letters and telegrams would be delivered but for most people it was the one sacred holiday of the year, often the only holiday of the year. Everyone prayed that the weather would be fine and sunny. How was Samuel to know that tomorrow the world would change beyond all recognition.

Samuel had followed the railway line from Thame to Tiddington and he guessed, from the position of the sun, that it was about five pm. He turned back towards Thame. Samuel was an excellent forager and over the years since early childhood he had learned how to harvest the countryside. It was his only heritage. He carried two bags, the one for foodstuffs the other for fuel. The fuel bag was light, after all he was dependent on the few nuggets of coal dropped by the passing trains. When he was closer to home he would find the best wood available otherwise the weight would hold him back. His wife Martha and his two girls would be waiting, hungry, so he stepped out.

The embankments, hedgerows and copses gave Samuel a steady flow of nature's bounty. Though the harvest was limited so late in the summer he had found plenty of pignuts and wild plums. Late nesting pigeons yielded some eggs, a previously set snare had provided a rabbit and to these he added some potatoes, onions and carrots taken from a nearby field. That, he thought, would keep the hunger away for a day or two. He knew that the next train down the line was not due until eight, while the next up train would pass at about seven. This gave him a good two hours to clear the track without being seen. The last thing he needed was a fine for trespassing, a fine he could not afford to pay, so that would mean prison.

The Peddelle's problems had started back in the early Spring. They had begun when a hidden and unsuspected nail had jagged deep into Samuel's finger as he repaired a boot. Septicaemia had taken hold. He had been so ill that he couldn't work for weeks. When he tried to go back to his old job, he had been turned away. An apprentice had taken his place. Samuel had prided himself on being a good cobbler and he and Martha, though poor, had subsisted in modest comfort. He could still remember the joy of their first born and even when the count had reached seven, he still considered each and every one a blessing. Denied a job, Samuel decided to set up his own business working from his parlour, their meagre savings had gone on tools and leather. Then disaster struck. Within days the scarlet fever had taken a virulent hold in all the children and he and Martha had watched in stunned and helpless anguish as five children died in a week. Burial costs added to the loss of wages had bankrupted them and despite the forced sale of most of their possessions, they had been unable to pay the rent.

Tuesday would see the bailiffs at the door. The choice was stark, it was either the highway or the workhouse; vagrancy on the open road or the house for paupers. Samuel sighed at the choice because with two small children there was no real choice. That choice was helped by the fact that the Thame Union Workhouse did not have a harsh reputation. Nonetheless, it was the place of last resort, a place of shame. There was also Martha to consider, because since the funerals she had been overwhelmed by shock and melancholy. Rarely did she speak to him.

Wearily, Samuel pressed on as fast as he could walk, reluctant for the day to end for tomorrow may well be his last day of freedom for the foreseeable future but he was concerned that there was no food in the house.

Martha and the two girls were waiting as he opened the door of the small terrace cottage in North Street. Wordlessly he handed over the bags and they disappeared into the kitchen. At that moment Samuel would have mortgaged his soul for some tobacco but there was none so he sat on the floor of the empty parlour and sucked his empty pipe, while shadows of the past danced around him. Why had Martha aged so much? So quickly! He could not think beyond those questions because those questions had answers he could understand. But Martha's whole life had been the children and their future and to dwell upon those matters opened his mind to questions that had no answer.

Even as Samuel sat thinking the world as he knew it was disintegrating. The telegrams and letters detailing the mobilisation were being processed. Germany had declared war on France and was making demands on Belgium that could only lead to hostile assault. Samuel knew none of this, lost in his own misery he did not realise that he sat on the very edge of a great powder keg and that the fuse had been lit.

Evensong at St Mary's of Thame had finished when Thomas Guntrippe stepped down from the train. The return from summer camp with his fellow territorials had been a long, tiresome and hot journey. Thomas was crumpled, sweaty, dirty and hungry; his boots still caked with dried mud. He did not like being so untidy and regarded it as being most unsoldierly. The quicker he could get working on his uniform with damp sponge and iron the quicker his pride would be restored. Thankfully he collected his bag and pack and stepped out towards his cottage in the nearby Park Street. Cheery but tired farewells sounded out as the men parted company. Little did they know that within a few days they would take the train away from Thame. As he stepped out, Thomas touched his jacket pocket once again to check that his pay was still intact, a habit so ingrained that he did it without thinking. Neither did he think about his comfortable worn boots. Soon he would have reason to bless them as he tramped through France. He let himself into the cottage. "I'm home, Rose."

Rose Guntrippe made no effort to stand up to welcome Thomas. Instead she remained seated on the chair close by the blackened range on which a pot and kettle gently simmered. Thomas had been proud to marry Rose; Rose stood five foot five, not beautiful, but well made, firm breasted despite the two children. "Don't make so much noise. You'll waken the lads."

Thomas dropped his pack, edged over and stooped to kiss her. "I'm hungry – not eaten since breakfast."

7

Rose turned her face aside. "Stop that nonsense."
"I thought you'd be pleased to see me."
"Sit down, I'll serve your supper."

Thomas and Rose had been married eight years but it had proved a marriage of opposites. Thomas was a quiet introspective man, easily contented with life and his lot. But he was not as Rose often said, a damn fool, easily pleased. The real problem was not one which could be said or spoken of publicly. It was a problem that both frustrated and annoyed Rose so in her eyes he was not a real man. He could impregnate her but not satisfy her. Thomas could not sustain more than three thrusts at Rose's juicy loins, then he was finished. She could not hide the scorn, nor could she bring herself to say the right words so she hid behind the condemnation of 'damn fool'. Most men she knew would have taken a belt to her but that was not Thomas's way and she mistook his gentleness for weakness. Thomas maintained his pride by pretending indifference, he burnished his pride by being a territorial soldier and in the appearance of the wagon and two shire horses that were the centre of his working life. The wagon and horses would not have been out of place in a Lord Mayor's Show.

Supper finished, Thomas stood up and smoothed down his jacket. "I'm off for a pint – the Four Horseshoes."
"Please yoursen. Don't come home drunk – and don't wake me. I must be up early."
Bank Holiday or no, tomorrow was wash day.

Alice Harty had gone to bed early but she found it difficult to sleep as the heat of the day had yet to dissipate. This had the advantage of keeping the animals in the adjacent pound peaceful, only a low rumble from one of the cows broke the silence. No, it was not the normal animal sounds nor even the heat that kept Alice awake. There was a far greater worry than that. In her mind she was troubled because two hours previously her husband Albert had marched off to his favourite pub, The Greyhound, at the bottom end of North Street. Albert Harty was the stockman in charge of the pound and Albert loved a pint, or two – or three!

Albert emptied himself out of the pub door. He was neither drunk nor sober but he was belligerent and the pub cat nearly inherited a boot as Albert let fly. There was no good reason to sing, in fact Albert was sure that he should not sing so his mind made up, he sang. His voice echoed around the adjacent cottages.

"We were sailing along – on – on – Moonlight Bay –eee
we could hear the voices ringing
they seemed to say – eeee . . . !"

Police Sergeant Cox gave a discreet but firm cough. "Ahem!" The singing stopped abruptly. "That's better, Albert. 'Tis a Sunday as you well know."

Albert tipped his cap. "Aye, so it is." Then he went quietly on his way. Sergeant Cox watched him till he was out of sight then he followed. 'Moonlight Bay', he thought, 'where do they think such things up? What is the world coming to?'

The sound of footsteps outside the cottage and the lifting of the latch of the kitchen door signalled that Albert was home. Alice froze and feigned deep sleep as Albert climbed the stairs and threw open the bedroom door with a bang. In the flickering candlelight Albert glared at Alice's still form. "'Tis no good you pretending to be asleep, woman!" The words spat out. "Speak to me, you cow!"

"I'm not well, Albert – not tonight, please!"

Alice had given birth to four children, one for every two years of marriage and she was terrified of yet another pregnancy. From her very first child, she had experienced cruel pain during childbirth and this had got worse with each succeeding child. The midwife had told her that another child could well be the death of her. She had tried to make Albert understand but Albert in a passion could not, would not, be denied his 'rights'. Tonight he was in a passion! The burning hardness he proudly brandished as he undressed, throwing his clothes carelessly on the floor, must be quenched.

Albert pulled Alice sharply around; squirming, she turned her head aside and crossed her legs in rebellion. For that she got a fist in the face and then Albert drove his right knee between her legs forcing them apart. At the same time he wrenched her nightgown up to her chest. His voice was harsh with anger and desire. "I said I want my rights, woman – keep those legs apart or you'll get my belt!"

Alice had cried out at the force of the blow to her face and her knees ached but she lapsed into resigned silence as Albert drove deep into her body and rutted away. There was no escape because Albert weighed nearly fifteen stone as well as being a powerful man. He held Alice down with the weight of his body and grunted in her ear. "Don't you sod me about, you cow."

"You're hurting me, Albert."

Albert appeared not to hear, nor was he deterred by Alice's resigned silence and unresponsive body.

Albert gave one last violent, convulsive thrust as he climaxed then he collapsed, pinning Alice even more firmly to the bed.

"Albert – please – I need to go for a pee."

With an exaggerated groan he rolled off and Alice fled the bed, a prayer on her lips and hate in her heart.

Sergeant Cox stopped by the charge desk. Constable Jones looked up to see a puzzled sergeant staring at him. "Can I help you, Sergeant?"

"This song we've been hearing. This Moonlight Bay. Where is it?"

"Can't say as I rightly know, Sergeant, but I believe that it just means a romantic place. These are romantic times."

"Uhm, I wonder why there would be screams on Moonlight Bay?"

* * * * * * *

Twayblade Stevens ate his fried breakfast with sober slow relish. Four slices of bacon, three eggs, two sausages and fried bread. An onlooker might have raised the question as to why he was so thin. Twayblade never questioned such matters, breakfast was his great pleasure but cricket was his love and the letter in his hand, delivered by the first post, gave him more satisfaction than any he had received in the past. Two of his lads were invited to an Oxford cricket trial. He sat back and read the letter again. Two of his lads chosen! A deeply contented happiness pervaded his entire body, from his toes to his tousled hair. Mrs Thatch, his housekeeper, put her head around the dining room door. "Have you finished, sir?" When she got no answer she retreated, grumbling. Despite the fact that this was a bank holiday, there was a great deal of work to be done.

Mr Stevens, Mr Alfred Stevens to be correct, games master at the grammar school, was known to all the boys as 'Twayblade'. Alfred had the endearing habit of lifting his chin, letting his arms flop out to his sides, palms outwards, then he would shrug whenever he was asked a question to which he had no answer. Early in his career an observant pupil had said he resembled a Twayblade, the wild orchid that grew in the nearby Chilterns, and so the nickname had stuck. There was no malice in it, only affection.

Alfred's thoughts were rudely interrupted as Mrs Thatch put her head through the doorway. "The Headmaster wishes to see you, Sir. Immediately!"

Sidney Barnes looked every bit the assistant gamekeeper on the Thame Park Estate that he was and had been for ten years. Baggy brown trousers and jacket that fitted loosely over his waistcoat, leather gaiters and peaked cap. Also he was a well-built handsome man with a trim moustache, his body fit from constant exercise but not the back breaking exertion of farm labouring. Generally Sidney was a placid man, it paid a gamekeeper to be attentive and subservient to his master and his guests and he had never before had a problem with deferring to his betters. Until today that is. Yesterday Sidney had mentioned to the Head Gamekeeper, Joss Parker, that the army may be needing fighting men if this talk of war became reality. Sidney hadn't even meant to suggest he might be considering leaving. Joss Parker gave him a hard look but said nothing at the time. This morning had been different. When Sidney called at Parker's cottage he had been given the plain unequivocal message. "The maister has said you cannot leave, the season will be on us soon. This talk of war is daft. If you go there will be no reference and no job when you return."

For the first time in his life, Sidney felt that he was a chattel, not a free man; a servant who had no rights but to serve and servitude. He had protested half heartedly but it made no difference so he bowed his head, touched his cap and ate humble pie. A threat to the livelihood of his mother and father who both worked on the estate underlined the message. Angry but impotent, Sidney loaded his shotgun and went out to fight the crows.

Many a wild 'villain' escaped that morning as Sidney brooded upon events. Suddenly he was dissatisfied; why had he never been more than ten miles from Thame and that only the once! From childhood memory he recalled that half the world was coloured red on the map. Suddenly he longed to be away.

"Vicky, I think we should go in the races. There are races for girls." Mary Peters still thought of herself as a girl, whereas her sister Victoria, a year older at sixteen, thought of herself as grown up. She squashed Mary with ease. "You know father would not approve." Several yards behind them Mr and Mrs Peters strode arm in arm. Apart from Sundays there were only two days each year when Mr Peters did not work, Christmas Day and August Bank Holiday Monday. Each time they passed a customer, Herbert Peters grocer, raised his bowler and smiled, then he would whisper 'never give offence, my dear', and Mrs Peters would give his arm a tiny squeeze of acknowledgement. "It's a lovely afternoon, Mother."

And so it was, a fine sunny afternoon, specially arranged by the Committee of the Thame Band Flower Show because today they had been accorded the privilege of holding the show in the immaculate grounds of the Prebendal. The tower of the nearby St Mary's church gazed down in approval.

"This rumour of war cannot be true, Father." Mrs Peters knew that no-one would want to go to war in such lovely weather.

"Of course not, Mother."

Victoria and Mary stopped and waited. "Father , can Mary and I go over to the flower show?" Both she and Mary knew that

Father would want to spend a lifetime inspecting the prize vegetables, so they crossed their fingers. Father looked troubled. "I'm not sure – so many people. You will get lost."

"Father, we are not children!" Mary tossed her hair in mock annoyance.

"No, Father, let them go. They will be safe here." For the first time this year Mrs Peters asserted herself.

Mr Peters' fob watch appeared in his hand. "The band concert starts at three – we will all meet there. Don't forget now." A great roar sounded as the first races started.

War had already started in the 'Produce Tent' and several irate men glared at the Steward. "How come that bugger Pullen have won again?" A finger poked at the Steward's chest.

"Aye, 'tis bloody nonsense!" Another finger advanced.

Steward Roberts held his ground. "The judges have decided. He said it was a day of hard decisions with so many fine specimens to hand."

"Well, 'tis bloody obvious he left his glasses at home. Those beans o' mine are the best in Oxfordshire."

Another man stepped aggressively forward. "Call they onions? If they be the best of show then I'll kiss your horse's arse!"

Mr and Mrs Peters walked into the tent and there was a sudden hush. The Steward gave silent thanks. "Clear the tent, gentlemen. The display is open to the public." He lowered his voice. "And there will be no language in front of the ladies."

The pride of the Lord Williams's School was the spacious and manicured cricket field. The field was bounded by the school buildings on the north side while rolling farmland to the other three points of the compass gave an impression of endless space and quiet. Only the occasional train along the hidden track on the south boundary disturbed the peace and overshadowed the skylarks.

Officially the school cricket season finished with the end of summer term but this year the team had emerged triumphant and unbeaten so Twayblade Stevens had arranged this day's special match. The ultimate test he could devise. Today his team played the might of Aylesbury. On the field the school team captain, Edward Holling, considered his tactics. The school team had batted first and scored a respectable one hundred and ninety all out, but now a determined resistance by two of the Aylesbury men had taken the score to one hundred and fifty for six. Unless a breakthrough could be accomplished the first defeat of the season stared them in the face, and that in front of several hundred assembled spectators. His tactics decided, Edward waved William Smithe to his side. "We must take a chance, Bill. Do you think you could tempt them to hit out?"

William Smithe was the team's slow bowler. A crafty bowler of off-breaks and top spin. "This wicket is a bit slow, Edward. It's taking a chance – but these two batting think they've got us on the run. They're over-confident."

Edward considered for a moment. "Round the wicket, Bill – toss'em up." Then he set about lining the leg boundary with his best catchers of the ball, then he turned back to mid-on. William Smithe curled his fingers tightly around the ball and shuffled forward, every fibre of his mind and body concentrating on the spot two yards in front of the leg wicket on which he wanted the ball to drop. The moment the ball hit the pitch, William knew he had won. An over-confident batsman swung his bat with deep contempt but the ball straightened up and the top spin hurried it through. Whack! The ball soared up and out to the boundary, straight into the safe hands of square leg. One hundred and fifty for seven. "You lucky beggar!" The batsman growled it out as he made his way back to the pavilion. William sniffed, 'They always say that', he thought but mindful of the school's reputation for sportsmanship he gave a guileless smile in acknowledgement. "Dreadful bad luck, Sir."

They sat together in the team room of the pavilion, bound by friendship and the elation of victory. In the centre was Edward Holling, to the right were John Howe and Freddie Coxe, sprawled on the floor to the left were James Pullene, William Smithe and Harold Jones. On the bench by the door sat Twayblade Stevens, a congenial look on his face. The younger lads had been sent to help

Mrs Thatch set out the visitors' tea. Freddie Coxe raised the great jug of cool beer he had liberated from the grasping hands of Mrs Thatch and took a long swig. Eager hands reached out as he paused for breath. The beer should have been heavily laced with lemonade but Freddie had been determined that no contamination would taint their victory drink. Twayblade watched with benevolent happiness, then cleared his throat. "Um-um! Well done, lads, this has been the most successful season ever – well done, every one of you."

John Howe began to sing and waved at the others, "For he's a jolly good fellow . . . . " Twayblade waved to silence them. "I've an important announcement! Two of you have been selected for an Oxford trial. Well done, William Smithe and James Pullene. One day I want to see you play for the county."

"Sir!" James Pullene stood up, "We have heard there is to be a war. There will be no cricket."

Twayblade took a few moments to reply. Deliberately looking around at each of the six, his face serious. "You should know better than that, Pullene. Cricket will never cease, never be stopped by war. It is too important in the shaping of our nation and the Empire. But that brings me to a matter I had intended to leave until later. The Headmaster came to see me this morning." He paused, seeing looks of alarm pass around the group. "It would appear that you all tried to enlist this morning – and offered false ages! Did you not know that the Recruiting Officer is a friend of the Headmaster? But the Head has no jurisdiction over you so he has sent letters to your parents – no doubt they will want some answers."

He was gratified to see the consternation on their faces. "Very foolish, lads. Sixteen is too young."

"Sixteen and a half, Sir." Edward expressed all their thoughts.

Behind his back Twayblade Stevens crossed his fingers. "Maybe there will be no war – no need for you to join. In any case modern warfare is far too terrible to last very long."

"How long will this war last, Sir."

Alfred Stevens did his best impression of a Twayblade. "I dunno – not long I pray."

John Howe looked disappointed. "We will miss all the excitement, Sir. We will never get a chance to fight."

Harold Jones spoke up. "Captain Hanks said we must wait till we are eighteen. I say we join then."

"Aye, that is it, all together." William Smithe sounded pleased at the thought.

Edward Hollings stood up and raised the jug. "I say we make a pledge. All or nothing. I say we all join together when we are eighteen if this war holds that long."

The six touched hands. "All together."

"Lads, no hasty judgements, please." Twayblade Stevens tried to hold the line, "Let's not be foolish. Now, enjoy the drink and don't forget the concert party this evening."

"We're all ready, Sir and we have rehearsed a new song. An American song called Moonlight Bay."

Twayblade Stevens sniffed. "American! What's wrong with a good British song?"

In the cottage towards the end of Park Street, Enid Oxenlade could contain herself no longer and she burst into the darkened bedroom. "Wake up, Peter! Wake up!" She threw back the curtains to let in the late afternoon sunshine and ruffled the bedclothes. A deep groan gave forth. Peter Oxenlade worked at the bakers every night except on a Saturday and then slept the following day.

"What time is it?", Peter growled.

"Time! Don't bother with time. War, Peter – war! War has been declared."

"Bugger the war. Have you woken me early?"

Enid was unimpressed by his surliness. "Get up. I've made a pot of tea. The kids are so excited."

Alice Harty looked at herself in the mirror while holding a cold flannel to her blackened eye. Her neighbour, Milly Orton, looked on sympathetically. "He shouldn't hit you is what I say. Not for 'that'." She emphasised the word 'that'. Alice applied more cold water. "He's not really a bad man. Many get worse than me."

"Have you caught again, Alice?"

"No, thank God. But when he's in a rage he won't withdraw. Says it spoils his pleasure."

Milly wrinkled her nose and peered over Alice's shoulder to see herself in the mirror. "When I say no – Henry knows I mean it."

"That's as maybe, Milly, but your Henry is a gent. Why , he's never hit you very hard."

"Is Albert in the yard?"

Alice nodded her head in sorrow. "Aye, he'll come in stinking. Even the soda doesn't get the smell from his clothes."

"You get some of that Rinso," Milly nodded knowingly, "these new washing powders save a woman a deal of work."

"Huh!" Alice grunted in deep scepticism. "Like my mother, I put my faith in good carbolic soap and a scrubbing board."

Milly made a most telling point. "You never see Mary Pickford washing clothes in the pictures."

Alice was silenced for a brief spell. "Aye, you'm right – it must be nice to be waited on hand and foot by a handsome man!"

"Never you mind, Alice, when women get the vote, we'll trade our men in for nice new models."

"Get the vote! Women!" Alice snorted in derision. "Umph! My Albert would never agree – he ses it's only women what can't get a man who want the vote."

"Perhaps you'm right, Alice not all women are as lucky as us."

Alice's laughter sounded throughout the house. "Gawd, we are lucky, Milly – that we are."

Sidney Barnes flicked the release catch of his shotgun, let the barrels drop then extracted the two cartridges before closing the gun. It was five in the afternoon and as his gun was unloaded he considered himself officially off duty, having been out since four a.m. this morning. The remarks made in the morning still rankled him but he had said nothing in retaliation throughout the day nor had he neglected his duty. After all, there still remained the chance that one day he could don the bowler hat, the mark of a headkeeper. There was only one blight on his horizon, his mother wanted him married. A matter which she raised whenever the chance offered, after all, as she pointed out, Sidney was now twenty-eight and it was about time he did his duty. As Sidney was leaving the estate the gatekeeper had spoken of the strong rumours that war had started but war held no fear for Sidney. Guns and shooting held no fear for him, he could take out the eye of a rabbit at one hundred yards. He stepped out from the gate lodge on to the Thame Road and headed back to town, to Park Street. As he reached the bridge over the railway line he had a good view of the allotments over to the left. There, paying no attention whatsoever and engrossed in his weeding, was George Coates, one of Sidney's near neighbours. Sidney resisted the temptation to wave. He knew that George had him marked and was simply waiting on his reaching home; then George would be off for a bit of poaching on the estate. Sidney pretended he didn't know because George wasn't greedy, he took mainly rabbits to help feed his family, so that saved Sidney work and cartridges. Besides which George was very discreet and only Sidney knew of his presence. Even Joss Parker had not detected George, which was just as well or George's backside may well have had ventilation holes.

Two minutes later Sidney reached the house and let himself in. "You'm been a long time."

Sidney smiled at the words and put out his arms to her. "You'm right, girl, but I'm ready for yer – and hard as hell."

George Coates walked in a nonchalant, leisurely way from his allotment to the railway embankment. He paused for a few seconds to look around to make sure no-one was watching then he slipped through the fence, quickly picked up his sack from the bushes and was on his way. George had already chalked up one conviction for poaching and he did not want another. If a police constable or a gamekeeper caught him with snares or game then the magistrate would convict him out of hand. It was not a question of whether or not he would go to prison but for how many days! From his vantage point on the allotments, George could not only ensure that Sidney Barnes was safely home but that the adjacent Police Station was deeply involved in the ritual of shift changeover. God bless

Sergeant Cox and his attention to detail and God bless Rose Guntrippe who now had Sidney clasped firmly to her bosom, he thought.

George stepped out, although certain he had more than an hour to himself to follow his trap line and set new snares. There would be rabbits for certain and with modest luck perhaps a pheasant. His labouring job at Blackditch Farm did not pay well but with twenty pole of allotment and the fruits of nature supplemented by the game of the Master of Thame Park, George's family at least enjoyed full bellies most of the year. There was many an occasion when George had blessed his countryman's skills. He could blend into a landscape, he knew the value of stillness, natural shadows and stealth. It was just as well because it kept him out of jail. The Thame magistrates took a hard line on theft, especially trespass with murderous intent on a gentleman's game.

As George reached the edge of the Thame Park Estate he stopped to listen for a good two minutes. He noted the call of a cock pheasant from a nearby copse. A nice pheasant would fund an evening in the Four Horseshoes and there were few things George enjoyed more than a pint of bitter and a game of dominoes. If only this constant talk of war would cease, he thought, they'll not catch me going off as a soldier. George was no coward but all his life he had been a free spirit. He accepted the need to earn a crust but discipline, being told what to do, well now that was a different matter and not something for which one volunteered. Naturally George knew his place in life. He gave every appearance of being obedient and subservient, very mindful of his manners to his betters, especially respectful to the vicar and the constabulary. But in the spirit of Agincourt the two finger salute of derision was always near the surface.

Certain that all was clear, George merged into the background and checked the first of his snares. He gave a small grunt of satisfaction as a plump rabbit dropped into the sack.

Sidney had lost all thought of gamekeeping, poaching, disagreements, Thame Park Estate, headkeepers and so on. All he could see were the pointed breasts and brown aureoles of Rose Guntrippe's nipples. His throat was dry. "God, you'm got lovely boobs, Rosie." His hands reached out to fondle them.

"Get those damn trousers off."

Already Rose had removed his waistcoat and shirt but the belt buckle needed more strength. Reluctantly Sidney transferred his attention to the belt, his fingers trembling In his haste. "'Tis alright for you, woman. Just a few laces . . . . " He tripped and fell over as Rose dropped her knickers and she stood watching him. His voice raised an octave. "For pity's sake, woman. Help me before I break something!"

Rose stooped and got hold of the offending boot and gave it a strong pull. Sidney's foot popped out and he quickly released the gaiter so the baggy trousers could drop. Rose moved in quickly, "Lie back." She pushed him down then straddled across his body. "Hold my tits, Sidney, hold them tight!"

Sidney reached up. "Harder – harder!" But Sidney was beyond hearing.

Miss Stokes gave a roll on the piano as the Vicar stepped forward. The audience quietened in anticipation. The church hall was packed and the Vicar was hugely satisfied. Competition from the Electric Picture House in the Chinnor Road was fierce and the manager was always trying to entice Miss Stokes into his establishment. There was no chance of that. Miss Stokes did the flowers and harvest festival arrangements at the church and besides which, she deeply loved the Vicar in her chaste fashion.

"Ladies and gentlemen, our next act is well known to you." He read from a piece of paper. "I am told that they are – 'A terpsichorean syncopated ragtime minstrel sextet'! Well I never, I thought they were six lads who sang a song together! Please welcome the Thamesian Belvederes."

Edward Holling, William Smithe, James Pullene, Harold Jones, Frederick Coxe and John Howe ran out on stage. Taking off his straw bowler, Edward stepped forward and bowed. "Ladies and gentlemen, our first song comes from America."

Miss Stokes set about the introductory lines with great gusto. In the audience Victoria Peters turned to her sister Mary, "I've made up my mind, Mary. I'm going to marry Edward Holling – isn't he most handsome?"

Mary gasped in shock. "Vicky – how can you say that, you're not even going out together. Anyhow you're too young."

Victoria was unrepentant. "I am sixteen."

> *"We were sailing along on Moonlight Bay*
> *We could hear the voices ringing*
> *They seemed to say – they seemed to say, they seemed to say"*

"Oh, Mary, he is so handsome."

> *"You have stolen my heart*
> *Now don't go 'way*
> *As we sang love's old sweet song*
> *On Moonlight Bay – on Moonlight Bay."*

At the back of the audience, Enid Oxenlade reached over and squeezed Peter's hand. "Thank you, Love."

Peter looked embarrassed, "It is a free show, Enid." Enid smiled, "No matter, it is nice to be taken out."

"Then I shall take you again – one day."

In the terrace cottage in North Street the kitchen was getting dark. The small fire was nearly exhausted and gave out very little light. Samuel and Martha sat side by side in the gloom staring at the embers. Already the night air was cooling and Martha pulled her shawl closer around her shoulders. Samuel put out a hand to comfort her. "I never thought it would come to this, Martha. I feel so ashamed to have let you all down."

For the first time that day Martha responded. "'Tis God's doing, not your'n, husband. Though why he should take the children and not me I cannot understand. I must have done something very wicked." She was silent for a while and Samuel could think of nothing to say, then she spoke very softly, "Tomorrow we must go for a holiday."

Samuel was greatly puzzled, they had never had a holiday. "A holiday, Martha?"

"Yes, all the children will be waiting there for us."

"The children are here – with us. Asleep."

Martha hunched her shoulders and slowly shook her head from side to side. "No, they are there waiting for us – all of them. Emma, Violet, Ivy, Doris and Mary will be there."

Emma, Violet, Ivy, Doris and Mary were the girls who had died. Samuel put his arm around her shoulders. "Of course, Love."

* * * * * * *

The Master of the Thame Union Workhouse was a sombre, grave man and his dark suit and bowler hat added to the illusion. He stared intently at Samuel Peddelle as if trying to read his mind. Samuel nervously twisted his cap in his hands. At his side Martha and the two girls clung together, hand in hand and silent.

"We – w – w we – have come to seek help, Sir." For the first time in his life Samuel stuttered as he spoke.

The Master's desk was a plain deal table that would have been more at home in a butchers than an office. There was a great deal of tutting and sniffing as the register was opened, page by page. While he was doing this his wife, the Matron of the House stood, hands clasped, lips pursed, her eyes unyielding. Samuel found himself looking at the floor. The words snapped out. "Out-relief or the House?"

"The – the House, Sir. Our home has been taken."

"Names!"

"Samuel and Martha Peddelle, Sir. Our daughters are Sarah and Jane."

"Married?"

"Yes, Sir."

"Church or country-style?"

"Church, Sir."

"Ages?"

"I'm thirty six, as is my wife. Sarah is seven and Jane is three."

Slowly the details were set down in the register then the interrogation continued.

"Why are you not working, Peddelle?"

"Lost my job, Sir. I cannot find work."

"Why were you turned out of your home?"

"Debt, Sir. Outstanding debts."

The Master stroked his left ear. "Ah – a spendthrift are you?" He turned to his wife. "We shall have to teach Master Peddelle economy and thrift, my dear." There was a hint of sarcasm in his voice and Samuel reddened. "'Twere not so, Sir, if I may beg your pardon. The debt arose because five of our children died of the scarlet fever."

Samuel was pleased with his reply but he simply could not win.

"Seven children and no insurance!" There was a sudden biting hardness to the Master's sarcasm, "Can you not control your lust, man?"

Eyes downcast, Samuel had no answer, the humiliation bit too deep. The Master had not finished. "There will be none of that in this House. There will be no time or place for lust in this House." He turned to his wife. "Take the woman and children away, my dear."

Briefly Martha turned to look at Samuel and for a moment Samuel thought she was going to kiss him but the blank look in her eye told him otherwise. Then, as the Matron took her arm she obediently followed out of the room. Samuel looked on in despair. The Master brought him back to reality. "Why don't you enlist, Peddelle? Are you not aware that a war has been declared?"

"I didn't know that, Sir – about the war, Sir. I did enquire before but they said they only took men over five feet eight inches."

For a few moments the Master's voice softened. "Your wife does not seem well."

"It is since the children died, Sir. She hardly speaks."

"I will tell the Matron."

"Thank you, Sir."

Enid Oxenlade stamped her foot. "I don't care if war has been declared, you are not going. We need you here."

Peter Oxenlade stared in puzzled amazement. "You talked of nothing else yesterday. Now you say don't enlist."

"I'm frightened, Peter."

"People will think I'm a coward."

"I know you're no coward!"

"I hope you are right."

Victoria Welcome Peters smiled at Edward Holling. "Good day, Sir, may I help you?"

Victoria had been christened 'Victoria Welcome' at her father's insistence. The day she was born he had lifted her up with pride and said, 'You are most welcome, Victoria Peters.' Then he had turned to Mrs Peters and said, 'We shall call her Victoria Welcome, Mother.' And so it had been.

Edward blushed slightly and looked hesitantly in the direction of Mr Peters, proprietor of the largest grocer's shop in the High Street.

Mr Peters was unmoved by this gentle supplication and rather pointedly ignored him. Of course, had Mrs Holling entered the shop that would have been a different matter. Mr Peters would have leapt to give her deferential forelock-tugging service, but then Mrs Holling was the wife of the wealthiest lawyer in the town. Victoria moved forward. "You were very good last night – at the concert. You have a good voice."

He did not say so but Edward was pleased. In his eyes Victoria Peters was the most desirable girl in town, with her blue eyes, dark hair, trim waist and grave even features.

"The vicar has said I'm the best tenor in Oxfordshire." He said it more in wonder than as a boast. "I would rather be a tenor than a solicitor's clerk." Edward was due to join his father at the end of the week and he was not enthusiastic at the prospect.

"Word has it you would rather be a soldier!" As she said it Victoria raised her eyebrows in mock surprise. Captain Hanks had barely time to throw the six lads out of his office before the news flashed around the town.

Edward looked wistful. "Aye, that would be an adventure. Now we will miss all the fun."

"I would miss you if you went."

"Can I walk you to church on Sunday?"

"You had best ask my father."

The brave warrior suddenly looked fainthearted. Mr Peters looked around, peering over his glasses. "What's that?"

"Mr Holling wishes to walk me to church on Sunday, Father."

Mr Peters gave Edward the sort of look that a lepidopterist gives a butterfly just before pinning it. "Does he now?" He was about to say 'No', but the look on his daughter's face told him otherwise. Wisely he changed his mind. "Yes, Vicky and I will look forward to seeing you on Sunday. Now, let's have some service, Vicky. I'm sure Mr Holling does not wish to spend his whole day in idle chatter."

Mr Holling, senior, sniffed disdainfully. "This girl – her father is a shopkeeper, you say?"

"Yes, Father. Her name is Victoria Welcome Peters. Mr Peters owns the grocer's shop near the Birdcage."

"I trust this is not serious, young man." He was about to remark that in his view the Peters were 'trade' and not much above rough trade. "Need I remind you that we have a position and reputation to uphold in this town."

Edward maintained a discreet silence having incurred his father's ire twice in a few days. The stinging rebukes arising from the enlistment fiasco were still fresh in his memory.

* * * * * * *

The large dray horse snickered in appreciation as Thomas Guntrippe fed him an apple core. The horse was one of a pair that Thomas had looked after for over five years with a deep abiding affection. He was never happier than here in the stable, brushing, cleaning and polishing. Away from Rose's sharp tongue and comments. Perhaps if he had married someone less sensual and demanding than Rose he may have maintained his manly pride intact. No matter how hard he tried he could not prevent himself ejaculating beyond the count of three thrusts, then he was finished. As Rose's frustration grew her scorn kept pace with it and Thomas's pride and manhood took a terrible battering. But today he could put that aside, salvation in the form of a mobilisation had arrived. His kit was already packed and his uniform ready. Later in the afternoon the band would see them to the station, the crowds would cheer. For twenty minutes he would be a hero and his two young sons would have reason to be proud. Their dad would be one of the first to go to war. Already he was planning a Christmas treat for them, when this was all over and he could regale them with tales of derring-do. He gave the horses one last pat on the head and he turned away. At the door he paused and looked back but the horses, muzzles buried in fragrant oats, ignored him. It was as if he was forgotten already.

Sergeant Cox, Oxfordshire Constabulary, dismounted from his bicycle, leant it against the Pound fence and removed his trouser clips. He was an imposing man standing six and a half feet to the top of his helmet. Albert Harty looked up as he approached and gratefully put down his manure fork; a break from the daily monotony, and a chat, was always welcome.

"Good day, Sergeant. No more strays for me, I hope."

It was rare for a day to go by without Albert being called out to impound a few animals. Though that rarely happened on a Tuesday morning, Market Day. On Tuesday morning a stray was unlikely to be noticed unless it got into a garden. It was when the visiting stockmen and the farmers had drunk themselves into gentle insensibility that the problems started. Sergeant Cox removed his gloves. "No, there are no strays that need attention – not at the moment."

Albert was puzzled. "You seemed set on business, Sergeant?"

"Aye, there is a matter we need to talk about, Albert." Sergeant Cox looked around and seemed satisfied, "This is best kept quiet." He touched his nose.

"You can rely on me – soul of discretion, me." Albert spoke with quiet pride.

"Umm. It has come to my attention that you are a fighting man, Albert."

"Oh no, Sergeant. I would not call me a fighting man."

"Oh yes, Albert. Quick with a punch and a belt buckle."

"I have never touched a man hereabouts with a buckle – on my word."

"'Tis not men we are talking about – 'tis women. You have taken to beating your wife to the distress of your neighbours."

"You'm treading on dangerous ground, Sergeant." Albert's voice turned angry. "You have no right to come between husband and wife."

"So you don't deny it then? Not that it would do any good if you did." He put his arm around Albert's shoulder so that he could speak softly in his ear. "I shall be watching you most carefully. If one more black eye or bruise is reported to me, I am going to make your life a misery, Albert"

Albert recoiled in shock, fists clenched. "'Tis agin the law to threaten me."

"You are a coward, Albert! D'you hear me? Only the worst sort of man beats a woman."

"'Tis a man's right to chastise – always has been."

"Perhaps you had better enlist, Albert. The army needs fighting men."

"You called me a coward!"

"Aye, that I did. So prove me wrong and enlist."

Thomas Guntrippe picked up his youngest lad and gave him a hug and kiss on the cheek, his oldest lad hung back uncertain as to how to react to this display of emotion. "Goodbye, son. See you both soon. Be good for your mother."

Then he stepped up into the carriage, clearly marked third class. Several hundred people thronged the platform and the town band was playing at full throttle. Rose Guntrippe waited until Thomas was on the train before she stepped forward and proffered a cheek for a kiss. Thomas leant out. "Don't forget. Go to the Town Hall on Friday to get your allowance."

"Don't you forget to write."

The whistle blew, the last door clanged shut and the engine shuddered. Slowly the train pulled away. Rosie had to shout. "Be careful, Thomas."

As Rose stepped back to leave the Town Mayor walked past. "You must be very proud, Mrs Guntrippe – very proud."

Rose did not answer but just nodded her head and gave a weak smile to show she was pleased at the acknowledgement. Suddenly the excitement did not really seem to fit the day. Looking around she knew that she was the only one to feel any apprehension.

Peter Oxenlade's allotment bounded the railtrack so he had a grandstand view as the troop train puffed its way to Oxford and beyond. He gave a wave but there was deep envy in his heart. Even now he could hear the music in the station yard and sense the excitement as the heroes left town. Reluctantly he went back to his hoeing. Another night beckoned at the bakery. Another night of toil. Another day of humdrum monotony. Peter yearned for some excitement. He could not understand Enid's objection to his enlistment, secretly he resolved to be away if the chance was offered. Should the war be over by Christmas perhaps it was already too late, he thought. By the time he had been through the enlistment procedure and eight weeks of training it would be time to go home. His heart ached at the thought.

William Smithe stared at the Agent in amazement. Mr Castle, Agent of the town cattle market and auctioneer extraordinary was not impressed. "Come on lad, move yourself. The sooner this is done the sooner we can be off." William's argument was somewhat subdued, he did not wish to give offence on his first day on the job. Notwithstanding he felt that he should at least indicate that shovelling cow shit did not fit the job of auctioneer's clerk as he understood it. "I'm sorry, Mr Castle, I didn't realise that shovelling was part of the job – isn't that what the labourers do?"

Mr Castle was neither impressed nor annoyed. "At the end of the day we must clean the market, then we can all go home. Custom and practice, Master Smithe, custom and practice. You all," he emphasised the word all, "help! Now, if this doesn't suit then you can speak to me in my office tomorrow."

William missed the looks of glee on the faces of the market staff. He did not realise that he had fallen for the old trick always played on new lads. William had seen the band march off towards the railway station, people cheering the heroes on their way; he silently cursed the trick of fate that meant he was sixteen, instead of eighteen.

James Pullene opened the ledger and dipped his pen in the inkwell. The high windows of the bank gave a fair light in which to work but the bottom halves were frosted so no life showed through. He sighed and meticulously entered the date. Was this to be his daily world he wondered, shut within a stuffy world of high collars, dusty books and money? How he longed for the spring when he would be able to put bat to ball; warm inviting days, full of cream teas and good fellowship. His reverie was abruptly shattered when a bristling senior clerk stood beside him. "Get on with your work, Pullene!"

The postman dropped the bag on Harold Jones' desk. "Damn bag gets heavier every day, Harold."

"There's a new regulation every day and five requests for official information." Harold emptied the bag of mail into a tray and handed it back. "I'll sort that lot later."

"Jones!" The Town Clerk stood behind him. "Get that mail delivered now."

"Yes, Sir." He quietly cursed as the clerk walked off.

The postman winked. "Proper sergeant-major that – you'd be better off in the army."

"Aye, you're right, Postie." He crossed his fingers, "Next year I shall be away."

The spanner slipped and Freddie Cox surveyed his skinned knuckles with dismay. His father had insisted he learn the trade.

"The car is the future, Freddie. It will change the world. It is the greatest thing next to flying!" Maybe, thought Freddie, when they work, but there was nothing more useless and stupid than a car that would not go. He blew on his wounded hand to ease the pain as his father entered the workshop. "Mr Wallace will be here in two hours for that car. Is it ready?"

"Not yet, Father."

"Well, get a move on!"

John Howe knocked on the door and waited, pencil poised over his notebook. The door reluctantly opened and Mrs Dobie appeared, rubbing wet hands on her apron. "Why do you always knock when I'm in the middle of doing something?"

John smiled, as instructed. "That will be tuppence, Mrs Dobie."

Mrs Dobie sniffed. "Insurance you call it. Bloodsuckers say I. All give and no take. When do I get a payout?"

"When you die, Mrs Dobie – which I hope will never happen."

"Course you would, more money for you isn't it. Never ending!"

She handed over the tuppence and her book. "Make sure you write it down proper."

"All done, Mrs Dobie. I trust Mr Dobie is well."

"No thanks to you lot!"

"Good day, Mrs Dobie."

Edward Holling settled in the corner of the rail carriage and relaxed. He counted his blessings. As the junior in his father's office it was his job to take the briefs to the various lawyers and barristers in Oxford with whom his father worked. A few hours of freedom, a chance to buy some song sheets and think of a future outside the dusty files of the law. Also there was the evening to look forward to, choir practice with Vicky Peters by his side. If only I could join the army, life would be perfect, he thought.

The drover had left his small herd in the auctioneer's pen and had been pleased when an hour later the cattle were sold and the bank draft was safely in his pocket. Pleased at the outcome he stopped at the Four Horseshoes to quench his thirst before leaving town. He downed half a pint in one gulp and turned to George Coates. "That was welcome, friend."

"Far to go?" George was not really interested.

The drover nodded. "A fair bit, friend but I shall take the train."

George had never been more than ten miles from Thame in his whole life, suddenly he felt mild envy of this stranger. "I've a mind to go to Oxford next month."

The drover finished his pint and beckoned for another. "You want to go further than that, friend. If you want to be treated fair, that is."

George bridled at this slight. "I get treated fair – none does me down!"

"I enquired at the market, the going rate for farm labourers is thirteen shillings a week except at harvest when you have to work double."

"There you have it, stranger, you were told true."

The drover took a long slow sip. "It's been a good day. Let me buy you a pint." Hastily George pushed his glass forward, this was a rare occasion. The drover raised his glass. "May you get a fair wage yet, my friend."

George supped his new pint. "I get treated fair, I tell 'ee."

"Men get one pound a week in most places."

"One pound – a week!" George gulped, "'Tis not true."

"Why should I lie? I tell you it is only hereabouts you are treated so. Bring your family to Wiltshire and you will see."

"Is that where you come from? Wiltshire?" George was about to ask where that was but suddenly he did not want to show his ignorance.

Another passing stranger down the bar butted in. "I had heard they only paid twelve shillings here, in my county they pay eighteen or nineteen shilling." He looked at George. "You are being cheated."

George nodded his head in acknowledgement and looked pensive. 'Have I been taken for a fool?' he thought, 'Have we all been taken for fools?' he thought. He could feel the anger rising in himself. 'Why have we been cheated all these years?' 'Why the hard days when there was no need?' In frustration he said a silent prayer. "Dear God, I have been a fool among fools, save us from ourselves."

John Howe sounded disappointed , in truth he was bitterly disappointed. Not once in his memory had the September Show failed to take place. Not once had the great funfair failed to assemble. "I never thought that a war would close the show." James Pullene and Harold Jones nodded in sympathy at this dreadful news. Freddie Coxe was the most disappointed of all. Last year he had won every race from the one hundred yards to the mile and he looked forward to repeating the triumph. Earlier he had seen his only rival, Thomas Guntrippe, march out of town. Even that rivalry was limited because Thomas's distance had been the mile.

Edward Holling noted Freddie's disappointment. "You must keep training, Freddie. They are bound to hold the county games."

"We must all keep fit if we are to enlist." Harold said what several had been thinking. "Captain Hanks is to open the office tomorrow to take volunteers."

Wistful looks flew around the room, the show forgotten. Edward returned them to reality. "We are here to rehearse. Now, close harmony."

"We were sailing along on Moonlight Bay – on Moonlight Bay. We could hear the voices . . . . "

* * * * * * *

Thomas Guntrippe had joined the 'Ox and Bucks' early in September as part of the first reserves to reach the battalion since it landed in France. The battalion had, like the rest of the British Army, taken a fearful hammering as it tried to halt the German offensive trying to smash its way to Paris. Normally reservists would be introduced by degrees, given time to acclimatise, a chance to settle in. Not at that time, no such luxury was possible, the reserves had gone straight into action. After intercepting the

German Army at Mons the French and British Armies had been forced back in a long retreat. When the day came to counterattack the allies had pushed the German army back to their new defence lines on the River Aisne. There both sides settled down to digging trenches and killing, often both at the same time. All that was now in the past, a period of ten weeks during which time Thomas had learned how to stay alive. Now it was November.

Early in his service it had been recognised that Thomas was a runner. Not that he could sprint at the top speed of his youth, but he had stamina and could run a mile with rifle and pack in five minutes. An ability that impressed his commanding officer, because with brigade headquarters a mile back, stamina was more important than speed as the messages went back and forth. On the 10th November, the German Army, determined to end the stalemate, launched a major attack about three miles east of Ypres. The attack, by the crack Prussian Grenadiers and Guards Divisions, broke through the British line defences near a spot known as 'Black Watch Corner' and swept forward into the wood of Nonne Bosschen and the edge of another nearby wood, Glencourse Wood on the morning of the 11th November. It was just bad luck that the reserve battalion for the broken line was the Ox and Bucks! They had just finished washing and breakfasting on a cold grey winter's day when the order to advance with extreme urgency reached them. It was a two mile forced cross country march to the tiny village of Westhock, right in the path of the German advance. As they approached the front they were dismayed to see the British artillery pulling back in disarray. Between Westhock and Nonne Bosschen lay five hundred yards of open ground, the first two hundred yards was gently rising ground to a slight ridge then the ground fell away to the wood. The ridge was being held by a motley rag-bag of wounded infantrymen and support staff. Every cook, bottle-washer, servant, quartermaster staff and a few junior nco's had been thrown forward, together with the walking wounded, a desperate attempt to hold the front. Over to the left a small group of Highlanders held grimly to a defensive ditch. Unbeknown to the Ox and Bucks, a company of Royal Engineers' sappers were holding desperately to the left flank at the edge of Polygon Wood, some half a mile off.

Within minutes of arriving at Westhock the Ox and Bucks Commanding Officer, Leiutenant-Colonel Davies had made his assessment and desperate for reinforcements had sent Thomas Guntrippe to the rear to the Brigade Headquarters with a message. With a quarter mile of the return leg of his journey stretching out in front of him, Thomas lengthened his stride, despite the rising ache, knowing that the reply message was urgent.

The shell hit the nearby roof of the farmyard barn and exploded, sending steel balls and shards flying all around. Thomas Guntrippe had heard the 'whizz' as the shell arrived and instinctively he tried to drop to the ground on his stomach. He was too late and although he was twelve feet from the explosion he was thrown forward with great force, smashing into a low wall. A piece of shrapnel sliced through his uniform sleeve and removed a sliver of his right arm, as if it were a scalpel. Thomas did not feel it, consciousness had left him a second before. He had no idea how long he had been lying there when he awoke but it took him a few minutes to gain control and even then his ears were ringing and his head ached from a great bruise across his forehead. His first inclination was to go back, away from the intense noise of battle but reluctantly he remembered his duty so he forced himself to his feet and stumbled on at a half run. As he neared the front line trenches the shelling intensified and there was a constant rattle of rifle and machine gun fire. He reached the battalion headquarters, a small dugout, the entrance of which was draped with a tattered old blanket. In his hurry to deliver his message, Thomas tripped into the entrance bringing down the blanket and lay sprawling on the floor at the feet of a stony faced Sergeant Major. "Ah! Guntrippe! You've taken your bloody time."

Thomas felt for the scrap of paper in his tunic pocket and handed it over, it was received without thanks. "Look at the state of you. Where's your hat?" The Sergeant Major turned. "Message from brigade, Sir!"

The commanding officer, Lieutenant Colonel Davies stepped over, took the paper and read it, shaking his head in sorrow.

Outside the noise of gunfire grew louder. The Colonel waved everyone closer. "Sergeant Major. You will go with Guntrippe and assemble every man not in the front line, arm them and be ready to move forward to the ridge in ten minutes."

The Sergeant Major picked up a bandolier of 303 rifle ammunition. "What men are excused, Sir?"

"None, Sergeant Major, none except the blind. Every man will fight – cooks, batmen, shit-house wallahs, runners, QM staff and the walking wounded. Get me a rifle as well." He turned to his officers. "I asked for reserves. There are none – not one man!"

He paused for effect. "None! However, luck is on our side. The Bosch have been attacking and fighting for over sixteen hours. That is why they are holding in the woods. Pulling their men together and having a rest."

"They are getting stronger all the time, Sir." The Adjutant intervened, "there must be over two thousand guards in Nun's Wood."

"There is no proper defensive line here nor is there time to create one. We have only one chance. We must clear that wood now – if not the Bosch will be marching on Paris this evening because there's nothing behind us to stop them."

"We are outnumbered four to one, Sir. It will be touch and go." The Adjutant had just returned from the ridge and had taken a good look at the German infantry through his binoculars, there was a touch of awe in his voice, "They are damn great men, all over six feet. They tower over our lads!"

"Good – it will be easier to shoot the beggars. Now, the Brigadier and I are agreed. This is a bayonet job. A rapid charge before the Bosch decide either to advance or dig in. In ten minutes, gentlemen, we will move forward to the edge of the ridge with fixed bayonets. A and B companies in the centre will lead the attack. C on the left, D on the right. C and D will give supporting fire until the leading companies reach the edge of the wood then they will follow in with the bayonet."

"What will be the signal to attack, Sir?"

"No signal, at three p.m. precisely A and B will charge."

"How far do we advance, Sir?"

"Clear the wood." He glanced at his watch. "Are we agreed, Gentlemen? It is now 14.45. At 1500 we go."

"It's three hundred yards from the ridge to the edge of the wood, Sir. It would be of great help if C and D fired fifteen rounds rapid." The commander of B company crossed his fingers.

"Agreed. C and D, fifteen rounds rapid, it is."

Fifteen rounds rapid was the classic British infantry tactic. Men spent hours practising to fire fifteen aimed rounds in sixty seconds. A well trained company of two hundred men could pour three thousand rounds of 303 at an enemy in a minute. Many a German Regiment thought they were being subjected to machine gun fire when an infantry company opened fire.

In the centre of B company, Thomas Guntrippe, fed ten rounds of 303 into his magazine, then locked the bayonet into position. At the last moment he remembered the old trick of holding down the rounds through the loading chamber as he slid the bolt forward an inch then he took a loose round and fed it into the breech and closed the bolt behind it. Now he had eleven shots instead of ten before reloading. Looking ahead he could see quite clearly a number of grey clad infantry were lining the wood and firing at them. For a moment he thought 'no one can cross this distance and live', but he forced it out of his mind. A few minutes later every thought but hate was forced from his mind as a fusillade of shots rang out and two companies charged forward with bayonets to the fore, a great surge of adrenaline urging them on.

By a small margin Thomas was first to the edge of the wood and with a great roaring shout he plunged in and loosed off a shot despite the fact that most of the German Guards he could see put their hands up in surrender. "Handy ho – handy ho!" He found himself screaming time and time again. His platoon sergeant appeared beside him.

"Line up, lads – line up!" Sweat was pouring from his face. "We must keep on – forward!"

Thomas calmed, his throat was hoarse and his mouth bone dry, he tried to answer but all he could do was croak. Ahead some

German Infantry tried to run and he raised his rifle to fire but the firing pin clicked into an empty breech. His magazine was empty, desperately he fumbled for a fresh clip of 303. There was blood on his bayonet. 'My God, how did that get there!', he thought.

"Forward!" The Sergeant yelled as loud as he could.

Thomas found his voice. "Bastards!"

It was quite dark but burning buildings, Verylights and continuous gunflashes gave sufficient light to allow the file of troops to move slowly forward to their front line positions. Despite the light they stumbled and cursed, although quietly. The rumble of guns ahead stifled any blatant display of martial spirit. This was reinforced by the arrival of a shell close by, making the men drop to the ground seeking whatever meagre cover was available. Over to the right of the road a bunch of men sat or slept on the ground, seemingly able to sleep despite the explosions and the cold of the night. They looked like a rabble, a dirty, dishevelled and exhausted rabble. One of the rabble shook the man sat next to him. "Tom, have you got a fag? I'd give a week's pay for a fag."

"And me, I'll ask these new lads." Thomas Guntrippe stood up and hobbled over to the advancing column. "Anyone got a packet of Woodbines, mates? We haven't had a fag for days."

His luck held, one man stopped and felt in his pouch. "Here y'are, soldier. What lot are you?"

"Ox and Bucks, mate".

"How'd you get in that state?" He pointed at Thomas's ripped, muddy and bloody uniform, "Ye look like mudlarks."

Thomas shrugged and took a cigarette from the packet. "Been in the line, got knocked about." He lit the cigarette and took a deep puff.

"Where's the rest of your lot?" The stranger continued to probe. Thomas waved at the fifty men behind him. "Gone – we're all that's left."

"Half your company gone then?"

Thomas shook his head. "No mate – this is the battalion."

"Good God, there's nobbut fifty!"

"Aye," Thomas agreed, "I shall have summat to tell my lad."

Joss Parker, head gamekeeper, stepped forward to the side of the automobile and took off his bowler hat. "Have you'm any instructions, Surr?"

Joss was a mite embarrassed, with the steady loss of men he was forced to undertake duties he would have considered beneath his dignity only a few months back. Now he was dusty from moving sacks of grain in his store; the chauffeur glared at him as he neared the car. Having just spent several hours cleaning and polishing the Armstrong-Siddeley limousine the chauffeur was not prepared to have Joss spoiling his handiwork, even if he was the head gamekeeper. Mr Wykham-Musgrave, owner of Thame Park, looked pensive. "I will return in the autumn for the shooting, maintain the proper standards, Parker."

"You'm can rely on me, as always, Surr. Haven't I served you for thirty five years?"

"Damn this war! The new tenant will be here in a few months but don't forget, you work for the estate, not him."

"What of Barnes, Surr?"

"Barnes as well – you know how to contact my agent?"

"I do, Surr. May I wish you'm a Merry Christmas, Surr – and your good lady."

"The old world is changing, Parker. Our world is changing . . . . "

"Surely not, Surr."

"I'm afraid so, it will never be the same again. Drive on, Barclay."

Chapter 2   1915: 'ONLY MAKE BELIEVE'

Miss Turle, Mistress of the first year pupils at the British School in Park Street, peered over her glasses. This was not easy because she was sitting on a high stool behind her elevated desk while the object she was viewing was only three feet from the floor at its highest point. "You may sit down, Robert. I am about to call the register."

Robert Guntrippe, aged six and four months, stood his ground with a dogged expression on his face. "Me Mam said I should ask, Miss." He held out a crumpled and grimy envelope.

"What is your question, Robert?"

"Dad has written us – from France."

"Good news, I hope."

"I doesn't rightly know, Miss. Mam cannot read proper. She said I'd to ask you."

"Put the letter here, Robert," she pointed to the desk top by her inkwell, "we will look at it at playtime."

"Me Dad has gone to fight, Miss. Me Mam said good riddance, Miss, but I miss him and want him to come home."

Miss Turle smiled, she had never heard Robert say so many words before. "There are many fathers away, Robert. Before we go home we will say a special prayer for them all and ask God to keep them safe."

Robert maintained a solemn face. "I spit on a stone and throw it over my shoulder, Miss."

"I think a prayer would be best, Robert."

"It's only make believe, Miss."

Robert reached up on tiptoe and put the envelope on the desk top, then whispered with pride. "I'm going to be a soldier, Miss, one day."

George Coates crouched, picked up the snared rabbit and loosened the wire noose. Deftly he dropped the rabbit into his sack and then wiped the wires clean before resetting the snare around the opening. He would have been and gone before now on most days, he preferred a dawn start in winter and early spring, but there had been an overnight frost and any footsteps on frosted grass would have left an imprint that could be seen for days. He could not afford to risk leaving such an obvious trail. Pheasants were scarce but he didn't mind that, he much preferred a tasty rabbit stew and hares were plentiful.

Suddenly George was aware of an unnatural quiet around him. No bird song or calls. Something was wrong. He suppressed the urge to turn and run, nothing would draw attention to him more quickly than a fast retreat. Movement and noise were his enemies. Senses fully alert, he looked and listened, his head still but his eyes scanning every bush, tree and shrub within sight. When he did move it was slowly and with extreme care. Three minutes later and one hundred yards away a rabbit emerged from a thicket and ears raised hopped hesitantly out into the open. George watched it intently and speculated. Was the rabbit just being naturally cautious or could it sense danger? He breathed a sigh of relief as the rabbit crouched to the grass and started to nibble.

George weighed his options. Straight on? Veer to the right, down the hedgeline. Veer to the left, go around the back of the thicket the rabbit had emerged from. Mind made up, he picked up his sack and went left, the safest route to his mind, follow his second trap line down towards Sydenham.

Headkeeper Parker had fashioned a small inconspicuous hide in the hedgerow thirty yards to the front of the rabbit. A week ago he had found a part of one of George's traplines. His practised eye told him that he had a habitual expert poacher on his hands and his whole professional being was affronted and outraged. Theft from under his nose, poaching right under his nose, from the estate he was paid to protect! So far Parker had not told Sidney Barnes of his find. He was convinced that the poacher was a townsman and he wondered if there may be collusion. Surely Barnes must have found signs before now and should have reported it, even if it were only a suspicion. In Parker's mind Barnes was either incompetent or turning a blind eye, neither was acceptable to him. Three days past

Parker had caught a brief glimpse of George, not sufficient to allow identification but enough to confirm his suspicions. He had been sure that today he would confront the thief. In more normal times Parker would have borrowed several keepers from an adjacent estate. That was impossible now, the men had gone to war and Parker was feeling his age. After keeping still for so long his arthritic hip was starting to hurt, he must move soon. 'Damn', he thought, 'I will get this bugger yet.' Angry with himself he thumbed back the hammer of his gun, raised it to his shoulder and in one fluid movement, sighted and fired. The one innocent party in all this, the rabbit, died without even knowing it was at risk.

George was nearly half a mile away when he heard the shot. He did not even pause or look back, he simply noted that he had been right to be cautious but it left him in a quandary. Was it an ambush or coincidence? He did not know but commonsense told him not to return for some days, the risk was too great.

The Master of the Thame Union Workhouse stared intently at Samuel Peddelle making poor Samuel both alarmed and guilty in equal parts but without knowing why, so he fidgeted under the close scrutiny. There was rarely much direct contact between Master and inmate and many months had passed since the Master had even acknowledged Samuel's existence. On receiving the summons Samuel had concluded that he had done something wrong or inadvertently broken one of the many rules. He racked his brain but to no effect, he could think of no reason, cause or wrongdoing but it did not quieten his worry.

The Master came straight to the point. "What I am about to say, Peddelle, should come as no shock to you." He paused to give Samuel time to digest his words. "No shock at all!"

Samuel stared back in astonishment. The Master continued, "I am referring to your wife, man – your wife!"

Samuel could only gulp. "My wife, Sir?"

The Master's voice displayed a mounting irritation. "Yes, Peddelle, your wife. Have you not noticed on your Sunday visits that her behaviour is odd – not the behaviour of a well person."

"She does not say much, Sir, but I did not think she were dying."

The Master's voice turned from irritation to exasperation. "Tch! She is not dying. We are talking of her unnatural behaviour. Can you not sense that her mind is unsound?"

Samuel hesitated, dredging up the courage to disagree. "No, Sir, not that surely. Since the children died it has been natural for her to say little. It is just grief, Sir."

The Master shook his head firmly, in disagreement. "If it were only that we would not be speaking. There would be no need of action. Unfortunately those responsible for her have noted a deterioration and she is getting worse. There is no alternative, I will get the Medical Officer to examine her next week."

"What of my girls, Sir?"

"There is no need of concern, they are in the care of the Matron. My wife is a God-fearing woman and she will see that they are properly mannered, scrubbed and diligent in their sewing. They will make excellent servants when they are old enough to contract out."

"May I speak to them, Sir?"

"There is no need of that, Peddelle. You have not set them a proper example. Sunday will be soon enough."

"Yes, Sir."

"That will be all, Peddelle. Back to work now, enough time has been wasted."

Edward Holling clapped his hands to get their attention. "The Vicar has asked that we sing at the Saturday concert. If you will look at the sheets you will find two new songs, we must rehearse those."

James Pullene pulled the stool up to the piano and opened up the keyboard. "These tunes are tricky, Edward. You had better get Miss Stokes to rehearse, you know her right foot is fierce."

It was well known that Miss Stokes could thump out a tune with a good strong beat, in fact it was difficult to get her to do otherwise as she possessed a strong martial spirit. It would take a deal of persuasion to curb her foot because since the war had begun Miss Stokes' martial instincts had been growing in dominance. As a result several men had suffered Miss Stokes' scorn and invective because they were not in uniform.

"I will speak to her." Edward tried to assert himself. "Now, let's try the first song. It fits in well with our minstrel songs, it's called 'Old Man River'. James, play the introduction please."

The parlour door opened and Mrs Pullene bustled in with a large tray of lemonade and cake, her weekly offering. A chorus of hearty 'thank-you's' followed her to the door. John Howe puzzled over the second song sheet. "This is going to be tricky. This is a duet for soprano and tenor."

Freddie Coxe was quite unconcerned. "We've done comic songs before – Bill can sing the high notes."

William Smithe bristled. "This is not comic – it's a serious song. Who will sing soprano seriously? Not me!"

There was great consternation all around. Edward had paid one shilling for the song sheet, suddenly it looked as if this great sum of money was to be wasted. Harold Jones voiced all their opinions. "Sorry, Edward, but I don't think we can use this."

With serious face Edward Holling gave the situation due and thoughtful consideration. "There is a solution if you all agree."

Five blank faces looked at him. "If you all agree I could ask Victoria Peters to sing with me."

"Oh dear. Are you sure she can sing." James Pullene sounded very doubtful. The others stood by him all shaking their heads and looking even more doubtful.

"She sings very well in church!" Edward sounded defensive. "She sings well I tell you, I would not . . . . "

He suddenly realised that the other five were all grinning fit to split their faces and he stopped and blushed. They had caught him out. James Pullene turned back to the keyboard. "Now that Edward has admitted he has a best girl we had better get on with this rehearsal."

Alfred Stevens leaned back in his chair, drew deeply on his cigar then puffed out a cloud of fragrant smoke. The Headmaster of the grammar school watched him indulgently. Alfred was his favourite member of staff and he looked forward to these monthly dinners together with the greatest of pleasure. Dinner finished, brandy to hand and cigars lit they both settled down to conversation.

The Headmaster raised his glass. "A toast, Alfred. This has been a most successful season, which after the cricket success is most remarkable. I am most proud, most proud."

"Thank you. Headmaster."

"I make no bones about it. It is very much down to your leadership and example that our boys have risen to the challenge. This success at football will stand them in good stead, this is what leadership is all about."

"If this war goes on we will need many leaders. Have you seen the lists of our old boys who have enlisted, Headmaster?"

The smile left the Headmaster's face. "My worry is that we will lose our brightest and best, so much for the thought that this would all be over by Christmas."

"That brings me to myself, Headmaster. You may recall that I spent time training as an officer cadet when I was at University."

"Yes, but that was a good many years ago."

Alfred paused before answering, he had not looked forward to this moment but there was no going back now. "I have been offered a commission. I do not see how I can refuse with honour but that would go against my conscience because I believe it is my duty to serve."

"I would never question your honour, Alfred, but I do have a concern if you will allow me to speak."

Alfred nodded in reply and the Headmaster continued. "My first concern is that you are thirty five which seems rather late for a soldiering career." He put his hand up as Alfred went to protest. "But that is not my prime concern. Can you not see that the boys of this school have a greater need of you – perhaps a greater need even than the army. Where will I find a dedicated and gifted master such as you?"

"I have thought long on this and my mind is made up. Can I go with your blessing? It means a great deal to me."

"Will you stay until Easter, Alfred? Give me time to find another master."

"Agreed."

The Vicar advanced to the edge of the stage. Miss Stokes gave forth a tinkle of notes to announce his presence and in return earned a grateful smile as the audience quietened. Miss Stokes' heart nearly burst with emotion as the Vicar raised his arms. "Thank you all for coming – we have raised the sum of one pound, five shillings and thre'pence for our brave soldiers." He paused as a great cheer went up from the audience. "Now don't forget, everyone. All the knitting must be at the Vicarage by Wednesday – I am told it takes a week to get to our soldiers. Also Mrs Bushell needs more volunteers to sew sandbags, please let her know if you can help. The last item concerns billeting. Two hundred soldiers will be arriving soon for several weeks, en route to France. Please give details of available rooms direct to the Town Hall."

He stopped and looked to the wings to make sure everything was ready; a thumb went up. "Ladies and gentlemen our next phantasmagorical vision will both delight and excite you. A new duo performing for you for the first time, please give them a warm welcome – Edward Holling and Victoria Peters."

Victoria stepped forward, her heart beating fast and Edward held out his hand to lead her on to the stage. She gave him a grateful look. When she had spoken to her parents they had not objected to her singing, it was singing with Edward Holling that made them hesitate, especially when they understood that the song was a 'love song'. In private Mr Peters had used two rude words to Mrs Peters, much to her horror, when she feigned deafness he had said the words again, – 'Chorus girl'. In the end Mrs Peters with her greater romantic inclination had won the argument, as she pointed out she intended to attend this concert and she expected an escort and a new dress. There was no need for Victoria to be apprehensive as she stepped forward on to the stage because at that very moment Mrs Pullene turned to her neighbour. "You must be very proud, Mr

Peters, such a beautiful and talented daughter, a great credit to you."

Mr Peters relaxed and hoisted his pride. "The talent comes from my side, Mrs Pullene, I had a rare voice as a lad."

Miss Stokes pounded out the two bar introduction but moderated her foot as she picked up Edward's warning glance.

"Only make believe I love you,
Only make believe that you love me,
Others find peace of mind in pretending,
Couldn't you, couldn't I . . . . "

Mrs Peters leant across. "This song makes me feel quite young and romantic, Father."

"Does it now – perhaps we can call in the Anchor for a port and lemon after."

"Make believe our lips are blending
In a tender kiss or two or three . . . . "

The night had been a tiring one for Peter Oxenlade, a long hard shift. He eased the tension by flexing his shoulders and he tried to remove the grit from his eyes by giving them a good hard rub. He had arrived at the bakery at ten o'clock the previous evening only to find that his assistant had failed to turn up. So the sacks of flour were still in the storehouse, the ovens were unlit, there was no warm water for the yeast and he had to search for the salt. Peter rolled up his sleeves and set to work. Throughout the night he toiled desperately trying to catch up but never quite succeeding. He was still hard at work when the shop bell rang insistently sharp on 7a.m. heralding the first customer. Lads from the hotels and bigger houses demanded their daily orders of fresh baked bread and rolls. "Come on Peter, the first residents are up and wanting their breakfasts!" Young children roused early from warm beds shouted for supplies of yesterday's stale bread, sold at less than half price. Extra hot rolls were wanted for 'The Swan' and 'Spread Eagle'.

Gradually the early rush subsided and Peter waited patiently for the proprietor, Mr Howes, to appear and take over the daily duties.

Then Peter could go home to his bed. That was when Miss Stokes appeared. "One large bloomer and a small wholemeal, young man – and no dirty fingers, thank you."

Dutifully Peter wiped his hands on his apron then placed the loaves in Miss Stokes' basket. "That will be sixpence, Miss."

Her hand went out to touch the bread. "As I thought, this bread is still hot! I want properly turned out bread that can be cut."

"Sorry Miss, there hasn't been time."

"Not time? Disgraceful! Have you been sitting idle instead of getting on with your job?"

"No Miss, the bread will cut if you wait twenty minutes. You are very early this morning."

"Don't be impertinent, young man. You should be grateful you are not in France where brave men are fighting for their country. Not skulking in Thame and making excuses."

On better days Peter would have bitten his tongue or quietly tugged his forelock in submission but he was tired and Miss Stokes had touched a raw nerve. "That applies to women too."

"How dare you – you – you cowardly scoundrel!"

"Yes miss, there are plenty of VAD's needed if you want to serve your country."

Miss Stokes clutched her bosom and closed her eyes. "Oh, you wicked, wicked man. Mr Howes shall hear of this."

"What has happened here?" Mr Howes filled the doorway.

"Oh Peter, how could you?" Enid Oxenlade could not believe what she had just heard. Peter Oxenlade stood there with a stupid grin on his face, pleased with himself and strangely elated. "I should have enlisted afore today. Now someone else can bake the bread, I've done with that."

"But why did you upset Miss Stokes?"

"She were the last straw I tell 'ee."

"Then you can go back and tell them you've changed your mind."

Peter waved the shilling at her. "Don't be daft – I'm a soldier. My train warrant is in my pocket."

Enid passed from anger to fear and the tears started to fall. "Miss Stokes is just an excuse."

Peter put his arms around her. "Nay – but there are lots like Miss Stokes, pointing the finger. I will not be called coward."

Enid could see only the possible hardships. "How will we manage on a soldier's pay? What if you are hurt?"

"Over one hundred have gone already – it will soon be over."

Enid wiped her eyes but was not mollified. "Everyone said it would be over by Christmas. Now the telegrams arrive and people wear black – widders' weeds."

"Give us a kiss, love and come to bed – I must leave on the first train in the morning."

* * * * * * *

The Ox and Bucks had been in reserve for four days. Long enough to get a change of clothes and dip in a bath, long enough for the lice to gain a new foothold in the seams of their clothing. More than long enough to get heartily sick of digging yet more trenches, a task that seemed to occupy most of each day. The only relief was that they were far enough from the front trenches to escape aimed shelling. They were far enough back to escape direct observation but not far enough to escape the occasional random or misdirected shell. Each explosion was sufficient to remind them constantly of where they were and what a return to the front line would entail. Thomas Guntrippe lived in the hope that salvation would arrive in the form of a summons demanding his services as a runner. His prayers went unanswered and the constant drone of the sergeant major's instruction and invective intruded on his thoughts. Dig! Keep digging! Dig faster! Dig deeper! Oh, grateful relief from the monotony. Fill sandbags! Fill those bags faster! Fill more sandbags! So the days went by, when they weren't digging or filling they looked for food or slept the sleep of the damned. Fitful uncomfortable sleep made worse by the cold, sleep that did not renew nor revitalise. The men still sang along during the work parties but there was no joy in it anymore, just a deep, deep longing to *'Take me back to dear old Blighty!'*

The sergeant major had long since given up on direct motivation, like all old soldiers they had perfected the art of looking busy and doing nothing. Now it was forty yards in a morning and six feet deep – measured to the inch. There was no escape, just the sergeant major's tantalising words. "Only another ten yards, lads, then its hot tea, a bacon sandwich and letters from home."

With a deep inward groan Thomas swung his pick to loosen more sub-soil. He thought back to the first time he had been sent into the reserve area, many months ago now and the company officer saying it was for 'well-earned' rest and recuperation. After several days of unremitting toil only utter tiredness and dejection had saved him from a charge of mutiny.

A heavy shell exploded some fifty yards away to the right and automatically the whole company dropped to the ground in one single fluid movement, learnt from months of exposure to danger. Thomas felt the ground tremble and a smattering of debris rained down. The whole company counted. If no more shells fell for twenty seconds they would carry on working. The count ended and the sergeant major was on his feet. "Up you get, lads – let's be moving."

Suddenly a shout echoed down the line. "Guntrippe! Report to the Adjutant." Thomas closed his eyes for three seconds and said a quick prayer of thanks to Lady Luck.

The Adjutant clamped his pipe between his teeth and puffed foul fumes at Thomas. Smoke filled the whole dugout, the Adjutant was of the firm opinion that tobacco smoke deterred rats, mice and lice. Thomas put his heels together and saluted, desperately trying to give the impression that he was bright and eager for duty. "Reporting for duty, Sir."

The Adjutant was not impressed. "Your uniform is a disgrace, Guntrippe. Did no-one tell you we have visitors?"

"No, Sir, been digging, Sir."

"Never mind. I've a special job for you. A party of the Middlesex are coming up the line. In one hour you will take them forward and familiarise them with the area."

Thomas's heart sank. "That will take all night, Sir!"

"There are times, Guntrippe when your astuteness and perspicacity of mind simply astound me. I fear you may have Staff Officer potential and we will lose you."

Thomas wondered whether he was being praised or not and he searched the Adjutant's face for clues. None were forthcoming.

"Be ready in one hour, Guntrippe."

Thomas's hopes faded. He had hoped that a message to brigade was required. A chance of freedom. A visit to the canteen two miles to the rear. A few hours in a bar even, a heavenly glass of beer. No, this is not fair, he wanted to shout out. Why should he go back to the mud, the danger, the noise and a night without sleep.

"Yes Sir, one hour it is, Sir."

Herbert Richard Peters, grocer and solid citizen, twiddled his moustache, frowned strongly making his forehead wrinkle, pulled at his left ear lobe with his right hand while jutting out his lower lip. He was thinking. Victoria could tell that he was giving her request the most deep and serious consideration.

"Don't you think you are rather young to be a nurse, Vicky?"

"Father, I am seventeen," Vicky tried to keep her exasperation from showing, "Nurse Healey needs all the help she can get at the new hospital – patients are arriving daily."

The whole town had collected money to set up a hospital in the old grammar school and already it was trying to cope with thirty patients. As fast as one left others arrived. Mr Peters was not convinced. "There are badly wounded men there – how will you cope with that? You will have to go into wards full of men."

"Nurse Healey has said I will just help – I will not have to deal with wounds until I am properly trained. No-one can be a proper nurse until they are twenty-one."

Mr Peters frowned even harder. "Tell me again what your duties will be."

For the third time Vicky explained. "I will go to the hospital on Mondays, Wednesdays, Friday and Saturday at six each morning to light the fires and get the men their breakfast."

"As I thought – you will be in the wards where the men are, all alone."

"No, Father, the night nurse will be on duty until eight when the day nurse takes over. Besides which the men are patients – wounded soldiers."

"How will this make you a nurse?"

"Nurse Healey has said I can go to her class for two afternoons each week."

Mr Peters gave ground, a little. "Perhaps I should speak to Nurse Healey. There must be no payment, of course – this must be voluntary. I cannot have people saying that we are profiteering from this war – nor taking bread from the poor."

Victoria relaxed, a little, she felt she was winning. "Of course not, Father. This is for King and Country. Nurse Healey tells everyone that we are the footsoldiers of medicine."

"I will speak to Mother. If she agrees then perhaps it will be alright."

"Mother has already agreed, Father. We have discussed it and Mary has volunteered to take my place in the shop."

"Umm! It seems my blessing is not really needed!"

Vicky smiled. "Of course it is Father – it will cost four shillings for my uniform."

Rose Guntrippe put her hands on her hips and glared at James Roberts of Newbarn Farm. "Do you or do you not want help, Maister Roberts?"

James Roberts decided that evasion would not work. "I put the word out for a man or at least a grow'd boy."

"An' no-one has applied," Rose pointed her thumb back down the road, "I can see – I've been watching all week."

James scratched his head in puzzlement. "I don't deny it but why on earth do you want a job?"

"I were brung up on a farm – it's what I know best. Besides which I need the money."

"You get an allowance surely!"

"Aye, you're right but my boys still go hungry."

Mrs Roberts appeared at the farmhouse door and vigorously shook out a mat, giving Rose a long hard silent look at the same time.

"Give me a few days to think on it, Mrs Guntrippe."

"You may take as long as you like but I'm going from farm to farm until I get work. My mind is set."

Mrs Roberts went back inside giving the door a good hard slam.

"I need help with the dairy herd."

Rose nodded in reply, "I know."

"Will you take on for seven days a week – help with the milking?"

"Aye."

"Can you make butter?"

"Aye."

"Two shillings a day."

"Agreed."

James hesitated. "I – I'd appreciate it if you wore trousers."

Mrs Roberts need have no fear of me, thought Rose. "Trousers it is Maister Roberts, just as the landgirl at Manor Farm."

The Master of the Thame Union Workhouse managed to convey a depth of sorrow commensurate with the task to hand, unfortunately it made Samuel Peddelle deeply apprehensive and his stomach churned. The situation was made worse because the only emotion the Master normally displayed was disapproval. The situation must be very serious indeed, Samuel concluded.

"The Medical Officer has examined your wife, Peddelle. Sad news I'm afraid."

"I see, Sir. Is she near death?"

The Master shook his head. "Worse than that. Doctor Edsell has said that your wife is insane. He has gone to prepare the certificate."

"Wh- wh- what does this mean, Sir." Samuel's heart had turned to stone, his breathing slowed making him catch for breath. Deep down he had known the situation was serious but hope had sustained a degree of optimism in him. He had kept telling himself that Martha would heal, that her long silences and inability to accept what had happened was only a temporary problem. Time would heal, time must heal, his prayers would be answered. Why, he only had to close his eyes and he could see a happy smiling Martha, surrounded by children. Laughter echoing around the kitchen. The Master cut through his thoughts. "It means that your wife must be close confined to protect both her and the public."

"Will she be sent to an asylum, Sir?"

"No, not that. The doctor has said there is no violence or danger and we will keep close watch on her."

"What of my girls, Sir? What is to become of them?"

"They are in the Matron's care. When they are twelve we shall find a position in service for them."

"May I see my wife, Sir?"

The Master pondered on that for a while. "If it is a comfort to you, you may see her for half an hour on Sunday afternoons. Do you or your wife have any family who may take the girls?"

"None, Sir."

Samuel turned to go. "Before you go back to work, Peddelle, hear this. When you see your wife do not encourage her in her fantasies."

"Her talk is not of fantasies, Sir. She simply talks as if the children are still alive – only make believe."

The Master sniffed. "That's as maybe, but the doctor believes it is harmful to encourage her."

* * * * * * *

The medical orderly tugged at the bloody torn uniform with a lack of compassion or concern that had developed over many months of dealing with wounded men. "Water." It was said with a hoarse whisper. "Please."

The orderly inserted the tip of a knife into the jacket and started to cut, even though he was most careful the man on the stretcher groaned in pain. The orderly leant over. "Hang on – no water, mate, not until the doc has seen you."

The torn jacket, then the shirt yielded to the knife, exposing a badly mutilated shoulder and arm. "There's shrapnel in there, mate." He extracted several pieces of dirty cloth making the man on the stretcher gasp with pain. "Sod you!"

The orderly assumed a pained expression. "No swearing, I'll have you know I'm a proper Christian. When I've cleaned you up I'll light you a fag – OK?"

"Thanks."

"Where'd you catch it then."

"Night patrol – up near Arras."

"What's your name."

"Tom – Thomas Guntrippe."

"What happened."

"Shell – right on our patrol – lucky to be alive."

A wedge of disinfected lint was laid over the wound and Thomas winced as the disinfectant touched raw flesh.

"Is it bad?"

"Seen lots worse, mate – you married?"

"Aye."

"Your missus will be pleased, there's no shrapnel below your belt – your marriage tackle is safe and sound."

"Lucky old me, eh!"

"Play up Thame, play up!" Albert Harty's voice roared out over the football pitch, then as the ball dropped to be trapped by an Aylesbury forward, he gave full vent to his loyal feelings. "OFFSIDE REF!"

On the pitch Harold Jones checked to ensure there was a player behind him then he moved confidently forward. Thame was leading by two goals to nil but with only five minutes left to play a goal now might raise the spirits of the opposition and just give them a chance to turn the match around. Harold moved close in, feinted to the left then his right foot darted out to take the ball, then he swivelled and pushed a long accurate pass out to Freddie Cox on the right wing. Three hundred voices roared out in unison as Freddie beat the halfback, raced on twenty yards and crossed the ball. The centre forward rose above two defenders and deftly nodded the ball into the net. Harold relaxed, this game was won. A few minutes later the final whistle was almost drowned out by the cheering crowd.

Second Lieutenant Stevens put his stick under his left arm and returned the salute of a passing soldier. At his side Edward Holling, John Howe, James Pullene and William Smithe fairly bubbled with excitement and admiration, both feelings mixed with envy. "Can you put in a word for us, Sir?"

Lieutenant Stevens gave Edward Holling a stern look. "Do you mean 'will I help you to enlist when you are too young'?"

"What difference does a few years make, Sir?" John Howe found it difficult to hide his disappointment, "We are all fit and we can shoot!"

Rifle shooting was very popular and the small range in Park Street was an excellent venue for martial spirits.

"There is more to soldiering than just shooting."

Lieutenant Stevens had been made aware of that much, to his annoyance and frustration, when his Colonel had assigned him to regimental duties. Despite his protests the Colonel was adamant. 'Organising our stores and supplies is a worthy task for your special talents. Men cannot shoot empty rifles, men cannot fight on empty bellies, men cannot march without boots. We have as much need, nay more need, of your organising skills as your martial spirits!' James Pullene intruded on his troubled thoughts. "Sir – Sir, when do you go to France?"

"Very soon now – as soon as the battalion is up to strength. Now let's find Harold and Freddie."

Edward said it with pride. "We all intend to join the Ox and Bucks, Sir, when our time arrives."

William Smithe echoed all their thoughts. "Aye, we shall join you soon. Then the Huns will get a fright."

Lieutenant Stevens stopped, wishing for the first time that he was not in uniform, that he could issue a housemaster's instruction with no right of appeal. "Finish your training before you enlist. Don't forget your careers. Also I want you all to apply for officer training."

"Left, right, left, right, left – pick 'em up, pick 'em up! Oxenlade, keep in step." The drill sergeant's irate voice sounded across the parade ground. "Platoon – halt!" Twirling his pace stick Drill Sergeant Benson stepped deliberately down the front rank until he reached Private Oxenlade, then he stopped and glared. The pace stick flicked at Peter's ankle. "Your puttee is loose." The pace stick moved and flicked at Peter's webbing belt. "Why is it, Oxenlade, that you always look like an sack of potatoes tied with loose string?"

"I don't know, Drill Sergeant!"

"Platoon – by the right, quick march!"

After half a dozen steps, Peter's boot caught the heel of the man in front of him, making them both stumble and lose the step.

"Platoon – halt!"

Drill Sergeant Benson stepped up to Peter. "Oxenlade, when you march you put one foot in front of the other at the rate of one hundred and forty paces to the minute. Why are you the only man in this whole battalion who cannot do this simple thing?"

"Don't know, Drill Sergeant!" Peter went red in the face shouting out his answer.

The drill sergeant moved his mouth closer to Peter's ear as if to speak in confidence. "Do you have a medical condition? Are your balls tied together with string?"

Peter's self esteem hit rock bottom as the rest of the platoon sniggered. Poor Peter was totally, completely and utterly dejected. For four weeks he had drilled, polished his equipment and marched, during that time he had been shouted at, abused, cursed and bullied but still he could not march in step nor maintain a soldierly appearance.

"No, Drill Sergeant!"

"Then why do you march as if your testicles are tied in a knot?"

"Don't know, Drill Sergeant!"

"Tell me, Oxenlade, enlighten me. What is your particular occupation?"

"Baker, Drill Sergeant."

"Why did you join this army, Oxenlade? Was it to give me nightmares? Or was it to turn me to religion?"

"No, Drill Sergeant, I wanted to serve my country. To fight."

"Do you now. Then I must do my best to preserve your life until we can set you on the Bosche. Report to the Cookhouse Sergeant. Tell him of your particular occupation and bake me a cake. Try to bring a little pleasure into my life. Fall out!"

Cookhouse Sergeant Hagen placed a cool glass of beer in front of Drill Sergeant Benson. "There you are, Charlie. A favour returned."

Sergeant Hagen was not well known for his generosity, Charlie Benson was a mite suspicious. "What favour was that?"

"That lad you sent me – the baker boy. What a find, he can bake like an angel."

"Oxenlade? He can't even march in a straight line."

"Give him to me then. With two thousand men to feed, this lad is worth his weight in 303 ammo."

"I will speak to Lieutenant Stevens – but you must promise to keep him away from the parade ground."

* * * * * * *

Captain Fairbairn, Officer Commanding, Thame Volunteers, could not believe his luck. Six willing fit lads stood before him. He was not ungrateful for his elderly volunteers but what if the Hun were to break our defences. What if they landed in England? How could they be repulsed? Captain Fairbairn was a sensible man, he knew that the defence of Thame should not rest on the shoulders of twenty four men all over the age of fifty, few of whom could run a hundred yards without pausing for breath or stumbling to a painful halt.

"Sergeant Major!"

Sergeant Major Simmons, veteran of India and Africa, came smartly to attention, marched over and halted. "Sir!"

"Fetch the register, Sergeant Major. We have six volunteers. Now, stand easy, men."

Edward Holling, John Howe, William Smithe, Harold Jones, James Pullene and Freddie Cox relaxed, they were in the army at last. Edward Holling stepped forward. "This terrible news from the front. This use of poisonous gas! That is what made us want to join, Sir."

"Yes, Sir, surely this is a criminal perversion." James Pullene sounded most concerned.

Captain Fairbairn stroked his moustache with his left hand. "Umm – you can be sure that British justice will prevail when we beat the Hun. With willing volunteers have no doubt – we will win."

Ever since his father had died thirty five years ago, George Bailey had been master of Blackditch Farm. He was attuned to the vagaries of the weather and the need to be flexible but there was one custom that never changed. A custom that confirmed his place as Boss, Farmer, Honest Citizen and Bountiful Christian Giver. At Saturday mid-day, at the back door of the farmhouse, he paid his men in silver and copper carefully counted out into each labourer's hand, for which he touched his forehead and said, "Thank you, Maister." Then the transaction was carefully and laboriously entered in the Cash Book. In years gone by as many as twelve men would have assembled but that number had dwindled to four. As George Bailey paid out the wages, he ruminated on the loss of men and the difficulties of coping; a year back he had operated as an overseer, now his working day started at five and finished when the work was done. And this at a time of life when he believed he had earned a rest.

George Coates, cap in pocket, stepped forward and held out his left hand. George Bailey felt in his leather bag and counted out. " . . . twelve shilling, thirteen shilling, fourteen shilling and . . . one, two, three, four, five pence." He looked up. "Is that agreed, Coates?"

George Coates pocketed his pay. "To the penny, Maister."

George Bailey noted that Coates didn't salute or say thank you. Furthermore George Coates had always added the words, 'God bless you'. Instead George Coates stood his ground, causing George Bailey to give him a questioning stare. "Is there ought wrong?"

"Aye. I have been at Blackditch these nineteen years – man and boy – but I shall not come again."

There was genuine surprise in George Bailey's reply. "Say you are leaving? Don't tell me you've enlisted?"

"Nay – not to soldiering. I'm to Pound Lane Farm where I shall be paid twenty one shillings a week, my true worth."

The other labourers stepped in closer so that they could hear what was being said.

George Bailey was shaken to his core. "Twenty one shillings you say! Why, no farm can afford this!"

George Coates remained very polite. "'Tis the going rate – and plenty of jobs too."

"I've allus been fair – none can say I haven't been fair."

"Aye, so I thought," George Coates was careful not to show temper or bad manners, "but at the last market you got top rates for your cattle and many around are saying you are making a fortune out of this war."

"This is tittle tattle and envy, George, but I will review the wages if you stay. I can't say fairer than that."

"I'm sorry, Maister. I have given my word."

"You'll regret this. Mark my word you'll be back with your tail between your legs. Begging for work. But if you go now you'll get no sympathy here."

"I bid you good day, Maister, afore mislike takes hold," George put his cap on, "good morrow on the Sabbath."

"This won't last, Coates – you're living in a world of make believe."

Albert Harty raised his fist and his voice. "Get up those stairs, woman or by God I'll give yer a beating!"

Alice Harty was frightened but tried to hold her ground. "The kids are not abed, I've not finished my work." She pointed to a pile of dirty dishes and pans. "Sit down, I'll get you some supper."

"Damn your supper, woman. Get up those stairs and spread your legs."

Alice appealed to his better nature. "I'm not well, Albert, my back is killing me."

Even though he was unsteady from the drink, Albert moved forward very quickly and lashed out. His open hand caught Alice high on the side of the head and the force knocked her into the kitchen dresser. She fell to the floor alongside the smashed crockery. Before she could gather her senses and run away Albert caught her by the arm and his hand banged into her mouth. Luckily he was unbalanced otherwise Alice would have lost teeth. She cried out in pain as she was dragged to the stairs.

Headkeeper Parker was angry and it showed. He had spent several weeks attempting to catch the poacher but had failed and his frustration mounted. Now his anger spilled out on to Sidney Barnes. "You've been out by the north coppice, as I told you?"

Sidney nodded, "Aye, Mr Parker."

"What did you find."

"Nowt of consequence. The new pen is holding the pheasants and I've taken the partridge eggs to the bantams."

"Are you telling me you didn't see the signs of the poacher – only a blind man could have missed them."

Suddenly Sidney understood, Parker had put him to the test. Parker was right, George Coates had set a trip snare in the pheasant wood. The area was set aside so that the pheasants would be attracted to the grain put out for them each day. Sidney had made a point of tripping the snare every day so no harm was done.

"Sorry Mr Parker, I should have told you."

"Who is this poacher? Out with it!"

"I don't know for certain – it's a local man, he comes in to take a rabbit now and then. No great harm."

"I had thought you were incompetent, Barnes. Now it seems you are dishonest. Poaching will not be tolerated. That's what you're paid to do . " He waited for Sidney to answer but none came. "I've a mind to dismiss you for dishonesty."

Sidney thought it best not to answer, it would be the end of his career if he were to be dismissed, however there was no one to take his place and it would be impossible for Parker to maintain the estate shooting on his own. Parker had considered that but his mind was made up. Either the poacher was caught or Sidney would go, Parker's pride would not allow otherwise.

"You've got two weeks. I want this poacher in front of the magistrate. If not, you can look for employment elsewhere!"

"This is unfair." Sidney found his voice.

"It's justice!"

Rose Guntrippe had spent a frustrating time waiting for Sidney, so much so that her initial passion had turned to anger. She had no idea that an equally angry Sidney would confront her. What angered Sidney as much as all else was the fact that the head keeper had guessed the truth. Sidney had not wanted to catch this poacher, knowing as he did that the man was a neighbour. He was almost certain that the man he must catch was George Coates. If he did then the other neighbours would turn against him. Why couldn't Parker live and let live?

As Sidney entered the house, Rose quickly stood up to give him a tongue lashing. He stopped her with a black scowl and a harsh tongue. "Say nothing, woman! Enough is enough in one day."

Wisely Rose resisted the temptation to match his anger. "Sit down and take off your jacket, gaiters and boots. Shall I get you some beer?" As she went to turn away Sidney gripped her hand and pulled her savagely back.

"Did you leave those damn bloomers and corsets at home, like I said?" His voice was harsher than she had ever known and his hand went under her dress and gripped bare flesh. "Just as well, you bitch!" Then he forced her down on her knees and threw the skirt up and over her shoulders.

Rose was alarmed. "Don't you dare beat me!"

Sidney carelessly ripped his flies open. "I'm not gonna beat thee." Then he knelt and rammed hard, grunting and thrusting. "This is purely for pleasure."

"Oh-oh-oh." Rose tensed as a deep sensual spasm convulsed her and she flexed her internal muscles to grip Sidney's penis. "Slow down, Sid – slow down."

It was rarely that Sidney was the master over Rose, so he slowed, not to please her but to prolong his domination over her. "Lift your arse, you bitch."

The doctor gave Thomas Guntrippe's shoulder and arm careful scrutiny, flexing the arm and gently probing at the wounds with his fingers. Despite the gentleness Thomas gasped with pain. "How do you feel, soldier?"

"Only fair, Sir."

"You're a lucky man, Guntrippe. We thought we had lost you." He pointed to the wounds. "This is mending well."

The doctor turned to the nursing sister. "This man needs time to recover – good food and exercise will see him well. If his temperature stays normal for thirty six hours I want him sent back to England. Have his documents ready when I visit tomorrow."

The nursing sister turned to Thomas. "Home for you, soldier. You'll be in Dover in two days."

"Thank you, Sister – I won't be a nuisance any longer."

The Sister looked pleased. "The good news is that the doctor thinks you'll recover and be able to go back to your regiment in six months."

The Vicar of St Mary's Church in Thame did not really look forward to his occasional Sunday visits to the chapel in the Thame Workhouse. Normally at the end of the short service he could hurry back to the Vicarage for a few hours rest before attending Evensong. Not today. An inmate had asked to speak to him; he resolved to get this meeting over quickly.

"Thank you for seeing me, Father. My name is Samuel Peddelle."

The Vicar checked his fob watch. "What can I do for you, my son?"

"My wife has been declared insane and will never leave this Workhouse."

"This was mentioned to me but surely this is the best place for her. She will be cared for and protected here."

Samuel sought for the right words. "My – wife is beyond help, Father. But it is not her I want to speak of – it is my two daughters."

"You need have no fear," the Vicar looked relieved, this was an easier matter to deal with, "the Matron will look after them."

"True, Father – but it is not as a loving home, with a mother."

The Vicar shook his head. "There is little I can do except take an interest in their welfare."

Samuel came to the crucial point and crossed his fingers. "I had heard that the church could arrange adoption, Father. Find them a home with a proper Christian family."

A frown appeared on the Vicar's face. "Our adoption service is for orphans, my son. Do you . . . ?"

"Yes, Father. I have thought hard on it – it is the only thing I can do for them. I beg you consider."

"You say Christian, my son. But I cannot recall that you were frequent visitors to our church."

Samuel tried to look suitably chastened. "There did not seem to be a need to come every week – but the fault is mine – none other. I would not want my girls to go to a godless house."

"I will seek advice. Did you speak to the Master on this?"

"Yes, Father." The Master had made it clear that anything that reduced his roster by two mouths to feed was welcome.

The two girls sat on the bench on the opposite side of the table. Apart from an occasional rolling of eyes they were very solemn. Samuel watched them and tried to gauge their feelings but had to admit failure. Over the months he and the girls had drifted apart, only the half an hour visit on a Sunday afternoon gave any sort of contact. He felt as a stranger; the girls submitted to a kiss on the cheek but that was the only physical contact and they gave no hint that they might be pleased to see him.

"Are you well, Sarah?" Sarah nodded dutifully, eyes unblinking.

"Are you well, Jane?" No answer.

Samuel paused, he did not know how to frame the words properly. "You know that your mother is – unwell, don't you?"

Sarah stirred. "Everyone ses that Ma is mad." She said it most matter of factly.

"Quite mad." Jane repeated it with moderate emphasis.

"Would you like to leave this place? Live in a proper home – with a family?"

Sarah wrinkled her nose. "Old Mother Shipley ses we will all die here."

"She ses it is God's will because we are sinners." Jane did not seem concerned at the severity of her words. "Old Mother Shipley ses there are only two ways out – the asylum or the box."

"Girls, you must take no notice of these sayings. I promise you will leave one day – to a better life. Promise me you will pay attention to your learning."

For the first time in months Jane volunteered some news. "I can say the alphabet, Pa."

She had called him 'Pa'. Samuel's hopes took wing.

* * * * * * *

Vicky Peters had been at the hospital since five a.m. It had been quite dark as she left home and there had been a bitter east wind blowing down Thame High Street. Since then she had cleaned seven grates, lit seven fires, tended the kitchen range, humped in buckets of coal, cooked and distributed thirty breakfasts, collected all the trays and was now in the kitchen up to her armpits in water and dirty dishes. She had never felt so happy, so needed, so wanted. Thirty helpless battered men had watched her every move and she had learned that a radiant smile, a word of praise and a cheerful comment was better than medicine. As she washed she hummed.

"That's a fine tune, Nurse. You have a nice voice." One of the walking wounded stood in the doorway. "We can hear you in the ward."

A flustered Vicky turned. "Oh, I am sorry I didn't mean to upset you all."

MY HEART AND I

"Upset, Nurse! Nay, we all look forward to the mornings when you are on duty. Best days of the week!"

Vicky blushed. "I'm not a nurse – just a helper."

"Will you come and sing a song for us?"

Vicky was suddenly aware that everyone in the ward must be listening because clapping broke out. "I – I – I don't know that I'm allowed to."

"It will please the lads – they all agreed I should ask you."

Vicky dried her hands. "I am taking you back to your bed!"

"Only if you promise us a song."

As they entered the ward more clapping and cheering sound out. "Give us a song, please."

"Quiet please, or I will get into trouble."

"Just one song Miss, then we promise we will let you go."

"You promise. One song, then you will be quiet?"

A chorus of, "Yes, Nurse," and, "Of course, Nurse," sounded around the ward.

Vicky waited for quiet. *"Only make believe I love you, only make believe that you love me . . . . "*

Lieutenant Stevens listened to Private Oxenlade's request with extreme patience. Considering this was the second time in a fortnight that he had heard this request he sat with remarkable fortitude and waited until Private Oxenlade had finished. He thought to himself that the request was couched in better and more fervent words than his own request to his Colonel only last week. Not feeling there was any need to be inventive he used the Colonel's words as the basis for his reply.

"I regret, Oxenlade, I cannot grant your request. In the first place you are already in an active service unit serving in the front line. Secondly you are undertaking a vital role in helping the battalion win this war. No, that is all!"

A downcast Private Oxenlade persevered. "I'm a good shot, Sir. I joined to be a proper soldier."

Stevens gave a wry half smile. "You are a proper soldier. Sergeant Hagen speaks well of you. He tells me you are the best baker in the British army – our men depend on you."

Private Oxenlade sounded as miserable as he looked. "I joined to fight, Sir. It don't seem fair."

"This is the army, Oxenlade, fairness doesn't come into it. March him out, Sergeant Major."

"It is quite simple," Edward Holling had explained. "You wait outside until you see she is at the counter, then in you go. Just ask her – that is all you do".

"What if she says no, what then?"

"Don't be a chump, John, Vicky has said it is expected – she likes you!"

It had all seemed so simple ten minutes ago but now a tongue-tied and embarrassed John Howe stood before the object of his affection and spluttered.

"A box of matches, Miss."

Coolly Mary Peters reached around and placed a box on the counter. "That will be one penny, Sir."

John fumbled for his money, found his penny and promptly dropped it on the floor. At the rear of the shop Mr Herbert Peters noted the confusion and walked around to join Mary.

"Now, now, young man – what is going on?"

John Howe found his penny and stood up, somewhat red in the face. "Found it, Sir!" He proffered the penny.

Mary took charge of the situation. "This is John Howe, Father. He is working in insurance."

Herbert Peters stroked his nose. "And what does that mean, young man?"

"I'm training as an insurance clerk, Sir."

Mary half closed her eyes in exasperation. "Father – John has asked if he can walk me to church on Sundays."

John Howe went even redder in the face.

"Is this true, young man? You are very forward." Herbert Peters sounded harsh, damnable young lads constantly chasing his daughters.

"Yes, Sir. I'm sorry, Sir. But it is more than that. Mrs Pullene asks if Mary can join the choir."

"Ah! Mrs Pullene you say. Now that is a different matter. Perhaps this will be possible – but I will speak to Mrs Pullene."

"Yes, Sir. Of course, Sir. Mrs Pullene said to say that choir practice is from six to seven on Tuesday evenings and she likes the choir to be in place fifteen minutes before Morning Service and Evensong."

"So, you are not asking on you own behalf."

"Oh no, Sir. Mrs Pullene has said I must be responsible for ensuring that Mary will get safely there and back."

Mary smiled. "How wonderful, Father, Mr Howe is being a proper gentleman and," she played a trump card, "there are no music hall songs at church."

"Yes, I dare say this is acceptable. But mark my words, young man. Any hanky panky and there will be serious trouble – serious trouble."

Mary stepped forward and kissed him on the cheek. "You are so good to me, Father – you must be the kindest and wisest father in the whole world."

"And you, young lady will remember you are not sixteen until the end of the week."

Police Sergeant Cox gave the prisoner a disdainful look before turning his gaze back to the arresting officer "What happened?"

"This man left the Greyhound Public House at 9 o'clock Sergeant, whereupon he did weave and stagger about the highway as if under the influence of alcoholic drink. When I admonished him he did raise his fists to me and said, 'Go fuck yourself!' Several members of the public then left the public house and this man did insult them and offered to fight them. I then put him under arrest for being drunk and disorderly."

Sergeant Cox returned his gaze to the prisoner, pen poised over the charge sheet. "Name?"

"You know who I bloody well are – 'an I'm not drunk!"

"Name?"

"Albert Harty."

"Address?"

"You fucking well . . . twelve, Pound Lane."

Sergeant Cox walked around the desk. "The constable has reason to believe you are drunk. You will walk the line."

He pointed to the long white line down the centre of the charge room.

"Not before time!" Albert stepped forward eagerly to the line. "Just say when, copper."

"You will walk the line, then stop. Each step must touch the line. Start now."

Albert stepped forward again, as he did so a heavy boot clipped his heel and he fell, sprawling on the floor. Temper roused, Albert lurched to his feet and fists flailing, launched himself at the Constable. He had the momentary pleasure in feeling one fist strike target then a sharp rap from a truncheon took him to his knees.

"Now, now, Harty," Sergeant Cox spoke very softly, "no more violence, please. Striking a police officer is not to be tolerated. Put him in the cell, Constable."

Albert Harty was wide awake when Sergeant Cox unlocked the cell door and entered. Albert looked pale and miserable, his night had been most uncomfortable. The sergeant handed over a mug of tea and a slice of bread and jam. "Get that inside you – I'll bring you a razor in a while."

Albert was not mollified. "I shall make a complaint. Even police are not above the law."

Sergeant Cox nodded his head slowly as if in understanding, even sympathy perhaps. "Umh. As I recall, Harty, this is the third time of late you have graced this cell. The first time you had a warning, then a fine. Now you have assaulted a police officer doing his duty."

"'Tis bloody lies – you have got it in for me!"

"You bring trouble on yoursen. You can't keep away from the drink."

"Sod you! Ever since you decided to come between husband and wife, which you've no right to do – there's been nowt but trumped up charges – an' you know it."

Sergeant Cox viewed Albert with unblinking eyes. "You have a choice. It's the magistrates at ten-thirty or the recruiting officer at ten. The choice is your'n."

"That ain't no choice, you bastard."

"'Tis the best you got!"

* * * * * * *

"Is that you, Thomas?" Albert Harty looked up at the pale face of the blue suited man stepping cautiously down from the train at Thame station.

"Aye, 'tis me, Albert."

Albert noted that Thomas's left arm was pinned in so the arm could not move and when Thomas reached back to lift his pack out, his stiffness was obvious.

"Good God, man! What has happened to you?"

"Bad luck, Albert. A shell got me – but I'm on the mend. Soon be back at the front."

"You'll not want to go back, Thomas, not now you're home."

"I thought Rose and my lads would be here to meet me."

"I've seen no-one, Thomas, but I had heard your wife was working at Newbarn Farm. Just over there."

"Perhaps you could give me a hand, Albert. I'd be grateful."

"Not me, Thomas. You're home – I'm just off." He touched his jacket pocket. "Got my one way ticket to the depot at Cowley Barracks. It's a-soldiering for me."

Thomas reached over to shake his hand. "Well done, Albert. You're a brave man. Every man is needed."

Albert drew back. "Christ, I didn't bloody volunteer! I were given no choice. It was join or go to prison."

"How did that happen?"

A whistle sounded and the train eased forward. Albert swung up into the carriage. "I'll tell you one day. But I'll tell you this, don't trust a woman – especially your Rose. She lies on her back too easy. She's too fond of Sidney Barnes – that's what!"

"What do you mean?" It was too late, the train was already pulling away. Thomas gave a wave and then turned to see a crowd of people appear in the station entrance. Outside a band started to play and flags waved. The Mayor stepped forward and shook Thomas's hand, "Welcome home, Thomas, welcome home." Then Robert ran forward and gripped his leg. "I've missed you, Pa. I told everyone you were coming home."

The band blared out a tune, *'Take me back to dear old Blighty'*. The Mayor grasped Thomas's arm and raised it up. "Our hero!" To cheers and applause the band stepped out. Thomas had no choice but to follow.

The seven black saloon cars proceeded out of Thame in sedate procession, under strict instructions not to exceed twenty miles per hour, in the direction of Princes Risborough. One or two pedestrians may have been forgiven for thinking it was a funeral procession but a quick glance soon dispelled that possibility – there was no hearse. Nor was black much in evidence among the passengers, twenty five men in blue suits, seven women in nurses uniforms, seven drivers in grey chauffeur's outfits.

"Where did you say we are going, Nurse?"

Victoria Peters pointed out of the window. "There – up on the hill. Can you see the white cross in the hillside."

"Looks very lovely, Nurse. What is it called?"

"Whiteleaf Cross. It is said it was made by the ancient Britons, but I don't think they were Christians."

"Never mind, Nurse. It's a lovely day for a picnic."

"D'yer mind if we sing, Nurse?"

"Nothing that will offend Matron."

"Right then Nurse. Now all together.

> *After the ball was over,*
> *after the break of day . . . . "*

The cars parked under the lofty beech trees near the Cross. Matron was the first out and grown men quailed before her firm commands.

"Two nurses take the walking wounded off for a stroll – not too far. Chauffeurs to collect wood and get a fire lit – yes, that means you as well, Mr Coggs, Mr Fairbairns instructions. Two nurses to get the picnic baskets unpacked and make the tea. Two nurses to organise the chairs for the disabled men."

One man stepped forward. "A bottle of beer would go down well in this heat, Ma'am."

"There will be no need for the stimulation of alcohol, young man. There's plenty of ginger beer and lemonade!"

"But we are army men, Ma'am. A drop of the brewer's delight is part of our pay."

"We are the Thame Military Red Cross Hospital, soldier, and alcoholic drink is only available on a doctor's prescription."

Since he had spoken to the Vicar, Samuel Peddelle had asked himself time and time again what he would do if the Vicar came back to say that adoption was possible, that his girls could go to a proper home. He had pondered and puzzled, even in the night he had examined endless arguments and possibilities. So much so that tired and exhausted through lack of sleep he had neglected his work, so that he had been admonished several times and been punished by the loss of meals. The loss of the meals had troubled him more than he thought possible, not realising that his stomach had become a creature of habit and he got gut ache and mouth watering if a meal was even a few minutes late, let alone denied. Despite all this deep thinking, denial and heart searching, he could not reach a conclusion.

What was the greater love, he asked himself. To keep the girls here or to let them go? His heart said keep them here, at least he could see them each Sunday. If he let them go, what then? Would they forget him, would they cling to some memory of him. The Vicar of St Mary's said nothing to help Samuel while the brooding Master of the Workhouse said nothing at all, he simply transfixed Samuel with an unblinking stare. The Vicar steepled his fingers as if in prayer. "My son, I have found a solution to our problem."

"Problem, Father?"

"Yes, the need for parents for your girls."

Samuel closed his eyes for a few seconds. 'Please God, not so soon.'

The Vicar leant forward. "That is what you asked me to do, was it not?"

"Yes, Father." Fear sounded in Samuel's voice, it showed in his suddenly trembling hands and nervous tic.

"You do still wish your girls to go to a God-fearing home where they will be properly brought up, do you not?"

"Where is this home, Father?"

"I cannot tell you that," the Vicar's face and voice remained expressionless, "neither can I give you names."

"Surely, Father, I have a right to know – a need to know."

"No, my son, these are our rules. We consider it best for the children and their new parents. Do you not recall my comments about orphans?"

"These are hard rules, Father – it may be I will never see them again, never to know they are well and happy."

"I will give you twenty four hours to decide if you wish."

Samuel steeled himself, mind made up. "No, Father, what must I do?"

"You must sign this document, the Master and I will witness it."

"When will the girls leave?"

"Tomorrow."

"May I have some time with them?"

The Master spoke at last. "Just ten minutes, Peddelle. This is not a Sunday."

George Coates could not explain it but he had felt uneasy since slipping through the hedge on to the Thame Park Estate. It was over a week since he had last slipped away from Thame to check his snare lines. Despite the better wage he was earning, his wife complained of rising prices and a few rabbits would fill the stew-pot, while a plump pheasant would mean an evening in the Four Horseshoes. George could go one of six ways. Line five would make it difficult to take a pheasant. The penny went up again. Tails, six! Heads, four! Heads. Line four it was. George relaxed, spat on the penny for double luck, then stepped out.

As he progressed eastward, George gradually relaxed. He blended so well into the landscape that rooks flew around unconcerned. A buzzard drifted over and two crows chased it over his head as he reached the edge of open ground before the east copse. Stooping down he moved carefully over the grass then stepped into the cover of a large oak. Over to his right a pheasant sounded so he moved carefully in that direction. Then he froze. The pheasant was tethered, it was a trap! He went to run but it was too late.

"Don't move or I'll shoot!" Headkeeper Parker could not keep the triumph from his voice.

George dropped his sack and made ready to fight.

"Stand still, George. There's no escape." Sidney Barnes stepped out behind George, shotgun cocked.

Headkeeper Parker stepped forward. "I know you, Coates. Thought you'd get away with it, did you? We'll see what the magistrates have to say. Bring that bag. Barnes, and take a hold of those snares in his pocket. We don't want any evidence destroyed or lost."

He waited until Sidney was ready. "Turn around and walk to the lodge, Coates. You can run if you want, but I tell you now, you'll look like a sieve!" Then he called back into the copse and a lad appeared. "Run on, lad. Get a constable to meet us at the lodge by the gate."

Nine months had passed by since Samuel Peddelle had seen his girls in proper dresses. Out of the drab grey workhouse clothes they already seemed brighter and more confident. At first he could think of nothing to say to them and they stood there hand in hand, puzzled looks on their faces. Forcing back his tears, Samuel stepped forward, knelt and took them in his arms. "Pa!" Sarah stared in confusion. "We are only going on holiday." Both girls nodded. "Just a holiday, Pa." "Only a few days." Samuel steadied himself. "That's right, girls, just a few days."

The Matron stepped forward. "It is time, the bags are on the trap." They must be very small bags, thought Samuel.

Jane took him into her confidence. "Old Mother Shipley said no good would come of this and Matron has stopped her dinner." Then she lowered her voice even more. "Mother Shipley said rude words!"

"Come, girls," the Matron put out a hand to turn them to the door and Samuel gave them a quick kiss. "Be good, girls." Then he watched them to the door and gave them a wave. Just for a moment the tears started to flow and then stopped abruptly. There was no need of tears, his girls were free.

Come Sunday he sat and told Martha but she gave no indication that she had heard or understood, just the quiet unblinking stare of last week and the week before. As he left Samuel took her hand. "Forgive me, Martha." Just for a second he thought a fleeting look of pain crossed Martha's face.

"What you doing, Thomas?" Rose stared at Thomas Guntrippe with alarm rather than concern. "Do you want to do yoursen harm?"

A startled Thomas coloured and stopped exercising. "I thought you had gone to the farm."

"So it seems. What are you doing?"

"'Tis obvious, woman," Thomas could not keep the exasperation from his voice, "My arm and shoulder are weak, the doctor has said this will make them stronger."

Rose was not deterred. "The wounds will break open unless you've a care."

Thomas turned his back on her. "The flesh is knitted." Then he proceeded to lift the weight taken from the kitchen scales.

"Is this so you can hurry back to war? Haven't you had enough? Or has being called a hero gone to your head?"

"I can't sit here hiding away!"

Rose watched him for a minute before speaking and when she spoke it was very quietly, quite unlike her. "You've never told me what it was like – out there at the front."

Thomas put the weight down and buttoned up his shirt. "I can't find the words – But I left good men – mates – behind. They need me."

"You needn't go to please me." Rose stared at him intently, as if willing him to understand, "You've done your bit, nobbut a fool would say otherwise. How many more have to die before you see reason?"

"When the doctor considers me fit I'll be sent back."

"You're not afraid then?"

Thomas thought on that. "Oh, yes. I'm afraid – I were never so afraid in all my life. Hundreds of men have died all around me."

"You've never said – except to Robert. Now he wants to be a soldier!"

"Never fear," Thomas spoke with total conviction, "'twill all be over before Robert is a growed man. There will never be another war after this – mark my words. He will be safe."

George Coates's temper had exploded when Sidney Barnes had walked into the bar of the Four Horseshoes. It was only the publican's insistence that prevented a brawl at the bar. A dozen stony faced neighbours circled the yard. Sidney could tell from their faces that they disliked him, and looked forward to him getting a beating. He had come to try and make peace but it was too late for that. At best he was a spy, at worst 'Judas'. George's fist lashed forward drawing blood from Sidney's nose but he had no time to recover. "You bastard! I'll fucking hang for you!" Blows rained on Sidney and he sank to his knees. "Fight, you bastard!"

Sidney put his hand up in surrender. "No. I had no choice, it was my job."

"Fuck you, Barnes! You sold me down the river for a bloody rabbit!"

"Poaching was your choice – not mine. You knew the risk."

Sidney wiped the blood from his mouth, desperately trying to summon up enough strength to jump to his feet and run. Then he looked around at the hard faces and decided it may be safer to stay.

"You're standing as witness – you want me in prison." George spat at him.

"I've no choice – but you have a choice." Sidney prayed, "You do have a way out."

"An' what choice be that?" George's voice was still thick with anger.

"Enlist."

A gasp of anger went up all around and one man kicked Sidney in the ankle. "You shit – this is deliberate."

George was doubly incensed. "You only want me out of the way so you can fuck Rose Guntrippe – I've been watching you over a year." George turned to the crowd. "He's been taking Thomas's place – even when he's bin serving in France."

There was outrage all around. One man stepped forward and grabbed Sidney's hair. "Is this right? Have you bin leching a hero's wife. A man serving his country at war?"

Another onlooker joined in. "Aye, that he has. There are a few know of this."

George stepped back. "I think as how it is our Gamekeeper who should enlist. What do you all think?"

"Aye's", went up all around, "and good riddance."

"D'yer hear that, Barnes. If you are still here by the end of the week, the whole town will know. And then by God, you'll get the beating of a lifetime."

"You'll still go to prison, Coates – there's more than me as witness."

"Then it seems we'll both be taking the shilling."

* * * * * * *

Head gamekeeper Parker was extremely annoyed, how was he to raise several thousand pheasant poults with thousands of intruders wandering the grounds at will. It hurt even more to be told that these intruders were welcome paying guests and considered much more important than pheasants. Only half an hour ago, he had found Robert Guntrippe, armed with a catapult and a degree of murderous intent, stalking among the oak trees. If Robert had accepted the confiscation of his catapult with proper resignation and apology all would have been forgiven and forgotten. However, the son of a hero was not prepared to take this rejection without protesting and Parker had learnt that he was an 'old fart far too old to serve his country' – or words to that effect. Poor Parker's heart nearly gave out. What was the world coming to!

The crowds steadily mounted as, almost without exception, everyone turned out for the Grand Fete in Thame Park. All the schools had closed for the afternoon. In the tent by the raised stage, which had the lake as a backdrop, the pageant players checked their lines. Miss Bates, organiser, moved among the players, conducting a roll call.

"Will Scarlet!" Freddie Coxe quickly stepped forward.

"Little John!" Harold Jones waved. "Here!"

"Friar Tuck!" William Smithe slapped his false stomach. "Here!"

"King Richard! . . . . "

Outside the silver band played out a rousing medley of tunes.

Edward Holling, senior, lawyer, inclined his head rather stiffly and doffed his hat. "Good afternoon, Mr Fairbairn, it is most kind of you to let us have our fete in your lovely grounds."

Steven Fairbairn, new tenant at Thame Park, nodded his head in appreciation.

"Kind of you to say, Holling. The truth is my wife and I love these events – though I did not think we would get over two thousand people."

"Everything is being done for a worthy cause, it brings out the best in people I believe." Mrs Holling gave her most gracious smile as she spoke.

"And what fine people, Mrs Holling. I'm especially pleased with your son – one of my volunteers, always willing to play his part, fine example to the others. He will make a splendid Robin Hood in the pageant."

A slight frown crossed Edward Holling's face as he remembered that the Victoria Peters girl was Maid Marion. "He is rather young, I fear."

Steven Fairbairn would not have it. "Youth is a state of mind – not a burden. I think you'll find he's man enough for whatever lies ahead."

Herbert Peters was not convinced. "Fancy having this on a Thursday, Mother! You know I always take stock on early closing day. Now I shall be all behind."

"Now, now, Father. There's a war – we must raise money." Mrs Peters spoke reassuringly. "The more money we raise the quicker this war will be over."

"Hmm. I'm not sure our Vicky should be in this pageant."

"Oh, Father! Mrs Pullene said that most of the players are girls – there aren't enough men available."

"Edward Holling is always available! He should be in the army."

"He is too young, Father. Now, come with me – I want you to spend some money on the stalls – I want you to win me a prize."

"Goodness gracious, Mother! There is a woman dressed as a man, in tights."

"Yes, Father – I know, don't forget I helped with the costumes."

"But tights, Mother! This will attract men of the wrong sort. What is the world coming to?"

"There aren't enough men of any sort, Father. Now don't fuss. You will have to get used to women running the world."

"I hope that doesn't include the vote, Mother, we can't have women deciding how the country is run."

There was a sudden surge of people and the word quickly spread. 'The pageant is to start soon.'

Miss Bates, narrator and mediaeval troubadour stepped to the front of the stage. A great hush descended.

"We present to you this day a pageant in six parts and set before you for your pleasure by kind permission of Mr Fairbairn." She waited for the band and audience to finish, 'For he's a jolly good fellow'.

"Good gentlefolk of Thame, we take you to a world of yesteryear when our good land was threatened and justice trampled down but then, as now, bold men did volunteer and we were blessed with Robin Hood and all his merry men to challenge that corruption and lay aside our fear."

Mrs Peters had the programme. "The first part is called, 'Under the Greenwood Tree', Father." Her finger moved on, "Then comes The Wedding."

Forty minutes later King Richard stepped forward and drew his sword. "Kneel, fair Robin, for this day I honour you in sight of all, that did so nobly defend this realm and confound our enemies."

Robin knelt. "I dub thee Knight – rise up Sir Robin of Loxley. Peace reigneth in this land of England and ne'er shall face again such perfidy while men such as thee defend it."

The narrator stepped forward.

"Fair Dames and Squires
In our pageant we have tried to show
some peacefulness of Merrie England long ago.
When Knights were fearless, bold and brave
'tis so today . . . . "

FIVE HUNDRED OX AND BUCKS MEN DUCKED AS THE TWO SHELLS EXPLODED IN FRONT OF THE TRENCH THEY WERE DIGGING OUT. FIVE HUNDRED MINDS THOUGHT AS ONE, WERE THE GERMANS JUST HAVING A GO, A RANDOM ATTEMPT AT DISRUPTION OR HAD THEY SEEN SOMETHING AND WERE GETTING THE RANGE. AS THE MINUTES TICKED BY THE MEN RELAXED SOMEWHAT AND CARRIED ON DIGGING. THEN A MORTAR SHELL DROPPED AT THE END OF THE LINE WITH A BANG AND FIVE SECONDS LATER THE CALL WENT OUT FOR STRETCHER BEARERS.

"On yonder Flanders plains
brave men are fighting
falling in our defence.
They chose the nobler part.
O, Youth of England unsheath the sword
Like Robin Hood . . . . "

"KEEP THOSE WAGONS MOVING – DO NOT BUNCH UP." THE QUARTERMASTER'S VOICE BELLOWED ALONG

THE LINE AS THE COLUMN OF SUPPLY WAGONS MOVED
CLOSE TO THE RUINED MENIN GATE IN YPRES. AT THE
REAR MARCHED SEVERAL HUNDRED EXHAUSTED
MUDDIED OX AND BUCKS MEN. THEY HAD SPENT
ALL DAY LOADING THE WAGONS WITH SUPPLIES AND
AMMUNITION. A MILE DOWN THE ROAD THEY WOULD
UNLOAD AT THE SUPPLY DEPOT. WHEN THAT WAS
DONE IT WOULD BE PAST NIGHTFALL AND THE REST
OF THE DAY WOULD BE THEIR OWN.

"Defend the maid, the poor, the weak
let no barbarian hordes these sylvan glades defile.
No ruthless Huns these ancestral homes despoil.
Let every man who loves his Country and his King
Cry with me – 'GOD SAVE KING GEORGE!'"

The band struck up the opening bars as the entire cast filed on
to the stage. Two and a half thousand spectators stood, men
removed their hats, boys their caps. Then all their voices sang out.

"Land of Hope and Glory, Mother of the free
How shall we extol thee, who are born of thee
Wider still and wider, shall thy bounds be set
God who made thee mighty, make thee mightier yet
God who made thee mighty, make thee mightier yet."

* * * * * * *

Herbert Peters clamped his pipe between his teeth and gave a
deep satisfying puff. How he looked forward to a smoke after
dinner and for the first time of the day he could relax in his
armchair. He opened the paper and read. Mrs Peters relaxed and
picked up her sewing, all was well in her world, father was at peace –
but not for long.

"Have you seen this news, Mother. Tut, tut!"

Mrs Peters did not look up from her sewing. "Now, Father,
you know I leave the papers to you."

"It says here, Mother, that the 'Ox and Bucks' have had over
two thousand casualties in the last year."

"Oh, surely not, Father. The war seems to be going so well."

"Well I don't think the Gazette would lie, Mother, what would be the point."

Mrs Peters looked pensive. "It would explain why the hospital is always full and Vicky has so much work to do."

Mr Peters gave his pipe a good knock on the fender. "Must be this poison gas we hear about."

"These Huns are savages, Father, uncivilised savages!"

"You are right, Mother. That's because they don't play cricket. We've civilised over half the world with cricket. Pity we didn't teach the Germans."

"What films are showing at the Electric Picture Palace?" Mrs Peters was partial to an evening at the picture palace. There was silence for a moment.

"With seats at one shilling I don't think we should go again this week, Mother."

The Regimental Sergeant Major stood rigidly to attention, pace stick under his left arm, and saluted with smart precision.

"Private Harty is charged under section five of Kings Regulations in that he did leave these barracks without permission and when arrested did cause bodily harm to the arresting Corporals of the Military Police."

The depot colonel, Commandant of the Etaples Training Garrison, shifted in his chair, read the sheet in front of him then looked at a bare-headed Albert Harty. Albert had eventually been beaten, overpowered, beaten again, thrown into a truck, thrown into a cell, receiving a few good kicks for good measure since he had been found in the Calais bar at about ten o'clock the previous evening. There were few bones in his body that did not ache and his uniform was ruined. Ramrod stiff, the Military Police Sergeant in charge of the arresting patrol gave his evidence.

When he had finished, the Colonel frowned and re-checked Albert's record. "You have been in the army only eight weeks, Private Harty. In that time you have done almost as much damage as a Hun Regiment. Belligerence and a willingness to fight are prime requirements in a soldier. However, such attributes should be used to fight the enemy. What have you to say for yourself?"

Albert tried to gather his thoughts. "Well, Sir, 'tis hard for me. I've never been allowed out of barracks since I enlisted an' it don't seem fair to me, allus bein' picked on and put to extra duty."

"Do you have any comments, Sergeant Major?"

"Yes Sir! Private Harty has no concept of discipline. He has a weakness for drink, Sir, and has got fighting drunk in the canteen every pay day."

"How does he perform on the range?"

"He finds it easier to hit the target with the rifle butt rather than an aimed round, Sir."

"There is a note here, Sergeant Major, from the Quartermaster. It seems that Harty has lost kit amounting to over two pounds."

"That is correct, Sir."

The Colonel turned to Albert. "Will you accept my punishment or do you wish to stand before a General Court Martial?"

"Accept your punishment, Sir."

"Twenty eight days 'Field Punishment Number Two'. March him out, Sergeant Major."

"Cap on! About turn, quick march! Left, right, left, right . . . . "

"Halt." The Sergeant Major marched up level with Albert. "Four weeks from today you will be sent to join your regiment. When you get there you will be a fit soldier or you may die in the attempt. You will double to your billet and report back to me in ten minutes, washed, shaved, tidy, properly dressed with pack and rifle. You will get no pay so if I smell drink on your breath you will be charged with theft. Do you understand me?"

"Yes, S'arnt Major."

"Louder."

"YES, S'ARNT MAJOR!"

"Do you have any tobacco or cigarettes on you?"

"Yes, S'arnt Major."

"Give them to me."

He ground the packet into the tarmac with his boot. "No smoking is allowed on Field Punishment – at any time, night or day."

"Ten minutes! Double march!"

Harold Jones, clerk to the Town Clerk, or perhaps more correctly clerk to the clerk to the Town Clerk, straightened his tie, rubbed the toecaps of his shoes on the backs of his trouser legs to give them a shine, put his clipboard under his arm and set out to do his duty. In a few weeks from now two hundred officers and men of the British Army would arrive in Thame and Harold had been given the great responsibility of organising and arranging their billets. So far he had listed one hundred beds but it was a task that got harder each day. Today he was bound for East Street and Park Street. A few minutes later he was at the first house in East Street, pencil ready he gave a sharp officious rap on the door. Silence. Another sharp rap. Slowly the door inched back and a deeply suspicious voice spoke out. "What do 'ee want?"

Several doors further down the street opened and a woman appeared in each doorway. The first door started to close so Harold quickly stepped forward. "Good morning. I've come from the Town Hall."

"Bugger off." The door shut tight.

Harold put a cross against number one and turned towards number two. The woman in the doorway folded her arms and watched Harold intently until he stopped in front of her, then she turned and called out to her neighbour. "Don't raise yer hopes, Ivy – 'tis only a boy in long trousers."

"Good morning, Mrs, I'm from the Town Hall. We need billets for visiting soldiers in two weeks time."

Number two called out to number three. "He's giving out men, Ivy. Can yer manage a few?" She turned to Harold. "How long?"

"Two weeks, Mrs."

"I may have room," she waited until Harold's pencil was poised in expectation, "or I might not."

"Oh!" Harold could not hide his disappointment.

"What sort of soldiers are you offering?"

"Men going to France, Mrs – prime volunteers."

"How much."

"One shilling and thre'pence a day."

Number two called out to number three. "D'yer hear that, Ivy. We can have a man for one and thre'pence." Her finger jabbed at Harold. "I shall want to pick my own."

Harold stuttered. "The-the-the army allocates the men, Mrs, not me. I do all the clerking and pay the amounts each week."

Number two looked at him with greater interest. "So it's you who has all the money, eh? I could offer you a nice warm bed. If'n you're of a generous nature, that is."

"No, Mrs – I don't think my mother would agree to that."

"In that case you can put me down for one – but make sure he's clean, fit and good looking or there will be serious trouble."

"I will do what I can, Mrs."

Harold marked his list. "Thank you, Mrs." Then somewhat relieved he turned and marched to number three. Ivy gave a loud and prolonged sniff. "Put me down for four."

"That's most generous of you, Mrs."

"Don't be daft – 'tis five shillin' a day. Just you make sure I get paid or you'll really know what trouble is."

During the first week of field punishment Albert Harty thought he was going to die of fatigue and lack of sleep as he performed drill, exercises and duties at the double from dawn until dusk, then at dusk he had to clean his kit to standards that would have met with approval in the Brigade of Guards parading at Windsor Castle. There was never a moment of peace and the corporals and sergeants appointed to drive him ever faster did their duty to the letter with the greatest zeal. In the second week as Albert gained in fitness, he lost several stone in weight and his muscles toned and strengthened. Then he found that he could cope easily with the exercise and he learned how to achieve perfection of kit and appearance with comparative ease. When he got to the third week the tables were turned, Albert found he could out-march, out-run and outlast his constant tormentors, nor could they find fault with his presentation, to their great frustration. At the end of the third week Albert chanced upon a bible while he was cleaning the chapel and, like many a soldier given an opportunity to misappropriate, the bible disappeared into his shirt front. He had no need nor desire for a bible other than the vague thought that it may be possible to swap it for food or fags. Naturally, he did try but not one person was interested in a second hand army issue bible, so that night he opened it and started to read. For reasons that he never understood he found that once he had started to read he could not stop. By dawn, Albert had found God, or as he liked to think, God had sought him out. The Orderly Sergeant doubled Albert to the cookhouse at dawn, the first day of Albert's new life.

Each man was entitled to a mug or dixie of tea, a fifth of a loaf and two rashers of bacon for breakfast, in two hours time the two thousand men would want their first meal of the day. In one and a half hours time the Company Orderlies would arrive to take the rations back to the tents and barracks. An amazed cook watched as Albert set to, bread was fetched, cut and counted out, giant urns were scrubbed, cleaned and filled with fresh water, fires lit and stoked, extra coal delivered. The cook had never had service like this and he sang as he fried the bacon. When all was ready he called out to Albert. "Breakfast ready – have some bacon, mate!"

Albert's taste buds had been tantalised into mouth watering activity as the bacon cooked, so, bread in hand, he quickly made his way to the range.

"Can I dip my bread, mate?"

Dipping one's bread in the hot bacon fat was an envied and rare breakfast feast, normally reserved only to the cook and the Orderly Sergeant of the day. The cook nodded, "You've earned it."

The new Albert was pleased, surely the Lord was showing the way, so he gave the cook the first benediction he was to give and the cook to receive. "Ye are the salt of the earth, the Lord's blessing on you, for blessed are the pure in heart for they shall see God."

"Dunno about that, mate, I've never seen God in a fucking Cookhouse!"

Albert wagged his finger in mild sorrow. "Do not mock God. Remember he is everywhere. It is written in the bible – 'Swear not at all'."

Later that morning Albert stood before the Regimental Sergeant Major. "The Orderly Sergeant tells me you are acting strange, Harty. It seems you have become a 'gospeller'."

"Permission to speak, S'arnt Major?"

"Keep it brief, there is work to do."

"Afore today, S'arnt Major, I have been a right hand that gives offence but I have been shown the proper way. It is said clear, 'blessed are those who hunger after righteousness'."

"Is this some joke, Harty, for if it is I will break you! You will go to the front, religion or no."

"God did not find me to take me from my duty, S'arnt Major!"

"Your duty is to fight the Hun, not the British Army!"

"The bible tells me to love my enemies and to bless those who curse you and pray for your persecutors."

"Ah, so you will not fight – is that it?"

"Oh no, S'arnt Major. I will love you and pray for you and the Military Police but the Huns break God's laws and must be chastised. Only when they are dead can they be received into heaven for they are Philistines."

Sidney Barnes gently aligned the rear and front sights of his rifle, his trigger finger automatically applied first pressure then he offset two points to the left to allow for wind and fired. The rifle bucked but the bullet had not even reached target before the bolt rammed another round into the breech and the rifle was cocked, ready for another shot. Six hundred yards down the range a triangular pointer briefly marked the centre of the target. Another bullseye Sidney noted without satisfaction, he knew the shot was only just inside the centre mark as the rifle had pulled very slightly sideways. It was the tight jacket that was the problem, Sidney had worn a very loose jacket for years and he could not get used to the restraint of a uniform.

The Drill Sergeant pacing the firing line, looked and grunted in satisfaction. "Umm! Well done, Barnes."

"I could do better if I could take my jacket off, Drill Sergeant."

"I daresay, Barnes, but the army does not allow nudity whilst on parade."

Twenty yards behind the firing line George Coates heard the remarks as he opened another box of ammunition, extracted a handful of bullets and patiently started to fill clips with five rounds. He had noted that Sidney Barnes was far and away the best shot among the men under training and had been since the first day. There was no rancour in that judgement. After two months of training during which the pair had been thrown together many times, the anger and animosity had died. Not completely in George's case, but a quiet unspoken truce prevailed between them.

"Coates!" The Drill Sergeant beckoned. "Five rounds for each man on the line."

George hastened forward. When he reached Sidney he bent over. "Rosie might like yer naked but if I see yer stripped off in the line I shall shoot yer left bollock off!"

Sidney sniffed disdainfully. "Yer couldn't shoot my bollocks off if they were hung on the end of yer rifle."

The Drill Sergeant made a note in his book. Some men would go straight from training to join the regiment in the line but he was always on the look out for men with special skills. Skills that could be improved by training. The army had an insatiable appetite for men but particularly men with specialist skills, skills whereby more enemy could be killed. He did not know it yet but Sidney Barnes was destined for the sniper school, while George Coates was to go for grenade training. George could lob a Mills Bomb thirty yards and drop it in a bucket. His records up to date, the Drill Sergeant called out to Sidney. "On yer feet, Barnes. Port arms for inspection."

Sidney jumped to his feet, rifle across his body and bolt pulled back for inspection. The Drill Sergeant glanced in the breech. "Order arms! Now, I want you to go down the line, coach each man in turn especially Mason, Billings, Cook and Fenny."

"Yes, Drill Sergeant!"

Thomas Guntrippe was determined that his departure from Thame would be the opposite of his arrival back six months ago. Then he had been met with a band and treated like a hero. His son had danced along at his side, filled with a proud excitement that Thomas could not share. Now the doctor had declared that he was fit enough to return to his regiment. It was a decision made with reservations but Thomas had pleaded his case and the doctor had reluctantly graded him B1.

Thomas had tried to explain his feelings to Rose but had failed. She had told him he had done his bit and got angry when he persisted. He had never told her of Albert Harty's remark but he noticed that Rose's temper was shorter by far since Sidney Barnes had enlisted. Thomas was sad because he was treated like a hero when he knew full well that he wasn't. Nor could he explain why home wasn't home any more and that went beyond Rose's unfaithfulness. At the front he had shared the dangers and hardships with men he regarded as comrades and friends. No one in Thame had that shared feeling or experience. Those that Thomas related to were at the front or dead, he could not remain in Thame. He must go back.

Thomas was alone on the station platform as the train pulled in. He threw his kit in through the door then stepped up into the carriage. As the train pulled away to Oxford he caught a glimpse of Robert, his face tear-stained, sitting on the fence just past the bridge. He wished he had waved, deep down he had a feeling that perhaps Robert was the only person in the world who loved him.

* * * * * * *

A frightened and distraught Constance Harper ran all the way from the women's dormitory to the Master's quarters, screaming all the way. Now she thundered on the door with both hands. "Come quick, come quick – 'tis terrible to see!"

The Matron of the Workhouse was very annoyed. She had promised herself a leisurely breakfast and a visit to St Mary's Church for morning service. The trap was being prepared and the

Master was fitting his tie. She hurried to the door and threw it open. "Can it not wait? This is Christmas morning."

Constance was breathless from the run. "Come!" The Matron was suddenly aware of the terrible keening wails coming from the women's quarters. Constance found her voice. "Old Mother Shipley ses it's God's punishment on us all."

The Matron started to get angry. "Talk sense. What has Mother Shipley done?"

"Her swinging, Matron – it is most horrible to see, an' on Christmas Day."

"Mother Shipley?"

"No, no, Matron. Martha Peddelle – from a beam! Her face is black."

The Matron turned. "Husband! Be quick now – we have terrible trouble."

The Master of the Workhouse glared at Samuel Peddelle. "Your wife has shamed us, taking her life on Christmas Day. My wife is deeply troubled and the house in hysterics."

"I am sorry, Sir. My hope is that she is at peace at last."

The Master was not mollified. "She leaves no peace here. All the women and children crying. Never did I think we would have to cancel a Christmas Day."

"May I sit with her, Sir."

"You realise there can be no Christian burial for her."

"I do not think she will mind, Sir. Christ does not seem to care for our family."

The Master gasped. "What a wicked thing to say, Peddelle."

Samuel's hands twisted in unison. "'Tis just the hurt speaking, Sir."

"The men will arrive with the coffin soon – you may sit with her till then."

"Thank you, Sir. It is in my mind that I should leave this house, if I may speak on it."

"There can be no release to vagrancy, Peddelle, It is against the law as well as commonsense."

"No, Sir, perhaps I could serve my country. It is not all good news from France."

"You were rejected before and I do not believe your health is good – the doctor has said several times that your chest is congested."

"If you will allow me to try it would please me, now that Martha has gone."

"You said once that she lived in a world of make believe. I trust you will not do the same."

"No, Sir. There is no place in this world any more for make believe."

The Quartermaster Sergeant knocked on the door and entered. "This list has just arrived, Sir. You recall that we have asked for replacements for months to no effect, well, we are going to be allocated two men. According to this note, one is a man called Guntrippe – he used to be the Brigade runner, returning from a 'Blighty'. The other could be a problem."

Captain Stevens looked up from his chair and pushed the ammunition list aside. "What sort of problem?"

"According to my information he's taken to religion, Sir. A note came down from base camp to suggest we keep careful watch on him."

"Who is he?"

"Private Harty. Seems to have spent more time on field punishment than anything else. Has a special dislike of Military Policemen apparently."

"I remember Guntrippe. He will be useful because he knows our ways. I will see them both as soon as they arrive."

The Quartermaster Sergeant saluted. "Yes, Sir. And may I wish you a Happy New Year."

"Thank you, Q, see if you can find a bottle so we can raise a toast."

The Quartermaster Sergeant touched his nose. "Already done, Sir. A nice drop of scotch."

"Before you go, Q. Have a word will you, down the line. We are in desperate need of a cobbler. If not half our men will be barefoot before this winter is out."
"Leave it with me, Sir."

"Sing for me, Edward, please sing. Just for me alone" In the dark, Victoria could ask without Edward seeing her faint blush. "Tomorrow is a new year. Father says the war will end then."

Edward stepped out, banging his gloved hands together, to get his circulation going. There had been a small fire in the church hall that they used for choir practice that gave out just enough heat to make them feel the cold as they left the protection of the building. The Church of St Mary's could no longer be used after dark. "Come on, Vicky, or we will freeze."

Victoria stopped. "I am not moving unless you promise me a song for New Year's Eve."

Edward stopped. "A song for a kiss?"

They had never kissed and Edward half held his breath, fully expecting to be rebuffed. Vicky reached out and touched his cheek. "Don't you know you can have a kiss at any time."

Edward stumbled. "You never said."

"Certain things don't need to be said."

"I love you, Victoria Welcome Peters."

"Then sing me a song – then I want to kiss you so you'll never forget."

"When I grow too old to dream
I'll have you to remember
When I grow too old to dream
Your love will live in my heart
So kiss me my sweet
And so let us part
And when I grow too old to dream
That kiss will live in my heart."

"I love you, Edward Holling. No more make believe."

Chapter 3   1916: 'ROSES OF PICARDY'

"Captain Stevens!" The Colonel beckoned Alfred to his side, "Well done, a splendid dinner. I will not ask how you managed it in case I may have to disapprove."

The Ox and Bucks had spent a dismal Christmas Day in the front line and Alfred, knowing that the battalion would be relieved and retire into billets for rest at the end of December, had organised a special late Christmas Dinner for New Year's Day. He had requisitioned the largest barn for the occasion and every man in the battalion sat down to roast beef and ham, followed by plum pudding well soused with brandy. Now for the final tribute, port for the officers and a bottle of beer for the men.

"Thank you, Sir, we felt that the men deserved it – I only wish we could do more. I have arranged for a pianist, shall we call Private Bates to lead the singing?"

"Excellent, call the men to order."

Alfred stepped out to the centre of the barn. "Order! Order! Pray silence for the Colonel."

The Colonel rose and a respectful silence fell. "Since we came to France we have lost many comrades and I salute their memory. But today is our Christmas Day and our thoughts rightly go to those we have left at home. Be upstanding. A toast! To our nearest and dearest far away and all those we love and care for – family and friends."

A roar went up. "Family and friends – God bless 'em."

The pianist hurried in and struck up a tune and Private Bates stepped forward to join him.

> *"Keep the home fires burning*
> *While your hearts are yearning*
> *Though your lads are far away*
> *They dream of home*
> *There's a silver lining*
> *Through the dark clouds shining*
> *Turn the dark clouds inside out*
> *Till the boys come home."*

"Right lads – enough of this old slop. All together now, 'The Woodpecker's Song ....

Oh, I put my pecker in the woodpecker's hole
And the woodpecker said, Why bless my soul
What is that? What is that?
Reee-volting
Oh, I ...."

Despite the night cold there was a moderate fetid warmth in the milking shed and the adjacent barn, winter sleeping quarters for the small dairy herd of Newbarn Farm. The milking shed had two stalls and one central oil lamp that gave sufficient light for the job in hand. Rose Guntrippe had arrived promptly at four a.m. and started milking, the other stall was occupied by a waiting cow but James Roberts was late. He had been late several times recently but he had never been this late before. Rose knew that James was awake because there was a lantern alight in the farmhouse kitchen. Three cows had been serviced and the milk safely in the churn before James appeared.

"You'm late, Maister – 'tis not like you."

Roberts grunted so Rose could not tell whether he agreed or disagreed. His subsequent silence worried Rose because her intuition told her that there was something wrong, perhaps trouble. She decided that it was best not to ask questions. When the cow was dry she took the bucket to the churn and the cow plodded off to the barn. James spoke at last. "Have you milked Sunset?"

"No, she's waiting on you'm." Sunset was a heavy milker but she possessed an uncertain temperament so Roberts had always handled her. As he said to Rose on the first day, "Yon Sunset, she has crinkly teets – doesn't like being touched so she needs careful handling. Leave her to me." Rose led another cow into the stall.

"It's a dark night, Maister – dawn will be late a'coming."

There was silence for some minutes apart from the milk hitting the pails. When Robert did speak there was a hesitant note in his voice. "I – I've put out the word for another man." He stopped and waited as if expecting Rose to object.

"As you'm please, Maister."

"The Missus is bad ill. The doctor has said her body has too much sugar. How can sugar be bad for a body?"

"What about a medicine? My mother swears by Goat's Rue and Knapwort."

"It has gone too far. I must get another milker."

"'Twill be hard, Maister. Why not get help in the house. That will free you."

"What of the poultry?"

"My Robert will do that for you after school."

Roberts thought hard, what Rose had said was right, a man would be hard to find especially one experienced in milking. "Aye, you may be right."

"Let me speak to Alice Harty, Maister. She's a fine cook. Her husband is away fighting."

"That will help but I shan't be able to do as much out here."

"I can do a full man's share, Maister."

"Then you will be paid a man's rate, Rose, 'tis only fair."

"An' thre'pence a day for Robert if he feeds the hens and collects the eggs."

"Done."

Samuel Peddelle had left the Workhouse with the full blessing and approval of the Master. Samuel had pledged to enlist and the Master had rubbed his hands with pleasure after he had struck Samuel's name from the register. One less mouth to feed, one less mouth to pay for! So Samuel had walked down the path from the main door, his heart bumping with emotion, turned right and walked to the Cowley Barracks by Oxford, the depot of the Ox and Bucks. He was free. What Samuel had not considered was a doubting doctor and standards of selection. The Medical Officer applied his stethoscope to Samuel's chest, tapped with a finger and listened, a look of concern on his face.

"Do you have fits?"

"No, Sir."

"Any pains?"

"No, Sir."

"When did you last go into hospital?"

"Never once, Sir."

The M.O. felt the muscles of his arms, then turned to the clerk. "This man is unsuitable. He is unfit, underweight and undersized."

"May I have a quiet word, Sir?"

"Sir, we need this man."

"Surely not, even you can see he is poor quality – no stamina."

"This man is a cobbler, Sir. There is desperate need in France. Word has reached us."

"This man is not fit to march two miles!"

"He walked ten miles to volunteer, Sir!"

"The best I can do is B3 – and that is generous, mark you."

"That will do, Sir. Unfit for combat but fit to cobble."

"Make sure he is looked after and given extra rations."

"Never fear, Sir, he will be fed on prime steak and wrapped in cotton wool."

Samuel Peddelle could not hear what was being said as he waited in a stew of fearful anticipation, hoping he would not be rejected. Already his stomach ached from the loss of his midday meal, conditioned as it was from eating to a strict timetable. There was one thing he knew for certain. He could not go back to Thame with all its associations with the past. The only matter he must carry with him was the thought that each day that passed took him further from his daughters and that was an easier burden to bear away from the Workhouse. There was, even now, no easy reconciliation with the knowledge that they were no longer his daughters and his mind rejected the thought. Silently he cursed his fate.

The Medical Officer returned. "Are you certain you want to enlist, Peddelle?"

"Yes, Sir. With all my heart, Sir."

"Very well, I shall grade you B3 – but mark my words – no heroics."

"Yes, Sir – sorry, I mean no, Sir. Am I accepted?"

"Yes but no combat duties. No shooting at Huns – and a good vapour rub on your chest, every day."

"Yes, Sir."

John Adams shivered as he removed his hat and overcoat. Then he moved briskly to the coal fire to warm his hands. "Damn this biting cold wind, Herbert. God knows what effect it must be having on our troops!"

Herbert Peters, grocer, hovered by the sideboard. "Sit down, John, while I pour a drink. Port?"

John Adams waved his pipe. "Do you mind?"

"Not at all, John. I always enjoy a pipe myself at this time of the evening. Now, what can I do for you?"

Herbert handed over a glass then made his way to the other armchair. "Mother will not disturb us, she's writing some letters."

John Adams sucked fiercely on his pipe. "As you know, the Military Service Bill has become law – in effect, conscription. Those who won't enlist will be made to serve. Subject to certain exemptions, of course."

Herbert lit his pipe. "There – has been – a lot – of talk about shirkers and religious types."

"See it all around, Herbert – 'tis a disgrace. Now, I have been appointed Chairman of the local tribunal to oversee the review of exemptions but I need half a dozen sound men to serve with me. I want you to volunteer, Herbert!"

"Eee – mmm – well, it is a lot to ask of a shopkeeper, John. I don't know." Herbert puffed his pipe and rubbed his hands in indecision. "I rely on goodwill – takes years to build goodwill, John."

"Your country needs you."

"Aye, But it will mean making judgements on neighbours and townsfolk – as well as customers. I am no saint."

"Duty, Herbert, duty. Conscience and duty call us all. We cannot fight, you and I but we can serve. Don't forget, we are told a million men are needed. I will not take no as an answer – this tribunal must have the weight of respect and contain the God fearing goodness of our foremost citizens otherwise it will lead to endless acrimony and argument."

"It is hard to resist a call to duty, John, though it gives me concern."

"I will enter your name," John Adams clenched his pipe firmly between his teeth, "Lord Kitchener has said we need these men – we must find them."

Herbert Peters sighed. "You had best put my name forward, I suppose, though I wish it could be otherwise."

"A letter of appointment will be drawn up – we start work in a fortnight's time."

Herbert could not suppress his surprise. "So soon!"

"The sooner the better – there are over two hundred claims for exemption already."

Captain Fairbairn, Thame Volunteers, smiled in understanding. "Are you sure of this?" The question was addressed to Edward Holling. "None of you are yet eighteen, Edward."

Edward held his ground. "Our minds are made up, Sir. I heard Mr Adams speaking, if we don't volunteer soon then we will be conscripted."

"True, but the result is the same, you will all be called for service."

"But not together, Sir. We want to serve together. We are pledged as friends, we have looked forward to this. Harold will be eighteen in April – he is the eldest, Freddie is the youngest, he will not be eighteen until July."

"I believe you are right. If you enlist under the Lord Derby Scheme then you can arrange to be called forward as a group. I can arrange it."

"Thank you, Sir."

"This is not entirely to my liking. Most of your group have officer potential and I can help in this if you will allow me."

"Thank you, Sir, but our minds are set. We have been comrades since we first went to school. We have played cricket together, learned to swim in Jemmett's Hole – we are friends, Sir."

"You realise you cannot go overseas until you are nineteen?"
"We know that, Sir, but we will be trained and ready. Perhaps we can do our bit before this war ends."

The parabolic symmetry of the flares rising and falling over 'No Man's Land' gave the frosted landscape an ephemeral beauty. Behind the flares the night sky was pitch black but the immediate landscape shimmered in the light and the ugliness seen in daylight was but a memory. The watching troops knew the ugliness would return at dawn and the barbed wire would regain its menace. George Coates sat on the firing step in the trench reassured by the knowledge that he was safe from hostile rifle or machine gun fire. He pulled on his balaclava helmet and then took out his mittens. How he blessed all those good ladies sat beside the fireside at home and their busy clicking needles as they knitted warm comforts with patriotic fervour. His face blackened with soot he blended into the shadows of the trench. Beside him five other men were going through the same motions. Only George, though, did not have a rifle. As the party's bomber George carried a dozen primed Mills Bombs in a canvas haversack that hung on his chest. The sergeant in charge of the party asserted his authority. "Everyone ready! What is the password?"
"Snowdrop."
"Lead out, Coates."

Several hours ago when the group had assembled, to plan the raid, the Sergeant had deferred to George, 'Listen to him, you lot. Bomber Coates has been out more times than you've had hot dinners'. George had patiently explained. "It's four hundred yards once we're through our wire. No crawling unless we're under fire, that's the quickest way to get caught up. Do a 'crouch' walk. Do not run – fast movement gives you away. If we get caught by a flare, just freeze and look at the ground – if you look at the flares you will be night blind. When we get near the German trench don't shake the wire – it will jingle and they will know summat is up."
"D'you get that." The Sergeant took over, "We want one prisoner."

"What if he shouts out, Sarge?"

"Don't worry, he'll be shitting himself with fright. Don't forget, if his mates open up on us, he's as likely to get killed as we are."

Despite the cold night air George had not gone more than forty yards before the exertion and tension brought on a sweat and a few seconds later he cursed quietly as the lice began to bite. Several times machine gun fire had shattered the peace of the night but it was not directed at the raiding party. George rightly put it down to nervous trigger fingers but it had the disadvantage that many more flares lit the sky as sentries searched for any attackers. Eventually the flares subsided.

"Let's go, Sarge. The Huns are on edge tonight so I'll go slow."

Already tired from loading the wagon Thomas Guntrippe pulled himself up on to the driver's seat and picked up the reins. "Jump up, Albert!" Then he urged the horses forward.

Thomas and Albert Harty were starting out on the nightly supply run up to the battalion in the front line. It was an odd union. Albert had no fear, totally convinced as he was that God had him marked for some special act and that he enjoyed a favoured protection. Thomas found that his fear grew each day, only a fraction at a time but growing all the same. He found that the first shell of the night triggered off a rising tide of fear that he could not subdue until he was safely back in the Quartermaster lines. Safely back he would use the cleaning and feeding of the horses as a form of therapy. Then after breakfast he could fall into a troubled sleep.

A random shell exploded some four hundred yards away and Thomas visibly winced. Albert reached out and touched his hand. "Fear not, Thomas. The Lord is our shield."

"I would rather he stopped the shelling and make this war end."

Albert shook his head in sorrow. "Nay, ye do not understand God's way. This war cannot end until we have struck down all the Philistines."

The wagon hit a patch of mud and Thomas had to crack the reins to urge the horses on. "We are fighting Huns – not Philistines!"

"This is just a beginning for it says in the Bible that 'nation shall rise against nation, and kingdom against kingdom'. This marks the second coming of Christ."

Thomas found himself perturbed by Albert's conviction and ready answers. "I've never heard of that!"

"Worry not, Thomas, I will save you. The Lord has said 'the strong must bear the weak'."

The horses struggled as the wagon hit a hole in the track, and Thomas had his reply, "Then you had better push or we'll not get there."

George Coates hugged the ground in a small depression about thirty yards in front of the German trench and listened intently. The minutes ticked by but he did not move or make a sound. There was no sign of any sentry but George knew that one must be present. But where? He waited. Seven minutes later a faint movement and a cough pinpointed the sentry's location and George motioned the Sergeant forward.

"Gawd, George, you take your time!"

"Shush." George pointed. "He's there – just beside that fallen sandbag. I think he's asleep – having forty winks."

"I'll move the men up. I'll leave Higgs with you to give us cover."

George put two bombs on the ground and held another two ready to throw. He watched the four men creep forward to the lip of the trench, then on a signal from the sergeant, they dropped into the trench. Suddenly a man started screaming out loud, "Hilfe! Hilfe mir!", and George could hear men running in from the right. Then a shot rang out and as the four raiders scrambled out of the trench and ran back, George dropped three bombs into the trench. The bombs exploded in quick succession as the four men, panting furiously, dropped down beside him. A machine gun rattled out some hundred yards away but the gunner was obviously shooting at phantoms. The sergeant touched George on the shoulder. "Let's get away."

"What happened?"

"We had to shoot the bastard – he woke up in a fright."

George dropped two more bombs into the trench. "Let's go."

The raiding party hadn't gone more than forty yards when the starshells cracked overhead and the night sky turned to daylight all around them. George dropped into a shell hole and pulled the sergeant in. "Wait here, it's too dangerous to move!"

"Keep down, men – no-one moves!"

"We'll get no prisoner tonight, Sarge. Might as well go back."

"Aye – it'll be like a bloody hornets nest out there."

"Give it a while. When the flares die I'll drop some bombs about fifty yards to our left, then we can be on our way."

The Company Quartermaster Sergeant slapped Thomas on the back. "Well done, Guntrippe. Am I pleased to see you, we lost half our ammo and rations from shell fire today. The lads will be hungry."

"There's letters as well, Quarter."

"That's a blessing – bucks the men up no end in the line. Now, let's get this unloaded then I'll do you a nice tot of rum."

"Kind of you, Quarter. But none for Harty, please."

"Where is Harty?"

"Gone to deliver prayer books."

The rattle of machine gun fire and exploding bombs drifted back from No Man's Land. "I hope Harty is not out there."

Thomas sniffed. "He's daft enough!" The night sky out in No Man's Land suddenly lit up again and a nervous machine gunner kicked off a dozen more in unison as he opened fire. Thomas could not stop himself shaking and found he was really looking forward to the promised rum.

George Coates peered out from the shell hole to check the source of the machine gun fire. Satisfied that they had not been pinpointed he drew back.

"Give it a while, Sarge – they're still very nervous."

"Captain Cross is going to be upset we've no prisoner but we just couldn't stop the bastard sentry screaming. There's a dugout just there and we could hear men coming up."

Machine gun bullets rattled the wire behind them and the party crouched lower. "I don't think we killed that sentry."

"Best not to try to bring a wounded man back."

"We tried – but he was too heavy."

"We've only fifty yards to go."

Another batch of starshells filled the sky. "Damn – we're stuck here for the night!"

In the silence they could hear someone singing a long way off but the song came through quite clearly in the still night air.

> *"Onward Christian soldiers, marching as to war,*
> *With the cross of Jesus . . . . "*

"Bloody hell, Sarge, who is that?"

A shell exploding drowned out the singer for a moment.
> *"Onward into battle, see his banner . . . . "*

George Coates lifted up. "We can go, Sarge. That's Private Harty going back down the line to the depot." More shells whistled overhead. "He makes a wonderful decoy."

Herbert Peters bustled forward to the counter, tying his apron in place as he did so, regretting that his midday cup of tea was only half finished. He disliked waste and wished now he had bolted the door to customers but it was so rare for someone to come before two p.m. The customer was a woman but Herbert had never seen a woman dressed like this in his shop. What is the world coming to, he thought, women wearing trousers! Trousers that had seen better days. He knew that he had seen the woman before but could not place her. Not a regular customer and several shades below the standard of those he normally welcomed. His deeply ingrained suspicion of strangers triggered, his manner was somewhat abrupt.

"Can I help you?" His voice was hard and unfriendly and he realised from the woman's reaction and startled look that his question sounded like a challenge. He quickly modified his tone. "How can I help you, Miss?"

On closer inspection he could see that his latest customer was a fine looking woman with a trim figure under the bulky working clothes. She caught him appraising her and she looked him straight in the eye and smiled in a knowing way. "Your shop was recommended. I want to send a parcel to France."

Herbert rubbed his hands and stepped forward. "Of course, we have made a name for our service. Our boxes of comforts are greatly appreciated by the troops."

"How much?" The abruptness of the question unsettled Herbert.

"Eh – from seven shilling rising to twenty-five shillings."

"I think twelve and six will be enough – a man cannot keep so much in the trenches."

"There is no charge for the box."

The woman wrinkled her nose. "I should think not. Now what will my man get?"

"I start with four tins of finest bully beef . . . . "

"No! My man cannot abide bully beef. When he was home he said they got it every day in the trenches."

"Corned mutton then, Miss. This is quality meat."

The woman's voice was scornful. "Corned mutton! 'Tis not fit for dogs."

Herbert coloured at the rebuke. "Of course – no mutton."

"It will be best if I choose. Best beef cubes. Yes, those."

"A tin of the Melbo, Miss – a good choice."

"Palmer's camp coffee and three tins of Nestles condensed milk. Some haste if you will, Mr Peters, I've to be back for the milking by three. Two tins of salmon, two tins of fruit – the nice ones with pears. Thomas has a sweet tooth so two pounds of sugar, cocoa powder, best Lyon's tea in a tin and a large tin of McVitie's biscuits – oh, and matches."

"May I recommend the dry soup tablets, Miss."

"Aye, put those in – an' some potted meat and relish."

103

Herbert was almost running to keep up with the stream of instructions.

"I shall go to the tobacconists to get some cigarettes. Thomas is fond of his Gold Flake."

"It will all be ready when you return, Miss."

"Thank you, Mr Peters. This letter has the address. Please put a note in the box." Herbert studied the letter.

"Just write it out, Mrs Guntrippe."

"I would be obliged if you wrote it, Mr Peters, I'm not clever with a pencil – an' worse with a pen."

"Of course – what shall I write?"

"From Robert and Edward – to the bravest dad in the world."

Robert Guntrippe crept sleepily down the stairs in his nightshirt. "I want a pee, Ma."

Rose Guntrippe had already raked out the range and set the fire and was ready to set out to the milking shed.

"Go back to bed, Robert – 'tis thick snow out."

Robert opened the kitchen door and peered out. "No school today, Ma!"

"Use the pot, Robert – you'll freeze out in the yard."

Robert was immediately on his guard, he was nearly grown up. "The pot is for babes, Ma. Pa never uses the pot."

The snow was still falling, great flakes steadily obliterating the outhouses and beyond, already it was almost a foot deep. "Your Pa would love a pot this morning – it will be cold in the trenches."

"Will Pa have the parcel by now?"

Robert was proud of his contribution, every penny he had earned had gone towards the parcel.

"I believe so, a hot soup will keep him warm this morning. Now, go back to bed and don't waken your Gran – she needs her sleep."

"If I don't go to school I shall write to Pa."

Sidney Barnes stared out over No Man's Land through the small aperture in his sniper's post, his eyes slitted against the glare of the snow. Satisfied that all was quiet he carefully unwrapped the specially oiled and cleaned rifle and checked the telescopic sight. Then he loaded a clip of ammunition and fed a round into the breech. From his post he could see along the trench in both directions and the lines of silent, staring men searching the land in front for signs of movement as the dawn came up. There seemed to be no danger of attack, he doubted if even a mouse could have moved unnoticed in that snowy landscape.

Ten minutes later the call went down the line. 'Stand down!' All the men on the firestep not on sentry duty stood down and exercised to get warm. A hundred yards off a rattle and clanking of ladles and cans announced the arrival of the CQMS with the morning's rum ration. Sidney gratefully supped his tot when it arrived. His 'spotter' ambled over.

"Periscope is in position, Sid. Ready when you are."

"Give me two minutes to get comfortable."

The two worked together, the spotter constantly searching the nearby trenches looking for troop movement, unwary sentries and working parties. As soon as the spotter sighted potential targets he would call out instructions and Sidney would quickly re-align.

"Jacko, let's concentrate on the angle."

The angle was a spot where the German trench suddenly turned at a right angle and a slight dip in the parapet gave the appearance of a flat narrow triangle. Troops moving to the rear turned at this point and in the elation of leaving the line were often careless. Sidney knew that, even if he couldn't see a person in the triangle, if he put a bullet into the trench by skimming the parapet he could make a 'kill'. Sidney trained his rifle on the lowest point of the triangle then watched the parapet to the left. Within a few minutes his finger tightened on the trigger. The tip of a Mauser rifle barrel showed above the parapet moving steadily to the right. Sidney counted off the imagined steps, one, two, three, four and then fired. He could tell from the quick flurry of movement in the enemy trench that he had probably scored a hit. Impassively he flicked back the bolt and reloaded. Jacko's voice called down the trench. "Well done, Sid – they won't call him Herman anymore!"

Chairman Adams called the meeting to order. "Attention please, gentlemen. As this is our first meeting please make sure you have a copy of the guidelines provided by our clerk, Mr Simmons. Also a warm welcome to our Military Representative, Mr John Clark Brown."

Adams had been of the opinion that the Town Hall Meeting Room was far too big and ostentatious for the needs of a Tribunal. But as he looked around he realised that if anything, a larger room might be needed. What with the press, the applicants and their dozens of supporters, friends, relatives and representatives, there were not enough chairs for everyone.

"Mr Simmons, call the first case."

"Mr Chairman, the first case is an application by Arthur Cornish for exemption from military service on the grounds that he is a sole trader with responsibility for his mother while his two brothers are serving soldiers."

"If Mr Cornish will step forward please."

A young man stepped forward, nervously twisting his cap in his hands. He had even put on a collar and tie for the occasion and was slowly strangling.

"What is you age?"

"Twenty six."

"Mr Simmons, please note that Mr Cornish falls within the age category for conscription. Mr Cornish, in your own words tell us why you wish to be exempted from military service."

"'Tis like this, Sir. I am a one man business now my brothers have gone to war, also my mother is dependent on me for money and help."

Chairman Adams glanced around the table. "Have members any questions?"

Before any could answer a voice boomed out from the back of the hall. "I want to know what as gives you'm the right to sit like Solomon in this yere place. You'm want to go afighting – not sitting on your backsides!" There was a splutter of applause.

The whole tribunal stiffened and looked offended. Chairman Adams glared at the speaker. "You will watch your manner, Heskey or I shall call the Constable to set a charge on you. This tribunal sits by parliamentary act, approved by the Lords and under the signature of the King. When you insult this tribunal you insult the crown! If there is another outburst then you will all wait outside in the road. Now, let us proceed."

Mr Godden picked up on the questioning. "Mr Cornish, you say your mother is dependent on you. In what way is this? Is she, for example, incapable?"

"My mother depends on me for money which is earned from the business which was started by my father. She has no other means of support."

"Is your mother incapable? Can she dress herself? Can she cook, do housework?"

"She is over sixty and frail but otherwise she is capable."

Herbert Peters intervened. "What exactly is your business?"

"Building supplies. I keep a small yard."

"Have you tried to find a person to run the business for you?"

"No, Sir."

"Why not?"

"It is hard to trust your livelihood and future to a stranger – what if they were dishonest?"

"Why cannot your mother check the books and money. I feel sure the bank would offer support." Tribunal member Mr Chapman made his point.

"I don't think a stranger would look after the business properly even if my mother was bookkeeper."

The Chairman gathered his thoughts. "Mr Cornish, let me put it to you straight. Where will your business be if we lose this war? What will you do if the Huns march into Thame?"

Arthur Cornish had lost his nervousness but now twisted his cap in frustration.

"I still say my mother is too old, Sir."

There was a hurried conference of the tribunal members, Mr Adams accepting points and getting agreement. Then he spoke. "Mr Cornish, you will be officially notified in writing that your application for exemption is rejected but your call-up will be deferred for two months so that you can find a person to run your business."

Subdued but nontheless angry muttering sounded from the back of the hall. "Silence! Next case, Mr Simmons."

"Mr Chairman, the next case is an application by Edwin Coker for exemption on the grounds of ill-health."

"Has Mr Coker seen the Military Medical Officer?"

"He has a letter from his doctor, Mr Chairman."

"Tch! This is not acceptable. The act does not allow this as a valid basis for exemption. Application denied, next case."

"Your honour!" Edwin Coker got to his feet. "A man what is ill cannot get to the Military Doctor."

"An ill man could not stand at this meeting. Next case."

"Mr Chairman, next is a plea by Edward Lawrence for exemption from military service as it offends his conscience and religious beliefs. He wishes to be identified as a conscientious objector as allowed by the Act."

John Adams' face assumed a serious frown. "Stand forward, Mr Lawrence and state your age and religious denomination."

"I am thirty and I have been an Anabaptist for sixteen years."

As he spoke, Edward Lawrence looked around at a hundred blank faces and he knew that he had no friends in this assembly. God has chosen a hard road for me to follow, he thought.

"State the beliefs on which you base your plea for exemption and the reasons why you should not serve."

Lawrence looked at each member of the tribunal in turn before he spoke. "Gentlemen, I believe totally in the Commandments of our Lord, the foremost commandment being 'thou shall not kill'. This war goes against everything in which I believe and every law of God I uphold. It is by its very nature an unChristian war. God said 'blessed are the peacemakers' – he did not say any word in favour of warmongers. My conscience will not allow me to kill my fellow man and if I did so I would have committed the greatest of sins."

Mr Wells of the tribunal looked up, as if from deep contemplation. "Are there no circumstances that might cause you to kill or say, resort to physical violence? What would you do if, for example, a man tried to rape your wife in front of you?"

"I have been asked that before. As it has not happened I cannot reply with absolute certitude but I believe I may react as other men."

"Ah! So you would fight."

"There is a great difference, Sir, between the defence of my family against a criminal act and the legalised killing arising in war."

"You will pardon me if I fail to see the difference," Mr Wells' voice took on a hard edge, "when our country is fighting for survival in a war we did not seek."

"Mr Lawrence, you say you will not kill but I feel you could serve," Herbert Peters' tone was more conciliatory than Mr Wells, "do you not accept that you can serve in a non-combat role?"

"No, Sir, surely the purpose of a military force is to seek violence. I see no difference between the hands that give a gun over and the hand that fires it."

"Do you pay taxes, Mr Lawrence?"

"I do."

"Surely then you accept that our taxes go to pay for our fighting men – so where does the guilt begin or end? Your taxes pay for men to kill and be killed so you are as involved as we are."

Edward Lawrence shook his head in sorrow. "It was our Lord who made this clear when he said 'give unto Caesar what is Caesar's'. My conscience is clear in this matter."

Mr Adams, Chairman, was clearly frustrated. "Let us end this or we will be here all night. Tell us where it states in the Bible that you cannot serve your country. You have told why you do not wish to kill. Tell us why you cannot serve."

"These matters are inseparable, Sir, like body and soul . . . . "

Mr Adams put his hand up. "It is clear to us that your conscience is strong in this matter." He conferred with his members for a short while then looked up. "Mr Lawrence, your request for exemption is denied. You will be noted as a conscientious objector but you will serve in a non-combat role as decided by the Military Authorities. Stand down."

"We shall be in the army by the end of July at the latest! Captain Fairbairn has arranged it." Edward Holling could not keep the excitement from his voice. As he spoke he held Victoria's hand and squeezed hard to reinforce the intensity of his feelings. "I know you said you did not want me to go but . . . . "

Vicky put a finger to his lips. "I understand, Edward. Other men have gone – I cannot hold you here – I would not want to, I shall be proud of you for doing your duty."

"I'll be home all the time. We're not allowed to go to France until we're nineteen." The disappointment showed in his voice.

Vicky squeezed his hand in return and then kissed him on the cheek. Everywhere we go, she thought, I see curtains drawn in sadness; why are men so drawn to war. "Promise me you will take care. As fast as one soldier leaves, another arrives."

"This must be over very soon, my love. W-will-will you marry me when this war is over?"

Vicky ruffled his hair. "You great silly. I have already decided to marry you – long ago."

"When did you decide this?"

"The first day that I knew I would love you forever."

George Coates rested wearily on his shovel. "Sid, if I'd known we would have to dig through the whole of France – well, I'd never have come."

Sidney Barnes eased his back and sounded of like mind. "Only a bloody fool would make us dig a trench when it is snowing. Why, it stands out like a sore thumb!"

Over four hundred Ox and Bucks men laboured today. Repeating what they had done yesterday and the day before and would do tomorrow. Four days of back-breaking rest. Exploding shells sounded some way off and then the explosions moved closer, making the men apprehensive. George looked at one of the men who reacted nervously. "No need to worry yet, mate."

"It's alright for you, Bomber, but I'm not used to this." He thumbed in the direction of the explosions, "I only joined five days ago."

"Hear that, Sid. Been here five days and still enjoying it. Look if you can last five days then six is easy. What do you say, Sid?" Sidney stopped digging. "I say this. We dig trenches. We build roads. We carry mine spoil. The Quartermasters pile up shells. There is something afoot, I can smell it."

George pulled a face. "What does it matter, 'tis all the same. We get paid a pittance – Albert Harty calls it a widow's mite. Not that Albert cares."

Sidney nodded knowingly. "Take my word, there's a big battle coming – we'll be in Germany by Christmas – or dead."

Captain Stevens, Quartermaster, had assembled his men to ensure that they were all briefed and knew what to do. He could not say exactly why all the work and preparation was needed but he was dealing with British 'Tommies'. There's was not to reason why! However it had just dawned on his men that this work of which he spoke was not an alternative, not an option but extra work.

"Sir." Thomas Guntrippe stood to attention. "Will we get help with this extra work – we are short handed."

The other men looked apprehensive, expecting Thomas to be struck down by an unseen hand for having dared to question orders.

Alfred Stevens did not react, without these men he would fail. He decided the best response was the truth. "No, I have already asked. We will work longer shifts. Also the dumps must be guarded so the Quartermaster Sergeant will prepare duty rosters."

Private Peddelle came to attention. "I would like to volunteer, Sir."

"Note that, Q, everyone will stand guard duty whatever their grade. Make sure everyone has a rifle, in good condition."

"Noted, Sir, with permission I will arrange some shooting practice. Some men haven't fired a rifle since leaving base camp."

Private Oxenlade came to attention, a touch of excitement in his voice. "Does that include cook staff, Sir?"

"Yes, Oxenlade. Cook staff as well. Put my name down as well, Q, and let's arrange a prize – for anyone who can make marksman."

Herbert Peters opened his Gazette and read. "Mother!"
"Yes, Father, what is it?"
"Terrible news, Mother, an entire battalion of Ox and Bucks men have been taken prisoner by the Turks. Bloody savages!"
"Now, now, Father. You know I don't like swearing." The needles stopped clicking. "Is that bad?"
"Bad! Very bad I should say. They are just part of the army that surrendered. Very bad show. Bad for the Empire."
Mrs Peters resumed her knitting. "We must organise some parcels – and a good supply of balaclavas."
"They are in a hot country, Mother!"
"No matter, they will enjoy a parcel."
"Aye, but where do we send them? We can hardly put 'somewhere in the desert' on the address."
"Oh, that reminds me, Father. Mrs Watson and Mrs Brown both complained about prices today. Prices seem to be going up every week."
Herbert gave a loud sniff. "It's not just prices going up. It seems to me that hemlines are going up even faster. Disgraceful!"
"Oh, Father! What harm is there is showing an ankle? I think its rather fetching – and its most practical. A woman can walk through the market without soiling her dress."
Herbert put his hand on his forehead. "What with the British Army giving in to savages, prices up, hemlines up and the August Bank Holiday cancelled, I can tell the country is going to the dogs. We'll get no holiday this year, Mother, why . . . . "

"I absolutely forbid this!" Edward Holling, senior, was livid with anger. "Do you hear me, Edward? You are still in articles. What possessed you?"
Edward Holling, Junior, stood his ground. "I'm sorry you disapprove, Father but as the law stands all men over eighteen and under forty one must serve or be conscripted, so I have enlisted under the Lord Derby Scheme."

"The law is clear to me. I had intended to apply for exemption while you finish your training, then go to the OTC. A deposition has been prepared."

"I want to serve with my friends, Father. This is the only way we can do it. The Recruiting Officer said we are now in the army, properly enlisted. The papers will arrive soon."

"Since you started associating with that Peters girl your judgement has been affected. No good has come from this."

"Victoria has never encouraged me to enlist, Father. In fact she has hinted that I should stay at home as you suggest."

"Then I apologise, Edward, I spoke from anger."

"Accepted, Father, because I intend to marry her when I am able to."

"You will wait until you have turned twenty-one. I will not allow you to marry until you have reached your majority, whatever the circumstances. This is my last word – no son of mine will make an unsuitable marriage with my approval."

"On that we are agreed, Father."

Several hundred solemn faces gazed up at the Vicar of St Mary's as he gazed down from the pulpit. Over five hundred townsfolk had followed the Thame Volunteers, headed by the Scouts Bugle Band, as they had slow marched from the Cornmarket to the church. Although the death of Lord Kitchener had been reported only a few days previously the groundswell of public distress and sympathy had culminated in a fine military parade. The Vicar glanced at his notes.

"The sermon today is taken from the Acts of the Apostles, chapter thirteen, paragraph thirty six. 'And he served his generation'. For does it not state that David, after he had served his generation by the will of God he fell on sleep and was laid unto his fathers.

Our nation mourns the loss of this great man, Lord Kitchener, who has fallen on sleep. Taken from us at the very height of his powers and in an hour of great need. But this is God's will, for it can be no other, no matter that we are distraught and in need of comfort . . . .

The hymn is 'Abide with me'."

"Abide with me, fast falls the eventide
The darkness deepens, Lord with me abide
When other helpers fail and comforts flee
Help of the helpless, O abide with me
. . . . "

Thomas Guntrippe trembled; only by exercising of a considerable degree of self-control could he stop himself from shaking. He feared that if he once let himself go and started to shake he would break into a thousand shattered pieces. For as far as he could see the forward horizon of night sky was one vast thunderflash as thousands of guns loosed off a bombardment. Palls of smoke hung over everything and the noise was overwhelming even though he was over a mile behind the batteries. Already the barrage had lasted for nearly two days. Worse still it was rumoured it was to last another week. Thomas should have been asleep but he found it impossible. He knew that under that pall of smoke there were tens of thousands of men waiting to advance. For weeks Thomas and his mates had laboured, delivering supplies and he knew that there was still more to do. At midnight the labour would start again. Peter Oxenlade stood beside Thomas, dusty with flour.

"There'll be no Huns left soon." Peter sounded quite pessimistic.

Thomas grunted then found his voice. "I'll pray for that – then we can go home."

"You'm don't understand, I've never been in the front line as you'm have. I joined to fight."

"There's no pleasure in it, Peter."

"Just one day, that's all I ask – just one day."

A loud voice gave out a hail a way off and Peter turned in alarm. "I must be off, the ovens will be ready."

Albert Harty marched up and gave out a great beaming smile of happiness. "How the good Lord smites the Philistines. He told Joshua that he would send in the hornets to drive out his enemies."

"You weary me, Albert. This is not the bible land, it is Picardy."

Albert was not crushed by Thomas's comment. "I will pray for you. Did not David say 'the Lord is my rock, and my fortress and my deliverer!' Trust in the Lord, Thomas!"

Thomas looked up at the sky. "The Lord has decided on rain – it is going to rain I tell you. How will we get the wagons to the front?"

"Not wagons, Thomas – chariots of fire. These be chariots of fire."

The send-off was a triumphal procession rather than a march to the railway station. Over fifty relatives and friends assembled to accompany the six lads on the start of their journey to the Depot. Edward Holling walked along, arm in arm with Vicky. Mary Peters held John Howe's hand. Mrs Pullene had insisted on packing a great hamper of food even though, as was said a dozen or more times, the lads were only going on a one hour journey. Mrs Coxe had insisted on knitting them each a half dozen pairs of socks and a scarf, even though it was the height of summer. Victoria had to swallow before she spoke. "Let's sing, Edward – I fear I may cry otherwise and I don't want you to remember me with tears."

"There's no need for tears, Love – we are only going twelve miles. I'll be back before you know it."

"Roses are shining in Picardy,
In the hush of a silvery dew.
Roses are flowering in Picardy
But there's never a rose like you
. . . . "

In Picardy, by the Somme, the British guns had gone silent just after dawn but it was a short-lived peace as the German batteries, in anticipation of the long awaited attack, bombarded the British lines. Just before seven o'clock a series of huge mines had exploded, throwing tons of earth and debris hundreds of feet into the air; at half past seven the whistles sounded and one hundred and fifty thousand men lifted up out of the trenches and advanced. Almost immediately the enemy machine guns opened fire.

In a reserve trench behind the front line, there was an instant relief that the advance had started. The Ox and Bucks were due to go over later as part of the second wave but they had no idea whether the attack was a success or failure, so within ten minutes the mixed reaction of the past twelve hours, boredom, frustration, anger, relief and fear, reasserted itself. The Colonel and the Company Commanders took their binoculars to the firing step enclosures and searched the ground ahead. At first, nothing happened but within an hour the first wounded men and stretcher bearers appeared and within a short while the initial trickle turned into a flood. The noise and thunder of the guns continued.

The Colonel confronted two stretcher bearers. "What is happening, soldier?"

The bearers did not stop. "Can't rightly say, Sir. Our battalion has disappeared, just hundreds of casualties – must go on, Sir, beggin' your pardon."

Herbert Peters rushed into the kitchen, leaving the shop unattended in his haste. "Mother! Mother, listen to this." He waved the Gazette at her. The Thame Gazette was Herbert's favourite paper and he swore by the contents. "Wonderful success in the Great Battle, Mother. It is all here."

"Let me put this cake in the oven – before it sinks."

"Listen to this. General Haig reports that thanks to our very complete and effective artillery preparation, and thanks to the dash of our infantry, our losses have been slight."

"That sounds very pleasing, Father."

"Pleasing! I should say so, at the very least. Our lads will be in Germany in a few weeks. All over by Christmas, just you see."

"How many men have we lost?"

"None reported, Mother – it must be a great success."

"Good afternoon, Nurse Healey, how can I help you?" Herbert Peters had made his way quickly to the shop counter, a welcome smile on his face as soon as Nurse Healey had appeared. Nurse Healey was in charge of the Red Cross Hospital in the Old Grammar School. She looked rather worried, he thought, so he eased the smile from his face in case she thought he was being disrespectful. She unfolded her purse and took out a telegram.

"So sorry to trouble you, Mr Peters, but this has arrived with a deal of urgency. The hospitals on the south coast are overwhelmed with thousands of wounded soldiers arriving from France. They need extra staff immediately."

Herbert could not believe it at first. "Are you sure? How did this happen? Thousands! Did you say thousands? What is going on?"

"My information is rather scarce, Mr Peters, but it has been confirmed that boatloads of badly wounded men are arriving at the ports and the Red Cross Commandant has issued a special plea for help."

Herbert rubbed his chin while trying to accept the news. "I'm shocked. I had no idea but I don't see how I can help."

Nurse Healey put the telegram back in her purse. "Not you, Mr Peters, Victoria. I wish to send Victoria to Dover. She is the only trained person who is single."

"Oh no! I'm sorry, Nurse Healey." Herbert reacted strongly. "She is a girl – far too young. Besides which she is not a trained nurse, she has told me so herself."

"You underestimate your daughter, Mr Peters. She is a woman, not a girl. She is advanced in her knowledge and mature in her judgement."

"How long will she be away from us?"

"How can I say for certain, Mr Peters." Nurse Healey gave a deep shrug and spread her hands. "This crisis cannot be judged from a distance but wounded men take time to heal."

Herbert dithered in silent anguish so Nurse Healey continued. "Her meals and accommodation will be provided, as will her travel and uniforms. She will also get a small payment for personal matters."

"My wife and I will need to discuss this. There is much to think on."

"I am sorry to be the bearer of distressing news, Mr Peters. Yesterday we were singing 'Roses are shining in Picardy'. Today I fear it is 'Roses are dying in Picardy'!"

Herbert retained a puzzled look. "I still cannot understand it. Why this lack of proper news? If what you say is true, then the curtains and blinds will be being drawn all over the country."

"I fear so, Mr Peters."

The journey from Thame to London and then from London to Dover was very tiring after all the excitement of the last twenty four hours and Victoria Peters found herself dozing as the train clattered through the Kent countryside. Her father had travelled with her to London and had seen her safely across to Victoria Station. In other circumstances the tiredness she felt would have lulled her to sleep but she was aware of the fact that she was on her own and a mild apprehension broke up any desire to close her eyes firmly. It was nearly one o'clock when the train roared into two tunnels in quick succession and that really woke her up. It was such a relief as the train emerged into sunlight and she could sense the train was slowing. A guard came marching down the corridor calling out in a harsh nasal tone. "Dover! Dover Priory Station! In one minute the train will be stopping at Dover, all passengers will disembark!"

Quickly, Victoria was on her feet and slid back the compartment door. "Guard! Can you help me please. I shall need a porter for my case."

The guard tipped his cap. "As soon as we stop, Miss. Just be careful, no more than a tuppenny tip now. There are some rogues about."

A large sign proclaimed the station name as Vicky opened a window in the corridor and she looked out in amazement as the train drew into the station, surely this cannot be right, she thought. The platform was covered with lines of stretcher cases, dozens of wounded men lying there, being tended by a handful of nurses. Men with bloody bandages and filthy uniforms. All was quiet apart from the hissing of the train.

A porter opened the door and touched his cap. "Take your bag, Miss?" Victoria stepped down on to the platform in appalled confusion. "These men – all these soldiers, why are they here?"

"Boat docked an hour ago, Miss. This train will take them to London."

"But why? There are red label men here!"

"Dunno, Miss. Not for the likes o' me to comment."

The red labels indicated that a man had a serious wound that may haemorrhage easily and required care. The porter averted his gaze as Vicky gave him a stern look. He did not know but his tuppence was at grave risk.

"I have to report to the Military Hospital. Please find me a taxicab or hansom."

The porter became more respectful. "No need for that, Miss, not for medical staff. There's an ambulance ready to go to the hospital. Follow me."

A dishevelled nurse in a well-worn and stained uniform helped Vicky into the back of the ambulance, there was barely room for her and her case between the two stretcher cases. "I'm driving. Watch the man on the left – he's unconscious and has lost a leg. Ease off the tourniquet for a minute. Don't let them smoke or drink."

The Matron stared at Victoria, then re-read the letter sent by Nurse Healey. "What can you do?"

Victoria squared her shoulders. "Bandaging, splints, dressings including poultices. Preparation of hot fomentations. . . . "

"Good. Why have you got blood on your coat?"

"I helped in the ambulance on the way here."

"Nurse Healey writes that you have a cool head and a good singing voice."

"I have sung at concerts, Matron. I like singing."

"Good. A singing nurse is as good as a smiling nurse. But a smiling nurse that can sing – now that will cheer the lads. You do smile, do you not, Victoria Peters?"

"Yes, Matron."

"Then smile – smile whatever you see, whatever happens, even when it hurts."

Matron clapped her hands, "Orderly!" An elderly man appeared in the doorway. "Take Miss Peters to the Nurses Hut, number three and make sure that Nurse Stanford meets her." She turned to Vicky. "For the moment you will work with Nurse Stanford as her ambulance nurse. Meet the boats coming in and take the men to the station for dispersal, where possible red label cases come to the hospital."

"Yes, Matron."

"You will be relieved at eight this evening."

"I haven't eaten since supper yesterday, Matron."

The Matron gave an airy wave and laughed. "None of us have." Then she turned serious. "The men will be lucky if they've eaten in the last forty-eight hours."

Nurse Ivy Stanford gave Victoria a hug. "Am I pleased to see you. I've been on my own for days. Can you drive?"

Victoria shook her head. "Sorry, no."

"Ah, well, no matter. I'll teach you. Now if we're very lucky the canteen lady will let us have a mug of tea and some toast. Come with me. Now tell me all about yourself."

The Drill Sergeant paused in front of the first of his six new recruits that made up the front row of the platoon, the latest men committed to his tender care. His pace stick reached out and touched the first man in the centre of the chest.

"Name? Keep your eyes to the front, firmly fixed!" He glared at the platoon. "Eyes will not roll around like marbles when on parade. Name!"

"Private Smithe, Drill Sarn't."

The Drill Sergeant's voice turned into a croon. "At last, after two years of patient prayer the Lord has seen fit to answer. He has sent me a recruit who knows how to address the exalted rank of Drill Sergeant. Where, Smithe, did you learn this soldierly skill?"

"We were taught drill by Sergeant Major Simmons of the Thame Volunteers, Drill Sarn't."

The Drill Sergeant closed his eyes in sheer pleasure for a few seconds, then moved two paces sharply to the right. "Name?"

"Private Coxe, Drill Sarn't."

"You have polished your buttons and shone your boots, Coxe! Why is that?"

"Yes, Drill Sarn't, Sergeant Major Simmons insisted, otherwise we weren't soldiers, he said."

The Drill Sergeant almost purred. "Quite right. Just as it should be." He moved another two paces to the right. "Name?"

"Private Holling, Drill Sarn't."

"And did you, Holling, take instruction from Sergeant Major Simmons, perchance?"

"Yes, Drill Sarn't."

"Do I detect affection when you speak of him?"

"Yes, Drill Sarn't. He is an Ox and Bucks man, held in the greatest respect, he served in Africa and India."

The Drill Sergeant moved on. "Name?"

"Private Pullene, Drill Sarn't."

A rough hand reached out and stroked James's cheek. "You have a hairy face, Pullene, a very hairy face. Why didn't you shave?"

"Sergeant Major Simmons said I had a face like a baby's bottom, Drill Sarn't and didn't need to shave."

"Ah, you have restored my faith in human nature, Pullene. I was beginning to think that Sergeant Major Simmons was a man without fault. Now I find his eyesight is failing. From today you will shave every day. Have you heard me?"

"Yes, Drill Sarn't."

"This is the British Army – not a collection of foreign pansies." He moved on.

"Name?"

"Private Jones, Drill Sarn't!"

"Can you use a rifle, Jones?"

"Yes, Drill Sarn't, Sergeant Major Simmons taught us."

"Ummm!" The Drill Sergeant moved two paces smartly to the right. "Name?"

"Private Howe, Drill Sarn't."

"And what did Sergeant Major Simmons teach you, Howe?"

"He said we were to keep clean and tidy at all times, obey orders and avoid loose women, Drill Sarn't."

"Well, well, well! It seems that Sergeant Major Simmons has done almost everything."

"No, Drill Sarn't, he forgot one thing. He never told us where to find the loose women."

The end of a pace stick appeared suddenly at the end of John Howe's nose. "If I hear one more remark like that I shall poke this stick up your nose and stir up yer inter-lects. Right turn!"

He marched out to the front of the platoon. "Raise your rifles above your heads with both arms – arms full stretch. Good. Now, on my command, you are going to double march around this square in a clockwise fashion until you all remember that my bite is worse than my bark. By the right – double – march!"

Two hours later the platoon sat on their beds in the barrack room, silent and exhausted. During their absence the Post had been delivered and Edward Holling picked up a letter and opened it. "It's from Vicky! Oh, lucky me." Joy turned to an ominous silence. "Oh, God!"

"Is it bad news?" The other five were concerned.

"It's Vicky – she has gone to Dover! Thousands of men, wounded men, are flooding in from France. She has gone to help."

"When will she be home?"

"She doesn't say."

Alice Harty ran all the way to the barn from the farmhouse. In her haste she ran straight through the muck, mud and water and her legs became splattered as she held up her skirt so she could run the faster. "Rose! Come quick! Rose!"

Rose emerged from the barn, alarm on her face. "What is it, Alice?"

"'Tis the mistress, Rose. She 'as collapsed in a faint. We dursn't know what to do – there's no waking her."

James Roberts looked distraught, his wife lay on the bed pale and unmoving. Rose wrinkled her nose, the stench of strong urine filled the room.

"I've sent Robert to fetch the doctor, Maister, I said to say it was urgent."

James Roberts twisted his hands in anguish. "Nothing seems to help. She's been in a coma afore now but not as this. Her breathing has almost stopped."

Rose bustled forward. "Let's lift her up. Alice, my mother swears by warm honey – go fetch some. It's worth trying, Maister. It often brings people around."

"Aye – I would pay the devil if it would help."

The doctor had been and gone. James Roberts sat by the kitchen table, a beaten man. "There is no hope. The doctor has said she will not last the night – her kidneys are destroyed, Rose."

"She does not seem in pain, Maister."

"I know but she will not waken. I cannot say goodbye – I wanted to say goodbye after all these years."

Three infantry brigades had already smashed themselves against the rock called Guillemont or as the Tommies called it, 'Gillymont'. In preparation for the attacks the German Army had spent months burrowing into the depths, reinforcing with steel and concrete, siting the guns and planning the zones of fire. The two hundred odd yards in front of the open, shell-marked, ground, that reached up to the wire in front of the defences was littered with the bodies of the fallen. The Manchesters, Green Jackets and the Royal Scots had manured the ground with their blood. Tomorrow was the turn of the Fifth Brigade with the Ox and Bucks men on the flank. It was dusk as the men filed forward into trenches in Trones Wood, burdened down with weapons, bombs, packs, tools and rations. They should have had a quiet night to rest and make their peace with whoever they chose. Unfortunately, the Germans got wind of the attack and in the night shelled the wood. The bombardment started as the Quartermaster's staff arrived with extra ammunition, rations and rum; the attack was planned for 4.45 and the Quartermaster's staff were due to stay on and collect all the large packs and great coats for safe-keeping.

Thomas Gruntrippe had barely time to hobble the horses and tether them to posts when the first shell arrived with a screech and shrapnel scattered around as it exploded only some thirty yards away. Thomas looked around in alarm and his body started to shake. Albert Harty grabbed hold of him and dragged him into cover by the side of the trench. "Stay under cover, Thomas."

Thomas went to run but Albert held on to him. "If you run the shells will get you – if not the police will."

The shelling continued but moved away. "Look after the horses, Thomas. I'll take the rum to the line."

Albert lifted down two large jars of rum. "Wait there – keep the horses quiet." He picked up the jars and started forward, he had just reached the junction with the main trench, about forty yards off, when a salvo of shells roared over and exploded behind him. As the smoke cleared Albert looked back and he could see Thomas lying in a tangle of harness and horses, the wagon a wreck. Albert dropped the rum and ran back as fast as he could.

He lifted Thomas's head. "Can you speak, Thomas?"

Thomas looked at him in silence for a moment then his eyes slipped sideways and his body went limp. Albert felt for a pulse but from the amount of blood and Thomas's mangled and shattered legs he knew it was a forlorn hope.

An hour before dawn shells began to fall on the defences on Guillemont Ridge. Out in No Man's Land, Sidney Barnes had taken position in a shell hole, his sniper's rifle trained on a likely target area but the defences were not manned that he could see. The shellfire had driven the defenders underground. Sidney noted with satisfaction that the shellfire was accurate but he quickly realised it was also futile. It was having no effect on the concrete bunkers. Somewhere to his left another five snipers were in position but he could not see them. Their chance would come when the battalion advanced and they could give some covering fire.

Sidney had been grateful when he was ordered forward in the night, pleased to get away from the nightmare of shelling in the wood. A bombardment that the battalion was still enduring. Not for them the luxury of deep dugouts and concrete cover. He maintained a careful watch to his front but he knew it was too early.

When the bombardment finished then he would get the chance, in the meantime the German troops were safely tucked away underground, certain that no-one could approach their lines through the shellfire. Before it was light the wind dropped and the air cooled rapidly. Within minutes the mist started to grow, surreptitiously spreading like a live white fungus; first filling the hollows and then slowly spreading over the valley. Sidney cursed, he would not find a target through this mist.

At 4.45 the British barrage lifted and already the battalion was feeling its way forward. Out in No Man's Land Sidney could hear the Guillemont defenders running to their positions and the guttural commands of officers and nco's as they readied for the expected attack. As the leading attackers reached him, Sidney jumped up. "Where's the Lieutenant?"

An officer stepped forward. "Are we in the right place, Barnes?"

"No, Sir. The line has slipped to the left."

"It's this damned mist . . . . "

He was cut off abruptly as defensive machine guns opened fire and several men nearby were hit. Sidney could hear the bullets striking home. "Down, Sir. There's seventy yards to go to the wire."

"Is it broken?"

"Some gaps, Sir – not broken."

The officer turned to a corporal. "Find Coates, Corp – and bring him here. Barnes, you know the layout, lead Coates forward. I want some grenades put in those machine gun posts as we move."

George Coates whispered. "I can see 'em, Sid. It's a long throw over the wire." Four grenades arced forward in quick succession and exploded. Sidney watched intently then cursed, the smoke was being rapidly cleared by a rising breeze and within a few minutes the mist started to disperse, rapidly exposing the lines of advancing men. Immediately, the German machine guns lashed out and the attackers dived for cover. The Ox and Bucks Lewis gunners quickly found position and gradually a return fire built up. Several attempts were made to charge forward but the defensive machine gunners stopped them in their tracks, they were simply in too strong a position and had a commanding field of fire. Sidney Barnes and George Coates were the furthest forward, crouched in a shell hole. A continuous stream of bullets whined overhead.

"How many grenades left?"

"Six."

"Drop 'em over."

"They'll spot us if I do. They'll see them coming over because I shall have to throw 'em high."

"It's stalemate, George."

"What do that mean?"

"They can't get us and we can't get them. We're stuck here until it's dark."

"It's going to be a long day, Sidney."

Captain Stevens stepped forward and saluted. It was nearly ten o'clock and quite dark, the battalion had just retreated back into Trones Wood after a bad day. "I have arranged food and drink a mile back, Sir. We lost most of our transport and horses last night."

The Colonel returned his salute. "As soon as I get word that the Middlesex are in position we'll march the men back." He sighed. "That was a bad time, Alfred, I lost most of my officers and over two hundred men."

"I'm sorry, Sir."

The Colonel looked pensive. "God knows what I shall be able to say to their families."

The muddy field made a poor parade ground and did little to raise the spirits and morale of the Ox and Bucks men formed up in three sides of a square formation. Facing them was their Brigadier, sitting on a fine horse. In front of the Brigadier the Adjutant's voice sounded out. It was evident to the listening men that the Adjutant was deliberately voiding his voice of emotion as he read out the notice. "In accordance with Army Regulations you are hereby notified that Private Lawton G and Private McCubbin B of the 17th Sherwood Foresters, having been tried by a Field General Court-

Martial were found guilty of cowardice in the face of the enemy and sentenced to death. The sentences being confirmed they were duly carried out on the 30th July."

As the Adjutant finished, the Colonel called the battalion to attention and saluted the Brigadier. "Battalion ready for review, Sir." The Brigadier edged his horse forward, the muddy ground making the horse skid but despite a few prayers sent up by the men, he remained seated. "Stand the men at ease, Colonel."

Sitting astride his charger, the Brigadier was an imposing figure of a man, his bright red tabs of rank making a small splash of colour in an otherwise drab landscape. The battalion looked tired, depleted and grim. Having lost over two hundred officers and men at 'Gillymont' they did not take kindly to being paraded to be told that the British Army was shooting its own.

"I wonder why those two poor sods were shot?" George Coates kept his voice low so only his immediate mates could hear. Sidney Barnes sniffed. "I expect the silly beggars didn't want to march into machine gun fire on the grounds that it would kill them."

The Brigadier's voice boomed out. "Yet again I have asked you to do the impossible and yet again you have done it. Yes, done it! A first class job, a first rate job! And in doing so upheld the finest traditions of the Regiment. Yet again you have proved your courage and discipline. The Hun is proving to be a stubborn foe but I do not doubt we will break him. Already he is reeling from the blows we have dealt him and will continue to deal him . . . ."

George Coates shut his eyes, Oh Gawd, he thought, another bloody attack coming up.

"Reinforcements are on their way and in a few days we will be back in the line. I know you are as eager to be back there as I am, giving the Hun the bloody nose he deserves. And have no doubt, as usual I shall be there cheering you on."

From the rear, thought George, as usual.

Sidney Barnes interrupted his thoughts. "Pay parade in an hour."

"Thank God – I'm broke."

"There's a bar in the village."

"I could murder a pint!"
Sidney wrinkled his nose in pleasure. "And a plate of chips!"

"This is from Vicky, Mother." Herbert Peters handed over the letter. "I hope this means she is on her way home."
Beatrice Peters inserted a knife in the envelope and slit it open. "You are right, Father, it is from Vicky."
There was a minute's silence as she read, a frown on her face. Herbert got concerned. "Not bad news, Mother?"
"No – Vicky is working very hard, she writes that there are lots of soldiers still arriving. She asks for paper, envelopes and stamps. Lots of men ask her to write home to their families and she has spent all her allowance."
Herbert scratched his head in puzzlement. "It is very hard to understand." He opened the paper. "The Gazette reports that the King has sent this letter to General Haig. 'The continued successful advance of our troops fills me with admiration and I send best wishes to all ranks'."
"Does he, Father! Well, it seems to me that General Haig needs a good telling off!"
"Oh, no, Mother. You don't understand, we men must make hard decisions in war time."
"We should let the women decide."
"We cannot do that, Mother! Women are not suited to decide on such matters."
"If men bore the pain of childbirth, they may be less willing to throw lives away."

Vicky removed the old dressing as gently as possible but still managed to draw soft moans from the prostrate man lying on the bed. His back was riddled with shrapnel wounds, each wound an angry red and most oozing watery pus. He winced in pain as one dressing stuck stubbornly to his skin but Vicky persevered in trying to remove it as she had been given strict instruction that every fragment of old dressing must be removed. "Not long now, nearly finished, then I can put on the new poultices."

Only two weeks had passed since Vicky had arrived in Dover but already she had become hardened to the broken flesh and bones that surrounded her. Only the face wounds gave her cause for concern but she had been assured that that concern would diminish in time. She had learned that keeping up the men's spirits seemed to be as effective a cure as medicine.

"Is it getting better, Nurse?"

She smiled in response – even though he could not see her face, other men were watching. "Well on the mend, a great improvement."

She picked up the first hot dressing. "This will be nice and soothing."

The soldier shuddered as the first dressing was applied. "Ouch!" Vicky's voice took on a stern aspect. "Don't be a baby. Sister has said you are to go in the salt bath in two or three days from now."

"I can stand that, Nurse. It's my chest that worries me, I got a whiff of gas."

"I'll tell Sister, she'll put you on the oxygen."

The men in the adjacent beds watched intently, one of them spoke up. "Sing a song, Nurse – please."

Several other men took up the plea.

"What song do you want?"

"Tipperary, Nurse."

"No, that will make too much noise, some men are asleep."

"How about the one about 'the old folks at home', Nurse?"

"Aye, that's a good one, Nurse."

"Way down upon the Swanee River
Far, far away
That's where my heart is turning ever
That's where the old folk stay.
All up and down the whole creation
Sadly I roam
Still longing for the old plantation
And for the old folks at home.
All the world is sad and weary

Everywhere I roam.
Oh! Soldiers how my heart grows weary
Far from the old folks at home."

It was unusual for Alice Harty to enter the milking shed. Her domain was the farmhouse kitchen. So when she appeared, Rose Guntrippe assumed there was a problem.

"The maister is down the meadow, Alice."

"'Tis you'm I seek." There was a deeply worried look on Alice's face and that made Rose apprehensive. Rose stopped milking.

Alice steeled herself. "'Tis terrible bad news I bring, Rose. I dursn't know how to put it."

"Has something happened to my boys?"

"No, not that. I've a letter from Albert. They have had a bad time in France."

"What does he say?"

"'Tis Thomas, Rose. Thomas has been killed. Albert writes that he died in his arms."

"I've had no telegram. It must be a mistake."

"Albert would not lie – not on something as this, so serious. It were shellfire."

"Thomas has not written of late – but that is like him. Letters have been few and far between." She paused as if accepting the news at last. "How will I tell Robert? He loves his father."

"What of you, Rose? You must feel the loss as well."

Rose reflected for a moment. "You may think this strange, Alice, but he is rarely in my mind. We have not got along these recent years and also he has been away a great deal. I am sad he has been killed for I would not wish it so – but I will not miss him."

"A woman needs a man, Rose."

"You have it wrong, Alice, very wrong. It is a man needs a woman. Never forget that for it is the truth."

The Colonel of the Ox and Bucks glanced at his watch. One minute to zero hour. The first small glimmer of dawn appeared, thin as a razorblade. He was glad his men had had a quiet night in Trones Wood, no artillery barrage had made the night a misery as it had the last time they had waited in this wood. Looking out he could see that the approach to Guillemont looked as daunting as ever. There would be no supporting bombardment this morning, it was hoped that the element of silent surprise would be their best concealment. He raised his hand and the signal went down the line. The nearest man stirred in anticipation and he found himself praying. 'Dear God, give us courage. Watch over us.'

"Go!" The lines of waiting men lifted up over the parapet and advanced. Twenty seconds later the machine guns started to chatter and the stretcher bearers went to work as the men of the Ox and Bucks beat themselves once more against the anvil they called 'Gillymont'.

The Chairman of the Thame Union Workhouse peered over his glasses. "Are we all ready, Gentlemen? Good."

The Committee gave him their silent respect and agreement.

"Are the minutes of the last meeting approved?"

Nods all round. "Note that, Mr Secretary."

"The Master is first on the agenda, Mr Chairman."

"Please proceed."

There was great pride in the voice of the Master as he spoke this morning. "Mr Chairman, members of the Committee. I have the most pleasant duty that I can recall for some time. It is to tell you that our past actions and policy in sending boys to the colonies has paid a dividend of which we can all be proud. Here is a letter from the Local Government Officer in Regina, Canada. He reports that George Edwards, who we sent to Canada five years ago, has repaid his debt to society by enlisting in the Canadian Army and is this day serving in France. This is, I believe, the most uplifting news we have received this year."

The Chairman nodded on appreciation. "Well done, well done. A good boy that. Are there reports of any other boys?"

"None as yet, Mr Chairman, but the Secretary and I will contact both Canada and Australia to see if any other boys have enlisted."

"Good. Pass the word around. This will encourage other boys to go to a new life and responsibility."

"Hold those rifles steady – steady, I say!" Drill Sergeant Crook's voice rumbled across the square at Cowley Barracks with penetrating ease and the whole platoon gripped their rifles in the on-guard position. It was not an easy task when eighteen inches of bayonet were locked to the end of the rifle barrel.

"Port – arms!"

Freddie Coxe let his thoughts wander. His mind, in fact his whole being, fixed on the thought that he was about to die of hunger. The constant drill and exercise allied to loss of sleep made the situation worse, his hunger increased steadily every day. Even worse, he was beset with hallucinations; he could smell his mother's steak and kidney pie, succulent with rich gravy and surrounded by creamed potatoes, carrots and tight Brussells sprouts. Then bliss on bliss – a great portion of suet pudding, liberally doused with honey, on the side.

"Coxe! Coxe! Are you dreaming or dead?"

Drill Sergeant Crook stood beside Freddie, blazing with indignation.

"No, Drill Sarn't."

"Then what is the matter with you?"

"I'm hungry and faint, Drill Sarn't."

"Oh, is that all. I feared you had died, Coxe. Do you know how many forms I must fill in if you die on parade, Coxe? Do you?"

"No, Drill Sarn't"

"'Undreds! Bloody 'undreds! Don't you dare die on me."

Drill Sergeant Crook about turned and marched to the front of the squad. "Now you lot. You are going to be the smartest and best drilled squad ever seen in Cowley. You will put the guards to shame! For the next twenty minutes you are going to drill with a clockwork precision never seen before. You are going to amaze me." He paused. "And do you know why? Because in twenty minutes time you are going to march to the Volunteers Canteen for a wad and tea. A canteen that is staffed by beautiful young ladies fit for a sultan's harem. Shoulder – arms! By the right – quick – march!"

John Adams, Chairman of the Military Service Tribunal for the Thame Area, rapped his gavel. "Gentlemen, this session is declared open. Mr Simmons, please will you call the first case."

"Mr Baldwin claims exemption on the grounds that he is a smallholder and also a sole trader so service will cause him extreme financial hardship."

"Stand forward and state your case."

"'Twas this, Sir. My sole living is my plot which I tend myself and my lease is my only security. If I am sent to war I cannot pay my rent and I will lose my lease."

"Let me see your lease." Mr Godden held out his hand. "I will read this while you continue, Mr Chairman."

Herbert Peters picked up the questioning. "How much is your rent?"

"Six pound a year at Michaelmas, Sir."

Mr Godden raised his hand. "I'm ready, Mr Chairman."

"Proceed."

"Mr Baldwin, your lease allows you to sub-let."

"It do, Sir. But I cannot make a living by letting."

"If you rent out your plot the rent will pay your lease and preserve it. Your need for a living will be met by your service pay and allowances."

"I cannot live on that!"

"Mr Baldwin, millions of your fellow countrymen have to."

The Chairman intervened. "Mr Baldwin, let us waste no more time, a solution has been found. There can be no exemption." He paused to hold a hurried conference. "You are granted four weeks to arrange a let. Stand down. Next!"

Mr Simmons, Secretary, pored over his papers. "Mr Elton claims exemption on the grounds that he is an essential worker on the farms he owns and runs. He is unmarried."

"Mr Elton state your case."

"My farm has but three men and a boy to serve two hundred acres. Unless I am there to organise the work and plan the crops the farm will fail and I shall lose everything."

Mr Wells spoke quietly. "But not your life, Mr Elton."

Herbert Peters checked his notes. "Mr Elton, Manor Farm, which is similar to yours is run by two men while the owner is serving in France. While you employ over three men and say you cannot serve. Can you explain this difference?"

"With more rightness on my side than you lot could offer, I believe. Sitting here on your fat arses in safety, making judgements on matters on which you have no understanding and sending men off to be slaughtered."

"Your remarks are out of order, Mr Elton." There was a distinct edge to John Adams's voice. "Every man on this tribunal is legally exempt."

"Bollocks, there are plenty of men serving at your ages. 'Tis just excuses because deep down there is cowardice here."

Mr Wells remained softly spoken. "Mr Elton we ask for reasons and you hurl abuse. Bad language does not grant exemption."

"I built this farm up from nothing, by hard labour and knowledge. It were nothing when I took it on. If I leave it will soon lie in ruin."

"If what you say is true, Mr Elton, then Manor Farm should be bankrupt by now. However it is not, it thrives."

There was a hurried conference. "Mr Elton, your claim is denied, you are given four weeks in which to appoint a manager."

"Well, I hopes you're all fucking satisfied. If I lose my farm I shall never forgive you – go to hell the lot of you!"

"Next case, Mr Simmons."

"Next is Mr Hewlett. He claims exemption on the grounds of bad health and that his job as a milker warrants exemption under the terms of the Act as an essential worker."

"State your case, Mr Hewlett."

"I dursn't know where to start, your honour. The doctor has said it is a miracle I can walk at all. He said my leg is weak from the ricketts as a lad."

Mr Weller, noted for his extensive medical knowledge interrupted. "Tell me, Mr Hewlett, how it is you can milk a cow but are unable to walk."

A pained expression crossed the supplicant's face. "Why, bugger me – dursn't you know as one sits a'milking!"

"How did you get here today?"

"I got a ride on a cart – an' I can tell 'ee now in case you envy him, the horse is buggered too!"

John Adams had had enough. "Mr Hewlett, this tribunal cannot exempt you on medical grounds. You will go to the barracks at Oxford to see the Medical Officer."

"An' how do I get there, your honour? I dursn't walk that far."

"Mr Simmons will give you a warrant to get there."

"Ah! An' how do I get back – tell me that?"

"If you cannot walk the Medical Officer will provide you with a return warrant. If he deems you are fit to serve you won't need one, you'll be in the Army. Next!"

"Next is Mr Holland. He claims exemption on the grounds of age. His employer also asks for his exemption on the grounds that he is an essential worker and is needed to fulfil existing contracts."

John Adams beckoned Holland forward. "What is this matter of age?"

"It were in the Gazette. Any person over forty one on the 15th August last year is exempt. Plain as that!"

"Mr Holland, the authorities have put your name down for service because the records show that you were born on the 16th of August and last year you were forty one."

"I tell you I were born on 14th August, my mother were ill when I were born and made a mistake when she went to register weeks later. I always give my birth date as the 14th August."

The Secretary checked his list. "Mr Chairman, the details we must abide by are provided by the Registrar. We have no authority to alter or change any name on the list unless a man is certified insane."

Holland's voice rose. "'Tis bloody obvious a man is too old to go to war at forty one – one day more or less makes no difference. I suggest this tribunal examines itself!"

"Ahem!" Herbert Peters felt compelled to speak. "We must abide by the law, Mr Holland, even if it is only one day that makes the difference. May we hear about the work matter, and the contracts."

A man rose at the back of the hall. "I employ Mr Holland. A year ago I had ten bricklayers and I took on contracts accordingly. Now five men have been taken and I cannot afford to lose any more. Skilled bricklayers are as scarce as hen's teeth."

"You are unduly worried. The emergency powers act does not allow any penal action when it derives from employees being called to the defence of the country. Bricklayers are not classified as essential workers. Exemption denied."

"Next!"

James Roberts of Newbarn Farm put his hand on Rose Guntrippe's shoulder as she stopped beside him to empty the milk pail. "Most sorry to hear about your man, Rose. These are not best days for us."

Rose put the lid back on the churn. "There are many curtains drawn these days, Maister. No doubt there'll be many more afore men come to their senses and end this war."

"I spoke to your son – he is bad upset."

"Aye, but he is lucky, he has only good memories of his father. I am not so lucky but I would wish him back for Robert's sake."

"You'm right, Rose, a lad needs a father. I wish I had a son but we were not chosen as parents. Still I were lucky, good memories now she has gone but there were times in the two years she were bad when I found myself hating her – I wish I had been more forgiving – more loving."

"Regrets can drown ye, Maister."

"My father loved learning and he said that regret is the mark of a civilised man."

"What of forgiveness, Maister?"

"Only a saint can truly forgive – only a saint."

"You look most upset, Father. What is it?" Beatrice Peters could tell at a glance, after twenty two years of marriage, when Herbert was upset or disturbed.

Herbert sat down in his armchair with a deep sigh. "It is most disconcerting to be called a coward. At forty five I thought I was past such foolish pride but I find I'm not."

"This is foolish, Father! What happened? Who said this?"

"At the tribunal. Men pointed the finger at us. Said we shouldn't send men to war if we didn't go ourselves, it was cowardly otherwise."

"But you're too old for war, Father. This is silly."

"No it's not, Mother. I shall join the Volunteers and be a soldier of sorts, that will show them."

"I'm sure you'll be most handsome in uniform, Father."

"Aye, we can't have our Vicky stealing all the glory, can we?"

"You must take me to see the new film, Father. The one called the 'Battle of the Somme'."

Herbert turned in alarm. "My goodness, Mother, I don't know as I should. They've put up the prices by tuppence a seat!"

"Prices are going up, Father. People are starting to complain – and about shortages. I hope no-one thinks we are making big profits."

"Never fear, Mother, I shall put up a notice. Right in the front window!"

Peter Oxenlade concentrated with all his might and waited as the wavering front and rear sights of his rifle aligned, then he hastily pulled the trigger. An inner hit was marked up in the butts and a look of sheer joy covered his face. He rapidly squinted to his left. "A hit, Corp! A hit!"

Lance Corporal Barnes nodded in satisfaction. "Well done, Peter. If only you would squeeze the trigger instead of jerking you will make a marksman."

"D'you think so, Corp. I never hit the target 'til today."

"Reload and try again. Careful! Don't swing that bloody rifle about. Now, get a firm grip with your left hand. Ready. Fire when ready." Crack! "Well done, another inner."

Sidney Barnes breathed a sigh of relief. He had been sent to help the Quartermaster staff improve their shooting and he appreciated the quietness away from the battalion, if only for a week. Over to his right a rifle sent a bullet ricocheting off the target frame and a white flag of surrender waved. "Samuel! Stop firing."

Sidney picked himself up and marched over to Samuel Peddelle. "Have you never fired a rifle before?" He glared at Samuel.

"Sorry Corp. No, Corp. They would never let me shoot until today."

Sidney groaned and dropped down beside Samuel. "Unload." He checked that all the rounds were accounted for and the breech empty. "Now Samuel, this is the foresight and this is the rearsight . . . ."

Alfred Stevens walked along the rear of the firing line, his mind elsewhere and full of problems that must be solved. The battalion was on the move to the north. But where? How far? When? His transport wagons were under repair and new equipment and horses were slow in arriving. New reserves were due. When would they arrive? What kit would they need? The Quartermaster Sergeant broke into his thoughts. "I've just had word we're going to Redan, Sir, in three days."

"Redan! Are you sure, is it official?"

"Not yet, Sir, but it is absolutely certain," he touched his nose, "my informant is totally reliable."

"Redan it is then, Q. Let's go and make a start. Leave the men to practice. Corporal Barnes has made a big improvement in our shooting, I must thank him before we leave. Now, what other information has your brother-in-law got for us?"

"My, you do look handsome, Father – Mary! Come and see your Father."

Herbert Peters, resplendent in his new service dress, puffed out his chest and pulled in his stomach. "A fine figure of a man – if I say so myself. And I do, Mother."

Mary looked in from the shop. "Oh, wait until we tell Vicky. You look so tall – just like a real soldier, Father."

"Now, now, young lady. I am a real soldier. Once Mother has ironed out these creases and hung it on the line I shall be fit for battle." Herbert stretched his neck. "If you could fasten these collar clips, Mother. Everything is so stiff at the moment. And as for these boots, well . . . . "

"I think you should wear it to the next tribunal, Father."

"Yes, Mother, let them stuff that in their pipes and smoke it."

His body ached from head to toe, but George Coates didn't mind. At least he was alive and only bruised. Last night he had been sent out into No Man's Land with a party of thirteen other men to seek out and capture some prisoners from the German trenches. The raid had proved a disaster. In the dark the party had been unable to locate a suitable gap in the wire, a working party had probably made furtive repairs earlier in the night. Despite George's misgivings the party had tried to penetrate the wire with the result that several men got caught on the barbs. Even so they may have been safe but one inexperienced man panicked and pulled savagely at the wire in a futile attempt to free himself. Immediately the metal warning 'chimes' hung on the wire began to clang and within a few seconds starshells burst overhead and machine gun bullets whizzed through the wire. Even then they may have got away 'scot free' except they were within bombing range and grenades started to fall among the party. In the melee two men panicked, tried to run and were shot down before they had gone five paces. George had kept the defenders busy by lobbing grenades into the trenches while the party struggled back but, even so, with two men killed and seven wounded it was a bad night for the Ox and Bucks men.

Come the morning, the relief battalion took over the line and George and his mates trudged gratefully back to billets in a rear village. What luxury. Some sixteen men, including George, found themselves in an old farm building. The door had gone and some tiles were missing but there was shelter from the cold of the night and a plentiful supply of hot food delivered. In the light of a spluttering oil lamp, the men settled down and the air soon filled with pipe and cigarette smoke. Someone started singing a doleful song but was silenced when half a dozen voices told him to 'pipe down'. Then someone had an inspiration. "Let's have a contest – best funny song!"

Someone else picked up the theme. "How about funniest song, poem or joke?"

"That's it. A contest – we all put in twenty centimes. Winner takes all." The Corporal put down his hat. "Everybody in!"

The 'Boy stood on the burning deck', got a good round of applause, as did 'The Highland Ball'. Next the 'Bollocks Song' got a rousing and rapturous support followed by a loud ovation but then they all knew the words, they had sung it before a hundred times on the march. Several novel and rude additions to 'Mademoiselle from Armentieres' got a good reception as did an updated version of 'The Army of Today's All Right' which gave rise to a thundering chorus. And so it went on until there was a silence.

"Well is that it then?" The Corporal in charge of the prize fund looked around. A voice at the back piped up. "George has not done a turn." Fifteen pairs of eyes turned on George.

"Nay, not me lads. You know I can't sing. Got a voice like a strangled parrot."

The Corporal pointed at the hat. "Now, now, George – no excuses. Poems and jokes is acceptable – so do your bit."

"Well, I'll do my best. I heard this one from those Aussies up by 'Gillymont'. Let me see now – oh, I remember."

He paused to light his pipe. "There was this General and his wife travelling across Africa when they came to this great sandy desert. Now this General is very clever, we must get camels, he said. So they went to the camel market. 'Sell me two camels', he ses to the camel dealer, 'so I can cross the desert.' 'Bugger off!' said the camel dealer. Well, you can imagine, the General was about to have him shot when he realised he was not in the British Army. So he pleaded, 'My good wife and I must cross the desert.' 'The desert is too big,' said the dealer, 'the camels cannot cross unless they are bricked and that will cost you a thousand pounds in gold.' 'Done,' said the General, he was a rich sod. Then the camel dealer picked out two of the biggest male camels and he takes them to the water and lets them drink. The two camels slurp up gallons of water, then just as they are drinking their last pint to fill their humps, the dealer creeps up behind them and claps them smartly across the knackers with two great bricks. Crack! Crack! The poor bastards gave great gasps, gulped hard and emptied the water trough. 'They are ready to cross the desert, the extra five gallons will see them through,' said the dealer.

'Why, you cruel, cruel man,' cries the General's wife, hitting the dealer with her umbrella. 'Surely that must hurt dreadfully.' 'Course not,' said the dealer, 'as long as yer don't get yer thumbs caught between the bricks'."

George paused to re-light his pipe. "Now the General was impressed. 'Brick me, camel dealer,' he said, 'so I can cross the desert.' That night the camel dealer went home and told his wife. 'We are rich. The General paid one thousand pounds for the camels, then an extra ten so I would brick him.' 'But, there is an extra fifty pounds here, husband, where did this come from.' 'Why,' said the camel dealer, 'the General's lady gave me a tip so I would brick the General trebly hard. She said it would save her from having to have a headache all the way across the desert. Surely, wife, with such leaders the British Army is invincible'."

The flood of battered and wounded men shipping in from France had slowed down. The numbers of wounded men were still beyond the capacity of the front line hospitals to cope but the work of receiving, patching up and passing on had eased, so Vicky was allocated more duties in the wards of the hospital. She had even managed to spend a little time exploring and getting her bearings. From outside the hospital she had a fine view of the castle dominating the left cliff top, down below was the port of Dover, on a good day she could see the cliffs at Calais and over to the right was the majestic Shakespeare Cliff with its hotchpotch of military buildings and barracks on the slopes behind. Now it was early morning and Vicky was desperately tired. Throughout the night she had kept a vigil beside a young man from New Zealand. A man who had lost the side of his face, two legs and seemingly the will to live. The amputations had been a desperate race against infection and the lad had cried when he recovered consciousness after the operation and realised what had happened. All night he had drifted in and out of consciousness. His one eye half opened. Vicky stroked his head. "Hold on, Charlie, hold on. Would you like some water?"

The arrangement had worked well for several days. One squeeze of her hand meant yes, two squeezes meant no. Two squeezes.

"Shall I write to your mother today, Charlie?" Two squeezes.

"Why not, Charlie – she may be worried?" No response.

Vicky wondered what she would say or do if it were Edward lying shattered beside her. "You mustn't give in, Charlie. In a month or two you'll be able to go home, as soon as you are strong enough. I bet your girl will be waiting for you – do you have a girl, Charlie?" One squeeze.

"I expect she's pretty, Charlie." One squeeze.

"So you have a girl, Charlie. Shall I write to her for you?" Two squeezes.

"Why not, Charlie? Why not?" No response.

Charlie turned his head away but before he did, Vicky could see the tears falling from his eye.

"May I sing to you, Charlie?" One squeeze.

"Soft and low, Charlie, we mustn't wake the others."

> *"Beautiful dreamer, wake unto me*
> *Starlight and dew drops are waiting for thee.*
> *Sounds of the rude world heard in the day,*
> *Lulled by the moonlight have all passed away.*
> *Beautiful dreamer, man of my song.*
> *List while I woo thee with soft melody.*
> *Gone are the cares of life's busy throng*
> *Beautiful dreamer, awake unto me*
> *Beautiful dreamer, awake unto – me."*

She squeezed his hand. "Are you dreaming, Charlie?" No response.

Vicky felt for a pulse, no pulse. Frantically her fingers probed his wrist. Nothing. She felt the base of his throat. He had gone and she could not stop herself crying. There was no noise, only a cascade of tears over which she had no control. Gently she put his hand on to his chest and pulled up the sheet. Then she kissed him on the cheek. "Goodbye Charlie from New Zealand."

Robert Guntrippe held out the scrap of paper. "It's the telegram, Miss. Ma said I could bring it."

Miss Crook, Mistress of the second year pupils at the British School in Park Street, accepted the offering, unfolded the paper and smoothed it out so she could read it. "I'm so sorry, Robert."

"It's all that's left of him, Miss. Mrs Harty said that Pa were blown into little bits, fighting the Hun."

"I'm sure he was very brave, Robert. We will say his name at prayers this morning."

"He were a hero, Miss. Will you say he were a hero, Miss?"

"Yes, Robert. There are many telegrams arriving. We will say a prayer, for they are all heroes."

"Dear Lord, today we received the news that Private Thomas Guntrippe died in the defence of his country. As a hero of our nation we ask that you take him into your care and keep him in your peace for evermore. Watch over all those who serve our nation so that they may return safely to us." Miss Crook raised her head and looked out over the assembly. One hundred solemn faces, eyes firmly closed, hands clasped, met her gaze. "Amen."

"Amen." One hundred voices spoke in unison.

"Now, children, we will sing the hymn, specially chosen by Robert Guntrippe." She signalled to Miss Turle on the piano.

"Onward Christian soldiers.
Marching as to war.
With the cross of Jesus.
Going on before!
Christ the royal master.
Lead against the foe.
Forward into battle.
See his banners go . . . . "

143

The Ox and Bucks had started moving forward late in the afternoon, a dull grey late winter afternoon nearing dusk but there was no singing. It did not seem to be appropriate as they were passing dozens of burial parties and the cartloads of bodies waiting to be entered into the ground. All the way from 'Gillymont', as they called it, they had suffered a long slog of a march along broken congested roads but they were grateful there had been no shelling. On reaching the second line trenches they had settled down to wait and the Company Quartermaster Sergeants had issued the rations of tepid food and drink. At ten fifteen that night they would move quietly into the front line trenches. They were under strict instructions that there must be no noise, no singing, no shouting and definitely no shooting, unless there was an emergency. The Brigade Commander hoped that the German Army would not be expecting an attack this late into the winter and they would be fooled into relaxing their guard. Bombing parties and sniper activity were prohibited so for once George Coates and Sidney Barnes could look forward to a quiet night, even if it was uncomfortable because there were several inches of water in the bottom of the trenches and only the constantly working pumps keep the water at bay. Sidney stood on the firing step taking his turn at sentry duty.

"Move out. Move out." The quiet commands sounded down the trenches, it was 10.15. Time to move forward to the front line. Many a quiet prayer was muttered in supplication to any God prepared to listen. Most of the prayers asked that there be no mud tomorrow. There was only one thing worse than trying to advance through mud and that was advancing through mud under fire. Along the German line nervous troops sent up starshells and tossed an occasional grenade out into No Man's Land. The Ox and Bucks kept their heads down and their hands in their pockets.

The battalion was already waiting with bayonets fixed and a tot of rum safely aboard when the Royal Artillery opened the bombardment at 5.45am. Sidney Barnes clipped his safety catch forward, his platoon officer was first up on to the parapet, "Let's go, lads."

Ghostly wraithes of mist swirled about the ground and thick mud sucked at their boots as the men advanced. One hundred yards! One hundred and fifty! The wire loomed up. Groups of men bunched up by the gaps in the wire then, as the barrage lifted and moved forward a hundred yards, the battalion surged forward and dropped into the German front line trench, so far there had not been even one answering shot.

George Coates stood by the entrance to a deep dugout, Mills Bomb in hand. Two comrades, rifles at the ready, gave him cover. In his best German he shouted down the steps. "Kom rous! Engerbay-me!" No answer. A grenade clattered to the bottom of the dugout and exploded.

A frightened voice sounded out. "Nicht shiessen, Englander."

"Kom-rous – hander ho!"

The company commander hurried along the trench. "Send the prisoners back immediately. Private White has a wound, he can escort them back."

"But there are two hundred prisoners, Sir." Lieutenant Harris protested. "What if they run?"

"We've no time to waste, we move forward in two minutes. Get the men assembled. The next trench will be tougher."

Herbert Peters put the letter aside. "Vicky has it right, I'm afraid, Mother, we've been duped. Tens of thousands of good men have been squandered for a few square miles of ground. Every week the Gazette has reports of our men lost."

"I do wish Vicky would come home, Father. I do miss her so." Mary felt the absence of her sister even more than her mother and father did, they had each other. It was even lonelier now that John Howe had gone to the depot to undergo his training.

Herbert puffed at his pipe. "She'll be home when this emergency is over."

Mary kept her fingers tightly crossed as she made her request. "John Howe will be home on leave soon, Father, can we invite him to dinner one day. He is a serving soldier now."

145

Herbert pondered on that for a moment. "Yes, I consider that suggestion is worthy of our approval. What do you say, Mother?"

"Oh yes, Father, he's such a nice young man – and you will have so much to talk about now you are a soldier too."

"There Edward – see, you can see France if you look carefully." Vicky held on to her hat as she pointed. They were standing beside the old Roman Lighthouse under the high walls of Dover Castle and the breeze, which was modest down in the town, had a stronger touch to it on the cliff top.

"I can see it, Vicky."

He turned and took her into his arms and kissed her. "It has been so long, Vicky – I never thought we would be parted so soon."

Vicky looked sad, "I am glad I came. So much suffering – how can men be hurt so bad and live? There have been times when I thought my heart would break."

"When I wrote I said I would stay for a few days. We had been promised a week's leave. Now I must go back tonight, we ship out to France on Tuesday."

"But why, Edward. You said they would not send you until late summer. That you had to be over nineteen."

"So many men lost, reserves are needed quickly. We must all go. It is our big chance."

"Hold me tight, Edward. There always seems to be so little time these days."

Chapter 4   1917: 'PROMISES'

"Dearly beloved," the Vicar of St Mary's in Thame raised his right hand to bestow a blessing, then continued, "today is the first Sunday of the New Year in which, if all our prayers are answered, this war will end. During the past year the terrible reality of this war has given us all cause to be saddened by the loss of life among our serving men. This is the time we must stand together, reach out in comfort to others and confirm our faith.

But in our hour of need, on our darkest days – what do I hear? Words of dissent, men unwilling to share the burden of service and the questioning of faith. Did not our Lord warn against a house divided? A congregation that does not pull together will fall – be pulled down." He paused to compose himself.

"Remember this, for not only did God give us the means to plough and harrow but in his love bestowed on us the four grains of virtue. Justice, prudence, temperance and fortitude. These were sown deep in men's soul to grow. When this had been done God instructed us to build a house to store the harvest. He gave us a wooden cross for timber, for mortar he offered mercy made from his blood and on this foundation we built walls made from his pain. When this was done he covered it with a roof fashioned with his holy words.

So was built God's house on earth and he called it Unity. Destroy our unity at your peril. Destroy God's unity at the peril of your soul. Let us pray and renew our promises."

The train drew into Dover Priory Station with a great hissing rumble, giving out clouds of steam that obscured the view of the platform. From the open window Edward Holling anxiously scanned the platform hoping that he would see Vicky waiting. It was a forlorn hope, his letter had been sent off late and then the date of embarkation had been moved forward by twenty-four hours. Edward's anxiety increased, there was no sign of Vicky, in fact the platform was almost devoid of people except for an officer marching up, calling out as he progressed. "Form up in the Station Yard – form up . . . ."

As the train stopped two hundred soldiers clambered out of the carriages on to the platform and the sergeant major in charge of the Ox and Bucks contingent turned to Edward. "Holling, check every carriage, make sure nothing has been left behind while I get the men formed up." The Sergeant Major, ex Drill Sergeant Crook, had been promoted and was on his way to join the Headquarters Company at the front. The men, all new recruits, were going to the training depot at Etaples.

Edward wanted to check the Station Yard so he completed his search in record time, then he grabbed his kit and ran out. Still no sign of Vicky, his hopes withered. Sergeant Major Crook barked out a command. "Fall in! Form three ranks! Left turn! Quick march!"

Down they marched to York Street, then along the Snargate. It was as the column turned right that Edward spotted Vicky standing on the pavement behind a raggedy group of children. Only the children waved, the adults had seen a million men go back and forth. As Edward drew level, Vicky waved.

Vicky gave a silent prayer. Only intuition had drawn her towards the harbour today. From the hospital she could see the ships going back and forth. When Edward's letter had arrived she had noted that a troopship was raising steam after being docked all night.

Later Vicky watched as the troopship headed towards the Channel, a watchful destroyer on the flank. From her vantage point on the Prince of Wales Pier she could still see the tiny figures of the men lining the side of the ship but she could no longer see Edward; so she waved and held tight to the memory of a one minute embrace, a kiss and a promise. "I'll be back soon. I promise."

"There is no need for concern, Mother – I will keep it safe in the small wardrobe." Herbert Peters held the rifle as if it might bite him while Beatrice Peters regarded both him and the rifle with some alarm.

"What does this mean, Father?"

"The Volunteers are now an official unit. We are real soldiers, responsible to the War Office. Captain Fairbairn said it is in recognition of our high standards, but there has been no inspection or evaluation!"

"What if they send you to France, Father! What will happen then?"

"No, not France, Mother. It is just that they are desperate to release younger men to the war, so we may be called for home duty."

"But what if you are sent away, Father? Away from here?"

"You and Mary can run the shop. There is no need to worry."

"That is all very well but there is talk of rationing by the issue of coupons. Every day now there are shortages and people complain. Oh dear, oh dearie me!"

"Now, now, Mother. No one has said I must go away. Captain Fairbairn only mentioned it as a possibility, he has promised that we will all serve in this area. After all that is why we volunteered – to defend our homes."

After several weeks of feeling unwell, Samuel Peddelle had been persuaded to attend morning sick parade. Only yesterday evening he had caused an alarm by collapsing at his bench. He stood, bare-chested, in front of the Medical Officer.

"How long have you been ill, Peddelle?"

"Only a little while, Sir."

The stethoscope probed at his chest. "Cough!" "Again." A look of deep concern crossed the Medical Officer's face. "Are you bringing up phlegm?"

"Once in a while, Sir."

"Pity. There must be a bucketful on your chest! The orderly sergeant tells me you were unable to do guard duty several nights ago."

"Only the once, Sir."

"No guard duties until I say, otherwise you may have to go to the hospital. Every morning and evening you must sit over a bucket of hot water with a towel over your head, for half an hour. And a good vapour rub, morning and night."

'Charlie, Charlie, time to get up! Charlie, Charlie, get out of bed!'

The sound of reveille shattered the silence of the night. Freddie Coxe dragged himself into consciousness, though it took a supreme effort. He was convinced, every morning, that the bugler had made a mistake because 'Lights Out' had sounded only minutes ago. Already the lamp was alight and Edward Holling pulled on his socks, trousers and boots. "Come on, Freddie – it's our turn to get the water." He banged a pail to emphasise the point. "Get a move on or the queue will be a mile long."

From 4.30 in the morning until 9.30 each evening the lads trained under the eagle eyes of half a dozen instructors, except when they weren't under training, and then, for the most part, they queued. They queued for water, for dry rations, for breakfast, for dinner, for tea, for issues from the stores, for canteen service and quite often, to use the field toilets. The outright misery of the first day had been put partly to rights by Edward, who got them organised – the object being that their group was always the first to arrive. Today it was the turn of Freddie and Edward to get the water for washing and shaving while William and James folded all the blankets and tidied the tent. Harold and John took all the jackets and hats in turn and polished all the brass. By the time Freddie and Edward returned it was a quick wash and shave, then jackets on before moving on to the mess hall for 5.20 ready for breakfast at 5.30. Freddie was always first. There were two reasons. First he was the fastest runner, secondly he was always the hungriest.

Freddie had quickly learned that first in the queue had his pick of the largest portions set out on the mess table. Then it was back to the tent to polish their boots, reload their large packs and clean their rifles ready for the 'On parade!' command at 7am. By 7.15 the inspection was over and they started on the one hour march to the training ground.

The milking shed was very quiet except for the 'squish' of milk into the pails and a muted cow noise from the adjacent barn. Rose was deeply engrossed in thought, the milking automatic. Robert was proving difficult and her mother-in-law's eyesight was deteriorating as the cataracts developed. Several seconds had elapsed before Rose realised that James Roberts was speaking.

"Sorry, Maister – I were thinking on problems."

"No matter, Rose – t'were of no great importance."

Rose stopped milking and gave James a direct stare and he shuffled his feet and looked embarrassed. "Things are best said."

James kept his eyes downcast. "There is a Farmers Union dinner next month, at the 'Spread Eagle'."

"Is that so, Maister."

"I did ask if you would come with me."

Rose gave a deep chuckle then abruptly stopped when she realised that she had offended him.

"Forgive me asking, Rose – I meant no harm."

"Asking or making fun, Maister? A woman does not take kindly to offers made in fun."

James stopped milking and turned to face her. "Nay – 'tis no fun. You'm a woman a man can admire. I'm too old for fooling."

"You'm not old, Maister! A woman be old at fifty but a man – why, a man is in his prime."

"I will take it kindly, Rose, if you will partner me."

"Men will speak behind their hand, Maister. Stain your good name iffen you take your milking girl on your arm."

"Pah! They will not – they will envy me, mark my word."

"Then I accept, Maister, for I have never been taken to a dinner afore."

"Thank you, Rose – if you will use my given name it will please me."

James Pullene tried without success to hold his breath but the cloud of tear gas made his eyes stream and his mouth burn. He was near to panic but by his side William Smithe held on to his arm. William went to speak but could only cough. Suddenly the shutter in the door of the dugout chamber swung open and a voice boomed out. "Respirators on!"

Like drowning men clutching at a lifebuoy, William and James fumbled to release their masks and fit them over their heads. As soon as the masks were fitted the shutter clanged shut and the ten minute countdown started.

Sitting on the grass of the embankment, Harold Jones and John Howe coughed and spluttered, they had been through their ordeal. Edward Holling and Freddie Coxe were next and already Freddie was feeling apprehensive, wishing that he had gone first so it would be over by now.

For three weeks the six lads had drilled, marched, exercised and trained continuously, without any relief or let up. The gas test was the last day of training. Tomorrow they would leave for the front.

Miss Hammond, Mistress of the third year pupils at the British School in Park Street had never in her life dealt with a major disciplinary matter. Certainly not an offence that may merit the ultimate punishment. Initially, when confronted by this crime, she had been speechless but that only lasted a short while before she gave a loud shriek. The six lads who were digging looked up in consternation while the rest of the boys and girls beat a rapid retreat. At last Miss Hammond found her voice. "What are you doing? Come out of that hole, the Headmaster will hear of this!"

The Headmaster had been unwilling to believe Miss Hammond and he had taken a few minutes to go out and verify the facts for himself. Now he had a face like thunder and the six lads standing before him started to look worried. The Headmaster was known to have a strong arm and a penchant for mild violence with a cane. "Who is responsible for this vandalism? Who was it suggested digging holes on our playing field?"

Silence. Several eyes studied the floorboards.

The Headmaster decided that Robert Guntrippe seemed a likely candidate. "Are you the ringleader, Guntrippe? Did you start this?"

"We were only digging a trench, Sir – in case the Huns attack Thame."

"Ah! So this is a trench, is it? Do you realise you have ruined our football pitch. This will cost a great deal of money to put right."

"My Pa told me what to do, Sir." There was pride in Robert Guntrippe's voice. "An' we all watched the battle at the picture house."

"This is very bad and deserves serious punishment. You will go back to the playing field and fill in the holes. When that is done you will come back here, to my office."

The Headmaster waited until the lads had raced off before speaking. "What do we do, Miss Hammond?"

"I don't know, Sir, but I don't think they are bad boys."

"Agreed, Miss Hammond. These lads want to be soldiers. They want to defend us. And what do soldiers do? They dig trenches and fight with machine guns – we have all seen it graphically shown at the 'Palace'."

"Will you let them off, Sir?"

"Goodness gracious, no! This is a caning matter. A public caning matter, in front of the school. Soldiers, especially young soldiers, need strong discipline."

Harry Payne had lived for forty-five years mainly within shouting distance of the Thame Courthouse and in all that time he had never appeared within its walls until this day. Now he stood in the dock, cap-in-hand, head bowed.

Sergeant Cox filled the witness box and addressed the bench. "Your Honour, I were called out in the afternoon of the thirteenth of this month, when in receipt of a complaint that a soldier, resident in the Red Cross Military Hospital in Thame, having been wounded in action and subject to the restraints on military persons was to be found in the house (stated as fifty eight the Lower High Street) in a drunken state. I did, with urgency, go to this house and found the door open; on entering I saw drinking glasses on the parlour table together with a half empty bottle of whisky and a large jug containing a quantity of beer. There was no sign of the soldier. In answer to my questions, Mr Payne admitted that out of admiration he had invited a wounded soldier to his house for a meal and a drink."

The Magistrate peered over his glasses. "The soldier in question, where is he?"

"Returned to his regiment, Your Honour."

"I see. Did he make a statement?"

"No, Your Honour. He were unwell when I went to the hospital and Nurse Healey would not allow me to question him."

"You believe he was drunk?"

Sergeant Cox shrugged. "I can think of no other explanation, Your Honour, as he were gone the next day."

The Magistrate turned to Harry Payne. "Do you admit that there was a soldier from the Military Hospital in your house?"

Harry puffed with pride a little. "That is what I told the Sergeant, Your Honour. He were from my old regiment, the Ox and Bucks."

The prosecutor stood up. "There is other evidence, Your Honour. I call the Vicar of St Mary's."

The Clerk administered the oath.

"Reverend Bird, will you please describe what happened on the thirteenth as you were passing number fifty eight."

"Yes, utterly disgraceful behaviour. The front door was open and I could hear men singing a bawdy song with words that have no place in a properly mannered society. It is my understanding that such songs are bawled out daily by uncouth men serving in the army but such profanities have no place here. When I entered the house, I saw an inebriated soldier in a blue jacket sitting at the table with a glass in his hand. Payne was sitting in an armchair in a similar state. When I told them to stop singing they both cursed me with vile swear words that I cannot in any circumstance repeat. So I went to find a constable."

"Thank you, Reverend." The prosecutor turned to the court. "Your Honour, it is an offence under the War Regulations to supply alcoholic drink to any member of the armed forces falling within medical jurisdiction and treatment."

Henry Payne began to feel distinctly uneasy as the magistrates held a short conference. The Chairman spoke. "We find the defendant guilty as charged. Do you have anything to say, Payne?"

"Yes, Your Honour. No harm were meant, no harm were done. I promise it will not happen again."

"Promises are too late, Payne. Such behaviour cannot and will not be tolerated. It is an affront to a Christian and God-fearing community. You will be imprisoned for one month with hard labour. Next case!"

The Clerk of the Court called out. "George Rogers, a person of no fixed abode, after seeking and taking refuge in the Thame Union Workhouse did refuse work as required by law."

"What have you to say, Rogers?"

"Beggin' your pardon, Your Honour, but I cannot work having received many wounds gained in warfare in the service of my country an' for which I were honourably discharged as unfit to serve."

The prosecutor stood up. "I call the Master of the Workhouse, Your Honour."

The Master stepped into the witness box and swore the oath, then the Prosecutor took over. "Mr Armstrong, please describe the events leading up to this charge."

"Yes, Your Honour. On the tenth of the month the accused, George Rogers, claimed entry to the Union House and stated he was homeless and destitute. He made no claim for any dispensation by either age or condition so the next day he was sent to the yard to break stones. The standard allowance of two and a half bushels of stone was given. However, he did no work that day nor any day since on the excuse that he was incapable of work because of disablement from war wounds. I called the doctor to examine him and he declared Rogers able to work. Rogers still refused any work."

The Magistrates looked most concerned; one shook his head in disbelief. The Chairman hunched his shoulders and leant forward so that he could get a better look at this miscreant. "Rogers, when were you discharged from the army?"

"In 1901, Your Honour – an honourable discharge."

"Was your discharge on medical grounds?"

"Yes, Your Honour."

"From what regiment?"

"The Fifty Second – the Ox and Bucks."

"Show me your discharge paper."

"Fell to pieces long ago, Your Honour, having been looked at so many times."

There was a brief whispered conference at the Bench then the Chairman addressed Rogers. "There is no evidence you are unable to work. There is the view of the doctor that you are capable of work. The Master of the House has given evidence that you have done none of the work allocated to you. If we allow you to deride society, the very fabric of our country will descend into chaos and ultimate ruin. Such idleness at the expense of honest ratepayers cannot be tolerated. Fourteen days with hard labour. Take him away."

"Keep moving along!" "Keep moving!" The muttered demands of the nco's sounded along the file of heavily laden men trudging through the night. For over a week the Ox and Bucks had been at 'rest', filing up to the front line trench to fill baskets with mine spoil and then carrying the baskets back over half a mile for dispersal. Unbeknown to the German Army a tunnel was being dug underneath their defences. The tunnel went down deep into the clay to avoid the soft sand of the upper ground, but the clay had a distinctive blue colour and a mound of it would have drawn immediate attention to the mining. So it must be taken away and hidden from the enemy's sight. When the mine was finished it would be packed with several tons of explosive ready to be blown up when some future attack was to be launched.

The six lads had arrived at the front to join the battalion on the first day of this new, tiring and uninspiring duty. Edward Holling and William Smithe had just arrived back at the dump having carried a hundredweight of spoil in the dark. They were sweaty, thirsty and exhausted but there was to be no relief. Once the basket had been emptied they would get fifteen minutes rest then it was back to work again.

The pair sat down on the upturned basket, William raised the matter foremost in their thoughts. "How many more nights on this fatigue, Sarge?"

"You've only been with us a few days – don't you like it!"

"No, Sarge – I don't." William was quite emphatic.

"Cherish it lad – we're not being shelled. Last week we lost ten men an' two of those were because of our guns."

Freddie Coxe and Harold Jones appeared out of the gloom. "We heard there is a canteen nearby, Sarge," Freddie was hungry, as ever, "no more than a mile off."

"Aye, that there is. A canteen and two cafes – an' nearby there's a fine knocking shop, called Ginger's, that does a splendid line in breakfasts – so I'm told."

Freddie closed his eyes in delicious anticipation. "That's for me, Sarge – a fine breakfast."

"You'll not afford their prices, lad. Why 'tis over forty francs!"

"A lot of money, Sarge," Freddie sounded most surprised, "Why, I should want a jolly fine breakfast for that much."

Several dozen men had arrived in the night listening to this conversation and they burst out laughing. Freddie realised he had made some sort of gaffe, so he kept quiet.

William was quick off the mark. "None of us have that amount of money, Sarge – but what if we have a raffle with the winner getting a night at Ginger's?"

"Good idea, lad. Let's see, if everyone in the Company put in twenty five centimes that would raise – forty two francs. We'll get organised as soon as we're back at the billets."

Samuel Peddelle had been conscious for a little while before he opened his eyes. The glare of unaccustomed bright lamps caused him to squint, slowly he focussed on his surroundings. Where was he? The bed was comfortable, the sheets clean. Sheets? He could not recall such a comfortable bed as this. He tried to move but the bed was tightly made and he found he had no energy to fight against it. How did he get here? He had not slept in a bed such as this since – painful memories crowded in and his troubled thoughts caused him to murmur somewhat. The two soldiers in the adjacent beds exchanged glances and looked concerned.

"Do you need a nurse?" One of the soldiers asked.

Samuel's reason returned. The clean bed. The quiet. The long bright room. The smell. Now he understood, he was in hospital but try as he might, he could not remember how he had got here. He turned his head so that he could see who was speaking.

"Shall I call a nurse?" The soldier asked again.

"No – I'm fine. How long have I been here?"

"Seven or eight days. They thought you were a goner, you know. Bad pneumonia."

A nurse appeared beside Samuel's bed and put a thermometer under his tongue. "No talking." She felt his pulse. "You had us worried, soldier – good, your pulse is normal." She removed the thermometer. "And your temperature is normal! How do you feel?"

"Just weak, Nurse."

"Not surprising, you've eaten nothing for days. I'll get you a cup of cocoa, that should help."

"Where am I?"

"The base hospital at Etaples, soldier. Now, you rest. The doctor has said you can go on leave as soon as you are able to travel."

"Oh!" Samuel sounded troubled, "I dursn't know about that, Nurse. I've no family."

The soldier in the next bed reacted. "You lucky bugger! I get a bullet and have to go to the depot next week. You get a bit of fever and a 'Blighty' for your trouble! Then you sound off-hand."

Vicky had jagged her left hand close to the base of the index finger with her scissors while cutting a dressing. It was one of those tiny incidents that should not have occurred, except that she was extremely tired and the tiredness made her careless for a fraction of a second. Even so, she scarcely noticed it though she had remembered to soak the hand in disinfectant before going to bed and an exhausted sleep. Perhaps in the full bloom of health that would have been the end of it but overwork and lack of food had lowered her resistance, overnight the hand started to swell and turn red. During the day the infection got rapidly worse and the pain slowed her down. Twice she tried to speak to the ward doctor but he had no time to stop and listen to a nurse's ailments. By the next morning the pain was so intense that Vicky had to seek out the Matron and ask to be relieved from duty. Within hours the hand had been lanced and drained but it was too late. The nurse needed nursing. Vicky had wanted to return to duty but the Matron was adamant. The diagnosis was exhaustion, fatigue and anaemia. There was no place in a military hospital to nurse a woman!

So Vicky found herself travelling, unwillingly, back to Thame. For the first time in six months she could put herself first. For the first time in six months her hands were idle but she did not know how to cope with the feeling of helplessness that overcame her. Gradually the rhythm of the train rocked her off to a shallow sleep. Every now and again as the train rattled over points, she would awaken with a start and her hand would ache and she would remember the faces of the men who had died.

Sidney Barnes could not believe his luck. He knew that every man was entitled to leave, he had even heard that some men had been given leave once but this was the first time since coming to France that he had become one of the chosen few. Home leave. It has been a pleasure to hump his kit on the four mile walk to the railway station. Then he had sat in a lather of suspense for sixty minutes, before the train pulled out for Calais, in case the whole thing was a cruel farce and he would be sent back to the front line at any moment. As the train pulled out, he kissed his pass before tucking it away in his breast pocket, then he and the other fifty men destined for England, gave a cheer.

Rarely did Alfred Stevens seek a meeting with his Colonel, except in exceptional circumstances; even more rare was the reverse, for the Colonel to seek a meeting with Alfred, except to issue pedantic orders. Today was that rare event. "Come, Alfred, and sit down." A smile and the handshake of welcome.

The battalion was back in reserve and for once it was a quiet peaceful day with no fear of shelling. A time to relax, to write home, to reflect, for re-appraisal.

"How long have you been Quartermaster, Alfred?" The Colonel's hand went up. "No, don't answer that!"

"It does seem a trifle long, Sir, now that you mention it. A good few years, Sir – though it seems longer."

"You've been a darn good Quartermaster, Alfred. Never let us down."

"Thank you, Sir."

"That brings me to what I want to ask, Alfred. A Major Harris will be joining us soon – coming out of retirement but he has Quartermaster experience. I can't put him in charge of a company – too old. I want you to step down."

"If you recall, I never wanted this job, Sir."

"True. As you know I lost Clement, my Adjutant nearly six months ago and Lieutenant William has been doing the job – but he's no administrator and I did promise him that the job was only temporary. I want you to be Adjutant."

"A pleasure, Sir."

The Colonel seemed lost in thought for a while before he spoke. "Do you realise, Alfred, that you and I are the longest serving officers in the battalion – I have lost so many officers I have forgotten most of their names."

"Not truly forgotten, Sir. Just buried by events for the time being."

"Perhaps you will remember, Alfred, that there was a time when you badgered me to be allowed in the front line – to be in the action as you said. Well, I can promise you'll get plenty of that soon. This war has a long way to go yet."

"May I buy you a drink in the mess, Sir?"

"Only if you can promise there is a decent gin on offer and some Player's cigarettes."

"That's one promise I can make, Sir."

Several years had passed by since the last social evening of the South Oxfordshire Farmers Union. Nor would it have taken place this year except for the donation of a prime bullock, also the good lady of the 'Spread Eagle' had scoured the district for best vegetables, cream and forced asparagus, which together with choice wines from her cellar completed a splendid meal. The results now graced the servery and tables of the assembly room.

Colonel Atwell, President, put out his hand to James Roberts. "Good evening, Roberts. So pleased you were able to come – and with such a lovely companion. I do not think we have been introduced, Ma'am."

James bent his head in acknowledgement. "This is Mrs Rose Guntrippe, Mr President. She has taken gracious pity on a lonely old man."

The Colonel bowed. "So pleased to meet you, Mrs Guntrippe." He stared at her décolletage. "Such beautiful – such a lovely dress."

Rose curtsied. "You'm most kind, ... " She was about to say Maister, but was suddenly conscious of her speech.

James intervened. "Mrs Guntrippe lost her husband in France, Mr President."

"So sorry to hear that, Mrs Guntrippe, but you must find consolation in the knowledge that he died in the service of his King and Country."

"Aye, there is that, Sir, but his son would rather he be alive to play football and take him swimming in Jemmett's Hole."

As a frown crossed the President's face, James took Rose's arm and gently guided her away to the bar. "A sherry will set up your appetite, Rose."

The three piece orchestra started to play. "If you say so, James – tell me, why do men always make so light of dying?"

"I think the President likes you, Rose."

"He likes looking at my tits – that's for certain sure!"

"That dress – it – it does show you to advantage."

"So it ought – it cost ne'er a week's wage."

"Aye, it do suit you , Rose. Such a pity we must leave by eleven but they cows cannot wait beyond that time."

"Doan you'm forget, James. I shall want a promise of a dance after dinner or you may be milking alone."

"If we dance, I shall not want to let you go – not wearing that dress."

Rose touched his cheek. "That's better – why I've not seen you'm smile as that for many a month."

"It has been hard to forget the past, Rose."

"No need to forget it – we belong to our past. Just look forward to tomorrow is what I say."

Lieutenant Wood turned and put up his hand. "Wait!" Fifteen pairs of ears strained against the silence of the night. The patrol had been sent out to probe at the German line, with the prime objective of getting a prisoner; or failing that, to cause as much mayhem as possible. Every man in the patrol was on edge, keyed up to react in the event of danger or attack; however, every man was greatly puzzled. They were certain this trench was empty. All the signs pointed to it being devoid of life. Had the Bosch been here there would have been some sign. A guarded light, a voice sounding in the dark or rising up from a dugout, a tidiness in the trench. The Germans were a tidy race. This trench looked as if it had been used as a rubbish dump. Old broken boxes and canisters littered the bottom of the trench.

"Sergeant!" The platoon sergeant edged forward to the Lieutenant's side.

"Here, Sir – there's summat wrong. This trench was occupied two nights ago. I'm certain."

"Are you sure we're in the right place?"

"I'll check with Bomber Coates, Sir but I'm sure this is right." He called down the file. "Coates – come up."

Cautiously George moved forward. He was feeling decidedly on edge and he felt certain this was an ambush. It was the stillness that did it. Not even a rat was moving. "Here, Sarge."

"Are we in the right place? The Lieutenant is worried."

"This is the right place, Sir. Quite certain of that."

"There's not a Bosch here! This is what we'll do. One bomber and a rifleman will go out on the flanks – about fifty yards. The rest of us will search every inch, check out all the dugouts. Use the torches – see what we can find."

"I tell you, Sir, the front line trench between markers 3 and 6 is deserted. Even beyond those points we could see nothing. The Bosch have vanished."

Lieutenant Wood had hurried back to make his report, his company commander had taken him to the Colonel. "Are you certain? Absolutely certain?"

"Yes, Sir. Bomber Coates pointed it out. There's not even a rat there. Every scrap of food, fuel, bedding and clothing has gone. We didn't find any ammunition – only a trip wire connected to a grenade in one of the dugouts."

"Any casualties?"

"Not one."

"There is another thing, Sir. We know that there are two Bosch support trenches behind their front line. Bomber Coates pointed out that throughout the entire patrol there was no sign of any activity in those places. It was all unnaturally quiet."

"Well done, Wood. I shall inform Brigade immediately. We will send out patrols over our entire front straight off." The Colonel turned to the Adjutant. "Issue an order for all the company commanders to get ready to move forward within the hour. Pass a word of praise to Bomber Coates – we must encourage the men."

When the others had left, the Colonel turned to Alfred Stevens, a puzzled look on his face. "If the section in front of us has been mysteriously vacated then it must go much further. Brigade will need to get everyone forward or our flanks will be exposed."

"If the Bosch have moved back it will explain why there were all those explosions over the last few days. Do you recall we were puzzled because there was no shelling. It must be significant that they have stripped the trench our men searched."

The field telephone trilled. "Brigade on the line, Sir."

The platoon sergeant stepped along the trench. "Holling – Pullene – Howe! Get ready, field marching order, keep your greatcoats on. Holling, pick up extra bandoliers of 303."

"What's happened, Sarge?"

"We've lost the Bosch. We are going to find them."

"In the dark, Sarge!"

"Best time to find them when they can't see us."

Though she tried to appear calm, Beatrice Peters could not keep the worry from her voice as Herbert Peters helped Vicky into the parlour. Beatrice swept forward. "Oh, my poor love. You look worn out. What have they done to you?"

Herbert was also concerned. He had waited at the station for over an hour awaiting Vicky's arrival, his anxiety growing inch by inch with worry, after receiving her telegram, made worse by the late arrival of the train. "She just needs rest and plenty of nourishing food, Mother. Then she'll be right as rain."

"But you have lost so much weight – and what have you done to your hand?"

Vicky sat down by the fire. "It's been a tiring journey." She held out her hand. "Some infection got in – the doctor has said I must rest."

"No need to worry now, Vicky. Now you're safe home we'll take good care of you. I've a good mind to write to that hospital and tell them off!"

"No, don't do that, Mother. It's not their fault, there is just so much to do – so many men in need of help. I must write to Edward soon."

"Come and sit at the table. Mary has made a lovely warming broth for you. You can eat it while Father changes, ready for rifle drill."

"Rifle drill?"

"Yes, Father is a soldier now, you know – he's got a uniform and a rifle."

Mary appeared in the doorway. "I've put a pan and hot bottle in Vicky's bed."

"Mary, you never wrote that Father was a soldier now!"

Mary laughed. "We wanted to keep it as a surprise."

"I knew that Father had joined the Volunteers."

"Well, now he is a real soldier but they have promised the Volunteers will only serve in Thame. Anyhow, Father is too old to go away!"

"Oh!" Beatrice Peters looked around in alarm, "Don't you let your father hear you say that!"

Vicky smiled. "It's so good to hear laughter."

Beatrice put an arm around her. "No worry now we've got you home. We'll soon have you put to rights or my name isn't M . . . !"

Mary laughed even louder. "Why, Mother, I do believe you've forgotten your own name."

Beatrice sat down in astonishment. "Well, I never! You're right. What will become of me?"

Vicky held her hand. "Good nursing will see you right, Mother."

"How many numbers have we sold?" The platoon sergeant was eager to make the draw.

William Smithe checked his pocket book. "One hundred and eighty eight, Sarge. Some have paid for more than one number. A few men asked for credit but I refused, as you said. There's forty seven francs in the bag."

"Let me check it."

William handed over the canvas pouch. "There. I've never seen so much money since we came to France!"

"You'm right, lad. Not since Corporal Carter ran the 'Crown and Anchor' board."

"What happened to him, Sarge?"

"Blown to pieces – never saw him, nor the money – nor the board ever again."

"The Company is waiting, Sarge. Shall I let the Sergeant Major know we're ready?"

The draw was totally illegal so it was important that all the nco's and warrant officers were included.

"Aye, tell him the 'Big Breakfast' is in the hat."

The 'Big Breakfast' was the name they had given the draw to hide the true purpose. The Sergeant sounded quite confident, after all, he had paid in a whole franc, he was half convinced the prize was his. "Holling, put the slips in a steel helmet."

"I've not paid for a ticket, Sarge."

"I know that – that's why I want you to do it."

The Sergeant Major put his hand in the helmet and stirred the slips, then picked one out. "Ticket number five and seven, fifty seven. Who's the lucky winner? Bugger, it's not me!"

Quickly the shouts sounded through the billets and an answering shout went up. "It's me! I've got fifty seven!" An excited Freddie Coxe came running down the road.

An aggravated Sergeant rounded on William Smith. "Smithe, I don't believe this – not ever hungry Coxe with the hollow legs. Tell me this is a joke. Tell me I'm dreaming."

William counted the money into Freddie's cap in front of over twenty envious men. The Sergeant was still sceptical.

"Are you sure you know what to do with that money, Coxe?"

"Yes, Sarge. I'm going to buy a woman and a breakfast."

"Have you ever been with a woman, Coxe?"

"Yes, Sarge – I mean no, Sarge."

The sergeant put his hand to his head. "What a bloody waste!" He appealed to the assembled men. "I think Private Coxe owes us all a proper report when he gets back" There was agreement all round. "That's agreed then!"

Freddie hesitated. "I don't know as I can, Sarge."

"Look here Coxe – we're all paying for this – for your pleasure."

Sidney Barnes had tried the house first but he didn't get much sense from old Mother Guntrippe except a rather vague instruction 'to try't farm'. His own father had sniffed disdainfully when asked, but eventually and grudgingly had replied. "You'll find her at Newbarn – don't be bringing her to this house. We'll not stand for it. You'll not shame us with your fancy woman – d'you hear me?"

Sidney found his temper flaring but managed to hold his tongue, obviously gossip had spread since he had left Thame.

Undeterred he made his way past the Police Station and along the Chinnor Road to the farm entrance. Carefully he picked his way across the yard. Silently he cursed the muck, this was nearly as bad as being in the trenches and he thought he had left that behind for a few days. Hearing a noise inside the barn, he stepped in. Rose was forking out hay to the cattle. She stopped as Sidney moved forward and looked at him accusingly. "You'm taken your good time, laddo!"

Sidney removed his cap and tried to look contrite. "Sorry, Rose!"

"You'm took off wi'out a word. Never a letter. Not even since Thomas was killed."

"Didn't know what to say. I'm no good with letters. I heard about Thomas but thought it might give offence if I wrote then."

"Oh, I take offence, Sidney Barnes. What do you want?" The last was said so sharply that Sidney grew alarmed.

"Start again, Rose – proper courtin' like. Pick up where we left off."

"Aye, you'd like that, wouldn't you'm. Just walk in. Lift your skirt Rose! Drop those drawers, Rose!" Rose threw down the fork, "No responsibility, eh! Well you'm can sling your bloody hook, Sidney Barnes – an' sling it far."

Sidney's dismay showed on his face. "This be my first leave. I looked forward to seeing you. I came straight here to ask you to marry me."

"Marry you'm? I wouldn't marry you if you were all that was left. I want more than to be a soldier's wife, never knowing from one day to another whether I'm wife or widow."

"We were good for each other, Rose. I'll not be a soldier for ever."

"Ahem!" James Roberts appeared in the barn doorway. There was a strained silence for a moment until Rose spoke. "This is Sidney Barnes, James. An old neighbour home on leave from France."

"Ah! Then you had best not waste time hereabouts when you could be off enjoying yourself."

Reluctantly Sidney put on his cap and turned to leave. "May I call at the house, Rose?"

"Yes, but speak to Robert. Tell him about his father. He misses him."

James Roberts saw Sidney to the gate. "I'd take it kindly if you don't come back here Mr Barnes. We have work to do."

"You speak as if we had never met, Mr Roberts."

"Of course we've met. I know you and you know me. That is why I want you away. Rose is too good for the likes of you."

"You speak like a husband."

"I wish it were true."

"The Hun are becoming very devious, Mother." Herbert Peters scanned the column in the Thame Gazette. "Do you realise they have built a new defensive line behind the old one and pulled back there before our men knew what was happening."

Beatrice Peters stopped knitting and looked puzzled. "Why would they do that, Father? What is the point?" The needles recommenced their rhythmic clicking.

"Surely 'tis obvious, Mother. They are drawing our troops into a trap. Cannot be trusted to fight fair."

"These things always have a name, Father – does this have a name?"

Herbert checked the paper again. "Hindenberg. That's it. Hindenberg! Damn Huns!"

"I expect it's a Hun name, Father. You did say it was behind the old line?"

"Yes, Mother."

"That will be nearer to Germany. Perhaps you can hand in your rifle now, Father. I really don't like it in the house. Not now that our Vicky is home. It's not safe having a rifle in the next bedroom – only a few feet from where she is sleeping."

"It's quite safe, Mother. We've no bullets!"

The Senior Nurse gave Samuel Peddelle a quick appraisal. She liked 'her soldiers' as she called them, to look spick and span when they left the hospital. Especially when, as in the case of Samuel, she and her staff had spent so much time and effort guiding them back to health. He still managed to look under-nourished and pale. It would be hard to find a man who looked less like a soldier than Samuel Peddelle, so the nurse had been mollified to learn that he was a cobbler and nearly as far from being a real soldier as the sheep in the nearby fields. However that did not allay her concern and she had persuaded the doctor to send Samuel on 'recovery' leave. This despite his protests that he had nowhere to go, no one to see. 'Everyone has someone', she insisted, 'Where do you come from?' 'Thame, in Oxfordshire! How lovely! A few weeks there with rest and good food will set you up, ready for work.' He had protested he could not afford it but to no avail, the Paymaster had told her that Samuel had never drawn his pay, so with nearly fifteen pounds accumulated, he could afford to stay in the best hotel in Thame.

"All ready, Samuel?" The Senior Nurse gave him a bright smile. "Don't forget your vapour rub. Every night!"

Samuel patted his small pack. "In here, Nurse."

"Pay?"

"In my pocket."

"Promise me you will come back fit and well. No work now! Lots of walks in the fresh air, plenty of food and a warm bed."

Samuel nodded. He found it hard to speak. It was the strangest feeling, he thought, to have someone care for you.

Sergeant Cox had made his way from the Police Station to the Four Horseshoes with some reluctance, as time went by the need to separate warring fools was beginning to pall on him but with his constables already out on patrol there was no alternative. As he arrived the landlord stepped forward quickly. "Good evening, Sergeant. 'Tis the same trouble as last night – Corporal Barnes has had a bit too much."

"Now I wonder as who supplied this excessive drink?"

"No need for that, Sergeant, I just try to make an honest living. It's not easy to refuse."

"You could make a greater effort. Now what has our Corporal done tonight?"

"Cleared the bar, smashed a chair, and thumped two of my best customers!"

At the end of the bar Sidney Barnes clung desperately to the rail and called for another pint. Sergeant Cox strode forward. "Enough of this now."

"Bugger off!"

"No more drink – its either home or a cell."

"Bollocks!" Sidney took a swing and missed.

Sergeant Cox moved in and took his arm. "I said enough, now come with me."

"They're all bloody cowards here! Send the bastards to the front!"

"They'll get their chance, Corporal. Now, let's find you a nice quiet cell to sleep this off."

The landlord edged along the bar. "Wants locking up and key thrown away is what I say."

Sidney's legs began to buckle. "S'that bloody cow, Rose! Threw me out!"

"Not surprised if you were in this state."

"I only wanted to bring a bit o' pleasure into her life!"

"I'm often told that women are a source of trouble but they are no bother to me, Corporal."

"Sarge – excuse me saying – but you must be too bloody old."

Samuel Peddelle stepped in the door and up to the bar. "Good evening landlord, I'm in need of lodgings."

The landlord gave him a hard stare. "Not another bloody soldier! We've just got rid of one of yours. Ox and Bucks!" He spat.

Samuel bridled. "You calling an Ox and Bucks man a bloody soldier? I'll not have that without official complaint."

The landlord retreated. "Sorry soldier – no harm meant. One o' the lads letting off a bit o' steam, that's all."

"What's this man's name?"

"Barnes."

"Ah, Corporal Barnes. A right hero I can tell you." Samuel gained in confidence. "I want a room with a fire and a decent supper."

The landlord tapped his forehead. "Right away, Sir. Will that be all, Sir?"

"A glass of best rum – the dark sort."

"This very moment, Sir."

"Where does Corporal Barnes live?"

"Across the road but you'll not see him tonight."

"Why not? Is he in the arms of a woman?"

"No, Sir – the arms of the law!"

Boredom drove Sidney Barnes out to the Thame Park Estate. He noticed immediately the signs of neglect. First there were the uneven hedges, then the dead wood lying under the trees where it had fallen, far too many rabbits and crows and not a pheasant to be heard or seen. No doubt, he thought, the gardens by the great house would be neglected as well. His father was still working as a gardener on the estate but apparently the estate was short of men and only absolutely essential work was done. Sidney made his way to the Head Gamekeeper's cottage and knocked. Mrs Parker seemed pleased to see him and sent him into the kitchen where Joss Parker was sitting, resting a gammy leg. Sidney removed his cap.

"Hello, Mr Parker, I thought I would look you up to see how you are doing."

Joss knocked the dottle from his pipe into the grate. "Is that you, Sidney? Why, so it is. Your'n father has told me of you. An' a corporal too. You'm are going up in the world."

Sidney noted the unusual use of his first name but made no comment. "Aye, this is my first leave but 'tis hard to settle."

Joss eased his leg and looked reflectively at Sidney. "You should not have gone when you did but I heard of events. Still, no matter now."

"I saw no pheasants as I came."

"No, there were none reared this last year. Mr Wykham-Musgrave has been ill and I could get no help."

Sidney did not want to ask outright in case of refusal, so he was cautious.

"I can see your leg is giving you some gyp, can I help in any way?" He waited while Joss appeared to think. "I've a week before I go back."

"Kind of you, Sidney, kind indeed. They damn crows and rabbits need knocking back. Also the enclosure where the pheasants run is in need of repair, in case I can get breeding this summer."

"I've got my gun at home, Mr Parker. I'll bring it this afternoon."

Joss waved at the cupboard. "Plenty of cartridges – the one thing as is always available. But no damn bantam feed."

"The rabbits will come in handy, Mr Parker – meat seems to be in short supply."

"Aye, take a few dozen up to the houses."

Joss filled his pipe while scrutinising Sidney. "I was thinking as how you'm might come back here when this war is ended. You were a good keeper till you'm went mad and buggered off."

"There were a time when I thought I should go off an' see the world – but now I've seen it an' I can't say as how I like it."

"Well, I can only last out a few more years – then this job could be your'n. I know the Master would agree."

"I should like that, Mr Parker."

Joss put out his hand. "We'll shake on it. 'Tis a promise now. An' seeing as how you've grown up and being a Corporal I feel you should call me Joss."

"'Tis a promise – Joss."

For three days Samuel Peddelle had led a quiet life trying to build up the courage to go and ask direct questions. He had even walked to the far end of Thame and stood outside the Workhouse. Once the Matron had walked right past him on her way to the High Street, but she had given no hint of recognition. She had seen thousands of nondescript private soldiers not worth a second glance her whole demeanour said. Eventually, Samuel had reasoned that the Master would not help even if he could, but it was unlikely that he actively knew the whereabouts of Samuel's daughters. There was only one person who could help, he decided, and that was the Vicar, provided that the same person still held the living. That was part of Samuel's reluctance. What if the Vicar were dead? Or had gone off so far that Samuel would not find him. What then? The disappointment would be too great.

There was no answer to this dilemma except to go to the Vicarage and find out, so on the fourth day, he made his way down Park Street, along the Upper and Lower High Streets until he came to the Priestend and down past the Prebendal to the Vicarage. At the last moment his nerve failed him and he turned back and went up the embankment to the church of St Mary's. First he searched for the graves of the five dead girls, but there was no trace. There had never been any marker stones, at last he went inside the Church. It was as he remembered it. He sat near the old font, where the girls had been christened and found himself lost in thought. What were their names? Emma? Yes, Emma. Mary – Ivy. What had they looked like? He wished that he could cry to release the anguish but the tears would not come. Why not, he thought, it is barely three years.

When the clock struck eleven he stood up and walked slowly to the Vicarage and rapped on the door.

"Good morning. I had hoped to see the Vicar for a few minutes."

The maid wrinkled her nose, a moderate disdainful gesture. "What name shall I give and what is your business?"

"Private Peddelle, Miss. A family matter."

"Wait there please." The door shut.

"I cannot recall you for the moment, my son, yet there is something familiar about you." The Vicar looked puzzled.

Samuel had taken the proffered chair. "It were a while ago, Father. I have been away in the army but you may recall that we last met in the Workhouse."

The Vicar stiffened. "Ah. Now I remember. Your wife committed the cardinal sin. I helped place your two young daughters."

"That's correct, Father. It is concerning my daughters that I wish to speak."

"The daughters who are now legally adopted?"

"Aye, that is it, Father. My position has improved – changed. What chance is there to get my daughters back?"

The Vicar shook his head in sorrow. "These things cannot be reversed, my son. Did we not make this clear at the time. Besides which, I cannot see what you mean by improvement in your position. You are a soldier, in France. Men die every day."

"It is hard to live without hope, Father."

"You may find it easier to marry again and have other children."

"I couldn't do that, it would be disrespectful to Martha's memory, but it would not erase the memory of the girls an' that is what eats at me, day in, day out."

"Will you believe me when I say I do not know the whereabouts of your daughters? These matters are dealt with by members of the adoption staff. The best I can offer is to write and ask that you either be allowed to know their new name or that they be told, when they are old enough, of their true parentage."

Samuel slumped in the chair. "I had hoped for better."

"There is no better, my son. Let me make enquiries and come and see me when this war is over. I promise that I will write and put your case."

Freddie Coxe walked timidly up the roadway to the entrance to Ginger's. On each side of him, Edward Holling held one arm while Harold Jones held the other, their duty was to ensure that Freddie arrived at his destination. There were two reasons for this. The first being that with forty seven francs in his possession, Freddie was liable to be robbed. Secondly, the whole company was deeply envious of Freddie and if he didn't go through with the visit to Ginger's and give a detailed report he was liable to get a good thumping. Edward and Harold were determined that Freddie was going to be safely delivered to the establishment. Only that day Edward and Harold had been called up in front of the company commander and promoted to the dizzy heights of temporary acting lance-corporal. Despite their protests they had been recommended for OTC training and these promotions would help develop their leadership skills. Freddie was more than aware of this and pleaded to be released but his two friends were implacable.

Edward summarised their views. "You needn't have bought a number and you needn't have taken the money!"

"But it's my money. I can do as I will with it!"

Harold was firm. "No. There's men back there as will crucify you if you don't go through with it."

"But I don't know what to do!"

"Well you'll soon find out."

Edward knocked on the door and it opened a fraction. The madam peered at him. "Officers only – fook off!" The door closed.

Edward hammered on the door. "Open up. We've got plenty of money!"

The door opened again. "It eese fortee francs."

"Show her the money, Freddie – there, see it. Good"

The door opened wide and Freddie was propelled inside.

Freddie had wandered back into the billets by mid-morning, a new silent subdued Freddie with only a moderate appetite. He spent most of the day avoiding contact with others. By sheer luck this was possible as the battalion had a genuine day of rest, free from all duties and fatigues. He even refused the chance to play a game of football, an unheard of event. His friends were convinced he was ill or at best, sickening. Edward and Harold were concerned and starting to feel somewhat guilty. The platoon sergeant sent for Freddie when the tea, bread and jam arrived at five. Over fifty men assembled.

"We're waiting, Coxe, to hear of your great adventure."

"I don't think as I should tell – 'twas quite shocking. That Mrs Ginger wore a gauze dress and had a painted face. She kept putting her hand in my trousers and saying lewd things!" Fifty men listened in complete silence.

"She kept asking, 'Ver is your cock, leetle man'. I had to keep my legs tightly crossed. Then she took five francs of my money."

"Well, what happened then?"

"She called in these four girls and demanded I buy a bottle of champagne so I had to give her another ten francs. Then those girls took all their clothes off and one sat on my lap and kept putting her tongue in my ear. It was quite revolting."

"Must have been a terrible hardship!"

Freddie did not seem to pick up on the irony in the remark.

"It were, because Mrs Ginger made me go upstairs with one of them to this bedroom and she started to pull my clothes off."

"Were she completely naked?"

"Oh no, she had stockings on."

"You lucky bugger!"

"You can say that but it was embarrassing standing there with no trousers and my cock sticking out – I felt a right fool. Then she demanded money. 'Thirtee francs, Tommee!' Thirty francs!"

"Well, what happened then?"

"Get on with it, Freddie!"

"She sat on the bed and counted the money – twice! She kept complaining that the coins were too small."

"Must have been a real hardship watching a lovely naked girl counting out yer money, Freddie."

"It were because I kept getting these terrible urges but I didn't know what to do until she took me into the bed. But it were beautiful – beautiful. I shall go again if I get the money. Mind you, it never cost me anything."

"What d'you mean, it didn't cost you owt?"

"Marie – the girl, she were pleased because she said I were a virgin. So I told her how we had sold draw tickets and I had won and she was so pleased she gave me my money back."

"You had a beautiful naked girl in bed – and your money back? By gawd, you have the luck of the devil, Freddie Coxe."

Freddie put his hand in his pocket and took out a coin. "There, see. She gave my twenty five centimes back! The cost of my ticket."

Edward Holling whispered in Harold Jones's ear. "Harold, I think we had better get Freddie out of here before he gets lynched by the balls!"

Sidney Barnes and George Coates passed like darkened ships in the night, unbeknown to each other. Sidney returning to the front; George on his way home for a well deserved leave, wearing his 'stripe'. He was especially pleased because word had gone around that the new adjutant was a first rate man. No longer the slapdash paperwork of the past, no more delays in promotions or vacancies unfilled, leave lists were up to date and fairly allocated and trivial orders lost in a bin. As Captain Stevens had said, George had been recommended for promotion twice before, his record was good and he was the longest serving 'Bomber' in the battalion. George's chest had nearly burst with pride, after all 'he was a first rate soldier who had displayed leadership qualities and courage in many difficult circumstances, especially during night raids on the enemy lines'. He felt a strange reaction as the train steamed into Thame Railway Station. Nothing seemed to have changed! It was the same when he walked out into the yard and up the road toward Park Street. Still nothing had changed. Everywhere quiet! He banged on the door of the cottage, number four Park Terrace. No answer.

A nearby door opened and Mrs Hammond peered across at him. "Is that you, George? Maud has gone to market – 'tis Tuesday." It was said in a very flat non-committal manner as if he had only been away for a day. He found himself getting exasperated so he did what he had always done in the past, he opened the door and marched in feeling quite deflated. Was this the hero's welcome home? Reason told him that none knew of his coming; but he still felt let down. A pot of stew was gently simmering in the banked range fire but there was no sign of the children. They must all be at school, he decided. Right, he thought, I shall go to the market and we will see if a hero is welcomed there!

The motley crowd of farmers standing at the bar of the Cross Keys paid little attention to George. Soldiers passed through and billeted in the town most of the time. George shouldered his way to the bar and ordered a pint of ale. He managed no more than a quick sip before a strong hand banged into his back and a voice boomed out. "Why! It's George – why bless my soul. Welcome back, me lad!"

To George's great surprise his welcoming assailant was his old employer, George Bailey from Blackditch Farm.

"Steady on, Mr Bailey, this is my first pint since I got back."

"Get it down you, lad – or should I say Corporal? Let me get you a whisky chaser to celebrate."

George's mind went back to the day, some years ago, when they had last parted company; his memory told him they had not parted entirely in friendship. But, what could he say, here was his old employer beaming a great smile of welcome and offering to buy whisky. Whisky! The world was changing. "Most kind of you."

"Landlord! A large whisky for a Thame soldier back from the war. Come and sit down, George. I've just spent two hours on my feet at the auction. Damned difficult to get good stock these days. Now, lad, tell me what you've been doing."

George noted the use of the walking stick and a stiff left hip. Sitting down for George Bailey was obviously a relief, getting seated was obviously painful.

"Trying to stay alive is the best way to describe the front, but this is my first leave, so least said the better."

George Bailey eased his leg. "There is a change in you, you've grown, you know – I can see the confidence in you."

"Aye, you're right. I shall not want to settle to labouring when this war is over. I've seen better things. I want some of them."

"I could see that as soon as you walked in – took me a moment to recognise you. That's what made me think. I want to retire, put my feet up. Ease these 'rheumatics' by the fire."

"Nothing to stop you, Mr Bailey."

George Bailey scratched his nose. "Can't do it at the moment, George. I need a good man – a foreman. Someone I can trust to run the farm properly."

George Coates supped his whisky and savoured the aroma. "Surely, you can get a man!"

"Nay. All the men are off fighting, like you. But this war has got to end sometime then I will be ready to hand over."

George called out to the landlord. "Two pints, Landlord."

"How about you, George, will you be my foreman? None know the farm better than you – other than myself of course."

"D'you mean it, Mr Bailey? If you do then I will accept."

"I were hoping as how you'd say that!" He held out his right hand. "Shall we strike on it."

"Aye."

"That's a promise then."

George Coates smiled as he replied. "'Tis a promise."

"Maud! Maud!" George Coates strode along the Upper High Street, waving. A way off Maud Coates caught sight of him and waved in excitement, then hurried to meet him. He grabbed her in his arms.

"Give me a kiss, George." George obliged. "I did not – how did – why didn't . . . . ."

"There was no time to write and I wasn't going to miss the train making out a letter."

"Let's go straight home – you will need a bite to eat."

"We're going straight home, Maud. But I should tell you I made a promise to myself."

"What's that, George?"

"I promised that the second thing I would do when I saw you would be to take off my greatcoat."

"Oh, George – we will need to be quick! The children are home from school in an hour."

"Well, let's bloody well run then!"

Peter Oxenlade had considered himself to be the forgotten man, denied every chance to destroy the Hun and subjected to endless days making bread, more bread and still more bread. Sometimes the monotony was broken by other cookery duties. When he had been called to the new Quartermaster's office he thought his wish to join one of the rifle companies had been answered at last. He was almost disappointed when he had been given a fourteen day leave pass and told to pack immediately. It was Sergeant Hagen who had advised him to send a telegram when he arrived at either Dover or Folkestone, 'make sure the family know you are coming, otherwise it's a great shock'. With growing excitement Peter mentally noted the stations as he neared Thame and when the train had pulled into the station there was Enid and the three girls all waiting and waving excitedly. He jumped down from the train and the girls overwhelmed him. Enid bustled forward and gave him a smacking kiss. The kids were yelling out 'Welcome home, Dad!' and Enid looked so pleased, it brought a tear to Peter's eye and he found himself with his arms around the girls blubbing like a young boy.

"It's so good to be home. It's been so long."

Enid was smiling when she said it. "You went quickly enough and left us."

"Never again, Love. When this war is over I'm settling down for ever."

The girls tugged at his hands. "Steady girls!"

Ivy, the oldest girl, tried to lift his pack. "Put it in the pram, Dad."

Peter was suddenly aware of the large perambulator a few yards off. "Pram!"

Enid took over. "Don't get worried, Peter – its not for carrying babies. We want no more of those – no more. Three is enough! This is to carry our kit and your kit." She lifted the pack and dropped it in the pram. "Let's be off!"

Peter looked at the pram, a small seed of concern was growing. "What are those garden tools for?"

Enid took his arm. "Because, my brave husband, we are going to dig over our new allotment."

"Allotment!"

"Yes. I queued at the Town Hall and managed to get twenty pole of new ground. There are lots of shortages you know, and we need the extra food. If we start now, it can be prepared and planted out to give us a good harvest this year."

"But I was hoping for a . . . . "

"I'm sure you were, Peter!" She cut in on him. "But the allowance is not enough so we are going digging. And we are going to keep digging until it's all done. Mr Roberts has said he will deliver a load of manure as soon as we ask and it will only cost half a crown as you're a hero."

Peter remembered that old saying that had been painted on the classroom wall, 'Hope destroyed makes the heart grow weak'. At last he knew what it meant.

"Is there no chance of a pint, Enid."

"There's a bottle of cold tea and some sandwiches in the pram. We've no time to waste."

Suddenly Peter had an inspiration. "Sunday. It's Sunday. We must go to church – we mustn't break the Sabbath."

Enid gave another smile. "The Archbishop of Canterbury has made a special pronouncement. Everyone can do allotment work on a Sunday – 'tis in the national interest, he said, an' the Vicar agreed with him."

Peter sighed. "Can we go home so as I can take off my uniform or it will get ruined."

"No need, Peter my love, your clothes are in the pram. You can change in the gents."

The girls went skipping up the platform as the train pulled out. "Come on, Dad – follow me!"

Enid grabbed Peter by the arm. "Cheer up. Let's sing a song."

> *"Take me back to dear old Blighty*
> *Put me on the train for London town*
> *Take me over there*
> *Drop me anywhere*
> *Birmingham, Leeds or Manchester*
> *I don't care"*

"Be careful with the pram, girls!"

> *"How I want to see my best girl*
> *Cuddling up as close as she can be.*
> *I ti-tiddly ity,*

Carry me back to Blighty,
Blighty is the place for me."

The field kitchen had been carefully sited under an old tiled lean-to shelter in a farmyard that had been shelled several times over the three years. Rain dripped through several holes and the wet wood used for the fires was giving off a tell-tale smoke, making Sergeant Hagen nervous. "Open up the dampers, get the fires drawing quickly or they'll start shelling us."

"The wood's drying, Sarge, and the rest is under cover." Peter Oxenlade stared bleakly out at the weather, a look of disgust on his face. "It will take hours to get the ovens hot enough to bake."

"You look as dismal as the weather, Oxenlade. For a man who has just been on a 'Blighty' leave you look bloody miserable."

"Just fed up with this weather, Sarge."

"Fourteen days leave should have set you up fine. Put you on top of the world. I bet your Missus made a fuss of you."

"I were too damned tired to notice. Never worked so hard in all my life."

Sergeant Hagen scratched his ear and raised an eyebrow. "Sounds like a tall story to me."

"No story, Sarge. My Missus had me digging a new allotment on rough pasture from the moment I got home till the minute I left. Proper slave driver. Said it was my fault for going off and leaving them short!"

"Well, she might have got you to work in the daytime but what of the night, eh, what of the nights?"

"I were too bloody tired – bloody well worn out. An' I was on a promise! It were a dog's life!"

"Well, brace yourself, the men are road building! I've never known appetites like it."

Captain Stevens, Adjutant, thumbed through the orders sent down from Brigade Headquarters. Now he must break the orders down for company use as well as highlighting all the overall co-ordinating orders. By the flickering light in the dugout he made a start. The battalion would advance in fighting order, no greatcoats.

Without thinking he crossed his fingers while wondering what the men would think about that with the attack due on Easter Monday at dawn and the weather damned cold. There had been constant sleet and snow showers and although the snow didn't hold, it was the sort of weather that made the teeth chatter, especially in that hour before the dawn, often the coldest part of the day. He made a note to issue an instruction that waterproof capes should be tied into the top of the small packs along with the obligatory 'two sandbags' that each man must carry. The rest was straightforward. Two Mills Bombs, one hundred and twenty rounds of ammunition, one day's rations and one flare for each man. That lot would give the new Quartermaster palpitations, he thought. He would have to go on bended knee to get the bombs and flares.

Alfred noted that the Brigade supply dump was too far back for comfort, getting additional supplies up to the front line and beyond was bound to create problems. He made a note to build up a reserve stock of ammunition and water near the battalion headquarters, where he could control them himself.

The dugout gas sheet swung back and the Colonel stomped in, hunching his shoulders and banging his hands together. "Where's Thomson, Alfred?" Private Thomson was the Colonel's batman.

"Heard you coming, Sir. Gone to get you a hot drink."

"Good! By the way, I've decided you and I are going up to have a look at the Harp in the morning. Need to get a good look and a feel for the terrain."

"What time, Sir?"

"Five thirty."

Inwardly Alfred groaned. "Five thirty it is, Sir."

The Corporal in charge of the Lewis Gun team was not an old hand at war. This was a war of young soldiers. They may be old in body but all were young in war. Today's assault against a strong point would test their mettle but the wait through the long night was worse, for it tested their imagination and nerve. That is why he had his team around him, together with the extra men detailed to carry surplus ammunition. Carefully and meticulously the group filled the circular magazines with ammunition. It gave the group something purposeful to do and while they were doing it the bonds of teamwork and friendship were strengthened by the knowledge that they were all dependent on each other. Even so, James Pullene found his throat getting so dry that he felt for his water bottle. A hand went out to restrain him.

"Try not to drink now – there'll be no water until the evening."

James knew why his throat was dry, it was the anxiety of waiting, he was sure a swallow of water would cure both, the dryness and the worry but he put the cork back in the bottle. "Sorry, Corp. This is my first time. I will be better next time."

The Corporal shook his head. "It never gets better," the men in his team grunted assent, "learn to keep your head down."

"I've never fired a revolver before, Corp!" James's rifle had been replaced by a revolver, but the weight reduction had been off-set by an additional five magazines for the Lewis Gun. The machine gun had an insatiable appetite and could consume a magazine in seconds on automatic fire.

"You'll only need the revolver if we get into serious trouble. I've told you several times and I'll say it again – follow me. Stay behind me – no rushing ahead. Keep your eyes open."

"I'll not let you down, Corp."

"I know that, lad. The Captain will let you go back to your section after this. The Colonel must think these bunkers are a problem because all the machine guns and bombers have been reinforced."

Further down the trench men sat huddled in small groups or lay back on the firing step in a fitful sleep, made more difficult by the coldness of the night. For those who were awake there was little to do except live in the hope that they were undetected by the enemy and as the night drifted by some men gradually allowed their optimism to build on the hope that this would remain a quiet night throughout.

The Battalion had taken extreme care to get to the front line undetected. First they had assembled in large caves near Arras before daylight on Sunday morning, then at midnight, after a good day's rest, they had moved forward in the growing darkness to their present position. There was hardly a man in the line who did not breathe a sigh of relief when the supporting bombardment thundered out and the countdown to zero hour started. At 7.34 the whole line lifted up out of the trenches without a spoken command and advanced across No Man's Land.

Edward knew at last what war was. It was thunder, blinding thunder, spiteful noise, weakening fear that sapped the muscles, confusion, elation to be still alive, hateful chaos – and death. In his endeavour to move forward quickly, Edward tripped headlong into the mud. It was then that he realised that no-one was moving forward. Behind him men lay unmoving on the ground. Over to the left a man jumped out of a shell hole and tried to run forward – but he had only gone a few yards when he stopped as though pole-axed and dropped to the ground. Suddenly it dawned on Edward that a man hit by a bullet stopped as if he had run into an invisible wall, and dropped on the spot. Machine gun bullets churned the ground nearby and in sheer desperation he rolled several feet to one side and fell into a shell hole. The entire attack had come to a grinding halt some seventy yards short of the concrete bunkers.

Twenty yards away in another shell hole William Smithe and Freddie Coxe huddled down. Only thirty minutes ago they had been stiff with cold, back in the trenches. Now they were sweaty with fear and exertion. For a minute or two they thought they were entirely on their own but then the distinctive rattle of Lee Enfield rifles and Lewis Guns built up and they forced themselves to check their rifles and started to look for a target.

On the far right of the line the Lewis Gun team had managed to get within forty yards of the bunker line and the corporal was quick to get the gun into position, then he started to pour bullets into the firing slit of the first bunker.

From a shell hole over to the left the platoon commander called out to Sidney Barnes. "Corporal Barnes, put some bombs into those Bosch guns while Corporal Wilson has them pinned down."

It took only seconds for the grenade launcher to be fitted to the rifle and ten seconds later a grenade crashed into the bunker and exploded. As smoke billowed out more Lewis Guns gained ascendancy and Sidney placed another grenade into the next bunker. Simultaneously the platoon commander leapt up and shouted the men forward. As the first men went into the trench and started bombing the dugouts the whole battalion advanced and the defenders were overwhelmed.

Edward was among the first to reach the trench and found himself taking the surrender of about thirty prisoners. Suddenly he was in control of himself, the fear suppressed, his mind clear. He motioned the prisoners up on to the parapet with his rifle. Further along the trench more prisoners were moving back.

The platoon sergeant marched down issuing orders. "Get this rear parapet in order – let's have some discipline, lads. The Bosch will hit back at any moment."

Edward got out his entrenching tool and pulled the two sandbags from his pack and started filling them with earth. Ten minutes later the German shells began to fall all around.

Throughout the afternoon Alfred Stevens had patiently gathered in all the information, sent out stretcher parties to bring in the wounded, passed on reports to Brigade and prepared his reports.

"My report is ready, Sir. Shall I read it out?"

The Colonel sat back for the first time today, lit a cigarette and nodded agreement.

"In the first place we met our objective and we have spent some time consolidating. Hostile artillery fire has had no effect. We have taken one hundred prisoners and captured a number of machine guns, three in total but a further nine were destroyed. All our casualties have been picked up and sent for medical treatment. Fifteen officers and six hundred and five men went into action. Our casualties amounted to one hundred and ninety two officers and men. I am taking statements regarding acts of bravery, it is my assessment that over thirty men are deserving of recognition. I do not think I have seen a more gallant action."

"We were lucky today, Alfred. Twice they could have caught us in a bombardment but we got away with it – thank goodness!"

The Quartermaster gave forth a genuine smile, after all this was a pleasant duty. He passed the precious slip of paper across his desk, or rather the cracked and dilapidated old table that passed as a desk.

"There you are, Harty. You are a lucky man – fourteen days leave."

Albert Harty remained rigidly to attention, a partial scowl on his face. "Thank you, Sir but I want no leave, Sir! The fight is not yet over. The Philistines have not been destroyed."

"This war is not over yet, Harty. It will not be over in a fortnight."

"But it ses in Revelations, Sir 'Be thou faithful unto death and I will give thee a crown of life'! I cannot go now in case the call comes."

The Quartermaster closed his eyes for a moment and took a sharp intake of breath to steady his nerves. "Harty, years ago and in its infinite wisdom the army invented leave. This was done to ensure the resting of soldiers to promote efficiency and restore health. It is also my belief that it is also necessary for the continuation of our race – now pick up that pass, dammit, and go forth and procreate!"

Albert Harty gasped in alarm. "You will send me to Delilah! She who cut the hair of Samson and then gave him over to the Philistines who put out his eyes!"

"I'm sending you on leave, Harty! Q!" The Quartermaster Sergeant appeared. "March Harty away and ensure he catches the first available train to Calais."

The Colonel gritted his teeth and tried to suppress his anger. He failed; the words almost spat out. "Give your evidence, Sergeant!"

The Military Police Sergeant came smartly to attention. He looked in quite good health except for a yellowing-blue eye and a plaster over his left eyebrow. "Sir, at 2200 hours on Friday the 20th of April my patrol was summoned by the civil power in the town of Calais. It was reported that a British soldier was destroying a bar and had done grievous bodily damage to several persons. As instructed by the Provost Marshall I did respond to this situation with the utmost urgency and attended with three men."

"What next?"

"The situation was found as reported. Inside the bar several men were lying unconscious and all the furniture destroyed. Private Harty was actively destroying the bar, including all the bottles. I called to Private Harty to stop but he ignored me. We then surrounded him and I said that he was being arrested for being drunk and disorderly and causing damage."

"Was he in uniform, Sergeant?"

"Yes, Sir."

"Carry on, Sergeant."

"On being told he was under arrest, Harty began shouting and raving. Saying that we were instruments of the devil and the antichrists, with that he began to fight. I ordered he be handcuffed, whereupon he went berserk and when trying to restrain him, two of my men received injuries that have caused them to remain in hospital since that night. A separate report is available from the Medical officer at the Base Hospital, he has stated that the condition of Corporal Higgins is serious. The civil authorities declare that the damage to property amounts to seven thousand francs and further charges for medical costs for the injured persons must be borne by the British Army, Sir!"

"What have you to say, Harty?"

Albert Harty peered out thorough swollen and blackened eyes. There was hardly a square inch of his face not cut and bruised, his nose was mashed and his lips swollen. It was obvious that he had difficulty in talking.

"'Twere – not – my fault, Sir. That were no bar but a place of harlots. There were nought but Jezebels and Delilahs enticing men. I asked for a room to sleep but they said I had lice and must have a bath and haircut. That was when the trouble started."

"I see. Over a bath and a haircut?"

"Yes, Sir, do you not see. It were Delilah making a mockery of the Lord, standing there half naked – the temptation of Samson. Once I knew their meaning how could I stand by and let them steal the souls of men and make us weak before the Philistines. But the Lord has made me his instrument and given me the strength to pull down these false temples."

The Colonel turned to the Police Sergeant. "Was Harty drunk?"

"I believe so, Sir, he smelled strongly of drink."

The Colonel turned back to Harty. "I was told you had forsworn drink! Why drink now?"

"I were not drunk. Drink were thrown on me."

"Then how do you explain your behaviour?"

"The message came clear from God, Sir. Seek out and destroy this temple of iniquity, evil and filth before the Philistines enter by the back gate and pull down the virtuous men who fight on our side."

"You are clearly mistaken, Harty. God has issued no orders for the destruction of our allies or their property. Had he done so this would have been restated and confirmed in Brigade Orders."

He checked a copy of King's Regulations. "Normally I would offer a choice of accepting my punishment or going to a higher authority. Due to the seriousness of the charges and the fact that you were sober throughout this destructive act means you will be tried before a General Field Court Martial. Until then you will remain in the custody of the Military Police."

"Surely there must be some mistake, Captain."

Captain Fairbairn, Officer in Charge of the Thame Volunteers, considered the point for a moment before replying, a frown on his face. "I'm sorry, Herbert, there is no mistake. The order from the War Office is quite clear and specific. Our unit is ordered to provide two men for coastal defence duties to commence in four weeks time – there then follows a description of the equipment to be taken. The only matter in which I have discretion is to appoint you to the rank of Corporal."

"That would give me a military responsibility for which I have no training or experience. But none of this alters the fact that we were all promised our service would be limited to the Thame area," Herbert started to get agitated, "I have responsibilities here."

Captain Fairbairn shook his head, "Sorry but I have already raised objections and made representations to the authority, but without any result. Norfolk it is and will remain, two men must go. There is an urgent need to release men for France."

"We are all too old for this foolishness!"

"That is why we drew lots, Herbert – to ensure fairness."

"I was not present, Captain."

"That was unfortunate, but I can give you my word that the draw was done with scrupulous fairness and witnessed by the eighteen men present. They can vouch for the integrity of the method used and verify the honesty of the occasion."

"So I must go off then, without knowing for how long or when leave of absence may be granted."

"That is the soldier's way, Herbert. That is the way that armies are run. Your commanding officer will be Major Harris, who is in charge of the south Norfolk coastal defences."

Herbert Peters was not placated. "As you say, Captain, but there would be no need to send old soldiers to war if so many young men had not been wasted for nothing."

Captain Fairbairn was shocked to his very soul. "Surely you cannot believe that when our country is under attack and our military honour is at stake."

"What do you want me to believe when tens of thousands of our young men are killed in a day and yet we are still held in Flanders?"

"That is modern warfare, Herbert."

"Men charging machine guns! That is not warfare, Captain, I would call it something else."

"Are you refusing to go to Norfolk – is that the whole point of this?"

"Nay, I'll go but do not make any more promises that cannot be kept."

The President of the Court-Martial intoned the sentence. "22084, Private Harty, having been found guilty on all counts is sentenced to six months detention in a Military Prison. However, as such a prison is not available you will serve the same period on Field Punishment Number One at the base camp at Etaples, and on completion of this term you will be dishonourably discharged from the army and handed over to the civil power for further trial. Is there anything you wish to say?"

"The Bible saith that 'man that is born of a woman is of a few days, and full of troubles', but I will not give up my faith. Forget not God's power. You pull down God's servants at your peril, for it is said clear, 'the ungodly shall not stand in the judgement nor sinners in the congregation of the righteous'."

The only light came from the gun flashes flickering against the night sky and the explosion of the shells. In the dark the Ox and Bucks men braced themselves because it was obvious the enemy suspected their presence and their guns were accurately aligned, though it was 'D' Company on the left flank that was suffering worst of all. Already two complete teams of Lewis Gunners had been destroyed and the casualty list reached fourteen men before the supporting bombardment started at 4.25 am. Eight minutes later the battalion advanced.

The enemy front line was reached with few casualties and Edward Holling organised his section. He and Harold had been designated to set up a relay post when the first objective was reached and the section were to act as runners between the attacking companies and battalion headquarters. He beckoned Freddie Coxe over.

"Freddie – go straight back to Captain Stevens and say that we have reached the first objective and the 'Blue Line' is taken. Casualties light."

"On my way, Edward."

"Well run like hell."

The group watched as the barrage lifted forward and the battalion advanced to the second objective. Already the mopping-up platoon was searching along the trench to seek out any enemy hiding deep down in the dugouts and the muffled explosion of Mills Bombs echoed up the concrete steps. The Battalion halted momentarily in front of the second objective then as soon as the barrage stopped the leading companies surged forward and dropped into the second line trench. Over to the left a number of Bosch machine guns started to spray bullets along the second line trench and men started to fall back from the next advance. Quickly Edward briefed John Howe. "Say there is heavy infilade fire from Oppy Village, I'll write down the reference, our men are held up at the second trench."

Hastily he checked the map and scribbled down the reference and the slip of paper was thrust into John's hand.

"Keep that safe – now go like double hell!"

George Coates beckoned William Smithe to his side. They had just helped to halt a counter attack by the enemy on the recently taken trench.

"You did well there, lad! Where did you learn to throw a bomb?"

William was very pleased. "It's just like delivering a cricket ball, Corporal."

"Have you had any training?"

"Only a few practice throws at the range during training."

George Coates nodded in satisfaction. "You're a natural, lad. I shall ask if you can join our team."

A shell exploding nearby drowned out William's answer and there was no time to repeat it as the shout went out that another attack was developing.

The Colonel peered over Alfred Stevens shoulder. "Have you finished that report, Alfred?"

"Nearly done, Sir. It's been a bad few days, we've lost over two hundred officers and men. A hundred or so prisoners have gone into the cage. I feel it's fair to say we did as good a job as the circumstances allowed."

"Headquarters won't be satisfied with a gain of eight hundred yards."

"We are in desperate need of replacements, Sir. We are five hundred under establishment, half our supposed strength."

"Replacements have been promised, Alfred. They are due now."

"We get a lot of promises, Sir."

"I know that Vicky is well, Mother, she has made a splendid recovery but now that I have to go to Norfolk she must remain here, in Thame." Herbert Peters felt he must put his foot down firmly as the master of the house.

Beatrice Peters was unsure. "Nurse Healey has said that Vicky is needed at Dover and the matron is asking for her to return."

"Our business is at risk! This war must end some time and our prosperity rests on the shop – and that includes Vicky and Mary. If I hadn't been instructed to go to Norfolk on this damn silly business it may be different. As the head of the house I will not allow Vicky to go back."

"She will be upset, Father."

"She can do voluntary work at the Thame Red Cross Hospital – as before. Surely the men there are in need of nursing!"

"What does the paper say about the war, Father?"

Herbert glanced down the columns. "Nothing much happening, Mother. Very quiet according to the paper. One wonders what is going on." He turned to the next page. "Oh, here's something. Mr Wykeham-Musgrave, owner of Thame Park, died peacefully in his home in Gloucestershire – four days ago. Now there's a thing. It seems like only yesterday when he were striding about here as large as life and trying to run us over in his great limousine."

As a mark of respect, Joss Parker removed his bowler hat before stepping into the Agents Office. "Mornin', Mister Sims. I came as soon as I were able. My leg 'as been a mite fractious of late." He hoped he might be offered a chair but no offer was forthcoming.

"Good day to you, Parker. This will only take a few minutes. You have heard of the master's death?" Parker nodded. "Good, I did not want to be the first to tell you."

"Aye, it were a great shock to me after all these years of serving him and his father before."

"Times are greatly changing, Parker. We must change with them."

"I hope as how the young master will visit afore long, so I can take him on a tour." Parker smiled, if a little sadly. "I can remember doing it for his father – as clear as yesterday."

Mr Sims coughed and shuffled his papers. "That will not be necessary. I have been instructed to close down all the estate operations. You will receive one week's pay in lieu of notice and you will vacate the lodge four weeks on Saturday."

"Upon my soul, Mr Sims, doan we even get a word of thanks for all the years . . . . this has been my life. It will come terrible hard after all this time. What does the young master say?"

"I've no idea, my instructions came from the main agent. Should you wish to vacate the lodge at an earlier date please let me know, so I can take stock and lock up."

"But what of the deer? Without constant repair they will be out through the fence before the summer is over and the farmers will complain."

"The deer are to be cleared out in ten days. Marksmen and lorries from the abattoir will be there at dawn. You are welcome to participate if you wish."

Parker gently shook his head in sorrow. "Nay, I could not bring myself to slaughter them."

Mr Sims stood up. "Well, it must be done! The world moves on. Good day, Parker. Please excuse me but other pressing matters need attention."

"But the dogs, Mr Sims, I cannot take the dogs into the town with me."

"There is a cottage empty – the old Attington Pike House. Tell Mr Price I sent you, I'm sure he will let you rent and there's plenty of space."

Rose Guntrippe was most concerned. Alice Harty had obviously been crying because her eyes were red raw from the handkerchief. Worse than that was her appearance, her face was gaunt and she had lost weight. When she saw Rose, she almost collapsed in anguish. Rose put out her hands to steady her.

"What's the matter, Alice? What has happened?" For a moment she thought that Alice had been told that Albert had been killed. "'Tis not Albert – is it?"

At the first expression of sympathy, Alice disintegrated into sobs and tears. "No, 'tis even worse, Rose – the bugger is still alive!"

"What's the problem then – what has happened?"

"Two weeks ago I went to get the allowance for me and the kids but there were none. It's been stopped – not a penny to be had!"

"But why, Alice, why? Did they say why?"

"He has been sent to prison for six months. There will be no allowance."

"You said a fortnight, Alice? What has happened since then, what have you done? Come into the milking shed and sit down."

"Now, wipe your eyes and tell me everything."

Alice slowly got her emotions under control and the sobbing died away. "At – at first it were fine. I had a few shillin' saved and I thought as how a mistake had been made and would be put right. But it were no mistake."

"You don't look well, Alice. When did you last eat?"

Alice would not look Rose in the eye, so Rose's suspicions multiplied. "As I thought – you've not been eating!"

"There is not enough money. I went to the Workhouse to ask for out-relief but the Union Secretary will only provide six shillings a week and when the rent is paid, well there's . . . . "

Her voice tailed off in despair. "I shall have to take all the children to the Workhouse."

Rose bridled. "Nonsense – I'll not have that. The Workhouse is no place for four young children. There's plenty here. Carrots, onions, cabbage and potatoes in the bottom field. Milk in the churn and eggs in the barn. Get off home now and bring a bag. And wipe those tears away – crying over a man!"

She watched Alice hurry away. As she turned back to work she was aware that James Roberts was standing at the entrance of the barn, silently watching her.

"Sorry, James. I did not know you were there."

He was silent for a while before answering. "Are you going to take on all the lame dogs of this world, Rose?" It was not said unkindly but Rose could see that he was serious.

"Not all the world, but Alice is a friend. A special case. Her husband was with my husband when he was killed. I don't know why her husband is in prison but I say this – he wouldn't even be in France but for this senseless, heartless war."

"He were not much of a gentleman from what I'm told."

"Alice do not want a gentleman – she 'as four kids, she needs a provider – or, better still, a job."

"Is there no place for a man in your life, Rose?"

Rose laughed. "What man will want a woman of my age with two boys and a dependent mother-in-law?"

"This man would."

"Are you serious – or . . . . "

"None more serious, Rose. Why, you are only thirty an' the sight of you gladdens my eyes and quickens my blood."

Rose gave him a long hard stare and he dropped his gaze before she spoke, as if embarrassed at his boldness. "Is it marriage you offer or a tumble in the hay?"

"I said serious, Rose. Marriage. Will you marry me?"

"It must be a full marriage, James. There will be no nightgowns and nightshirts in my bed but plenty of loving. Do you agree."

"You will be my joy."

"Then I accept, James Roberts." She stepped forward and grabbed the front of his shirt. "Kiss me!" Her hand felt at his belt buckle. "It will be fifteen minutes afore Alice can get back, show me how you make love."

"There be no time, Rose – what if someone comes in?"

"Then they'll see your backside going up and down, so stop worrying."

"But I worry for your reputation, my love."

She released his belt and dropped her hand down his trouser front. "You only need have one worry – that's if they don't hear me groaning with pleasure. Now get those trousers off!"

Because the weather was chilly for the time of the year and to placate her mother, Victoria Peters had wrapped a scarf around her neck and put on a pair of mittens. She left the shop and proceeded down the High Street to Church Lane, then turned along to the Red Cross Hospital in the old school house.

Nurse Healey was so intense in her scrutiny Vicky could almost feel the searching eyes probing at her body, so she felt compelled to speak. "I trust you did not think me forward, Nurse Healey, in asking to see you but I really do feel able to resume my duties."

Inside the mittens she kept two pairs of fingers crossed.

Nurse Healey reflected for a moment. "Let me see your hand." Her fingers probed at Vicky's left hand. "Does that hurt?"

"No. The hand is a little stiff – that is all."

"Good, the inflammation has receded and the scar has knitted together."

"You will let me come back then?"

"Give it another two weeks, Vicky. Best to be on the safe side though goodness knows we need your help."

"I had thought you might want me to go back to Dover."

"The Matron has said she will ask if there is an emergency, in the meantime she has asked me to give you more training – she believes you will make an excellent theatre nurse one day."

Vicky smiled her appreciation. "I hope that is a promise. Father wants me to stay at home but . . . . "

The 'A' company commander studied his watch. The covering bombardment had been falling on the enemy trenches for over seventeen minutes. On eighteen minutes he would signal the advance. The seconds ticked away. He wished the return fire was less intense, already he had lost three men. Six, five, four, three, two, one. Go! As he went over the parapet he could see that the company to his left were already on the move. Forty yards to the rear the two remaining companies and the runners moved forward. Edward Holling overcame his desire to run as enemy shells and machine gun fire shredded the leading companies despite the covering bombardment raking the German positions. Over to the left, more enemy machine guns opened up from an old factory building and the wood further up looked forbidding.

The whole attack ground to a halt in the shell holes that marked the sloping ground. John Howe leaned over and shouted to make himself heard above the noise.

"Shall I go back and report, Edward?"

Edward Holling shook his head violently. "No, we've strict orders not to report until the first trench is taken."

Nearer to the front a few enterprising men found a way to crawl forward in the mud and they got a toe-hold in the first enemy trench. Within minutes another platoon made a desperate attack and as the Germans retreated the two leading companies ran into the first objective but the return fire was too strong for any of the men to go further.

Captain Alfred Stevens pondered on his responsibility, the letter to Brigade still unfolded. The letter requested the early transfer of Edward Holling and Harold Jones for officer training. Mind made up he twisted the letter and lit a match. The burning letter gave him no great satisfaction but it eased his conscience. There was no greater percentage of casualties than those that occurred among the newly joined Second Lieutenants. Today they had lost four, not one over the age of twenty. No, he decided, the six lads were safer where he could keep an eye on them. He felt he owed them that much. His thoughts were disturbed as the Colonel stepped inside the dugout.

"Diary complete, Sir, and report ready for Brigade if you will sign it."

"We could have held out, Alfred, if only we could have got some ammunition forward. Brigade will roast me over this loss of the two Vickers."

"Brigade are always disappointed, Sir, but the facts speak for themselves. We lost three hundred men – that's fifty eight per cent of our total! Our men couldn't have done more."

The two men puffed cigarettes while contemplating the situation.

"The world is full of bloody promises, Alfred. D'you know that? We are promised more replacements. The Bosch are nearly done for, we have found a way to reduce casualties, the war will be over this year, we can retire for a rest, the Americans will be here soon – nothing but bloody broken promises!"

Beatrice Peters dissolved in a flood of tears when Herbert embraced her as the train pulled into Thame Station. A newcomer to the station may not have taken much notice, it was a common daily sight as soldiers left to rejoin their units. In this case though, they may have pondered a little because the uniform was new and ill-fitting, the peaked cap rather flat, and the man rather old to be going off to war. "Now, now, Mother, what will people think! I shall be home in no time – just you see."

Herbert turned and kissed Vicky and then Mary, on the cheek. "Take care of Mother. Now don't forget, you must get the order to the wholesaler, sharp, every Wednesday." Then he turned his whole attention to Mary. "And no credit, young lady!" Mary had a soft heart. "And don't be sending free parcels to that young man of yours. That's the army's responsibility –why you're not even engaged!" Mary wrinkled her nose in reply and that did nothing to relieve Herbert's concern.

Vicky put his case in the nearest compartment. Herbert had refused to limit himself to an army pack, that would seem to acknowledge that he was a real soldier and there were certain comforts that he would not leave behind.

Beatrice continued to sob. "We've never been parted, not once in twenty four years."

Mary put her arm around her. "Father will come to no harm. Not in this lovely weather." The sobs became louder.

Herbert stepped up into the train and closed the door. The train gave a convulsive judder and steam billowed up. The guard waved his green flag and blew his whistle and the train pulled away. They stood waving until the train was out of sight.

"Where did Father say he was going?" Beatrice continued to dab at the tears with her handkerchief.

"Waxham, Mother," Mary took her arm, "by Yarmouth."

"Oh, I do hope he'll be alright."

"The weather's fine, Father will be beside the sea. It will be just like a holiday for him."

Beatrice brightened. "D'you think so, Mary? It will be a comfort if it is true."

Vicky took Beatrice's other arm. "It will be a nice holiday by the seaside."

To the south of Ypres on the western front the thunder had continued for days as thousands of guns poured tens of thousands of shells into the German defences on the ridges that overlooked the British lines. Each day more guns came into use and the violence escalated. There was no escape from the thunder by either defenders or attackers and it went on for twelve days. Two miles behind the front line the Ox and Bucks men listened. Tired men who had spent days and nights moving supplies forward and mining spoil back to be hidden from enemy eyes. At three in the morning of 6th June, nearly twenty great explosive mines were detonated under the German positions and the ground moved as if struck by an earthquake. The prelude to Passchendaele, the attack on the Messines Ridge, had begun.

The letter was unexpected and Sidney Barnes scrutinised it for some minutes before breaking open the envelope. He suspected that the handwriting was his father's, as usual the writing was neat italic script, and a quick glance at the letter confirmed his suspicion. It was the news that shook him to the core. The master was dead! Joss Parker had been thrown out and the Park and House were up for sale with the whole estate. Farms for miles around included. Many in an uproar at the loss of tenancies. Sidney read the letter over and over but the words never varied. His father still had a job to help maintain the gardens but who could say what a new owner would do! And all the deer slaughtered! Sidney felt his hopes for the future wither and die. Since returning from leave he had known a brief period of intense happiness with the feeling that his future was assured. In his mind he had planned the future of the game facilities on the estate, he would make it the best shoot in Oxfordshire. Now it was all dust in his mouth. He was somewhat relieved to get the order to report to the Adjutant, but puzzled to find George Coates had got the same order and was waiting by the Headquarters dugout.

A few minutes later Sergeant Major Crook called them in. Alfred Stevens looked up from his mass of papers. "Stand at ease!"

George Coates could not contain himself. "Have we done summat wrong, Sir?"

"No, nothing wrong. You're both needed to train others. It will mean going to Etaples for four to six months. However, the Colonel has said this duty must be voluntary."

George Coates could hardly contain himself. "I'll go, Sir." Already he could feel the welcoming embrace of a friendly bar, a warm bed and decent meals.

"You will be promoted to full corporal for this duty. What about you, Corporal Barnes?"

"Aye, I'll do it, Sir."

"You don't sound pleased, Corporal."

"'Tis not that, Sir. I was but thinking I had best use my skills while I can. There will be no use for a man with a gun when this war is finished."

"There will surely be a need for a skilled gamekeeper when this war is over, Corporal."

"Have you not heard, Sir. Thame Park is to be sold, the word is no keepers are required."

William Smithe opened the notebook. "How much?"

The Corporal sucked his teeth. "What's the odds?"

"Twenty to one the Sergeant Major, ten to one Sergeant Hobbs, nine to one Corporal Peel, seven to one Barclay, Warren and Crewe. Two to one Coxe. The rest five to one."

"I'll have a franc on Warren."

James Pullene checked the takings. James was good at arithmetic and it was his job to make sure they made a profit. "I wish there was a cricket match. Why do we always have football?"

The Battalion was at rest and today was its sports day. Already the first round of the inter-company football matches had been played. Now it was the turn of the athletes. Over on the firing range the rifles cracked out as the finalists of the inter-platoon shooting match tried to bring down the falling plates within the set minute.

Freddie Coxe had already won the quarter mile race. If he continued with his usual form the 'Book' would make a handsome profit. The half-mile race was about to start as William and James made their way to the track to cheer him on.

Captain Stevens barred their way. "I'll have ten francs on Freddie for the half-mile."

"Ten francs, Sir – you'll break the book!"

"Five francs then."

"I'll mark it down, Sir. If we could stand by the officers' enclosure it would better the odds, Sir."

"You mean you want me to approve of illegal betting? What will the Colonel say?"

"His servant has just bet on A company for the football and mc in the 'Bombers' competition, on behalf of the Colonel, Sir."

"I should have insisted on more discipline when you were at school."

Herbert Peters felt utterly miserable and far from home. Not only that but the futility of his duty gnawed at his respect for the sense of his superiors. The sea wall to the north of Waxham stretched out in front of him and despite the fact that it was August he could feel the chill in the wind and rain coming in off the North Sea. The rain dripped from his waterproof cape.

Apart from a few seabirds he could have been the only person in the world. He wondered what he would do if an invasion started. First there was the problem of recognition. He had no binoculars. Then there was the telephone. That was a mile away, a mile over shingle. Shingle that sapped the energy and, because of its instability, could easily lead to a sprained ankle. His personal assessment told him that should a German invasion fleet appear out of the haze the invasion force would have landed and been on its way to London before his ageing commander had got his twenty geriatric guards together to repulse it.

A ringed plover startled him as it flew up from under his feet and he listened for its call but all he could hear was the wind and the lap of water on the foreshore. He plodded on, praying that it would soon be mid-day and his relief would take over and he could climb aboard on the old truck and trundle back to base for a cup of tea.

It was then that the awful reality struck him. This was August. English summer! What would it be like in October and November? He shut his mind to it, for the moment.

"Sergeant Hagan tells me you are an excellent cook, Oxenlade."

Peter Oxenlade was very nervous, he would probably have quaked in terror except that he had met Captain Stevens when he was Quartermaster.

"Thank you, Sir."

"Where did you learn your trade?"

"From Sergeant Hagen, Sir, afore that I were a baker. I really wanted to be a rifleman, Sir. That's why I enlisted."

Alfred Stevens sighed gently. "Yes, you have told me a dozen times, Oxenlade but we must do the job we are best at. However, I do want to ask you to do a different job."

Peter Oxenlade brightened considerably. "Anything you say, Sir."

"I know that it is normal in the army to give an order and expect it to be obeyed. This is a different situation. I want you to volunteer to cook for the Officers Mess. When we are in the line you will be with headquarters company and you will make sure the officers are fed – but cooking will be limited. Behind the lines we will operate normal mess routine."

"Do you'm mean I will be in the front line with the battalion, Sir?"

"Yes."

"I accept, Sir – its what I've always wanted."

"Good. You are promoted to Lance Corporal with immediate effect and you will take over tomorrow. Now go and speak to Corporal Sims and find out what the Colonel likes – and more important, what he doesn't like!"

"Send the next man in, Sergeant Major."

James Pullene stepped in the doorway and saluted.

"Ah, good morning, Pullene. If I remember correctly you had excellent results in Maths and English at school. You went to the bank, I believe?"

"Yes, Sir."

"Good. I am going to appoint you Orderly Room Clerk, with immediate effect."

James Pullene showed his disappointment. "I'd rather not, Sir."

Alfred Stevens brushed his remark aside. "That's an order, Pullene. You are promoted to Lance-Corporal with immediate effect. Now go with the Sergeant Major, try to look cheerful, and he will explain your job to you."

"Even without more rain the ground is the worst I've ever seen, Sir."

'A' Company Commander voiced the views that most of the other officers held but in the main suppressed. "The shell holes are already filling with water."

The Colonel of the Ox and Bucks nodded in agreement. "The saving grace is that this advance will take all the high ground in four days right through to Passchendaele. Then it will be our turn to put the Bosch on the anvil."

The Commander of 'B' Company voiced his concern. "Our men are very tired. Bringing up supplies through the mud has been a real trial and we lost sixteen men in that last gas attack."

"Alfred, you had better have your say."

"Thank you, Sir. As you know I have had the Scout Parties out inspecting the front for several days. Our objective is the village of

Langemarck. The whole assembly route has been checked and the markers are in position. The main problem is the Steenbeck, it's only a large brook but the ground around it is marshy. We were told that the KR's were over the brook and it had been bridged. Neither is true. I have found extra bridging materials but we will need to delegate one platoon in each company to carry the boards forward and construct a bridge."

"Can the bridges be made up and taken forward ready assembled?"

"The tracks are narrow, only part assembly is possible."

"What if we do this in the night before the attack?"

Alfred Stevens made a note. "I shall talk to the Engineers today. It would really help if we could get across in the night and make some strongpoints on the far bank. If only it would stop raining."

A gloomy 'D' Company Commander peered out of the dugout door. "My men say this is set for several days – and they are rarely wrong about the weather."

The telephone gave two rings, Alfred picked it up. "The 'show' is delayed, Sir. To give the weather a chance to improve."

James Roberts rose to his feet and rapped the table with a spoon. "Ladies and . . . . "

The assembled company paid him no attention. Robert Guntrippe was busy punching a cousin who had made a rude remark. Old Mrs Guntrippe was still waiting for someone to cut her meat into small pieces and was complaining loudly and bitterly at the delay. James's brother-in-law was engaged in a wrestling match with two of the waiters over the retention of two bottles of champagne he had liberated from the bar without paying for them. The brother-in-law's wife was trying to kick the nearest waiter whom she thought was unjustly attacking her husband. The dining room manager of the 'Spread Eagle' was desperately trying to organise the serving of wine for the toast but one waitress had run off into the kitchen to bathe a swollen eye and most of the wine had already been purloined from the servery.

James tried again. "Ladies and gentlemen!"

Alice Harty gave a whoop. "There's none o' those here!"

James persevered. "Today is a happy occasion. I . . . . " He was drowned out as his brother-in-law was floored by a blow to the head and the guilty waiter was stunned by a bottle to his left ear.

Rose Roberts, nee Guntrippe, put out a hand and pulled James back into his seat. "No matter, Husband, let them be."

James looked chastened. "I wanted this to be a special day, not a battlefield!"

Rose put a finger to his lips. "It is a special day – an' doan you forget it." She looked around at their riotous guests and family. "Tomorrow they'll remember nothing, but let them be. I've not had such a good laugh for many a day."

"Perhaps you're right, Rose, there is so little laughter these days. I just wish so many had not forgot their manners."

"Get the pianist. Let's get them all dancing."

"Do you mind, Wife?"

"Nay, this be a bag o' moonshine day now the vicar has had his say." She waved her left hand to show her wedding ring. "An' tell the pianist – no military two-steps!"

The battalion had spent the previous night carrying dozens of pontoons from the Engineers camp to a forward dump. Ready for the attack. It had been a memorable experience in the thunder and blustery rain. Not that tonight was a great deal better as the troops huddled in the front line trenches, except that a small party of men were taking advantage of the dark foul night to lay a small bridge across the stream that flowed northward. Some men were already across and cutting the wire that blocked further progress.

Edward Holling and the headquarters' runners blessed their luck. For once the Headquarters was established in an old German concrete blockhouse. There was little in the way of comfort but at least it was large enough for all the headquarters' staff, including both the Runners and Scouts, to be sheltered from the worst of the weather.

At 3.45 the Royal Artillery opened the bombardment and it was no longer possible to either sleep or speak and be heard. An hour later, the battalion moved forward, struggling to keep on the duckboards while the leading men put the pontoons into position. It was not yet daylight but the enemy had got wind of the attack and huge numbers of starshells were fired over No Man's Land to provide illumination. So great was the relief at moving forward that almost without exception every man lit a cigarette and, despite the clinging mud, made a determined effort to stay as close to the rolling barrages as the Artillery cranked up the elevation of the guns on a minute by minute basis.

In the second line of advance, Edward Holling kept his small group of runners under tight control and within sight of the Colonel in case a message needed to be relayed on. Enemy machine gun fire was intense but luckily, it was mainly directed at targets to their right. Suddenly over a hundred prisoners appeared out of the gloom and Edward was ordered to take the runners forward into the shelter of a captured blockhouse.

As the light strengthened the left flank company began to suffer heavy losses and Edward could see the bodies lying on the ground and men dodging from shell hole to shell hole, but men had reached the first objective and could be seen consolidating their defences in case of counter attack.

The Colonel called to the Intelligence Officer. "Henry, take two runners forward to the left and check on the precise situation in C and D Companies. Send a runner back as soon as you have made an assessment. Check on the progress of the KR's." The Intelligence Officer called out. "Corporal Holling. Bring one man and follow me."

Freddie Coxe was already half way back to the blockhouse when the German counter-attack started. A and D Companies had one hundred casualties but, most important, had maintained contact with the Somerset Light Infantry on the left so the flank was safe. Edward had the satisfaction of helping A Company throw back the German attack and was somewhat disappointed when the Intelligence Officer decided to carry on up the trench line to the right so he could check on the right flank. As they set out the German artillery opened fire on the newly taken positions.

Edward and the Intelligence Officer had reached Alouette Farm and turned back towards base when the shell caught them in the open. Edward had heard the shrieking 'whizz' as the shell arrived and had automatically ducked down.

Through the mist of pain and shock, Edward could hear someone talking to him. Then he was aware of being lifted. Once he regained consciousness but it was dark and he could not see the faces of the four stretcher-bearers taking him back to the field dressing station. It was the beginning of a journey that would take several days. A painful journey relieved by morphine, of partial and disjointed memories that had no beginning or end.

Back at the front the battalion was already marching back to sanctuary, glad to leave the front line but one hundred and ninety men did not march with them. Harold Jones, John Howe, Freddie Coxe, James Pullene and William Smithe were especially subdued. They could not believe that one of their number had been struck down, they had no knowledge of Edward's whereabouts or what had now happened to him, except that he had been wounded. Only one man in the whole battalion was exhilarated. Peter Oxenlade had been instructed to prepare menus. He was going to earn his stripe by the provision of proper meals for the officers after weeks of cutting sandwiches and making tepid stews and weak tea.

Edward Holling knew that he was dreaming. The dream faded then strengthened, sometimes he could hear voices. There was one that persisted, a woman's voice that called his name and begged his attention. He wanted to respond but somehow he was unable to move. Once he opened his eyes but he could see nothing against the blinding glare that surrounded him. Edward pondered this problem but could make no sense of it so he pushed it to one side and surrendered to the dark.

"Edward! Edward, please speak to me." He could feel the tugging at his hand then a cool touch on his face. He knew that voice, it was his mother. The voice spoke again. "How is he, Doctor? Will he get well."

"I think he stands a good chance, Mrs Holling. He is young – and strong."

Edward opened his eyes and focussed. Mrs Holling gave a sob of joy. "Oh, Edward – you're awake!"

"Where am I?"

"In hospital – Boulogne."

Edward was suddenly aware that someone else had answered. Then he understood. It was his father.

"What are you doing here?"

"We got a telegram to say you . . . . were unwell. So we came straight away." Mrs Holling wiped a tear from her eye.

"Everything will be fine now, Edward, now you are on the mend." Edward Holling, Senior, sounded as sombre as ever.

"What of Vicky? Has Vicky been told?"

The silence told Edward more than a spoken answer. "Vicky has . . . ."

"Miss Peters is not family, Edward. She has no need to know. This is a family matter!" Holling, Senior, tried to end the subject.

"I will not forgive you if she is not told." Edward started to twist in the bed, his mind told him that he must get up.

A nurse stepped forward. "I think it best if you leave now, Mrs Holling. He is still very weak."

Captain Alfred Stevens read the report from the base hospital and noted that Edward Holling was listed as wounded. He said a quiet prayer of relief, pleased that he would not have to write a bereavement letter to his parents. Then he returned to the matter in hand as John Howe appeared and saluted.

"The Sergeant-Major said you wished to see me, Sir."

"Yes, Howe, very serious news I'm afraid. Your mother is dangerously ill and the Vicar of St Mary's has asked that you be given compassionate leave. Did you know that your mother is ill?"

"The last letter said she was unwell, Sir – but not dangerously ill."

"Normally I could not let you go but as we are at rest, and with God's blessing, liable to be here for several weeks, I am going to grant you two weeks leave as a special privilege."

"Thank you, Sir."

"When you reach Thame I want you to go and see the Headmaster for me. Will you do that?"

"Yes, Sir."

"Give him this letter and tell him how we are all doing. Above all, say we are winning – do you understand?"

"Trust me, Sir – I'm your man!"

Mary Peters nearly vaulted over the counter as John Howe marched into the shop.

"You never said you were coming home, John! Oh, I'm so glad to see you."

He pursed his lips. "Do I get a kiss – a hero's welcome?"

"Oh, you saucy thing." But she kissed him all the same.

John dropped his pack. "I've come straight from the station. On my way home but I had to drop in to tell you about Edward."

"Edward! Vicky is beside herself with worry, Edward hasn't written for over three weeks."

"Has no-one told you, he was wounded during the attack on Langemarck. We've heard nothing since but he must be alive!"

"Vicky will be so pleased." Mary frowned. "Why are you home now?"

"Word came that my mother is very ill. Captain Stevens gave me special leave."

The welcome vanished entirely from Mary's face. "Have you not heard, John? The letter must have been delayed. Your mother died ten days ago and the funeral was last week."

John Howe looked dejected. "I had no idea, Mary – I must hurry home. Do you know what happened, this all seems so sudden."

"Vicky spoke to your father. Your mother had to be taken to hospital – her heart. She passed away very quickly."

"Tell Vicky I will call later but tell her that Mr Holling must know, the army always tells the next of kin."

Victoria had been shown into Edward Holling's study by a rather subdued maid. Edward Holling, Senior, did not stand to greet her but motioned to a chair. "Please sit, Miss Peters."

"Good morning, Mr Holling. I think you know why I am here."

"Yes, Miss Peters, I can guess. What I do not understand is why you consider you have the right to intrude on the grief of my family."

Vicky gasped in shock. "You mean that Edward is dead?"

"No, Miss Peters, but he is seriously ill. It is my contention that this is the concern of his mother and myself, though I do not take exception to enquiries. After all, this war is of concern to us all."

"I had hoped you would tell me how Edward is and give me his address so that I can write to him."

"You must appreciate that I do not, and will not, approve of any relationship between you and my son. Edward is as well as can be expected having received serious wounds. This is not the time to subject him to emotional and futile attachments that have no place in his future."

"You have not answered my question, Mr Holling."

"And you, young woman, are impertinent. The best I can say is that Edward is progressing – slowly. The doctors believe he will recover."

"Thank you, Mr Holling. I should like to write to him."

"I will consider your request, Miss Peters."

"You do realise that Edward and I are promised to each other, Mr Holling?"

"Empty promises. Like so many others in this world today. Good day, Miss Peters." He rang the bell.

"Please show Miss Peters to the door."

John Howe had found his father grieving but it had been a grief he did not want to share, that he seemed unable to share. John found that strange because he had never considered his father as an emotional man. He had always seemed to be a tower of silent strength following quietly behind the more vivacious personality of his wife. Now that she had gone there seemed to be no purpose to his life and although John had tried to talk to him, there was no response. He voiced his worries to Mary.

"Father is becoming a recluse, Mary. He never wants to leave the house."

"He misses your mother, he just needs a little time."

"Do you think he loved her? I never thought there might be love between them. They seemed so old."

Mary smiled. "I do believe you wouldn't recognise love if it smacked you right between the eyes."

"I love you, Mary."

"Will you love me for a lifetime? When I'm grey and wrinkled? As your father loved your mother."

"Aye – I will. If you will let me!"

"Then you had better ask me – that Ernest Shaw at the pork butchers keeps coming to the shop and making eyes at me – and hinting."

John sniffed in disdain. "Ernie Shaw – pah! He's an old man. When this war is over we shall be wed."

"I haven't said yes."

"Then you better had, my girl, afore I get snapped up by another. I'm back to France tomorrow."

Mary ran from the shop through to the kitchen. "Vicky! Vicky! A letter from France."

Vicky opened the letter with trembling hands, tearing the envelope in her haste. There were tears in her eyes when she looked up. "Oh, Mary. It's from a hospital. Edward is safe." She read to the end. "He asked the nurse to write to me to say he is doing well and I am not to worry." She laughed out loud, "Not to worry – how can I do anything else!"

Beatrice Peters had listened to all of this with great concern. "Where is he, Vicky?"

"He is in the Military Hospital at Boulogne. I must go and see him, Mother. I must, I really must."

"Of course you must. We can manage for a few days, can't we, Mary. Especially now I've got the measure of these ration cards."

"Then I will speak to Nurse Healey today. I'm going whether Mr Holling approves or not."

John Howe sat with the other runners from midnight on as they awaited the zero hour call to advance. This waiting was always the worst part of any attack. Tonight was made worse by the falling gas shells and the men had to sit or stand around in gas masks for hours on end. In their packs were the dry rations that had been issued before assembling, but none could be eaten. All the men had been briefed on what lay ahead and John wondered if the defences ever varied. Yet again, they would be advancing against concrete pill-boxes and blockhouses. The assembly route had been thick with mud, often several feet thick, the assembly trenches were heavy with mud. They had every reason to believe that No Man's Land would be worse. Once the supporting bombardment started the noise was so great that, even without gas masks, talk would have been impossible. Harold Jones lifted himself up and gestured at John and the other runners. It was time to move forward. There was no sound of prayer but many a silent prayer was repeated. Full of hope they surged forward. There would only be two hundred and nine casualties today but for the moment hope reigned supreme.

"How many acres have we, James?"

James scratched at his temple before answering, as if to stir up his memory. "Well it depends. Own or lease?"

"Both then." Rose remained calm although she had been about to say a sharp word. James was always evasive when asked direct questions about the farm.

"You don't need to worry on such matters, Rose."

"How many acres?"

James downed the last of his breakfast. "Fifty acres is owned clear including the house and buildings. Then there is the meadows, they be near eighty acres and the arable is twenty acres which are held on tenancy."

"Mr Sims tells me that Thame Park is for sale and the parcel of land to the east, along past Blackditch, is for sale and that twenty farms are closing nearby."

"Aye, that's true. Though I cannot see why it interests you."

Rose gave him a sharp look. "As I recall we are married."

James pushed his plate to one side and patted his stomach. "True, and a fine wife you are."

"Doan you'm butterball me! What's wrong with getting more land?"

"How can we cope. 'Tis hard enough now even with Alice's help and young Robert doing what he can."

"With the farms closing there'll be animals and equipment going cheap, men will need work. This is the time to expand."

"'Tis not possible! This war makes men uncertain."

"I thought better of you, James. There's a fine team of horses at Swan Farm going begging. Mr Sims tells me we will get the east land for a thousand pounds, perhaps less."

"Why is that? I'll tell you. Because this is not the time to buy."

Rose gritted her teeth. "This is the very time. The sooner you agree, the sooner this will be settled."

James drew himself up. "This is not a wifely matter!"

"This farm and its future is a wifely matter."

"I never thought of you as a Suffragette!"

"Then you are due a few surprises, Husband."

Edward Holling could not bring himself to speak for several minutes as he clung to Vicky. The nurse looked on in some concern.

"He is still very weak, Miss. We mustn't overtire him."

Vicky pulled back. "Don't worry, Nurse. I understand."

She gazed at Edward. "I thought I had lost you, my love."

Edward held fast to her hand. "It seems so long – so long."

"I came as fast as the train and boat would travel."

The nurse interrupted. "I can only allow twenty minutes – doctor's orders!"

Vicky nodded. "Twenty minutes it is." She turned to Edward. "I'm not going back until I'm sure you're properly on the mend."

Edward was sleeping when Vicky spoke to the nurse. "I'll be off now but before I go tell me exactly what happened."

"Edward tells me you are a nurse."

"Yes."

"The shrapnel wounds were not so bad but he was not found for some time so he lost a lot of blood and dirt got in the wounds.

By the time he reached us he was in shock and the gas gangrene had taken hold. But I'm certain he will get better now – he couldn't understand why you didn't write or visit."

Vicky squared her shoulders. "No matter now. I shall stay until he is well on the mend. Now I must go and write to my mother."

"Royal Mail for you, Peddelle." The Orderly Sergeant dropped the letter on Samuel's work-bench.

"For me, Sarge?" Samuel Peddelle never got mail.

"Strange as it may seem, yes!" The sergeant marched on and Samuel cautiously inspected the letter. Yes, the letter was for him but the postmark was blurred; slowly he opened it and read.

'Dear Peddelle,

Further to your representations to me earlier this year, I have approached our adoption services administrator to discuss your change of circumstances and put your case to be given knowledge as to your two daughters whereabouts, and/or details of the adoption arrangements including the possibility of divulging their names and addresses. It is with regret that I have to tell you that no such information can be given now or in the future. I am assured that the two girls have settled down happily with their new parents and are in good health. You need have no need for concern regarding their future happiness. The only matter which the adoption service is prepared to consider is that your daughters will be told of their natural parentage when they reach their majority.

Yours faithfully
Dr J Bird.

Samuel read the letter twice. The first time he didn't want to accept the message. The second time he refused to accept it but he was pleased that the Vicar had kept his word. His pride mended a little. Another pair of watertight boots dropped on to his ready pile. Later today the CQMS would collect the 'repairs' and say a few words of mild praise. Odd words of praise like, 'if these fall to pieces overnight I shall tell the Bosch your co-ordinates'. Then they would laugh and Samuel knew he was needed and respected. One day, he decided, he would see his girls again. That was a promise he told himself.

Nearly a couple of months had gone by since the Ox and Bucks were last in action. They had needed time to induct hundreds of reinforcements and consolidate their training. Now they were back in the front line waiting in reserve, as the German army attacked. For several days the Ox and Bucks companies surged forward to reinforce the regiments holding the line. This went on for a week. To and fro, attack and counter-attack, in miserably cold weather as the Third Battle of Ypres drew to a close. The Battle of Passchendaele was over. A year that had promised so much drifted to an end.

Chapter 5   1918: 'WE BAND OF BROTHERS'

Despite its lateness the delayed Christmas dinner had met with universal approval among the men of the battalion, after all, it was the one day in the year when everyone would sit down together to eat, drink and be merry. Today there had been plenty to eat even if it was plain and simple fare, but where, oh where were the barrels of beer! Drink was in short supply. But the concert more than made up for that as the cigarettes were distributed. Soon they were all singing.

> *"There's a long, long trail a-winding into the land of my dreams.*
> *Where the nightingales are singing and a white moon beams.*
> *There's a long, long night of waiting until my dreams all come true.*
> *'Til the day when I'll be going down that long, long trail with you."*

As the melody faded the Master of Ceremonies stepped to centre stage. "Thank you Private Bates, give him another clap, lads! . . . . Now the next act you've heard once or twice before but this time they have written new words to some old songs. Give a warm welcome to the Thamesian Belvederes!"

> *"If you were the only Hun in the world.*
> *And I had the only gun.*
> *Nothing else would matter at the front today,*
> *I would simply shoot you in the usual way.*
> *A bayonet for breakfast, a mortar for tea*
> *With nothing to spoil my aim . . . . "*

James Roberts read the letter with studied care before speaking. "The solicitor has asked us to call to see him when our business is done at the market. The deeds must be signed and the monies paid. Once that is done the new land is ours in freehold."

The post had not been delivered until breakfast was in progress and Rose and James had already been up four hours, morning work done and prepared for the weekly market in town. James had his eye on a dozen prime bullocks for fattening while Rose had twenty pounds of butter to sell. Rose bustled over from the kitchen range.

"Is the trap ready, James?" Rose enjoyed riding in the small light cart which always drew envious glances from the old neighbours.

"'Tis ready. On reflection, it was a good day when you persuaded me to offer on that extra land. I ne'er thought it would go so cheap. Why, I reckon we can double the dairy herd."

Rose bent over and kissed him on the cheek. "This farm will be the envy o' the district. Mark my word. We'll be winning prizes when the Thame Show returns."

"Oh, I dunno about that!"

"Now, James, are we agreed there'll be no arrangement with the Factor to sell the harvest before it comes in."

James shook his head and ruminated for a moment. "Well – er – that is a time honoured practice and shares the risk."

"Nonsense – prices are going up all the time. We must not sell short, we need the money!"

"For what do we need more money, Wife – we are comfortable."

"More land."

"More land, Rose!"

"You'm heard. More land. I want our sons to be farmers, not soldiers."

"There is a glory in soldiering. Why, there is little but mud and muck in farming."

"I'll tell you what is so, Husband. Having nothing is poverty an' there is more death than glory in soldiering."

James was not convinced. "More land means more work!"

Rose would not concede. "Aye, but land can be touched. Land endures and secures the future. Now, are you ready? When we have been to the solicitor I shall want to speak to the Agent."

Sergeant-Major Crook emptied a basket of wood on to his privileged fire and warmed his backside with evident pleasure. "Welcome back, both of you. I trust you enjoyed your leave!"

The two recipients of this warm greeting were unmoved, either by the sentiment or the inaccuracy of the words. Both were thinking that the softer life of the depot may be better than back here, near the front line. There was no evidence that life at the front had improved. Unperturbed by their silence the Sergeant-Major continued.

"You will not be going back to your old companies. Captain Stevens wants you to take charge of the Scouts."

"Oh!" George Coates was not sure that being under close observation by the headquarters staff was to his advantage. Sidney Barnes said nothing, preferring to wait on events but without committing himself.

The Sergeant-Major rubbed his hands together and flexed his fingers, he was constantly troubled by the pain at the base of his thumbs. "We've lost so many men over the last six months. Lack of experience is our problem. Plenty of young lads, plenty of enthusiasm but no experience. Sidney, you will be promoted to Sergeant. George, you will keep your second stripe."

Sidney brightened at this news. "I was thinking of staying on as a regular when this war is over, this may help me."

George Coates was appalled. "Regular! Gawd help us, Sidney, but you can't do that!"

"Now, now, George," Sergeant-Major Crook looked mildly affronted. "I'm a regular. Sidney could do worse. Why, I shall get my pension in two years, then I shall put my feet up."

"Well, I'm going home I tell'ee. As soon as the final bloody whistle is blown – I'm off." George sniffed in disgust. "First chance I get!"

The Colonel Commandant of the Depot maintained a severe expression, his lips hardly moved as he spoke. "The Provost Marshall has seen fit to make representations to me, Harty, regarding your time in punishment."

Albert Harty maintained a fixed expression on his face. An expression that attempted to convey that his total silence was a result of his deep respect of every word said to him and most certainly not dumb insolence. The Commandant continued.

"He reports that you have taken your punishment as a soldier should – with diligence, discipline and humility. He recommends that you be allowed to return to your unit rather than be discharged."

Albert had marched in fully expecting to be ignominiously discharged and handed over to the French Police to stand trial before a civil court. He had been warned to expect a lengthy jail sentence.

"Beggin' your pardon, Sir, but I want to stay in the army until this war is over."

"Your response is noted. However, this is the second time you have been punished. That reflects no credit on you or the army."

Albert wanted to go down on one knee but wisely remained at attention. "I have learned my lesson, Sir. I will not offend again if you will give me another chance. As God is my witness, Sir, and may he strike me down if I transgress."

"Good, that is what I like to hear, Harty." The Commandant walked around from his desk so he could speak quietly. "If you stand here once more I shall personally horse-whip you – d'you hear me, soldier?"

"Yes, Sir!"

Albert was so overcome with relief a tear appeared in his eye and trickled down his cheek.

"You had best be contrite, Harty – a few more tears would not go amiss. You will return to your regiment immediately, under escort. Sergeant Major!"

"Sir!"

"Have Private Harty removed from my camp within ten minutes."

The Medical Officer had given Edward Holling a minute and careful examination. "Lift your arms out to your sides – up level with the shoulders. Good. Try and hold it for a count of ten."

"My walking is better, Sir, I managed two turns of the hospital without halting."

The Medical Officer was a bit sceptical. "With the help of the nurse, no doubt."

"No, Sir. I won't get better that way."

"You've made remarkable progress, Corporal. The wounds have healed over – but no violent exercise. Now that you're able to travel, I'm sending you back to England."

"Where to, Sir?"

"That – that is out of my hands, but as you only need nursing it will most likely be one of the smaller hospitals."

"Mother! Mary!" Vicky rushed from the shop into the kitchen waving a letter in great excitement. "Edward is being sent to England – he is well enough to travel." She started to cry as Beatrice Peters put her arms around her.

"When is he coming back? Where is he being sent?" Mary found herself getting caught up in the excitement. Vicky re-read the letter.

"He doesn't say – only that it will be soon."

Beatrice had the solution. "I'm sure his mother must know – we can ask her."

Mary caught Vicky's look of alarm. Vicky had never told her mother of the meeting with Edward's father, only Mary.

"No, I don't think we should do that, Mother. Mr and Mrs Holling will have enough to consider. Edward will write soon. Nothing else matters now he is safe."

Captain Stevens had taken nearly three minutes to read through the list of reports detailing Private Harty's military career.

"You seem to take a delight in beating the living daylights out of military policemen, Harty. Do you realise you have spent more time on 'Field Punishment' than the rest of the battalion all put together? When is this going to end?"

The object of his scorn remained silent, at attention. "What have you to say for yourself, Harty?"

"I am like Daniel, Sir, who were cast into the lion's den, but God has delivered me up to serve his purpose, for, like Daniel who could not be hurt because of his belief in God, so am I."

"You are well versed in Bible sayings, Harty. It is a pity you show so little real understanding of them. If it were within my power I should refuse your release to this Regiment, however, no-one else will have you. Sergeant-Major!"

"Sir!"

"Private Harty is to be the battalion sanitary man. We will have the best kept bog-holes in the whole of France. March him out and put him to work!"

Victoria had no difficulty in finding the hospital in Dover, it was the very one at which she had served earlier. As she walked down the ward she noted that there was a calm that had not existed before and many of the men were sitting up and several were out of bed. One or two of the men even recognised her and cheery words of welcome followed her down the aisle.

Edward was thirty yards away when she first saw him and her heart bumped so hard she was sure that everyone could hear it. Then pleasure turned to alarm as Edward stood up and put out a hand to her, making her run the last ten yards to grab his arm.

"Take care, Edward – be careful!"

Conscious of the many watching eyes, Edward kissed her on the cheek. "I've been watching for hours – I wanted to surprise you."

"You've certainly done that – are you sure you're allowed up. It seems so soon!"

"The doctor has said the more I exercise, the quicker I will be discharged."

"You must still be careful, my love."

"I will – don't fret now. Let's walk on the balcony."

"Kiss me, Edward – there's no-one looking."

"I don't mind if there is. The doctor has said he will discharge me in four weeks time if I keep up this progress – he's going to give me a week's leave before I go back to the depot."

"Surely you will be discharged!"

"No – not for me, Vicky. Discharge would mean I'm disabled –
I'll not have that."

"Where is the depot?"

"At Cowley, love, not far from you."

"Well, I hope they keep you there until this war is over."

"Will you come to Dover when I get my leave. Stay with me, I
don't want to go home. There'll be nothing but arguments with
Father."

"I'll speak to Mother."

"Is your Father still in Norfolk?"

"Yes, and thoroughly fed up. Twice he was promised he would
be relieved and twice let down."

Edward Holling eased himself into the privileged seat in the
stalls having ensured that Victoria was comfortably seated. Then he
gave her a small bunch of flowers passed on by the manager.
Edward had protested but the manager insisted. Wounded soldiers
dressed in regulation blue were honoured guests, even more so when
accompanied by a young lady wearing a Red Cross pin. So
Edward's money had been firmly refused and then the manager had
sent an usherette with the flowers.

Edward had met Victoria at the railway station just after mid-
day and had organised a taxicab to take her to the small hotel he
had chosen for their week's holiday in Dover. Initially, Vicky had
been reluctant to come, but when Edward had insisted on taking his
leave alone if she did not come, she had capitulated. After all,
someone had to keep a nursing eye on his progress. This evening's
outing to the 'Hippodrome' Music Hall in Snargate was a special
treat. Vicky had never been to a real Music Hall before.

The Master of Ceremonies rapped his gavel. "Laydees and
Gentlemen – at vast and prodigious expense we bring you that lady
with the golden voice – a voice to melt the hardest heart. A veritable
nightingale of melodious virtuosity. A warm welcome – please –
Miss – Pearl – White!"

Miss White floated on to the stage as the band played the
opening bars. Vicky held on to Edward's arm. "This is a nice song,

Edward. I will sing it to you some day. I'm really looking forward to hearing Harry Lauder."

> *"Dear face that holds the sweetest smile for me,*
> *Were you not mine how dark the world would be.*
> *I know no life beyond that goodly place,*
> *Life's radiant sunshine in your dear, dear face."*

Then in complete harmony the whole audience joined in the chorus and Vicky and Edward sang along, the pleasure showing on their faces.

> *"Give me your smile the lovelight in your eyes,*
> *Life could not hold a fairer paradise.*
> *Give me the right to love you all the while,*
> *My world forever – the sunshine of your smile."*

Edward squeezed Vicky's hand. "I'm taking you for a special treat later."

"And what special treat is that?"

"There's a shop not far away – they do a lovely faggot and pease pudding supper!"

"Did you enjoy that?" Edward sounded concerned.

"The supper – or the Music Hall?" Vicky kept a straight face even though she wanted to smile.

"The supper, silly!"

Vicky gave the matter due consideration. "Ummm. It fills the tummy. I loved the Music Hall, so gay. I wish we had one in Thame."

Fifteen minutes ago they had left the shop to come and sit in the alcove on the sea front promenade to eat their supper of faggot and pease pudding. Edward had chosen the alcove because it gave a view of the harbour and protected them from the night breeze. They had waited over ten minutes to get served. The lengthy queue was testimony to the fact that hot pease and faggots was a favourite Doverian dish. Naturally the canny and informed locals presented a basin to hold their supper and produced a fork from their pocket to eat it with. Edward and Vicky were unprepared so they had to buy two commercial wooden forks for a happenny and forego the rich gravy on the faggot. During supper they had been entertained by the muted call of ships horns drifting mournfully across the harbour.

Edward put his arm around her shoulder. "I'm so glad you came."

"I nearly said no – Mother has been unwell, so unlike her." She turned and kissed him on the cheek. "But I couldn't let you go off alone."

"I would have come to Thame. Not that I wish to see Father!"

Vicky took his hand. "He spoke to me – your Father. Even if we marry he will never accept me."

Edward was appalled. "Father said that!" He shook his head regretfully, "When we marry it will be different."

"Must you go back to the army, my love?"

"Yes – there is no other way until this war is over."

"I cannot bear the thought that I may never hold you to me."

"That will never be – I promise."

"You have been injured once – it can happen so easily."

Edward kissed her. "I love you – no matter what."

"Take me to bed, my love."

"Are you sure. What . . . . "

She cut him short. "I want these few precious days."

As Edward and Vicky stepped into the hall of the guest house in Granville Gardens, the proprietor, Mr Grimmond, put his head around the kitchen door. "Did you enjoy the show?"

Edward removed his cap. "Splendid show, Mr Grimmond."

"There is no supper I'm afraid – these war ration restrictions are a problem." He touched his nose and whispered. "I've put a bottle of Guinness in your room – and some lemonade in Miss Peter's room."

"Thank you, Mr Grimmond."

"Goodnight, then. Mrs Grimmond said to remind you that breakfast is at eight sharp." The kitchen door closed, firmly.

"Help me undress, Edward."

He tried to release a clip but failed. "My fingers are trembling."

Vicky maintained a practical outlook. "Take off your boots. They make so much noise."

Edward pulled at the laces, the boots eased off. "I wonder if the Grimmonds have gone to bed?" He slipped his shirt over his head and tugged at his vest.

Vicky carefully stepped out of her skirt and hung it neatly, best clothes were expensive and must be cared for. Her blouse followed the same routine as she watched Edward. "I hope you're not coming to bed with your trousers on!"

"Of course not." The trousers dropped. "I feel shy, though I don't really know why."

Vicky removed two petticoats. "I feel shy too. It's because you are watching."

Edward stepped forward and put an arm around her waist. "I will always watch you."

"Why are you shaking, my brave soldier lad?"

"Just . . . . you." His hand gently stroked her shoulder and arm. "Your skin is so smooth – all silk and velvet – so warm."

"Your hand is cool. Help me take off this bodice."

"I don't know how."

Vicky took his hand. "Let me show you – see – it's easy."

"May I hold you?"

Vicky nodded and he cupped a breast in his hand. "You feel so . . . . wonderful."

She closed her eyes and buried her face in his neck. "You are making me tingle all over."

"Shall I stop."

"No . . . . it's quite lovely."

"I will never forget this night, Vicky."

"Nor will I. Sing to me . . . . please."

"The Grimmonds will . . . . "

"Soft and low, my love – soft – and low."

"So deep is the night, no moon tonight . . . . "

Major Harris, commander of the east coast defences near Waxham, put out his hand. "Thank you for helping out, Peters.

Things have not been easy I know. Where would this country be without its volunteers."

After several months of complaining, Herbert Peters felt he could be gracious at last. "I'll not say it hasn't been a trial, Sir, but now it's over I must say thank you for obtaining my release."

The Major blew his nose. "Damn cold! Sorry. I was promised that no man would serve more than six months. I hope your wife is better when you reach home."

"Mother – sorry, I mean my wife, is rarely ill so I'm sure she will be well soon, especially now this worry is over."

"Thank you again, Peters. The truck will take you to Yarmouth Station in the morning. You'll be home for tea."

The Orderly Sergeant looked Edward Holling up and down. "Are you sure you have been posted here? And where's your kit?"

Edward felt in his pocket for his pass. "This is Longfield Barracks. My instructions are to report here at the end of my leave. It is quite clear, Longfield Barracks, Dover. I was in the Red Cross Hospital until a week ago."

The Sergeant shook his head in exasperation. "You should have gone to Cowley for re-kitting. Is this all you've got?" He pointed at Edward's small pack.

"Sorry, Sarge. I was knocked over last August and the stretcher-bearers found me and took me back. Don't remember much until I came to in hospital."

"That's why you should have gone to the depot."

Edward was puzzled. "What do I do now, Sarge?"

"You luck has run out, Corporal! Normally the duty officer would give you a pass and send you off. Not now though. Everyone is being sent out to France – even the instructors are being pushed out of their cosy billets. You'll be back in the front line within a week."

The doctor looked most concerned as he mounted his horse. "I will send out a nurse as quickly as I can, Major. In the meantime the men must stay in bed. Plenty of rest and warmth – oh, yes, and plenty of liquid."

Major Harris was devastated. "How can I cope? How did this reach Norfolk? What shall I do?" Every one of his 'volunteers', all sixteen of them, were lying in the barrack room that now seemed more like a hospital. Several hours had passed since he had learned of the catastrophe that had overwhelmed his small garrison. The whole barrack room of men was down with influenza.

The doctor tipped his cap. "These men are far too ill for duty – could be a fortnight." Then he whipped his horse. "I'll be back tomorrow!"

Sergeant Major Cook handed over the list. "Six replacements have just arrived, Sir."

Captain Alfred Stevens ignored the offering. "Any men with experience?"

"Five have come straight from training, Sir. Only Lance Corporal Holling has seen service. You may recall he was with us last year and was wounded."

"Of course I remember Holling – one of my school lads. Excellent young fellow! Allocate the five riflemen to A and B Companies, Sergeant Major. Detail Holling to join Sergeant Barnes and say I shall want to see him after supper."

The Colonel focussed his binoculars while Alfred Stevens fretted with concern. "It would be best to move on, Sir." Periodic sniper fire was a continual worry.

"It's quite calm out there. Nothing moving." The Colonel jumped down from the fire step. "Damn rumours! Half the time I think this talk of an attack is thought up by our generals, just to keep us on our toes."

"The question is, 'Who is going to attack?'. I've noticed lots of supplies coming up and replacements arriving."

"One thing is certain, Alfred. It's far too calm out there. The Bosch are trying to fool us."

A runner appeared and saluted. "The Sergeant Major told me to find you, Sir. A message from Brigade."

The Colonel opened the letter. "It is thought there will be an attack within twenty four hours. Burn all code books, documents and battle instructions! Let's get back and do something useful – at least we will have a fire to keep us warm."

"It will be useful if we get more water and ammunition brought up. The Redoubt needs strengthening."

"What do you make of that, Alfred?" The Colonel pointed at the sky. "There are dozens of our planes up there, keeping a watch. I hope this is not another 'cry wolf' situation."

"Whatever happens, Sir, we'll be ready. Everyone is working on our defences. That reminds me, Sir, your 'Sam Browne' is in need of repair, so I've sent for the cobbler to come up. The man made a special request to visit the line and as it's a quiet day I thought it best to get the man to do something useful."

"Damn good idea, Alfred. Good for morale. Shows a bit of spirit."

Alfred Stevens checked his watch. Two am. He stopped by the sentry standing watch on the fire step. "Anything happening, soldier?"

"Mist is getting worse, Sir – and I can hear transport wagons moving a way off."

Alfred had been unable to sleep so he had decided to make a tour of the front line trenches with the Intelligence Officer and Sergeant Barnes. This was the sixth sentry in a row to report suspicious noise from the German lines.

"What do you think, Bill."

Bill Lyons, the Intelligence Officer, needed no convincing. "They're getting into position to attack. I think we should get Brigade to put some artillery to work."

"I agree. Sergeant Barnes, is it too late to make a prisoner raid?"

Bill Lyons intervened. "I don't think it will help at this late hour. The report from Brigade shows there are a lot of different Bosch regiments in front of us. It will be better to put up more wire."

Alfred Stevens agreed. "Sergeant Barnes, go back to the Redoubt and get the men to work – put out as much extra wire as you can."

As Sidney Barnes departed, the sentry spoke up. "Any chance of some grub, Sir, we're starving."

"When did you last eat?"

"Not since midday, Sir."

"Where's the CQMS?"

"Forty yards down there." The sentry pointed.

Alfred roused the sleeping man. "Q – what's happened to the men's rations?" Bleary eyes peered back at him. "Men haven't eaten for over twelve hours – why?"

"Beggin' your pardon, Sir but you should know. Orders came from HQ to bring up extra ammunition and water. We hadn't enough transport to do more."

"What have you got locked in the canteen stores?"

"Usual comforts, Sir. Rum, biscuits, cigarettes, some canned meat and soup tablets."

"Open up. Distribute everything to the men except the rum. Save that until dawn."

"We can't do that, Sir. Everything has to be accounted for to the last match! It's more than my pension's worth."

"If the Bosch get into this trench tomorrow I don't think they'll pay. Give me a 'req' and I'll sign it. Now get moving and feed our men. Right, Bill, let's get along to the next company."

"Private Peddelle, what are you doing here?" His voice sounded harsher than he had meant but Sidney Barnes was troubled. All the indications seemed to point to a German attack and there were hundreds of men in the battalion who were new to the front and had never faced an attack. It was always those first crucial few minutes that were so vital to living or dying, success or failure.

"Where's your respirator?"

"Over there, Sarge. On the ledge."

"In the front line you carry it with you at all times, now, go and fetch it."

"I'm helping to string more wire, Sarge. The Sergeant Major said I could stay and help."

Sidney shook his head, three slow shakes that said in three seconds all he was thinking. 'I bet you don't know what to do, Sam

Peddelle, if a shell drops on us or ten Bosch bastards appear out of the ragged mist and what will you kill them with, Sam Peddelle, your bloody hammer? No, Sam Peddelle, you should be way back tucked up in bed, safe and sound.' "Corporal Coates! Get one of the lads to look after Peddelle."

Sidney went to the edge of the defensive wire and looked out toward the German front. No starshells! He could see neither the German line nor their own line some two hundred yards away, all was dark and quiet. But Sidney knew there was danger around. He could sense it. It was just like a night at Thame Park when he had waited in ambush for a cunning fox. Somehow he had always known when the fox was close by. The senses heightened. The ear tuned to every nuance of sound, the nostrils flared and picked out every element of scent. Even the skin on your hands and face seemed to reach out and touch the air to sample any strangers in it. And Sidney knew there was grave danger in the air.

* * * * * * *

During the hours of darkness, on the evening of the 20th March the German Army moved into their final positions for the great attack. Thousands of guns were made ready and nearly a million soldiers assembled. Massed in front of the thirteen divisions of the British Fifth Army were forty three divisions of the German Army. In the British line, near St Quentin, stood the Ox and Bucks.

* * * * * * *

Captain Stevens fell off his narrow camp bed as the earth shook and every moveable item trembled and vibrated. "What the hell!" His surprise and confusion made the situation worse as he scrambled in the dark to put on is helmet and drape his gas mask over his shoulder. Every candle had been extinguished in the dugout and it wasn't until he was able to find his precious torch that he could get himself organised properly. Outside the noise continued unabated and he could not recall a bombardment as fierce and loud as this. Another officer banged into him in the confusion and he found himself shouting. "Calm down!" His watch showed 4.45 and a glance out of the dugout door showed it was still dark. As he stepped outside he could see that the entire eastern sky was lit up as hundreds of heavy guns thundered out. The Colonel appeared and Alfred stepped forward. "Shells are going over, Sir."

The Colonel agreed. "They're hitting our artillery and support lines. We're safe for the moment."

"Shall I send runners to the front line companies to get reports?"

"Yes."

Freddie Coxe was there and back in ten minutes. "Bad mist, Sir. Good job I know the way. Captain Hammond said that a few mortar bombs are coming in but there is no gas and no sign of the Bosch, Sir."

In the front line the CQMSs got ready to dole out the rum ration while the companies stood the dawn watch. Fifteen minutes later the German barrage switched from the rear support areas and concentrated on the forward trench. There was chaos as men dived for shelter as the high explosive and gas shells pounded down. Dying men littered the bottom of the trenches and wounded men, unable to don their gas masks, gagged on the poison gas.

From the Redoubt that housed the Headquarters Company they could only watch in horror and amazement as the front line trenches disappeared under a never ending barrage of explosions and smoke. Shells were falling in quantities that none had ever seen before.

Down in the headquarters' control dugout the field telephone buzzed, Alfred picked it up and listened. "Brigade on the line, Sir. Urgent!"

The telephone link was their only certain means of communication with Brigade Headquarters, thanks to a deeply buried cable that had so far defied the bombardment. Alfred listened to the one-sided conversation as the Colonel took the phone. "Is that you, Harold? Where's the Brigadier?"

"Oh! Let's hope he pulls through. No, the barrage hasn't stopped. The Bosch are destroying my forward companies!"

"I can't pull them out – nothing can be done until this barrage lifts."

The Colonel spoke to Alfred. "The Brigadier is wounded – taken to hospital. Major Howitt is in charge." He turned back to the telephone. "That makes you a General, Harold. What do we do now?"

"Orders as before – hold you say! There's nothing to hold against at the moment – not a Bosch in sight."

He put the telephone down. "Harold reports chaos at the rear. We'll be lucky to get artillery support. Meantime we are to stand fast as per the last order."

"I understand, Sir. Is Major Howitt in contact with Division?"

"No. It seems we are on our own. All Harry knows is that the attack is all along our front."

"When the Bosch have mashed our front line they'll turn the guns on us." Alfred glanced at his watch. "Seven ten. Shall we disperse D Company to the outposts and get our men to dig more shelters along the rim?"

"Yes, but only the machine gun teams are to be sent out and no further than forty yards while this mist holds, otherwise it will be difficult to maintain contact."

There was a brief lull in the bombardment of the front line.

"Sergeant Major! Send a scout forward, I must know what is happening to A, B and C companies."

Edward Holling and John Howe maintained a lonely vigil by the steps that led out of the Redoubt to a gap in the wire that marked the route to the front line trenches. Freddie's greatcoat was folded on the ground beside them as he found it easier to move quickly without the heavy overcoat to hold him back.

"He should be back by now!" Edward searched the mist for the slightest sign of movement.

Ten minutes after Freddie went forward a heavy bombardment started again. There was less gas this time but many more heavy mortar shells designed to penetrate deep into the ground and pulverise the dugouts.

"How can anyone live through that." John pointed at the smoke and debris rising above the mist.

Edward stood to get a better view. "This must be the 'Big One' the lads have been talking about."

John nodded in agreement. "You're right – we had better say a prayer for Freddie."

Their hopes were lifted for a whole minute as the barrage stopped and there was an unnatural quiet. But it was only a lull as the unseen batteries made adjustments and then renewed the barrage with even greater ferocity, only now the explosions were coming closer.

Edward clenched his teeth. "Now it's our turn!"

John was already moving under cover. "Get in here, Edward." John crawled into the shelter under the rim of the Redoubt.

"What about Freddie?"

John leaned forward, grabbed Edward's collar and heaved him into shelter. "We'll . . . . " His words were drowned out as several high explosive shells detonated close by.

Sergeant Major Crook called down into the scout's dugout. "Sergeant Barnes! You there?"

"Here."

Private Harty was pushed down the steps. "Harty is joining your section. Look after him."

"Why me, Sarn't Major?"

"Captain Stevens orders. He's no use with a rifle but there's no place for slackers today."

"Corporal Holling!"

"Here, Sarn't Major."

"These two men are detailed to you, to guard this section of the rim."

As Sergeant Major Crook made off Edward emerged from the shelter to find Samuel Peddelle and Peter Oxenlade standing uncertainly before him. The thought 'scraping the barrel' came to mind but he pushed it aside.

"Have you got your gas masks?" He checked their packs and rifles.

"303?"

Peter Oxenlade proudly displayed three full bandoliers. "Here!" Then he played his trump card as he opened his haversack. "An' some cheese sandwiches courtesy of the officers' mess. How about that?"

"Corporal Oxenlade, you're a flamin' genius." John Howe was hungry and quite sincere.

"What about you, Sam?"

"Got my rifle and forty rounds, Corp."

"Can you handle . . . . " Edward knew he sounded sceptical but a proud Samuel cut him short. "Sergeant Barnes taught me – nearly got a first class badge."

"Good. When the Bosch come, aim for the body." He pointed to his solar plexus. "Right here!"

The bombardment had now reached half way from the trenches to the Redoubt and Edward's last remaining hope for Freddie was fading fast.

A salvo of shells exploded with dull thuds near the Redoubt. That meant gas. Within minutes the light breeze wafted the gas into the Redoubt and the cry of 'GAS' echoed around the perimeter and dugouts. Alfred Stevens checked that the gas blanket covering the dugout entrance was securely in place, then made his way over to the Colonel. "All the men are under cover except the men at the outposts, Sir, but there was a clear warning so they will have their masks on."

"Well done, Alfred. I've just spoken to Harold Howitt. He has confirmed that I can order the men back if the gas is bad. The Sergeant Major and I have checked outside. What with the smoke, fog and gas, it's impossible to go anywhere. So here we stay."

Alfred checked his watch. "Seven o'clock, Sir. I'll check on the gas every five minutes. I know we're safe from attack for the moment, but I think the Bosch will advance as soon as the gas clears."

George Coates gave Albert Harty a hard look. "Follow my orders – to the letter. D'you understand? These are dangerous."

Albert responded vigorously. "I'm your man, Corp."

"Maybe. But do exactly as I say. Follow me, take the bomb in the left hand with the pin level with the top of the thumb. Now put the screw head in the split end of the pin and give it a slight twist. Not too much!"

"What's that for, Corp?"

"It puts a slight bind on the pin so it's secure – much safer this way. Now, unscrew the plug cap and insert the fuse. Detonator end first. Well done! Now replace the plug."

"Now I'm in the section – can I be a 'Bomber', Corp?"

"Prime this lot while I think about it."

"Do you think the Philistines are coming, Corp?"

"Aye. They're coming – that is certain."

"Have no fear. God is on our side."

Alfred Stevens moved quickly down the dugout steps. "Barrage moving on, Sir, but no sign of the Bosch yet."

"How many men have we lost?"

"A few men affected by the gas, Sir. We are checking the outposts now."

"And the fog?"

"Still holding. Visibility poor."

"Has the scout returned from the front line."

"No, Sir."

In the front line trench a lone platoon commander staggered through a mass of splintered and battered timbers and the ragged remains of sandbags. The Second Lieutenant had searched his own section without success but he was having difficulty in walking, a piece of shrapnel had sliced into his foot and his sense of balance was impaired from the explosions. He limped along calling out, more from a sense of duty than any hope. "Anyone there?" "Can you hear me?" One hundred yards along the trench he was answered by a low mournful call. "Help!"

A soldier, three quarters covered with mud and earth put out a hand. The Lieutenant took the hand and tugged the man clear. "Can you stand, soldier?"

The soldier tried to stand but failed. It was obvious that one leg was broken and his face was covered with blood where a bulk of timber had dropped on his head. "God, it hurts!"

The Lieutenant bent over. "Put your arm around my shoulder – let's try to get back. The shelling has stopped."

"What about the other men, Sir?"

"I've passed dozens of dead men. I think we're the only ones left."

"This is only my third day at the front, Sir. Is it always like this?"

"Englanders!" A rifle bolt clicked. Three German soldiers had suddenly appeared on the edge of the ruined parapet.

The Lieutenant shut his eyes for a moment in sheer frustration. "Sod it! I thought we were going home."

The call echoed around the Redoubt and down into the dugouts. It was now 7.30. "Stand to! Stand to!"

John Howe stared out into the mist. "Can you see anything, Peter?"

"I can't see a damn thing. What about you, Sam?"

"Not a thing!"

"Quiet now," Edward asserted his authority, "Listen."

"Not one man has come back from the trenches!" John whispered the message without further explanation but they all knew what he meant. Four hundred men had gone forward. None had come back so far.

"The shells have blown half our wire away."

Suddenly the quiet was broken as machine gun fire rattled over their heads and several men passing behind them were scythed down.

Further along the perimeter, to the left, George Coates listened to the machine gun, then, having decided on its location, hurled three grenades in rapid succession. He was rewarded by shouts that he took to be curses but the gun continued firing. Over to the right Sergeant Barnes placed his men at two yard intervals.

"All ready? One grenade each. Twenty yards out. One – two – throw." A dozen grenades flew out and exploded. He relaxed. The Germans had not reached the wire yet.

George Coates moved his 'Bomber' section in beside Edward Holling's section.

"Hey, Corp!" Samuel Peddelle could not keep the excitement from his voice. "I can see something."

Edward Holling moved quickly to his side. "Where?"

"There, Corp."

Over to the left a sunken road passed the Redoubt on its way to Holnon, although the visibility was poor, Edward could clearly see a large group of men advancing resolutely forward.

"Bosch!" He swung up his rifle. "Fire at will!"

Four rifle shots cracked out and George Coates ordered his bombers into action. William Smithe threw four grenades in rapid succession and the column of men disintegrated. He called over to Edward.

"Well done you lot – first blood to us."

Peter Oxenlade turned in triumph. "I got one – I got one!"

Edward went to motion him down but it was too late as a bullet took Peter in the ear and he slumped forward, dead before he hit the ground. George Coates was watching the front. "They're coming again!" As the grenades hit the road, George grabbed hold of John Howe. "Go tell Captain Stevens or the Sarn't Major we need a Lewis gunner here." Then he turned to Harty. "Go and fetch more boxes of grenades."

The Colonel picked up the telephone. "Enghein Redoubt here, Harold. There's heavy movement of enemy infantry to our front. We need artillery support."

A sudden charge by German infantry through the mist in front of Sidney Barnes' section had got right to the edge of the Redoubt and there was fierce hand to hand fighting with rifle and bayonet. Luckily the wire constrained the attack and Sidney was able to stand back and shoot down the attackers as his section held them back. This was something he could do quickly and accurately with just a few seconds taken out to recharge his magazine. Over twenty attackers were already down and the section was starting to cheer when a dozen grenades were lobbed forward out of the mist. Sidney had no chance as the grenades dropped all around him and he had made only two strides to escape when they exploded.

All along the front and the two sides of the Redoubt concerted German attacks were building up and desperate fighting was taking place, but it was heaviest on the left where the road made an easier route forward. From the centre of the Redoubt, Alfred Stevens could see the attacks building up but he was worried by the pressure on the left side. "Sarn't Major! Get four men from the rear perimeter and follow me."

As they ran forward half a dozen machine gun bullets took Sergeant Major Cook across the chest. Alfred grabbed a rifle that was lying on the ground and started shooting. "Bomber, get those grenades going!"

Albert Harty delivered more boxes. "Can I help, Sir?"

"Yes. Get over here – bomb that far side of the road."

"Bless you, Sir. *Onward Christian soldiers, marching as to war, with the cross of Jesus . . . .*"

A random bullet caught John Howe in the throat and blood spilled out all over his uniform. Edward Holling turned and caught him as he fell and he fumbled for a field dressing. "Sit still, John." He slipped the dressing inside John's collar to staunch the flow of blood. "The stretcher-bearers will soon be here."

The attackers fell back but a well thrown grenade hit the parapet and skewed sideways several yards catching George Coates unaware. He was just reaching out for more grenades when the explosion took him full in the back.

The Colonel emerged from the signals dugout. "Corporal Jones!"

Harold Jones ran over. "Here, Sir!"

"Take one man and check the rear outposts. I must know what is going on behind us."

Cautiously Harold led James Pullene over the rear perimeter of the Redoubt and made his way forward. The first outpost had been destroyed, three men killed and the machine gun wrecked. Although the mist was starting to clear, visibility was still down to forty yards. The ground in front of the outpost was littered with dead German Infantry. Quickly they moved on to the next outpost jumping from shell-hole to shell-hole. The next post was manned. Harold cupped his hand over his mouth to direct his voice. "Corporal Benn. We're coming in."

"Who's there?"

"Harold Jones. Headquarters' Scouts."

Harold could see that the defences in front of this team were still intact and bodies of several German Infantrymen were on the wire.

"The Colonel wants a situation report."

"Tell him we're holding. Outposts two and three are in place. We don't know about number one. There are some Bosch in front of us."

" . . . . That's the situation, Sir." Harold Jones made his report to the Colonel. James was sent to bring Captain Stevens to the meeting.

"Alfred, I've decided to go and look at Holnon to see if there is a route out of here and where to call in the artillery. I shall take just my batman. This fog is lifting rapidly and when it does, the attack will intensify. However, I want Corporal Jones with one man to show me out to outpost one and wait there until I return. Can you use a Lewis gun, Corporal?"

"Yes, Sir."

"Good. We will move out in five minutes. Be ready."

Over to the left of the perimeter William Smithe had tossed out half a dozen grenades in quick succession when a bullet from the unprotected side caught him in the shoulder and he just had time to call out as several Germans closed in. Edward Holling and Samuel Peddelle turned and concentrated their fire bringing most of the attackers down, then Albert Harty tossed out two grenades and the remaining attackers retreated.

As Edward turned back to his front he sensed that Samuel Peddelle had been hit. Samuel fell slowly to his side, a look of surprise on his face. Edward knelt. "Where are you hit, Sam?"

"How did I do, Corp?"

"You did well, Sam. You did well."

"Tell Albert to sing louder." His body slumped and he let out a great sigh.

Harold Jones and James Pullene had only been in position for five minutes and the Colonel and his batman had disappeared into the distance when a breeze began to cut lanes of vision into the mist. As it did so they could see lines of attackers moving towards Holnon.

"Look at that, James! Bloody hundreds of them."

"What do we do, Harold?"

James's question was answered because a Vickers machine gun at outpost three stuttered into action and one line of German Infantry swung left to attack them. Harold was concerned about the ammunition, in the short time they had been given to prepare they had found only five panniers of ammunition for the gun. Harold swung the gun around and sighted. "As soon as this magazine is empty you must fill it as quickly as possible."

James broke open a bandolier. "All ready!"

Harold squinted through the sight. "Here goes!"

The signals clerk cranked the handle of the field telephone. "Major Howitt on the line, Sir." He handed the phone to Captain Stevens.

"Harold – we are surrounded. What are we to do?"

"Where's the Colonel?"

"Gone to check the route to Holnon but the mist has cleared and he won't be able to get back."

"What's your position?"

"I'm the only officer left. About forty to fifty men are still fighting."

"I'll ask Division to allow a withdrawal. I will call you back."

"Grenade!" Albert Harty gave a great roar as the grenade hit the rim of the Redoubt and bounced forward, then he threw himself on the ground. Bang! When he picked himself up he glanced over the rim and could see a line of grey clad men advancing towards him. William Smithe had been caught in the blast and his life was ebbing away as blood poured from his body.

Albert grabbed a grenade, pulled the pin and tossed it out into the road. Another – and then another followed in quick succession. "Bless you, God. A hundred Philistines are smitten! Praise the Lord!" He was so exultant he didn't see the prone rifleman take careful aim and put a bullet through his forehead.

Harold Jones squeezed the trigger. Tat – tat – tat – tat! The gun stopped. He flicked the breech back. Empty. "Magazine, James."

"All gone!" James lifted his rifle. "I've ten rounds left."

Harold checked. "We've two grenades. I'll cover you as you drop back."

"No, you go. I'm the better shot."

In the short lull two German soldiers had crept forward on the flank. As Harold went to push James out of the post, two grenades dropped just behind them and to the front a line of men lifted up and charged forward. Harold just had time to lob a grenade before the explosion caught them.

The signals clerk picked up the telephone. "Enghien Redoubt."

"Major Howitt speaking. I must speak to Captain Stevens."

"We're under heavy attack, Sir."

"Give him this message. He is authorised to retreat – now. Good luck."

As the clerk reached the top of the dugout steps he could see Edward Holling running across the Redoubt to the sand pit, the only place that still seemed to have defenders. He raced after Edward and they fell into the pit together.

Alfred Stevens picked them up and the clerk shouted out the message. "Major Howitt has authorised the retreat, Sir."

Edward Holling looked distraught. "Sorry, Sir. I couldn't hold any longer."

"D'you hear that, lads?" Alfred looked about him at the remaining dozen men. "We can go now."

A battered and bruised Sergeant wiped his face with his sleeve. "Has anyone told the Bosch, Sir?"

"No, I don't think so."

A wave of German Infantry swarmed over the Redoubt perimeter that Edward Holling had just vacated. "Ready, lads. On my command. FIRE!"

The last thing that Alfred Stevens did was glance at his watch, it was 5.15, and he gave a smile of satisfaction. They had held the advance all day. He put out his hand to touch Edward Holling and say 'sorry', but he never made it.

He that outlives this day and comes home safe.
Will stand tip-toe when this day is named,
And rouse him at the name of Crispin.
He that shall see this day and live old age.
Will yearly on the vigil feast his neighbours,
And say, Tomorrow is Saint Crispin,
What feats we did that day.

This story shall the good man teach his son,
And Crispin Crispian shall ne'er go by.
From this day to the ending of the world,
But we in it shall be remembered.
We few, we happy few, we band of brothers.

And gentlemen of England, now a-bed.
Shall think themselves accursed they were not here,
And hold their manhood cheap while any speak
That fought with us upon Saint Crispin's Day.

[HENRY V – WILLIAM SHAKESPEARE]

Beatrice Peters was distraught. "How can it be? What has happened?"

She crumpled the telegram and threw it on the floor. "I don't believe it." Nontheless the tears flooded out and great sobs racked her body.

Vicky tried to console her. "Mary is making a cup of tea, it will help to calm you." She knew it was a vain hope. She did not want to believe the news herself. Father should have arrived home eight days ago. When he didn't arrive they had all been concerned. The next day enquiries had got them nowhere. It was only when the telegram arrived that the reason for his non-arrival was clear. Father had succumbed to the Influenza, along with a number of his comrades.

Beatrice sobbed even louder. "I can't even go to his funeral – what am I to do?"

Vicky was beside herself with worry. The newspapers were full of the news of the German onslaught in France. The last letter from Edward had said he was on his way to the front. Mary was concerned about John Howe, but John had been at the front many months unharmed, so Mary tended to dismiss the danger, 'John will come to no harm, I'm sure.' Vicky had another reason for worry, another secret reason. She was pregnant, or as her Mother always called the situation, 'with child'. A letter to Edward sat on her dressing table but she had decided not to post it until she was absolutely certain.

"But you can visit Father's grave, Mother. Mary will take you to Norfolk. I will look after the shop."

The sobbing abated. "Do you think so, dear. It would make a world of difference."

'ARMISTICE'

The town celebrations had started but Vicky Peters could not bring herself to join in. She understood the feeling of relief now that the war was over and realised that the joyful procession and bonfire were expressions of relief and thanksgiving rather than jingoism. Besides which, baby Edward was only two weeks old and Vicky could barely allow him out of her sight, let alone subject him to the vapours of a cold evening and even the remotest possibility of danger. That was why she had agreed to allow Edward Holling, Senior, to visit. Certain that she would be at home. Nonetheless she puzzled over his request, because since the report of his son's death he had made no attempt to contact or speak to her. She half hoped that his visit may be an attempt at reconciliation but could not bring herself to raise her hopes so high. At the appointed time it was Mary who answered the door and showed Edward Holling into the parlour and then, as agreed, had retired to the kitchen to sit with her mother.

Edward Holling removed his hat and gave a slight nod of his head. "Thank you for seeing me, Miss Peters."

He made no attempt to extend his hand, so Vicky remained seated. "Please be seated. What can I do for you, Mr Holling?"

"I wish to speak to you privately, concerning your child."

There was no warmth in his voice and Vicky's hope of reconciliation half died so she corrected him. "My son, Mr Holling – his name is Edward."

Edward Holling stiffened. "Oh! I had hoped you might choose a different name – in the circumstances."

"He is named after his father – your son!"

"My son is not here to defend himself. It falls on me to defend his honour and my family's name. If you call the child Edward, people will assume my son is the father."

"There is no dishonour to your son. My son is a fine boy and Edward would have taken pride in him."

"What proof have you got that my son is the father!"

"The proof as you call it is my word, the love your son gave me and our son, who will grow in the image of his father. My only wish is that your son had lived so that we could have married."

"I would never have consented to this marriage, Miss Peters."

Vicky shrugged and sighed. "It is too late. He is gone. My future is my son, Mr Holling. What is your future?"

"I will never acknowledge this child. Never!"

"That is for you to decide. My son," Vicky emphasised the 'my', "will not lack for loving care – with or without you." She shook her head in sorrow, "Your son was a wonderful man, you should not soil his memory nor his honour."

"You plot to bring a bastard into the world, to trick my son into marriage and you have the effrontery to talk of honour. He never spoke to me of marriage."

Vicky tried to remain calm. "Your son loved me as I loved him – love him still. I would give my life for his if it were possible."

For a moment Edward Holling looked contrite. "It seems you are saying I did not love my son enough. But then it seems to me you loved him too much."

Vicky rose from her chair. "There you have the right of it, Mr Holling. Excuse me if I say I had the better of it. I will bid you, Good Day."

Edward Holling put on his hat. "Good Day, it is."

"Do you wish to see your grandson?"

"I have no grandson – nor ever will."

Down on the Show Ground a great roar went up as the flames reached the effigy of the Kaiser and it quickly burned away. The bells of St Mary's rang out and as the flames died back and the embers glowed, the crowd began to sing.

> *"And did those feet in ancient times,*
> *walk upon England's pastures green,*
> *and did the holy lamb of God . . . . "*

Chapter 6   1999: 'AT THE GATE OF THE YEAR'

A worried and concerned supervisory nurse had telephoned at nine o'clock from the John Radcliffe Hospital in Oxford. Victoria Peters was failing. Despite the fact that this news should have come as no surprise to Margaret she could not suppress a feeling of alarm. Her Great Aunt Vicky had been ill after a fall on Christmas Eve. The fall outside the Co-op in Thame High Street had been an accident but the old lady had defied everyone's expectation of a rapid recovery by failing to respond to treatment. For some time Margaret had remained optimistic, after all, Aunt Vicky had proved to be both strong and resilient throughout her life, never more so than through her nineties as she had clung to a precarious independence. Surely if Aunt Vicky had reached one hundred and two then a few more years was both her right and Margaret's reasonable expectation. Even the frailties of old age must retreat when confronted with such an implacable evasion of reality!

The staff at the hospital had aided Margaret in this expectation and they had used every bit of their professional skills and modern medicines to keep the old lady alive. It was a battle they now realised they were losing. The self evident truth was there for all to see. Victoria Peters did not want to live any more. Modern medicine and skill versus willpower.

When Victoria had first spoken of dying, Margaret had said all the usual soothing, protective words. "You will be fine". "You will be home soon". "Don't be silly now, you have years yet". The words and variations on them had been repeated many times until Victoria had gripped Margaret's hand and said very gently, "Let me go, Love – it is time for me to go."

"Nonsense," protested Margaret, "a little rest and you will be as right as rain – you'll see!"

Victoria had shaken her head very slowly and replied, her voice firm "It's been over eighty years without the man I loved – 'tis time enough."

For once in her life Margaret had no answer. It was obvious that the immense willpower that had seen Victoria through the twentieth century would now see her out of it. Even when faced with such evidence Margaret could not understand this desire to be done with the world. She resolved to have one more try, always provided that Aunt Vicky was conscious.

Margaret's concern and desire was understandable. Victoria Welcome Peters, to give her full name, had been as much a mother to her as her own mother, Alice. It had started when Victoria's sister, Mary, had died in 1922 giving birth to Alice. Victoria had raised Alice and even when, during the Second World War, Alice had married Douglas Tilling they had lived with Victoria. So when Margaret was born in 1947 she had grown up in a household where she considered that she had two mothers. The early childhood bond had been reinforced even further in 1990 when Alice had died, struck down by an unspeakable cancer. Margaret could barely remember her father who had died when she was five. As a young girl Margaret had asked her Aunt Vicky why she had never married. Victoria had made a joke of it, "No-one was silly enough to ask me", this while pulling a funny face. So the subject had been pushed aside and Margaret had never raised it again directly, somehow instinct said this was not a question that could be asked. Later in life Margaret had pieced together the story.

Victoria Peters had lost her young man, Edward Holling, at the end of the Great War of 1914-18 when she was pregnant but unmarried. A son, also named Edward, had been born but he had died somewhere in France, following on the D-Day invasion of Normandy in the Second World War. Margaret had often wondered why her great-aunt never spoke about them. She could only sense the overwhelming hurt of their loss because their photographs were kept hidden in a bedroom drawer. It was as if the memories they evoked could not be borne.

Only once could Margaret remember Aunt Vicky letting her feelings surface and that was as they had watched the television news in the aftermath of the Remembrance Sunday bombing in Enniskillen, in Northern Ireland. Victoria's voice became hard and critical, "They have spat on the memory of brave people. I will never forgive the Irish!"

Margaret had ventured reconciliation but Victoria remained unforgiving. "These bombers want to change history, the one thing that cannot be undone. Yesterday is set in stone forever, if it were not I would have changed many things. Now the Irish and their American paymasters have made terrorism acceptable and the innocent die!"

Margaret put the thoughts aside, none of it made sense to her; only the two faded photographs that were now displayed on Aunt Vicky's bedside locker made sense and she wished that she might have known them. Her thoughts returned to the present because it was now New Year's Eve and it seemed that Victoria Peters might not last into the new century. Margaret remembered Victoria's favourite poem. Perhaps if she recited the words once again, Victoria would gain heart and try to live. There was so much that Margaret did not know and she wanted the answers to a thousand questions about the past. A past that Victoria had been so reticent about. The few questions that Margaret had asked had been brushed aside. "Never mind the past, Love – there is so much new in the world. Look forward."

Was the past too painful, Margaret thought, still too fresh in the memory? Perhaps the real answer lay in Victoria's answer to Margaret's question about the poem. The poem mentioned God and when quite young, Margaret had asked, "Which God did it mean?" "The one in your heart", Victoria had replied.

Several days ago in one of Victoria's more lucid moments Margaret had plucked up the courage to ask some questions. "What was my grandmother like, Aunt Vicky?" Victoria had looked puzzled for a moment, "Ah! You mean Mary – my sister, Mary."

Margaret tried to sound casual, as if the answer did not really matter. "That's right – Grandmother Mary. Tell me about her, please."

For once Victoria had responded without any hesitation or prevarication. "She was a lovely person – fair – like your mother, only fairer. Full of ideas. She was going to marry John Howe – she really loved him . . . . but he died in the war as so many did."

"But she did marry, Aunt Vicky – she married my grandfather, Ernest Shaw – in 1921, I believe."

There was silence for a while before Victoria responded. "Aye, that she did – more's the pity. She couldn't stand the loneliness so she agreed to marry Shaw. He were a widower, twenty years older than she was."

"But why, Aunt Vicky – why?"

"'Tis plain, surely – not enough men, too many killed in the war. Mind you, she would have lived if the medicines of today had been available – no antibiotics in those days."

"What happened to my Grandfather?"

"Drank himself to death." Victoria suddenly realised she sounded pleased and moderated her tone. "I took Alice in but not him – not him – he were vile!" This was said with a finality that made Margaret realise that further talk about Ernest Shaw was ended.

Margaret put aside all these disturbing and disparate thoughts, put on her coat and went out to her car. She had left a message on the kitchen table in case one of her erstwhile sons came home unexpectedly. They had gone away for the New Year celebrations, so there was little chance they would return tonight. Her sons, like most of the townsfolk of Thame, were engrossed in their New Year's Eve Millennium celebrations. Already fireworks lit the sky and loud bangs reverberated over the rooftops. As she drove, Margaret thought of the right words to say to her great-aunt. Surely if she said the right words, Aunt Vicky would rally. Margaret could understand the loss of the man she had loved but surely that was too long ago to be relevant. After a century of rocklike dependability and resolute courage, Victoria only needed to hear the right words. Margaret resolved to find them.

It was about ten o'clock as Margaret walked along the corridor of the hospital. The subdued lighting and the general quietness gave the place a ghostly aura. Not a fearful aura, more a sleepy one. Her shoes clipped on the plastic tiled floor leaving a faintly echoing trail behind her. Ahead she could see a nurse at the ward reception desk.

As she approached the nurse looked up and gave a reserved smile of welcome. Margaret overcame a strong urge to make a flip remark to ease the tension that she felt. Wisely she suppressed it. She suddenly had the feeling that she would need the help and goodwill of every person and being in the universe if she was going to survive this night in hope rather than despair.

"Good evening, nurse – I've come to see Miss Peters – Victoria Peters – my great aunt."

Two serious grey-green eyes gazed at her. "I'm so pleased you've come. Victoria is in no pain but has seemed distressed. She is – slipping away from us."

"May I see her? Is she conscious?"

"She is drifting in and out of consciousness – the injections help but she is having hallucinations. Perhaps it is to be expected – one hundred and two is a great age."

"How long will she last, nurse?"

"Hours! – But if she rallies possibly days or weeks even."

"I had hoped she might listen to me – I feel so sure she could live if she wanted to."

The nurse nodded in understanding. "We had hoped she would want to see in the New Year, it is nearly midnight, – a new millennium. Is that worth a try?"

The nurse left Margaret at Victoria's bedside after checking the patient's pulse and respiration. "There is no change – I will be back in a while. Call me if anything happens." Then she was gone.

"Aunt Vicky! It's me, Margaret. Can you hear me?"

Margaret stroked Victoria's hand and then her cheek. Victoria responded, half opened her eyes and looked at Margaret without recognition.

'*Where am I? What was that? What is happening!*'

Confusion reigned in Victoria's mind for a while, then slowly she began to understand. She was still alive. She was still in the hospital. She tried to cry out but her throat was parched. Her hand went out to the glass on the locker. Margaret realised what was happening and gave her a few sips of water.

"I was so worried, Aunt Vicky. How do you feel?"

There was no response. "It's New Year's Eve – a new millennium. A new century."

Victoria closed her eyes as if rejecting the idea. Margaret tried again. "Aunt Vicky, it's New Year's Eve – don't you remember our special poem – the one you taught me, that was so special for us?" She waited for a moment then felt Victoria's fingers tighten on her hand. Hope soared. Margaret recited from memory.

"I said to the man who stood at the gate of the year
give me a hand that I may tread safely into the unknown.
And he replied, go out into the darkness and put thine hand
into the hand of God. That shall be to thee better than light
and safer than a known way."

As Margaret finished Victoria's head nodded twice, very slowly, in acknowledgement then she whispered. "Let me go now, Love – I have had enough of loneliness." Margaret reached out and touched her lips, "Shush now – or you will make me cry."

Victoria opened her eyes and looked up. Edward Holling stood beside the bed, looking at her but not smiling. He looked just like the man in the photograph beside the bed, unchanged after all these years. Victoria tried to reach out to touch him but failed. Edward made no effort to help her. At last he spoke. "You look so old, Vicky – you have grown so old."

"It has been a long time, Edward, my love."

There was a peevishness in Edward's voice as he replied. "I have been waiting for you."

"I still love you, Edward – I have always loved you."

Edward remained as stern as before. "How can I love you, Vicky – you are so old and ugly. You have waited too long!"

A tear formed in Victoria's left eye and she tried vainly to wipe it away but the tear dropped and others followed in a steady trickle down her cheek. "Don't leave me, Edward – don't leave me again."

"I don't want to leave you, stop this crying," there was deep scorn in Edward's voice, "but what use is a tearful old woman to me?"

"Don't go, Edward – I won't always be old."

"Soon it will be too late – the new century is close. We are people of this century, not the next."

"I am coming, Edward."

Margaret stroked Victoria's hand. "Aunt Vicky! What is wrong? Why are you crying." There was no response.

"Aunt Vicky – I will take you home soon. As soon as you are well. It will be the year 2000 very soon now – fancy that, you will have lived in three centuries."

Edward took Victoria's hand and she could feel the cool pressure. "Oh Edward, you haven't changed since you went off to war."

He looked at her for a moment before replying. "You have, Vicky. You had skin like velvet and firm breasts that fitted to my caress – now look at you, old and flabby – full of brown marks!"

"I have never loved any man but you, Edward."

"It has been lonely waiting, Vicky."

"It has been even lonelier living."

"Come with me, Vicky – it is time to go."

"I'm coming, Edward. In a little while."

Margaret could not keep the concern from her voice. "What are you trying to say, Aunt Vicky?" She rang the bell for the nurse. "She is trying to speak I think, but I can make no sense of it except she is agitated."

The nurse checked the monitor. "Her pulse is slowly fading – I could give her another injection but the last thing she said was that she didn't want any more medicines."

Margaret picked up the photograph of Edward Holling. Why was it, she thought, that the old faded sepia brown photographs always seemed so serious and romantic, never a belly laugh, always so posed.

Edward stared at Victoria for some time before speaking. "I am puzzled, Vicky." Victoria could think of nothing to reply that made any sense, Edward continued, "Yes, Vicky, puzzled. Why did you want to live so long? Still, I suppose you must have seen many new things."

"Truly marvellous things. Men have walked on the moon!"

"What did these men do on the moon?"

"I think – I think they played golf."

Edward's voice rose. "Men went to the moon to play golf, Vicky – golf! What a waste."

"Also men of science have made a sheep."

"Cannot sheep make sheep anymore?" Edward's voice was most scornful, "have men turned into tups!"

"No, Edward, don't be so silly. It is just that it is hard for me to explain."

"But what of war, Vicky, what of war? Surely mankind has abolished wars and their senseless killings."

Vicky shook her head in sorrow. "I am sorry – there have been many wars – horrible wars and monstrous weapons."

"The world has learned very little then," Edward looked dejected, "was our sacrifice in vain?"

"There is not enough love in the world, Edward – but I did my best – I loved those around me – I never forgot you, I still carry the memories in my heart."

"You were my heart, Vicky. Why have you waited so long to join me?"

"You do not understand, Edward. At the beginning I had the courage to join you but there was our son – you did not know of our son, Edward, did you?"

"Our son!" Edward recoiled in shock. "You never told me."

"I sent a letter – it arrived too late. That is why I had to endure, care for our son."

There was a bitterness in Edward's voice that Victoria had never experienced before. "So you saw fit to bring a bastard into the world!"

"How can you say that – our son! As fine a son as any man could wish."

"I am sorry, Vicky, forgive me. I did not speak as a man. What is our son called? Where is he?"

"He was called Edward, as you. I had such hopes for him."

"Where is he?"

"Killed, Edward – killed in the second Great War. Such a waste."

"A second Great War, Vicky? How can mankind have been so stupid? Could you not have stopped him going?"

"Edward, think back, how can a woman stop a man going to war?"

Edward nodded in understanding. "The young are so easily caught up. There is no sense to it."

"Sing to me, Edward – it has been so long since you sang to me."

"Which song, Vicky? We sang so many."

"You choose, Edward. Please."

"I know the one, Vicky. This lonely night is ending for us.

So deep is the night, no moon tonight
No friendly star to guide me with its light
Be still my heart.
Silent lest my love should be returning
From a world far apart
So deep is the night, Oh lonely night
On broken wings my heart has taken flight
And let me dream.
In my dream our lips are blending
Will my dream be never ending
Will your memory haunt me 'til I die
Alone am I, deep into the night
Waiting for the light, alone am I
I wonder why, deep is the night."

"Do you remember that night, Vicky?"
"How could I forget?"

"In all my dreams our lips are blending
Pray those dreams will have no ending
I will surely love you 'til I die
My heart and I, waiting just for you
Longing for the light, alone no more
My heart and I – my heart and I."

"I never forgot those words either, Edward my love."

"I know, I know. That is why I have come for you. Come with me now, Vicky. Let us go and find our son."

Margaret held her breath as the nurse checked Victoria's pulse, then re-checked. "She has gone, I'm afraid. Just slipped away. I'm so sorry. Your aunt lived in Thame, I believe."

Margaret nodded in agreement, she could not speak. The nurse continued, "I meant to ask your aunt if she ever knew my grandmother, she lived in Thame as a young girl. She was a wonderful grandmother – her maiden name was Jane Peddelle."

Outside the night sky was lit by a myriad of exploding fireworks and the brilliant colours sent scattered patterns of light dancing around the ward. "Only a few more minutes, Aunt Vicky, to reach into the New Year. The gate of the year is open."

Epilogue: ALL ARE HEROES NOW

This story has not been written to illustrate or glorify the role of the Oxfordshire and Buckinghamshire Light Infantry in the First World War. That role needs no help from me. Their service, heroism and honour is unblemished and secure in history. Neither is it meant to overshadow or diminish the role of other Regiments with local affiliations who made such great contributions to our force's efforts. The first 'Ox and Bucks' men landed with the BEF in France in August 1914. From then on they were actively involved in fighting for the duration of the war. Over 200 men were killed in the first few months, by the end of the war the total had risen to over 5800. I will mention only two events. In November 1914, some Ox and Bucks men stood with a few other badly depleted battalions and repulsed a major German Army attack at Nun's Wood, near Ypres. There were no reserves to their rear, only an open road to Paris. Had they given way the war may have had a different ending. The second event occurred near the small town of St Quentin in March 1918 as the last great German Army attack of the war smashed through the British defences. The Ox and Bucks were told to stand to the last man – and they did.

Since August 1914 a torrent of words have been written about World War One. So many words but I can find no sense in those that try to say how the war started. To me, it seemed to stem from a class of person thought to have the 'divine right to rule'. A group of people endowed with an unquestioning self belief but without some sense or perception. Ordinary people got swept up in a conflict that 'authority' said was both right and righteous – and that on both sides! Nonetheless men flocked to enlist and to fight. Naturally so, they felt their country was threatened. Throughout their youth they had been schooled in an abiding belief in King, Country and Empire. Every schoolroom had a map that showed half the world as pink. Our place in history was under attack! Out of the suffering that followed the start of war came some of the most beautifully poetic words ever bestowed on our country. Tales of heroism abound but they mask the slaughter, waste and a multitude of lost, maimed or saddened lives.

Looking back I wonder at the 'might have been' with so many brave and adventurous men and women lost. And most of all so many left to carry the burden of loss, guilt and regret. But there can be no weeping now, surely, for tears are in the past. What of anger? Anger is so negative. Should we not lay sorrow down, for sorrow has no place now. And what of fear? There is no room for fear, not when freedom has been won and the price full paid.

REMEMBER

COME NOVEMBER THE ELEVENTH
UPON THE ELEVENTH HOUR

WEAR UPON YOUR BREAST WITH
PRIDE A CRIMSON POPPY
FLOWER

AND PUT ASIDE TWO MINUTES OF
YOURSELF IN CONTEMPLATION

FOR ALL ARE HEROES NOW WHO
SERVED OUR NATION

THE OXFORDSHIRE AND BUCKINGHAMSHIRE LIGHT INFANTRY

BATTLE HONOURS OF THE GREAT WAR

Mons	Retreat From Mons
Marne, 1914	Aisne,1914
Ypres,1914	Langemarck, 1914
Gheluvelt	Nonne Bosschen
Aubers	Festubert, 1915
Loos	Mount Sorrel
Somme, 1916	Albert, 1916
Bazentin	Delville Wood
Pozieres	Guillemont
Flers-Courcelette	Morval
Le Transloy	Ancre Heights
Ancre, 1916	Bapaume, 1917
Arras, 1917	Vimy, 1917
Scarpe, 1917	Arleox
Menin Road	Polygon Wood
Broodseinde	Poelcappelle
Passchendaele	Cambrai, 1917
St Quentin	Rosieres
Avre	Lys
Hazebrouck	Bethune
Hindenburg Line	Haurin Court
Canal Du Nord	Selle
Valenciennes	France and Flanders,1914-18
Piave	Vittorio Veneto
Italy 1917-18	Doiran, 1917
Macedonia, 1915-18	Kut al Amara, 1915
Ctesiphon	Defence of Kut al Amara
Tigris, 1916	Khan Baghdadi
Mesopotamia, 1914-18	Archangel, 1919

During the war over 1,000 Medals of Honour were awarded to the Officers and Men of the Regiment.

In 1966 the Regiment was integrated into a new Regiment, The Royal Green Jackets.

WHISPERED STORIES TOLD LEST
WE FORGET THE PAST

THREADBARE MEMORIES TEASED
OUT, RE-CALLED AT LAST

TALES OF BYGONE MISTY DAYS,
SO FAINT REMEMBERED

TAKE TIME TO REMINISCE WITH
CUPS OF TEA AND TALK

FAMILY AND OLD FRIENDS
PASSING BY, A LIFETIME'S
WALK

AND TO BE THERE ONCE AGAIN,
SO FAINT REMEMBERED

THOSE LONG AGO THEIR
HAPPINESS AND SORROW
FADED FAST

MEN AND WOMEN DANCING BY,
SHADOWS FROM THE PAST.

RECOLLECTIONS FROM THE
HEART, SO FAINT
REMEMBERED.

WILL YOU REMEMBER THEM?

Brian A F Elks – 2001